VITA BREVIS

BY THE SAME AUTHOR

Medicus
Terra Incognita
Persona Non Grata
Caveat Emptor
Semper Fidelis
Tabula Rasa

VITA
BREVIS

A Crime Novel of the Roman Empire

RUTH DOWNIE

B L O O M S B U R Y
NEW YORK · LONDON · OXFORD · NEW DELHI · SYDNEY

Bloomsbury USA
An imprint of Bloomsbury Publishing Plc

1385 Broadway   50 Bedford Square
New York   London
NY 10018   WC1B 3DP
USA   UK

www.bloomsbury.com

BLOOMSBURY and the Diana logo are trademarks of Bloomsbury
Publishing Plc

First published 2016

© Ruth Downie, 2016

ISBN: HB: 978-1-62040-958-9
     ePub: 978-1-62040-959-6

LIBRARY OF CONGRESS CATALOGING-IN-PUBLICATION IS AVAILABLE.

2   4   6   8   10   9   7   5   3   1

Typeset by RefineCatch Limited, Bungay, Suffolk
Printed in the U.S.A. by Berryville Graphics Inc.,
Berryville, Virginia

To find out more about our authors and books visit www.bloomsbury.com.
Here you will find extracts, author interviews, details of forthcoming
events and the option to sign up for our newsletters.

Bloomsbury books may be purchased for business or promotional use.
For information on bulk purchases please contact Macmillan Corporate
and Premium Sales Department at specialmarkets@macmillan.com.

Remembering Teresa Vance,
a good friend to Ruso, to me, and to many.

. . . medicoque tantum hominem occidisse inpunitas summa est.

. . . only a doctor can kill a man with complete impunity.

Pliny the Elder, Natural History

VITA BREVIS

A NOVEL

IN WHICH our hero, Gaius Petreius Ruso, will be . . .

Accompanied by
> Tilla, his wife
> Mara, their daughter. See also "Entertained by/worried by/kept awake by"

Commanded by
> Accius, a former legionary tribune

Entertained by
> Mara, his daughter

Obeyed by
> Esico, and Narina, two British slaves

Questioned by
> Metellus, a security advisor

Disapproved of by
> Sabella, a bartender

Worried by
> Mara, his daughter

Puzzled by
    Kleitos, a doctor
    Birna, a man with a limp

Brushed off by
    Curtius Cossus, a wealthy building contractor

Kept awake by
    Mara, his daughter

Annoyed by
    Simmias, a fellow medic
    Sister Dorcas, a follower of Christos
    Tubero the Younger, a poet
    A slave from the Brigante tribe
    Minna, Accius's housekeeper (whom Tilla calls the Witch)

Employed by
    Horatius Balbus, a property owner

Assisted by
    Phyllis, the neighbor upstairs
    Timotheus, Phyllis's husband, a carpenter
    Firmicus, Balbus's steward

Used by
    Horatia, Balbus's daughter

Kept in order by
    Latro, Balbus's bodyguard

Informed by
    Lucius Virius, an undertaker
    Xanthe, an expert on medicines
    Gellia, a slave girl

He will never know the real names of the following, who appear in
the story without them:
    Squeaky, a large man with a small voice

a boy, nephew of Birna
a building caretaker, married to Sabella
another building caretaker with scummy teeth
a third building caretaker with a jug of wine and high hopes
a porter with a stylus behind one ear
a pregnant girl from the fifth floor
a toy seller
a sausage seller

He will fail to meet the following characters whom his author devised but barely used:

Doctor Callianax, a medical demonstrator
Delia, Kleitos's wife

And neither will he meet the following, even though he really did exist:

Marcus Annius Verus, the urban prefect, in charge of law and order in the emperor's absence. Verus had family connections with Ruso's hometown of Nemausus. This was something the author felt sure she could exploit but she never quite worked out how.

1

ROME, APRIL, 123 A.D.

T HE SHORTCUT WAS a mistake. They had almost lost the barrel down the steps after it rolled over his uncle's foot. The boy was still shaken by the thought of what might have happened. What if the two of them hadn't been able to catch up as it clunked away in the gray morning light? The boy could picture it tumbling over and over and finally smashing against a wall, leaving the thing inside flopped out across the pavement among a scatter of wooden staves.

What he couldn't picture was what they would have done next, and he thanked the gods that he didn't have to. He had flung himself at the barrel, while his uncle—who had earlier made him promise not to say a word until they were safely home again— yelled curses that echoed between the walls of the apartment blocks. The boy put his weight against the barrel while his uncle hopped about on one foot, still swearing. There was a scrape of shutters above them. Someone shouted, "Keep the noise down!" and someone else wanted to know what was going on out there.

His uncle shouted, "Sorry!" It was a word the boy couldn't remember ever hearing him use before, but it worked. The shutters slammed, and the alley returned to silence, except for the sound of the uncle sucking in air through his teeth when he put his foot back on the ground. Nobody bothered them as they eased the barrel down the last few steps and onto the main street. Then there was the long push up the hill, where it lurched about, sent this way and that by the great uneven stones and ruts in the road.

The noise of wheels on cobbles was more irregular now. The sun was almost up and the drivers of the last few delivery carts were hurrying to get out of the city gates by dawn. They were too busy avoiding traffic fines to pay any attention to a man and a boy delivering a barrel. A couple of slaves out early to fetch water eyed them for a moment and then turned slowly to go about their business, compelled to move gracefully by the weight of the jars perched on their shoulders.

The boy held his breath as a dung cart rumbled past, and then they rolled the barrel across the street. His arm hurt after that near miss at the steps. His uncle was still limping, his sandals slapping unevenly on the stones. They set the barrel against the lowest point on the curb and then heaved it up and under an arcade that ran in front of a row of shops.

"Right," grunted his uncle. They swivelled it—the boy was getting the hang of steering it now—and then trundled it past the closed shutters of the bar on the corner. His uncle gave the order to stop. They set the barrel upright and he gave two sharp taps on the nearest door with his knuckles.

The light was growing into day. Even under the gloom of the arcade the boy could make out the figure painted on the wall: a snake twisting around a stick. "This is a doctor's!"

"What did I tell you about keeping quiet?" The uncle gave the two taps again. Louder.

"Perhaps he could look at your foot."

"Very funny," said his uncle.

The boy, who hadn't intended to be funny, decided he would do as he was told and say nothing from now on. Nothing about what they had crammed into the barrel. Nothing about how pointless it was to keep quiet if his uncle was going to curse in the street and bang on doors. Nothing about how anyone who wasn't as tight-fisted as his uncle would have hired a donkey and cart to move a barrel this size. He wouldn't say a thing, because Ma was right: A boy with a big mouth could get himself into a lot of trouble.

Ma also said that any work that paid money was honest work, and if he wanted to eat, he had better go and find some. He certainly did want to eat, but now look where it had got him. He wanted to tell her that his uncle ought to be paying him a whole lot more for this, but then the boy would have to tell her what *this* was, and the thought of telling anyone made his toes curl against the cold paving. He tried not to think about ghosts.

The slaves had stopped at the fountain on the corner, only a few paces away. He could hear the low murmur of voices and the splashing of water. While one was filling his jar, the other would be lolling against the wall and gazing at anything that might be the least bit interesting. Like a man knocking on an unanswered door.

Glad he was under the arcade, the boy leaned back against the broad pillar where the slaves couldn't see him, folded his arms, and pretended he could read the faded letters painted on the wall. The uncle was using his fist on the door now. Then he put his mouth to the gap where the latch was and shouted, "Delivery!"

It was plain they were wasting their time. The household slave should have been awake, even if no one else was, cleaning out the hearth and getting breakfast.

The uncle was making too much noise to hear the creak of hinges from the bar next door. The boy stepped forward and tugged at the side of his tunic. A hefty woman came out of the bar and glanced across at them but said nothing. She started lifting the shutters from their grooves and moving them indoors, opening up the whole of the entrance. It was going to be another warm spring day.

Finally, to the boy's great relief, his uncle stepped back from the door and beckoned him to follow. The woman called after them, "Hey! You can't leave that there!"

"We'll be back later," the uncle told her without turning around.

The uncle was limping and scowling all the way home, which was a longer trip than it should have been, because he led the boy along a street that passed a big house and down beside the market halls before doubling back down an alleyway, like he always did when he thought somebody might be watching. The boy trudged along beside him in silence, cradling his sore arm and trying not to think about the dead man in the barrel outside the doctor's front door.

2

GAIUS PETREIUS RUSO gazed up at the outside of Rome's colossal amphitheater. He could make no sense of what he was seeing. Were they preparing some sort of acrobatic performance up there? Or was it a bizarre and creative form of punishment, like the horrors this place was built to display?

Curious, he had lingered at the edge of the crowd that had gathered to stare up at the second tier of stone arches. Now he was hemmed in by a sweaty throng of morning shoppers, slaves on errands, inquisitive children, a man whose clean toga and annoyed expression suggested he was delayed on the way to something important, and others who looked and smelled as if they had nowhere better to go. Behind him, a couple of youths had somehow managed to scramble up onto the plinth of the sun god, and were mimicking the pose of the golden giant towering above them while trading insults with the crowd below.

Ruso shaded his eyes from the brilliant blue of the spring sky, squinting to see what was going on beside a statue that stood in the shade of the arch. A young woman swathed in layers of cloth like an Egyptian mummy had been tied to the ladder. A golden-haired man draped in bloodred was directing a pair of slaves whose plain tunics bore matching red stripes. They were checking the knots.

"One moment, friends!"

The group around the girl all turned to see where the voice was coming from. The crowd also shifted its attention to an arch farther along, where a slave with his arms held aloft was shouting, "This time tomorrow, friends! In the Forum of Nerva, a live anatomy demonstration from the famous Doctor Callianax! See the doctor separate a living pig from its squeak and bring it back again!"

The rest was lost as the red-striped slaves appeared in the archway, pounced on the intruder, and attempted to separate him from his own squeak, but his work was done. The crowd cheered. The anatomist would have a good audience tomorrow.

Back in the original archway, a pale woman leaned over to speak into the ear of the mummy and groped under the cloth for a hand to grasp.

"They'd better have measured that rope," observed an unshaven man at Ruso's side. His tone suggested a certain relish at the prospect of what would happen if they had forgotten. "I heard they drop them headfirst."

Ruso said, "They drop them? What for?"

"*Succussion*, they call it," said someone else.

"What?" Ruso twisted to face him. "Are you sure?"

"It's a cure for bent backs," his informant told him. "It comes from Hippocrates. He was a famous doctor."

"Hippocrates didn't approve of it," Ruso said, glancing at the crowd and wondering what to do.

"Know all about bent backs, do you?"

"Enough."

Someone in front of them managed to turn 'round far enough to ask, "What would you do, then?" When Ruso did not answer he said, "Eh? If you're the expert, what would you—Hey! There's no need for that! Come back here!"

But Ruso was already out of his reach, worming his way forward by a combination of shoving, apologizing, treading on toes, and shouting the surprisingly effective "Let me through! I'm a doctor!"

Up in the archway, an older man who might have been the mummy's father or husband stepped forward and laid a hand on her shoulder.

Below, Ruso was still some distance from the front. "Let me through! I'm a—"

"Piss off, mate. We were here first." A man with a military bearing and a bad haircut moved to block Ruso's progress.

"I need to get past!" Ruso craned over the enormous shoulder in front of him. Up in the archway, the red-striped slaves stepped forward and lifted the ladder. They tilted it over the edge of the railing so the young woman's head hung above the street. The crowd gasped.

"I'm a doctor," Ruso urged, trying to squeeze sideways around the man. "And I have to get to the front!"

A hand clamped onto his shoulder. "I'm a wrestler," said a voice in his ear. "And no, you don't."

The murmur of the crowd grew louder. Above them, the patient was vertical, with her swathed head pointing toward the stone paving and the soles of her feet toward the sky.

"We have to stop this! Let me through!"

A voice said, "Let him through!" and someone else said, "*You* let him through!"

The young woman's relatives were leaning forward to watch, the man gripping the railing, the woman with her hands pressed against her face.

Below, more slaves were shouting at the crowd to stay clear of the drop. Ruso found himself forced to shuffle backward. "Stop!" he yelled as loudly as he could, writhing free and fighting to clamber onto the shoulders around him. He managed, "Don't do it! You could kill her!" before he was dragged down into the heaving, airless press of bodies.

Struggling to get back on his feet, the noise of the crowd above him coalesced into a roar of "Go! Go! Go!"

He managed to get his head up in time to see the ladder shoot down the side of the building. It jerked to a shuddering halt a few feet from the ground. A scream rang out into the sudden silence. Then one of the slaves in the street reached up and briefly drew back the white cloth from the patient's face. He shouted something up to the waiting group in the archway.

The master embraced the patient's family. Cheering and applause broke out in the street, and the crowd surged forward again, pushing and shoving to get a better look. Everyone except the

slaves now gathering up the loose rope had vanished from the arch:
The others must be scurrying down the stone steps.

Ruso finally managed to catch a glimpse of the patient through
the excited crowd. To his amazement, she was neither in a state of
collapse nor in obvious agony. Instead she was massaging the back
of her neck with both hands and smiling, while her parents
embraced her—from either side, so as not to spoil the spectators'
view—and led her forward. The girl broke away from them and
removed her stole to reveal the perfect alignment of her shoulders.
Then she delighted both parents and crowd with an impromptu
twirl before rejoining her family to walk away.

"It's a miracle!" declared someone nearby.

"It's a trick," Ruso told him, convinced that the slaves must
have put extra padding on a healthy girl beneath the mummy
wrapping. "The only miracle is that she can still walk."

"Eh? So the straight back, that's a trick too, is it?"

"Did you know her before? Did anybody?"

"We all saw what she was like," insisted the believer.

"It's a trick!" Ruso called, louder.

"My friends!"

Everyone turned. The man draped in red had somehow managed
to get across to the sun god. The youths had vanished, and he
had been hoisted up onto the plinth in their place. "Many of you
think you just saw a miracle." He waited for the cheering to die
down before continuing. "And some, like our friend here, will
say you saw a trick." He lowered his voice. "Let me tell you this.
You saw neither." He let the suspense build for a moment, then
continued. "What you saw here, friends, in front of a thousand
witnesses, was a cure. A cure that other doctors said was impossible, and why?"

"Because it doesn't work!" Ruso shouted.

Several people turned to glare at him, but the man was smiling.
"Because other doctors don't know how to make it work," he said.
"Because they listen to people like our friend here, who can't
accept the evidence of his own eyes, and to their own ignorant
teachers, instead of studying for themselves!"

A murmur of appreciation ran through the crowd. The speaker
bent forward, surveying them as if he were addressing them one by
one. "Tell me now, friends. How many times have you heard of a

gang of doctors standing 'round some poor patient's bed and arguing with one another?"

Judging from the laughter, everyone knew exactly what he was talking about.

"Friends . . ." His voice grew quieter, so that they had to strain to listen. "I'm not one of these so-called healers who wastes his time criticizing his rivals. I'm not part of some fancy school of philosophy that I have to defend because I have a book to sell. You deserve better than that! And that's why I've spent years of study and travel finding out for myself *what works*."

Ruso felt his teeth clench. Like the most pernicious lies, the man's claims had a superficial coating of truth and an appeal to common sense.

"You saw it for yourself, friends! Let us see if we can help you like we helped this young lady. Every medicine I will give you is guaranteed blessed by the goddess Angitia, every treatment taken from the genuine writings of Hippocrates himself! No problem is too large or too small! We're only passing through, so seize your chance—don't go home today without speaking to me!"

"Stay away from him!" Ruso shouted. "He's dangerous!"

He was aware of a silence falling on the crowd. People were turning to stare as the showman offered him an even broader smile.

"Might you be a medical man, my friend?"

Vaguely aware of the distant tramp of marching boots, Ruso took a deep breath. Leaving out the word *former*, he called, "Medical officer with the Twentieth Legion."

The showman extended an arm from on high as if to present Ruso to the crowd. "My friends, you see how it is! Jealousy! Your own doctors don't want you to come to me and be cured. And why not? You know why not! Because they'd rather keep taking your money!"

The sound of boots on stone was louder now. Someone had called out the troops of the urban cohort to keep order. Ruso yelled, "If you're so good, why don't you stay in—" But *one place?* was lost under the relentless rhythm of sword hilts beating on shields and the cries of the crowd. The men of the cohort charged. The people fled. In moments Ruso was standing alone in an empty expanse of paving with only a scatter of debris and the stink from a trampled dog turd to indicate that anyone had been there.

Having averted the riot, the cohort was reassembling under the deserted sun god. Ruso leaned against the plinth to rub his grazed knees and pull his tunic straight.

"You there!" roared a voice, its owner striding toward him. "You deaf or what? Clear off home!"

Eyeing the centurion's raised stick, Ruso chose not to argue. He had barely taken ten paces when a voice from a shadowed doorway across the street said, "I see you're still causing trouble, Ruso."

3

BROWN HAIR, AVERAGE height, faded tunic, battered sandals . . . had it not been for the voice, Ruso would never have noticed him. How long had he been standing in that doorway?

Metellus, looking faintly amused, nodded a greeting to the centurion. Then he took Ruso by the elbow as if they were old friends and steered him toward the clatter that had resumed on the demolition site across the road now that all the excitement was over. "I heard you were in Rome."

Anyone who did not know Metellus would have taken this to mean *someone happened to mention you*. Anyone who had served in Britannia during Metellus's time as security advisor to the governor would interpret it as *I have an informer at the port who sends me lists of disembarking passengers*.

"So," Ruso said, because it was best to be the one asking the questions, "what are you doing these days?"

"Oh, this and that," said Metellus. "Fortune has been kind. You?"

"I've made some useful contacts," Ruso assured him, wondering if Metellus wanted to know anything in particular, and for whom, and how to avoid telling him.

"Really?" Metellus sounded surprised. "Who?"

"I can't say anything just yet," Ruso told him. "You know how it is."

"Indeed."

Ruso hoped he didn't. "Sorry I can't stop and chat," he said, waving past the sun god in the direction of the emperor Titus's splendid baths, and not caring that this was an obvious lie from a man who moments ago had been loitering in the street. "I have to see a man about a job."

Metellus said, "I'll walk with you."

Ruso glanced across at the demolition site, where a man in a battered straw hat was supervising a crane team as they cranked up a boulder to load into a waiting cart. Pushing aside a fantasy of what might happen if Metellus stood underneath it, he headed in the direction of the baths. His destination was up the Oppian Hill and with luck Metellus would get bored before they got there. If not, well, Kleitos was the sort of doctor who would happily spend an hour talking about the medicinal properties of thistles or the finer points of treating prolapsed hemorrhoids. That should see him off.

They waited for two men to lug a bulbous oil amphora past, and then stepped into the street. Metellus said, "And how is your wife enjoying Rome?"

"She's very busy with the baby," said Ruso.

"Oh, dear, yes. I heard something about that."

"Parenthood is a marvelous thing," Ruso assured him. "You should try it yourself."

"I'm glad to hear it," Metellus told him. "Especially after the rumors."

Ruso said, "It never pays to listen to rumors."

"Actually, I find it pays rather well."

Ruso tried, "And what are they saying about you?" but there was no reply.

Smells of woodsmoke and perfume and stale sweat wafted into the street from Titus's bathhouse and the one behind it which, being built by a later emperor, was of course spectacularly bigger.

"I was told," Metellus began smoothly, "that the child isn't yours."

Ruso took a slow breath, savoring the memory of the day his patience had snapped and he had shoved Metellus into the nearest river. "She's not Tilla's either," he said. "We adopted."

"Ah. I did wonder, but one never knows what to expect with the Britons."

"My wife is a Roman citizen now," Ruso reminded him.

"Of course," Metellus continued smoothly. "Remarkable. I don't think I ever congratulated her. Please pass on my good wishes."

Ruso had no intention of ruining Tilla's day by telling her the man who had once put her on a security list of Undesirables to Watch was in Rome.

"If there's anything I can do," Metellus continued, "just ask. I know one or two people who could offer you work."

"Thank you, but I don't think it'll be a problem."

"I do hope you aren't relying on Publius Accius just because he encouraged you to come here—I believe that's how it was?" When Ruso did not reply, Metellus added, "Accius was a big man back in Britannia, but you'll need far better connections than that to get on in Rome. Especially with his tendency to make unfortunate remarks after too much wine." He glanced back at the amphitheater. "I take it you've tried the gladiator school?"

"I'm on their list."

Metellus said, "I may be able to help with that."

"Please don't." Facing a crocodile was one thing. Putting your head between its jaws was something else entirely.

Metellus shrugged. "As you wish. But the offer is there. You can always contact me via the urban prefect's office. Your wife won't want to stay in that rather unpleasant boarding house forever."

And with that the man was gone, brown hair and average height and faded tunic lost among the shoppers in a shady side street. The whole exchange might have been a hallucination, except now the tightness of Ruso's fists and the soreness of his grazed knees was accompanied by a deep feeling of unease.

He forced himself to take a couple of deep breaths and relax his shoulders. He was not involved in anything that could possibly interest the urban prefect, whose job it was to keep order in the city while the emperor was away on another of his foreign tours. If indeed Metellus really was working for the prefect. No, it was far more likely that Metellus had been drawn by the crowd, had spotted an old adversary, and decided to enjoy spoiling his morning.

4

IT WAS EASY to pick out Kleitos's apartment on the busy Vicus
Sabuci—it was the door under the arcade that had two holes
clumsily bashed through the wall above it so extra windows could
cast light into the surgery. To Ruso's disappointment, it was locked.
There was a large barrel half blocking the entrance, and there was
no reply to his knocking. He was surprised: On his first visit he
had been introduced to a couple of apprentices as well as Kleitos's
wife and children. He would have expected one of them to be
there in the middle of the morning to take messages, even if the
little Greek himself was out seeing a patient.

He hoped there was nothing wrong. Kleitos had seemed a
decent man: an enthusiast who had plied Ruso with questions
about military surgical techniques and the plants and minerals that
could be found in Britannia and had made scribbled notes of the
answers on scraps of parchment and the unused corners of writing
tablets. He had recommended reliable suppliers of roots and herbs,
and his promise to send a message if there was any work had
sounded genuine. He had also seemed sincerely sorry when he
explained that he could not send any of his patients to Ruso's lodgings, because none of them would dare to go there. But staring at

the locked door, Ruso felt that if this was how Kleitos went about his business, it was hard to imagine he had a thriving practice.

The blank face of the hefty woman serving in the bar next door told Ruso it was a mistake to ask for information without first ordering a drink. The purchase of a cup of spiced wine loosened her tongue a little, but not in a helpful way. She didn't know where the doctor was, and they didn't run a message service. "Come back this afternoon."

The wine was better than he had expected, which might explain the busyness of the surrounding tables: It certainly wasn't caused by the warmth of the welcome. He took the cup across to where he could loll against one of the pillars of the arcade and keep an eye on the doctor's front door. He might as well wait and have a chat with Kleitos now that he was here.

As he watched, another visitor arrived. She could not have been more than fourteen. Somebody seemed to have glued a perfectly rounded pregnant belly onto her underfed frame. She knocked, waited, knocked again, tried to peer around the edge of the door and called, "Doctor! Doctor, are you there?" before glancing 'round in an agitated manner.

Ruso stepped toward her. "Can I help?"

She turned, startled.

"I'm a doctor myself," he assured her. "I'm just—"

But she had fled. Ruso, still clutching his drink and marooned in the middle of the arcade, attempted a casual return to the pillar.

"Nice try, pal," suggested a voice from a nearby table.

Another voice said, "You again."

"I really am a doctor," Ruso insisted, not pleased to recognize the man with the bad haircut who had refused to let him past in the crowd at the amphitheater.

"So you keep saying." The man indicated Ruso's empty left hand. "Where's your box of tricks, then?"

"I'm visiting Doctor Kleitos."

"Feeling poorly, are you, Doctor?"

Ruso downed the rest of his drink in one gulp. "Not now," he said, putting the empty cup down on their table. In his haste to get away he narrowly missed falling over that wretched barrel outside Kleitos's door.

Around the corner he bent to tighten a loose bootlace before trudging back down the hill past the bathhouses. The larger of the two had been commissioned by an emperor Ruso had actually met, although the aftermath of a massive earthquake had been no time to exchange pleasantries. Much to his first wife's disgust, he had failed to exploit this brief acquaintance with Trajan, and by the time Hadrian had risen to power, he and Claudia were divorced. So she was spared the awful knowledge that he had failed to ask Hadrian for a promotion too. It was something that he was now beginning to realize might have been a major mistake.

Despite what he had told Metellus, this morning's outing had been a waste of time. There was no vacancy for a surgeon at the gladiators' training camp beside the amphitheater. The clerk had indeed offered to put his name on a waiting list, but when asked about the length of the list, the man had raised both hands and stretched his palms apart like a fisherman demonstrating the size of the one that had got away.

Ignoring the cries of the souvenir sellers, Ruso headed along the Sacred Way toward the business center of the city. The glare of sun on marble made him squint, and it occurred to him that Tilla was right. When they first arrived he had wandered down this most famous of streets, gazing at the marvels he had heard described so many times, barely able to believe that at last he was here, seeing for himself how everything was more glorious than he had imagined. Three weeks later, he was beginning to share his wife's view that Rome had too much of everything. Too many columns and statues and temples, the public buildings gobbling up so much space that ordinary people's lodgings were stacked five or six high on top of one another with cramped courtyards in the middle to let in some daylight. Too many smells, especially where the sewer vomited its waste into the river. Too much noise.

Worst of all, there were too many people who called themselves doctors. It was a sad state of affairs when a man who had run several military hospitals and who had prior experience of patching up gladiators could get no work, but some smooth-tongued charlatan in a fancy red outfit could drum up trade by dropping a young woman headfirst from the arches of the amphitheater.

His first wife's urgings echoed in his memory: "You must put yourself forward, Gaius!" But he could not think of any crowd-pleasing, patient-attracting miracles to offer. He certainly wasn't about to start dissecting live animals or tying women to ladders. He wasn't going to ask Metellus for help, either.

Passing through the shade of a ceremonial archway and back out into the glare, he averted his gaze from a couple of day laborers, who were still hanging about in the diminishing hope that someone would offer them work. He knew how they felt.

Ruso's own hanging about was less public, since it was done in the somewhat gloomy private residence of his former commanding officer, but it was hardly less humiliating. In the weeks since their ship had docked over at Portus, it had become obvious that he was an embarrassment—like a souvenir from a foreign country that didn't look as exotic when you got it home.

Unfortunately for Accius, Ruso was not the kind of souvenir that could be resold, as he had come here voluntarily. The voice of the first wife urged Ruso to remind Accius exactly whose idea it had been for Ruso to leave Britannia. Exactly who had insisted on pulling the strings that had released him early from his latest contract with the Twentieth Legion, and whose moral responsibility it now was to offer him work. But Claudia was not here to explain how this might be done without wrecking any chance of future employment.

Even if she had been, she might have struggled to be heard above Tilla, whose determination not to say, "I told you so!" had finally cracked over the stale loaf that was this morning's breakfast.

"But why did he offer you a job if he did not have one? And why did you not ask what it was before you said yes?"

Ruso, who had already considered these questions many times, especially in the long watches of the night, had no answers to offer. He was still trying to remember why coming here had seemed like a good idea when Tilla closed her eyes and sighed, "Just like a man!"

"What else should I be like?"

She lifted up their daughter and pointed the chubby face toward him as if the baby wore the terrifying stare of a Gorgon.

"We have Mara to care for now! You must be more responsible! You are a father!"

But not, it seemed, a satisfactory one.

He had abandoned breakfast and clattered away down the

apartment stairs as angry with himself as he was with his wife. She was right. He had persuaded her to come to this place. Now those eyes that bore the changeable colors of the sea had dark hollows around them, and she was thinner than he had seen her in a very long time.

So, here he was, turning in yet again at the plain doorway that led to Accius's family home. The owner of the shop next door nodded a greeting. The aged doorman, who had seen him almost daily for the last three weeks, stepped back and gave a bow that managed to be both respectful and supercilious at the same time. Or perhaps Ruso was starting to imagine things. Each of them was obliged to report to Accius, but the doorman had a job, whereas Ruso came here freely in the hope of being given something to do, but left empty-handed.

The scowl that Accius had probably been born with had grown deeper as the days passed. Doubtless Ruso's visits were the reminder of a bad decision and of a disappointment. On his return from military service, the former tribune had expected better than to be put in charge of Rome's Department of Street Cleaning.

Still, until this morning's conversation with Metellus, Ruso had managed to hope that Accius had a bright future. Admittedly he was not among Hadrian's staunchest supporters, especially since one of the men who had been executed shortly after the new emperor came into power was a relative. But Hadrian had been swift to express his disapproval of the killings. Then, in case anyone harbored any lingering doubts about his right to rule, he had arranged a massive public bonfire made up of everyone's outstanding tax bills.

In this atmosphere of forgiving and forgetting, it had seemed possible that Accius's aristocratic connections could still lift him to places high above the Department of Street Cleaning. Places in which, as he had assured Ruso, he would be in need of a Good Man.

Meanwhile, Ruso regretted ever mentioning his own family in the distant south of Gaul. Accius seemed to assume their modestly sized and debt-burdened farm was some vast estate like the ones that generated his own income, and that Ruso was able to drift around Rome indefinitely on a regular flow of unearned cash, indulging an occasional hobby of treating the sick while he waited to find out exactly what a Good Man did, and to be given the chance to do it.

Accius had not been brought up to understand money. He did, however, understand social obligation. Yesterday he had gamely offered, "Ah. Ruso. Yes. I haven't forgotten you," although clearly he wished he could.

Today, however, after Ruso had negotiated his way 'round the spluttering marble fountain and stepped aside to allow some visiting aristocrat to shuffle past clutching his toga, he was greeted with a cry of "Ah, Ruso! Just the man!"

5

WONDERING WHAT HE was just the man for, Ruso stepped into the grim austerity of Accius's study. The former tribune was sitting forward with his elbows resting on a desk that looked as though several generations of ancestors had used it before him, and not kindly. Still, the scowl was lighter than usual, and his hands were clasped together as if he had trapped some good news between them.

Evidently the news was too good to release straightaway. "How's the family?"

"They're very well, sir," Ruso lied, picturing Tilla in the cramped tenement room, trying to stop Mara from smearing porridge in her hair while keeping a nervous eye on the cracks in the wall lest something should crawl out. He dared not complain: They might have still been living in this large, gloomy house had it not been for Tilla's announcement that she would soon be punching Accius's housekeeper on the nose if the woman did not mind her own business.

"Good man," said Accius. "Now." He opened his hands. "Fortune has smiled on you. You'll remember Doctor Kleitos, my personal physician?"

"I was just there earlier, sir."

"Really? Did you know his father is very ill?"

So that explained the locked door. And perhaps why no one had taken in the barrel outside. "No, sir. There was nobody in."

"That's not the fortunate part."

"No, sir."

"This is." Accius reached out a hand. His clerk stepped forward to present him with a little scrap of rolled-up parchment, which he passed to Ruso.

Ruso fumbled with the knot in the frayed twine and gave up, sliding it over the top with the loop still intact. Then he held the curled scrap open with his thumbs.

The Greek words *a coldness of the limbs and sweating on the forehead almost always followed by death* had been ineffectively scraped off, and underneath was a smudgy note repeating the news about Kleitos's father. He went on to read in Latin, "'I would therefore be grateful if you would take over as much of the practice as you are able until my return. The apartment will be empty, and you are welcome to bring your family. The key will be with the caretaker, whose wife runs the bar next door. He is expecting you.'"

Ruso blinked and read it again. He still didn't believe it. Most men would have entrusted their patients to a known and reliable colleague, but Kleitos, on the strength of Accius's recommendation and one informal visit, had put both his livelihood and his accommodation into the hands of a stranger.

"This is a great honor, sir."

"I thought you'd like it," Accius said casually, as if he had arranged the whole thing himself. "Of course, I told him a while ago that you were a good chap. You'll have to move out when he gets back, but I gather the father lives several days away, so you should get a good run at it."

Ruso carried on reading.

"Is there a problem?"

He glanced up. "It's very generous of him, sir."

"Good." Accius settled back in his chair. "Frankly, I was beginning to wonder if I'd made a mistake in bringing you here."

"So was I, sir."

Accius paused, as if it had not occurred to him that Ruso might have an opinion. "Of course, I'm assuming he's already cleared it with his patron. You won't let me down, will you? Kleitos's patron is the father of a very lovely young lady, and she wants me to make a good impression."

"I'll do my best, sir."

"In fact, perhaps I should take you over there myself so you can meet him. Horatius Balbus is a fine man. Talks a lot more sense than some of these political types."

Ruso swallowed. "Horatius Balbus?"

"Ah, yes, of course. I forgot: He let you have one of his apartments. Have you met?"

"No, sir." Although Ruso had spent some time planning what he would say if they ever did.

"Well, you should. I'll let you know when we can call." Accius glanced over his shoulder at his clerk. "Have the next chap sent in, will you? Sorry, Ruso. No time to chat. Another bloody meeting. You'd think it would be a simple enough business keeping the streets clean: Just send a few slaves out with brooms. But no. Let me know how you get on. Meanwhile, don't let me down."

Acknowledging the doorman's bow as he left, Ruso had to admit to himself that the slave had never been disrespectful. The condescension had been in Ruso's own mind. And now what should have been in his mind was unadulterated joy and relief. Except that the end of Kleitos's note, which he had not read out to Accius, was less encouraging than the beginning.

He waited until he was around the corner, out of sight of the doorman and the bored shopkeeper next door, before pausing by a fountain to roll the note open again.

The Greek at the top—the business about cold limbs and death—was almost certainly from some sort of medical text. Kleitos was just reusing old writing materials. But the Greek at the bottom was in the same fresh ink as the message, and it said,

Be careful who you trust.

6

.

TILLA HAD CHANGED her mind about bathhouses. Now, at last, she understood why a woman might spend a whole morning dawdling in the changing rooms and meandering around the warm halls, listening to the babble of many tongues echoing from the high ceilings, and chatting idly about babies to other mothers with their hair wrapped in towels. It was better than fighting your way around the shops when you had no money or pacing stone streets till your feet ached or strolling through the public gardens at the mercy of strange men who thought you might want company. It was certainly better than sitting in a dingy tenement room, picking the remains of breakfast out of Mara's hair. But now Mara had the restlessness of a baby who was too distracted to sleep. She needed her bed.

Tilla scooped the baby up against her and the halfhearted wailing stopped. One of the other mothers helped to tie the shawl so that it held Mara in place, and she wished Tilla luck.

"Kick him where it hurts," suggested one of the new friends, helping herself to another of the raisin cakes they were sharing from the snack stall.

"I will," Tilla promised, pulling the linen stole up over her head

like a respectable Roman wife and remembering the days when
she would have advised exactly the same thing.

Reminding herself to turn left by the bakery, she wondered
where her courage had gone. It seemed to have slipped overboard,
unnoticed, somewhere on the long sea voyage from Britannia.

She paused again by a fish seller's stall, looking up between the
high buildings to check her bearings, and preparing to follow the
stone legs that held up the snake of the aqueduct. It would lead her
back to the place she was never going to think of as *home*.

As if to echo her mood, Mara began to wail again. "You are
not the only one who is hot and tired," Tilla assured her in British.
She had never realized what a precious thing sleep was until she
came to this terrible place.

She was a midwife. She was used to delivering babies in the
night, and she had expected Mara to wake at all hours. On
the journey here, Accius's horrible housekeeper had taken great
pleasure in trapping her in some corner of the ship and warning
her about the traffic rattling through the streets of Rome after dark
and the late partygoers and the clumping boots of the night watch.
Naturally in a busy lodging house there would always be someone
coughing or crying or arguing. Sometimes giving birth, although
Tilla's help was never needed. All this she could have grown used
to. But when she settled down to rest, the cockroaches came out.

Cockroaches were even worse than mice. She had tried sleeping
with a light burning, and then lain awake, worrying that the place
would catch fire and the night watch's ladders would not reach the
fourth floor. She had tried calming doses of poppy, but there was
always the worry that she would not wake if there was a crisis.
She had tried taking Mara into the bed and pulling the sheet tight
over both their heads in the dark, but after a while it was difficult
to breathe, and besides, who knew what was scuttling over the
bedding? Meanwhile, her husband had slept beside them like a
dead man.

Sometimes she wondered if he was only pretending, and that
secretly he too was lying awake, wondering how they could raise
their daughter in this place. Surely everyone knew that a healthy
child needed somewhere to run and jump and roll in the grass.
How would Mara learn that not all wild birds were pigeons or that
a dog could be your best friend or that you could make a hand-fed

lamb's tail wiggle by stroking its neck? Here the neighbors grumbled if you fed the birds, and you could not even tie a simple pot of lettuce seedlings onto the windowsill without the people below complaining every time you watered it.

As if she might find it reassuring, her husband had told her that there were people who cooked up the insides of cockroaches to treat earaches. When she pointed out that none of them had an earache and he had hardly any patients, he did something more useful and went to see the caretaker. The caretaker promised to come up and inspect the room later.

Of course he waited until he had seen her husband go out first. Tilla had watched from the safety of the doorway as the man's hairy hands turned over their possessions and groped the bed in a way that made her want to boil the sheets afterward.

Then, with a smile that displayed the yellow scum coating his teeth, he told her she had nothing to worry about. There were cockroaches everywhere in the city, and most places were a lot worse. She would soon get used to it.

She dared not complain again for fear of another visit. Nor did she dare to tell her husband about the way the caretaker spoke to her. It was no business of anyone else's if she was a natural blond, even if she did sometimes forget to cover her head. Her name was not Curly, and it wasn't Blondie either, and if the caretaker was stupid enough to believe the things he claimed to have heard about British women, she was not going to waste her breath trying to correct him. Still, she hoped her husband would not find out, because if he did there would be trouble, and then they might be thrown out, and what if most other places really were a lot worse?

Her new friends at the baths had assured her that not every apartment block was running with cockroaches, but then someone else had added, "But lots of them are," and someone else had told everyone about a friend of a friend who had woken to find a huge one nibbling the eyelashes of her sleeping baby. It was the sort of story that still made her shudder even though she told herself it probably wasn't true.

Kick him where it hurts.

Tilla glanced around to make sure nobody was looking, then paused in the street and tried lifting one leg. As she had thought, with a baby strapped to her chest it would be hard to kick anyone anywhere without falling over. Besides, the man would deny that he had done wrong. He would show his scummy teeth and say he hadn't meant any harm. She was just a foreigner who didn't understand a Roman joke.

There he was. Hanging around with some other men on the pavement outside the tenement steps. As she watched, an African in a work tunic emerged carrying a box, and squatted to place it next to a pile of luggage against the wall. Somebody must be moving out.

She glanced left down a narrow street. If she made her way around the back of the block she could enter from the other side and not have to pass them.

Tilla let out an "Oh!" of exasperation, as much at her own cowardice as from seeing the man who had forced her to confront it. "This is foolish!" she murmured to Mara. She was even letting that man take control of where she walked now. "I am ashamed." She slid two fingers inside her purse and stroked the little wooden horse her brother had carved. Then she squared her shoulders and went forward.

"Blondie!" The caretaker stepped into her path and gave her a cheery display of dental scum. "Where have you been? The boys have been waiting for you."

She was about to stride past without speaking when it struck her that there was something familiar about that box. She felt her courage flood back as she surveyed the rest of the items on the pavement. "Those are our things!"

The oldest of the "boys" fingered the writing stylus propped behind his ear. "We'll have to charge extra for the packing, missus."

She turned to the caretaker. "Our rent is paid!"

Instead of answering, he leaned closer and patted Mara's head with a hairy hand. "It's been a pleasure having your lovely mother here, little miss."

She stepped back to get her baby away from him, then twisted 'round to snatch at the case that held her husband's expensive medical instruments. "Give me that!"

But the African had a firm grip on it.

"Steady on, Blondie!" said the caretaker.

Someone picked up the box of crockery that had been a wedding present from her husband's family, and then placed her own bag of healer's necessities on top. Another two seized the rope handles at either end of the box that held her husband's kit from the Legion: the kit Tilla had come to treasure in the hope that he might find some way to put it on again and march them away from here.

She stood with her back to the wall, wrapped her arms around Mara and said, "If you do not give me my things right now, I will report you to Tribune Publius Accius as thieves."

The men seemed more puzzled than impressed. Perhaps she should have said that her husband would report them.

"Miss." The man with the stylus behind his ear spoke slowly and evenly, as if he were trying to calm an animal that might bite him. "Your husband sent us to help you move house."

Tilla blinked. "My husband?"

"What did I tell you?" the caretaker said to him. "British, see? They can't help it." He leaned closer and said in a stage whisper, as if he was afraid it might enrage her further, *"Highly strung."*

7

WHAT MARA WANTED was what usually happened at this time of day: a quiet doze. Instead, she was being bounced around as Tilla tried not to trip on the uneven paving, dodging passing pedestrians and veering 'round the bearers of fancy chairs that took up half the street.

Mara began to cry.

Tilla was perspiring inside her tunic of good British wool, and the wretched stole kept sliding off the back of her head. She could not stop to adjust it because she had no idea where the porters were taking them through the airless maze of buildings.

Mara's protests grew louder. None of Tilla's caresses, pleas, or promises of being nearly there made any difference. She side-stepped to scoop cool water from a street fountain and splash it over her own head and Mara's, then hurried to catch up. Finally she was close enough to call, "Where are we going?"

The last man swivelled around, and she gasped as he nearly lost his grip on the box of crockery. "The other side of Trajan's baths, miss. Vicus Sabuci."

She had no idea where that was, but she thanked him anyway, and resolved not to distract him from the crockery again.

The porters strode on, sweat making dark stains down the backs of their tunics. Tilla began to wonder if they were lost. All these streets lined with shadowy shops and bars looked the same. Had she not seen that display of brass pans before? Those bright bolts of cloth hanging from poles? She was sure she recognized the wilting wreath on that shrine. She had seen that slave with the basket of fruit on her head several minutes ago.

Finally Mara gave up crying and filled her cloths before dropping off to sleep. Tilla was wondering if she could persuade the men to stop by a latrine so she could change the cloths, when they came to a halt under the shade of an arcade. They were standing outside a closed and shuttered shop front with a snake on a stick painted on the wall.

While the head porter was banging on the door, Tilla sank down to rest on a barrel that had been left outside. She had no idea why her husband was not here to greet her, but she would worry about that later. She was going no farther.

The porters hurried away, already late for another job. Tilla was on her own in this unknown place, guarding an assortment of possessions and a smelly baby. There was a scribe's shop on the other side of the concrete steps to the next floor, but the man inside did not even glance up from his writing when he told her he had no idea when the doctor would be back. The woman at the bar on the corner seemed annoyed with her for asking.

Drinkers came and went at the bar tables. Beyond them, the entrance hall of Trajan's baths was so big that the figures passing underneath looked as though they were creeping into the house of a giant. Tilla kept looking up and down the arcade, hopes rising every time a figure came into sight, and falling when it was not him.

She began to wonder if the porters had taken her to the wrong doctor. What if her husband was expecting her somewhere else? She could not leave the luggage piled up out here beside the barrel for thieves to help themselves. Somehow, she would have to send word to Publius Accius's house, and ask the horrible housekeeper for help.

Across the road, people trotted up and down a set of steps to an opening with PORTICUS LIVIAE engraved on the wall. Livia, whoever she was, must be very generous to allow all those people to wander about in the shade of her portico.

A couple of women arrived and asked where the doctor was. When she said she did not know, but she was a healer and could she help, they went away again. The scribe shut up his shop and left. The shadows of the arcade's columns had moved across the paving stones. There was no sign of her husband.

A worse thought struck her. What if the caretaker and the porters had played a trick on her because of her complaint about the cockroaches? Even if her husband found her before nightfall, they would have nowhere to sleep, and it was all her own fault. She fingered the little wooden horse in her purse and tried not to think about being trapped in this hard stone city a very long way from home.

8

Ruso's opinion of Horatius Balbus was not improving as the afternoon wore on. When Balbus had sent his own steward rather than a junior slave to fetch the doctor immediately, Ruso had assumed it must be urgent. Instead, the afternoon was drifting past and he was stuck here among an overblown collection of sculptures, surrounded by walls painted to resemble marble in colors that shouted at one another and made the slaves look dingy by comparison.

He was not especially worried about Tilla making her way to Kleitos's surgery, even in Rome. If there was one thing army wives were good at, it was moving house on their own at short notice. In fact he was feeling faintly smug about what she would find. He would not, of course, voice the words *I told you so*, but it was just the sort of home a responsible citizen of modest means might arrange for his family: an apartment in what seemed like a good area with a bedroom separate from the kitchen, and no obvious signs of disrepair or vermin. Ruso felt a deeply unprofessional hope that Kleitos's father would be ill for a very long time.

He was less immediately concerned by the absence of Tilla than by the fact that she had his medical case. There had been no time to go back and collect it. Nor had there been any time to find any patient records, assuming Kleitos had left some. Almost as soon as the door was unlocked Balbus's steward had turned up to collect him, and been unhelpfully vague about what was wrong with his master.

A quick hunt around the rooms had failed to reveal any surgical instruments or many of the common remedies that Ruso would normally take on a call. Instead there were wide spaces on shelves that he remembered as crammed with bottles and boxes. Kleitos must have taken a lot of emergency supplies. For a man rushing to tend a sick father he seemed to have burdened himself with a vast amount of luggage: not only equipment, but most of the furniture as well. It all suggested he was expecting a long absence.

Recalling Accius's orders to make a good impression, Ruso had grabbed one or two items from the shelves and stuffed them into a battered leather satchel he had found hanging on the back of the door. He would have to worry about buying supplies later.

Now he was standing under the shade of Horatius Balbus's colonnade like one of the statues: *Doctor with Satchel over Shoulder.* Doctor with no more idea than the other statues of why he had been brought here. Doctor wondering how much of this place was paid for by rent from cockroach-infested tenement blocks. *See how cleverly the sculptor has captured his expression of boredom and disgust!*

Somewhere beyond one of the doors, a young woman was giving orders. Moments later a door creaked open and a round-faced slave girl scuttled toward him carrying a pile of linen.

"Hello."

The girl looked around to see if he was talking to someone else.

"Can you tell the steward—the one with—" The gesture was meant to indicate the striking dark eyebrows that looked like smudges of charcoal beneath the graying hair. "What's his name? Firmicus?"

If she knew, she was too nervous to tell him.

"Can you tell him," he persisted, "the doctor's still here?"

The girl hurried away without a word, vanishing through a doorway in the far corner.

Ruso decided to count to fifty and then leave. Accius could make his own good impression. Balbus clearly wasn't in need of urgent help, and other patients with more pressing needs might be waiting at the surgery. As might Tilla.

Twenty-nine, thirty.

He turned at the sound of the door in the far corner opening again. A different girl slipped into the courtyard, clutching a scroll rather than a pile of washing. She reminded him of his youngest sister: about the age, in other words, when a father needed to settle upon a reliable son-in-law before she flung herself at someone totally unsuitable.

The soft brown eyes narrowed, perhaps to get him in focus. The voice he had heard earlier asked, "Who are you?"

That complicated arrangement of curls must have taken hours. He wondered if she was expecting company. "I'm the doctor. Ruso."

"Why? Did Gellia send for you?"

"I was sent for," he agreed. "I was told it was for Horatius Balbus. I don't think he knows I'm here."

"Oh, I expect he does. Pa always knows everything. Or at least, he thinks he does."

Somehow he had known she would have dimples when she smiled.

"It's all right," she said. "You don't have to answer that. Why aren't you the usual doctor?"

"Kleitos asked me to fill in while he's away." No doubt he would be saying that a lot over the next few days. "Publius Accius was going to introduce me, but I've been called here anyway."

The girl brightened. "You're from Accius! Did he send a message for me?"

"No."

"Oh well." The girl reached up to pat the hairstyle as if it had just landed on her head and was still settling in. "I expect he's busy."

Ruso, realizing he had been accurate rather than tactful, said, "He didn't know I was coming here."

"Oh."

"I'm sure he, ah—" He stopped, not at all sure that Accius would have sent a message without the father's permission. "I could tell him you were asking."

"Oh, yes! You could tell him—" She paused to think. "Tell him I hope he's well, and tell him I'm looking after his present very carefully just like he said." She held out a slender wrist encircled by a jet bracelet.

Ruso recognized the sort of fragile luxury that soldiers bought for their girls back in Britannia. For the first time it occurred to him that Accius might have been harboring secret thoughts of this young woman all through the long months of his service in the provinces.

"Isn't it beautiful?" said the girl, turning the bangle around her wrist with her other hand. "I love how smooth it feels. It was my birthday present."

"It's very nice," said Ruso, who had long ago learned to exercise caution when any woman sought an opinion on her personal adornment. Too little enthusiasm led to accusations of *You don't like it, do you?* while too much brought on the curious complaint of *You're just saying that.*

"Accius brought it home for me. All the way from the seaside in Britannia."

Clearly this needed a better response than *Ah*, but Tilla was not here to tell him what it was. So he tried, "It's really very nice," and to his relief she lowered the wrist so he was not obliged to stare at it any longer.

Somewhere behind him, Ruso heard the click of a latch. A soft voice called, "Mistress Horatia?"

Horatia—of course, she would have her father's name—straightened her shoulders. There was a scuffle of footsteps, and a very small woman bustled past him into the courtyard. "Mistress, you are standing in the sun! And your tutor—"

The dimples were gone now. "I shall be out of the sun in just a moment. I am just consulting the doctor about my terrible headache. He says I must lie down, and unless it gets better I can't possibly go out to dinner with that awful old builder tomorrow night. And he says Greek is very bad for headaches so you can tell the tutor to go home."

Instead of hurrying away to deliver this message, the little slave took up a position beside her mistress and gave Ruso a look that said if he didn't leave them both alone, she would turn him to marble like the other figures around the courtyard.

The girl said, "Well, Doctor, I expect you're very busy, with your, ah—"

"Waiting," he said.

"Yes. Thank you for your advice. I shall do as you say." With that she hurried away, the heels of her delicate sandals clacking on the paving. The slave followed, closing the door firmly behind her.

Thirty-one, thirty-two . . .

Balbus's doorman looked shocked when he said he would call back later. "But, sir, the master—"

"He doesn't need urgent medical attention," Ruso assured him, but the man had cocked his head to listen to an order being barked from the street. He leapt forward and lifted the bar, dragged the heavy door open and stood back to bow.

A bodyguard barged past Ruso, followed by a bald figure in a purple-edged toga announcing, "Because if he doesn't, tell him I'll find someone who will."

The slave to whom this was addressed scuttled back into the street. The door was slammed behind him, leaving Ruso standing inside the porch watching the man who must be the famous Horatius Balbus—his patient, his recent landlord and Kleitos's patron—stride away into the house without a second glance.

"He wasn't here?" he said, incredulous.

The doorman said, "He is now, sir."

Ruso sighed and returned to the courtyard.

9

"WHAT A LOVELY baby!"

Tilla jolted upright on the barrel.

"How old?" A young woman with a droopy eyelid was bending sideways to admire Mara's sleeping face.

Tilla adjusted her skirts and tried not to look like someone who had been feeling sorry for herself. "Seven months."

"Oh, the best age! I'm Phyllis. Are you waiting for the doctor? He's not here, but there's a new one coming to help."

"Tilla," she said, relieved. "The new doctor is my husband. They said he sent for me, but I don't know where he is."

"Oh, you poor thing! How long have you been stuck out here?" A hand rested on her shoulder, and the kindness very nearly released the tears of self-pity Tilla had been holding back.

"You wait there," said Phyllis, as if there was any chance of Tilla running away. "We'll find him. Sabella might know. Her husband is the caretaker."

Moments later the woman from the bar appeared and demanded, "Why didn't you say you were his wife?" The thick black hair tumbled forward as she groped in the folds of a linen work shift and produced a key. "I'm Sabella. He's been called away." Unlocking the door herself rather than handing over the key, she said, "So, how well do you know Delia?"

Tilla said, "Delia?"

The woman paused in the act of seizing one of the bags. "You *are* the new doctor's wife?"

"We are both healers."

Sabella looked her up and down. "Germania?" she guessed.

"Britannia."

Sabella, who was the same width sideways as forwards, grabbed the sack of bedding with one hand and the clothes bag with the other before turning to a scatter of black-haired children who were watching from outside the bar.

"You lot," ordered Sabella, "come here and sit on the rest of this while I'm inside, and don't you dare move." Turning to Tilla, she said, "You can't be too careful around here, girl. You're not in Germania now."

Tilla said, "Britannia," but Sabella was halfway across a white-washed room set up with shelves and a workbench and a scrubbed table with a telltale tray of sawdust beneath it. At the far end of the surgery she swung 'round to shove a door open with her backside. Tilla heard the crash of shutters being flung open, and then a cry of "Where's everything gone?"

From behind a box of bandages and dressings, Phyllis called, "What is the matter?"

"Where's the furniture?"

Phyllis paused to look closely around the surgery. "Doctor Kleitos's seat is gone," she observed. "And the stool his patients sit on."

"And the saucepans!" called Sabella. "They've only just left, and somebody's been in here and had the lot!"

"And his weighing scales for the medicines."

"All the bowls and the knives and spoons!"

Tilla put her crockery box down on the scarred surface of the operating table. She could make out the shapes of missing bottles in the dust on the shelves. Below the workbench, a bucket with a broken handle contained a soiled bandage and three blood-stained teeth.

Phyllis said, "They've moved out."

"They can't have. Delia would have told me." Sabella stepped aside to allow them into a back room that was a kitchen and living space. "Even the pot's gone!" she declared, lifting the blue curtain that sagged across the corner to allow some privacy.

Phyllis said, "Who would steal a smelly pot?"

"The back door's barred from the inside," Sabella confirmed, giving it a good rattle to make sure. "Nobody's been in the front. We'd have seen them moving stuff out. Only your husband, and he was hardly there, so he can't have—" She stopped short of suggesting that he might have stolen the furniture.

Tilla said, "They must have taken the things themselves."

"The note said to expect a temporary guest," said Sabella, adding, "They never said a word to my husband about subletting," as if that made such a thing impossible.

Phyllis was busy surveying the kitchen. "A hearth and a grill! You will be able to cook at home!"

Tilla, who found cooking a very hit-and-miss affair, reached up to run a forefinger along the rough wood of the kitchen shelf. She examined the faint line of dust that stuck to it. Tentatively, she pushed a jar away from her. Nothing scuttled out.

Behind her, Phyllis said, "Are you all right?"

Tilla lifted the jar and examined the handful of flour inside, as if that was what she had intended all along.

She peered through the window grille at a courtyard much like the one she had left behind at the old apartment, except that instead of a pile of rotting scraps in the middle there was a water-spout over a trough. The balconies above were festooned with washing. There were rows of windows where mothers could lean out and keep an eye on their children, and the curious and the lonely could sit in the shadows to watch the comings and goings of their neighbors.

We could live here.

Returning her attention to the kitchen, she caught sight of a series of unevenly spaced lines scratched across the doorpost. The highest was level with her waist. "Does your friend have children?"

"Only two," Sabella told her. "Lucky girl. I tried the same stuff but it never worked for me."

Tilla remembered standing by a rougher doorpost in a faraway land, and being told to step away while her mother cut a new line in the wood, saying, "Look how you've grown!"

We could make a home here.

"I don't know how we didn't hear them," Phyllis was saying, fingering a string of onions that hung from a nail on the wall. "Our rooms are up above. We usually hear everything."

Tilla glanced at the ceiling joists and imagined the alarming sounds that might rise from a doctor's surgery during working hours.

Phyllis let the onions fall back against the wall. "Soft," she declared. "Not worth taking."

Sabella appeared from the adjoining room and announced that the mattress and the clothes chest had gone too.

Phyllis said, "Perhaps Kleitos is in some sort of trouble."

"We'd have known," Sabella insisted.

"Perhaps they were in debt."

"Never!" Sabella insisted. "Well, no more than anybody else. His bar bill's nothing. Besides, Balbus looks after them."

"Well, something is very strange."

Tilla said, "Balbus?"

"Horatius Balbus, the landlord," Sabella explained. "Kleitos used to be Balbus's slave. Now he's Balbus's freedman and Balbus is his patron. That's how it works here in Rome, see. A bit of luck and the right attitude, even foreign slaves can work their way up."

Tilla was not going to bother pointing out that she was not a slave.

"Mind you," Sabella was saying, "some of the riffraff we get here, I should think their owners were glad to get rid of them. We've had them chopping up doors for firewood, and all sorts. Only yesterday my husband had to tell a woman on the top floor to get rid of a goat. You should have heard her. Mind you, it was all in some jabber nobody speaks, so she was wasting her time."

Tilla thought, *Well, at least one person speaks it,* but Sabella had barely stopped for breath.

"You know, I thought there was something funny going on when Kleitos left the key under the door. It's not like him. They always leave one of the slaves to mind the shop when they go away."

Tilla pulled open the little cupboard to one side of the raised hearth. The shrine inside was painted like a garden, with faint lines hinting at a trellis and bright red and yellow dots filling it with flowers. The picture was stained with soot from a vanished lamp. Beneath it, the shelf was empty.

"They've taken the gods as well!" cried Sabella. Then, "She was supposed to be looking after my kids this afternoon." She glanced at Tilla. "I don't suppose— No, you'll be busy."

Phyllis said, "I will look after—"

"Never mind. They'll have to go to my sister." Sabella bustled out to where her children were squabbling over whose turn it was to clamber on top of the barrel and jump off. "You can all get down!"

Tilla followed her outside, glad she was not being asked to look after Sabella's children. She did not want to be plunged into the middle of some sort of dispute between neighbors before she had even unpacked.

Sabella was sniffing the air. "You need to change that baby, love. Your first, is it?"

Tilla nodded. Mara's history was too complicated to explain. "I didn't want to wake her."

"She'll get a rash, and then you'll wish you had." Sabella pointed indoors at the operating table. "You can do her on there while we get this barrel in. Phyllis, give me a hand."

Tilla's protest that the barrel was not hers was swept aside: It had been delivered for the doctor this morning. "Can it stay out there? It smells."

"Make sure you give her a good wash. I'll see if I can see what's in here."

Tilla, too tired to explain that a midwife did not need to be told about babies and rashes, hauled Mara's bag up onto the table, wondering yet again why, even though Mara was a fraction of the size of an adult, the bag with her belongings in it was twice as big as all the others. Busy untying the soiled cloths over wails of protest, she was only vaguely aware of figures moving around outside.

Moments later Sabella was back. "Whatever it is, it's going off. I've put a bag of charcoal on top to try to keep the air sweet, but it won't last."

"We could prize the lid up," Phyllis suggested. "It's only nailed on."

"I will ask my husband to see to it," Tilla promised. "Thank you for trying."

"You'll need to move it," Sabella told her. "You can't leave it out where the sun'll catch it. It's not like where you come from, with all that snow."

Phyllis said, "Perhaps we could drag it farther away from the door."

Moments later they were back inside the surgery, Sabella wiping her hands on her skirts and Phyllis massaging her own shoulders as if to loosen them after an effort. Tilla braced herself for further advice on the care of babies, and found herself unreasonably irritated when none came. She thanked them again for their help, but the helping was not yet finished.

"If I were you I'd put an old sheet over it to keep the flies off," suggested Sabella. "Then wait till dark and dump it a couple of streets away. The cleaning gangs will have to get rid of it."

"I will ask my husband to deal with it," repeated Tilla. She was not going to let someone's rubbish and a lack of furniture spoil her relief at finding a place to sleep where there were no cockroaches and no obvious sign of mice.

Just then someone knocked on the door of the surgery. A wiry man in a work tunic was silhouetted against the bright street.

"The doctor's gone away," Sabella announced before Tilla could answer.

"But the new doctor will be back soon!" Tilla called. "Will you come in and wait? I am a healer also. Perhaps I can help."

The man peered in at the three women and the baby having her bottom washed on the operating table. He mumbled something about coming back later and disappeared.

"Ha!" said Sabella. "We saw him off!"

"That is not the idea," Tilla told her.

"You can't go letting strange men in when you're here on your own," Sabella pointed out. "You're not in Germania now, girl."

"What if he is ill?"

Sabella was unrepentant. "That one won't pay you. You should see what he owes on his bar bill."

At the back of the surgery, half a dozen laundered bandages hung from a line slung between the rafters. Tilla reached out, hoping for something cool to press against her forehead, but they were stiff and dry.

"Such a beautiful little girl!" Phyllis reached out and gave Mara a tentative pat on the knee.

"The gods have been kind," Tilla agreed.

"You're too late for the market," Phyllis told her. "And the bakery. I shall bring you some bread. And tonight we will pray to Christos for you and your family and for Kleitos and Delia and the children."

Tilla thanked her.

"And I shall pray to Diana!" declared Sabella.

Phyllis was hardly out of the door before Tilla felt a hand on her arm. "You need to watch out for that one," Sabella told her. "Especially around the baby."

"Has she no child of her own?"

"They act friendly to draw you in. That's how it starts."

"Who?" Tilla knew only too well the ache of a woman with no child: something Sabella would never understand. "How what starts?"

Sabella stepped away and adjusted one of the pins in her hair. "I'm not one for passing on gossip," she said. "I'm just saying, be careful. And if you want a decent meal tonight, we do a good salt pork stew. Very filling." She paused in the doorway, surveying the surgery. "It's not like Delia, you know, going away like that and not saying a word. I don't know what my husband's going to say about it. What about the rent?"

Tilla, hoping Delia and her family were gone for good, thanked her again for helping. The rent was like the barrel: something that could be dealt with later.

Now it was Sabella who moved close. "If you do get any trouble with debt collectors," she said, "send them next door. We'll tell them Kleitos has done a runner and none of this is his stuff."

The street door clamped shut, and the surgery was plunged into gloom.

"Well!" Tilla spoke British into the sudden silence. "What do you think that was all about?"

But if Mara had an opinion, she was keeping it to herself. Tilla carried her through into the kitchen, laying her on her fleece on the tiled floor. Then she went through all the bags until she found the box with the dried leaves from the oak tree outside her family's house, and the bronze figure of Mercury that came from her husband's home in the south of Gaul. Taking the little wooden horse from her purse, she placed them all in the shrine by the hearth, leaving the doors open so they could watch over her while she set up her new household.

10

"THE MASTER WILL see you now." Firmicus, despite being a muscular man in possession of striking eyebrows and greater than average height, had a steward's talent for being unobtrusive. "Come with me."

More loud paintwork. More columns. More statues: one of a satyr doing something deeply undesirable to a goat. It occurred to Ruso that if he were Horatia's father, he would have put that somewhere she couldn't see it.

A second, more private, courtyard garden, where the cooling splash of a fountain into a basin full of fish and the chirruping of caged sparrows sweetened any residual noise from the street. Meanwhile the high walls hid any reminder of the tenants who paid for it all.

The man who had swept past Ruso on the porch earlier was sitting on a marble bench near the fountain, under the dappled shade of a leafy arch. It was difficult to see any resemblance to his daughter. The bald head squatted on a thick neck, his chest seemed to have slumped into the folds of his toga, and he sat with his knees spread to accommodate his paunch. Ruso was obliged to stand in the sun as the steward introduced him and was then ordered to leave.

Ruso was aware of movement in the shadows and realized that

other attendants had been present. As far as he could see only one figure remained: a hard-faced man with a club stuck into his belt, who was watching them from the far corner. Out of earshot, but close enough to intervene if there was trouble.

Ruso waited for his patient to speak. Balbus was overweight, but his stride had been vigorous and his complexion was healthy. Whatever was troubling him was not obvious.

Balbus picked an invisible piece of fluff off his toga. "Doctor Kleitos," he said, "has looked after me and my people for twenty years. For twenty years, I've looked after him in return." He dropped the fluff beside him. "Today he left Rome without having the courtesy to consult me."

"I believe he had a family emergency, sir."

"So I'm told."

Whatever snub Kleitos had offered his patron, it had nothing to do with Ruso. "How can I help, sir?"

Balbus's deep brown eyes looked into his own, and Ruso had the impression of a man who was far more perceptive than he looked. "I like to do business with people I know."

"Doctor Kleitos asked me to fill in for him, sir. Publius Accius can vouch for me. I served under him in Britannia."

"Hm."

Ruso wished he had waited before sending that hasty summons to Tilla. This man was Kleitos's patron: He could make things very difficult if he decided he did not want a stranger running Kleitos's practice.

"Ruso," said Balbus. "Didn't I find you an apartment?"

"Yes, sir."

"How was it?"

If he was honest, he might end up back there. If he lied, he might retain the job. Either way, the vermin would retain control of the apartments. "A bit of a problem with cockroaches, sir."

Balbus grunted. "Bloody nuisance. We do our best, but you only need a couple of tenants who don't clean up after themselves, and they're back again. It's hard enough stopping the buggers from burning the place down with cooking fires. We can't stop them from taking food in."

Ruso assumed the *buggers* were the tenants rather than the cockroaches.

"You were doctor to Publius Accius out in Britannia?"

"I was medical officer in charge of several hospitals for the Twentieth Legion, and I dealt with the casualties during the last rebellion."

"But you weren't his personal physician."

"He didn't have one." It seemed Ruso had not been summoned here to treat the sick, but to be interviewed for the job of replacing Kleitos. "If he'd been ill, he would have come to us."

"So what did he bring you over here for?"

Ruso said truthfully, "I can't tell you, sir."

To his surprise, Balbus nodded approval. "At least you know how to keep your mouth shut."

Since opening it was unlikely to get him any farther, Ruso remained silent.

"Who else knows you in the city?"

"Quite a few doctors and patients, sir."

Balbus's sigh was so exaggerated that he seemed about to deflate, leaving the toga collapsed on the bench. "Anyone I've heard of?"

Ruso cast his mind back over the plumber with the crushed foot, the woman upstairs with a bad fever, and the youth who was losing his hearing. Then there was the man who had arrived clutching his back, who explained that he didn't expect much because all doctors were useless. And all the spectators from outside the amphitheater this morning. "Probably not," he admitted. Then, just to get it out of the way, "There's a man called Metellus. He was in Britannia too."

"Never heard of him. What do you know about poisons?"

"I'd recognize the common ones. Anything obscure I'd refer to a specialist."

"So," said Balbus with the air of a lawyer summing up his case, "You know nobody, and nobody knows you, and you don't know much about poisons, either."

"That's about it." Which was unfortunate, since both Accius and Tilla were depending upon him to make a good impression. "Kleitos never mentioned poisons."

Balbus scratched his chin and appeared to be considering this dire state of affairs.

His caution was inconvenient but understandable. This morning's charlatan with the ladder was not alone. Only last week Ruso had listened in amazement as two self-styled experts debated the content of human arteries: one vehemently denying the other's assertion that they contained milk because, as anyone with any sense knew already, there was no room for milk when arteries were full of air. Neither man seemed ever to have attended an injured patient, nor watched any of Famous Doctor Callianax's public anatomy demonstrations of nonsqueaking pigs.

"Well," said Balbus finally, "that could work to our advantage."

Ruso did not dare to ask how.

"Any family?"

"A wife and child here," Ruso told him. "The rest of my family is in Gallia Narbonensis."

"I expect absolute loyalty and discretion."

"I do my best for my patients," Ruso assured him, suspecting it was wise to define the difference between *absolute loyalty* and *utter servitude*, "and I don't discuss what I know about them with anyone else."

"Not even Publius Accius?"

Ruso tried to imagine a situation in which Accius might be interested in other people's fevers and fractures and bunions. Then it occurred to him that the state of Balbus's health would be of enormous interest to Accius if he succeeded in marrying Horatia. Presumably she would inherit all this wealth when her father died. "Not even Publius Accius."

"Good. You can fill in until Kleitos gets back. I'll see to it that my people look after you and your wife and daughter."

Ruso's "Thank you, sir," was heartfelt. For however brief a period, he had got Tilla out of that crumbling, verminous tenement.

"But if you let me down, believe me—I will find out."

Ruso did not doubt it.

Balbus was reaching under the folds of the toga. "To business." He held out a square green bottle with a dribble of dark liquid in the bottom. "I've run out of this."

The glass was warm to the touch. There was no label. Ruso twisted out the stopper and sniffed. He could detect several kinds of foulness but could only identify poppy. He held the bottle upside down so the liquid trickled down toward his waiting finger. It tasted bitter and sickly at the same time, and he longed to spit it out and rinse his mouth under one of the streams of the fountain. "What is it?"

Instead of answering, Balbus raised a hand to gesture around himself. "All that you see here," he announced, "is the fruit of one generation. My father was a slave, my mother was a slave, and I was born here as another man's property." He indicated the purple stripe on his toga. "Now I'm master in the house I served in, I'm a priest in the cult of Augustus, and young Accius isn't the only eligible suitor with designs on my daughter."

So Balbus was a freedman. That explained the determination to swelter under the hard-earned toga even at home on a sunny morning. Ruso made the expected murmur of admiration and wondered if Accius knew he had competition for the hand of the dimpled Horatia.

"I have forty-three domestic slaves," Balbus continued, "and fourteen apartment blocks spread across the city with another three hundred or so slaves and freedmen working in the business. And it's no secret how I did it."

As he paused for effect, Ruso guessed that the next words were unlikely to be *fraud* or *extortion* or *befriending rich people with not long to live*.

"Hard work."

"Very impressive," Ruso agreed.

"And providing what people need," added Balbus. "The property business is all about demand and supply."

Ruso, realizing he was expected to comment, said, "Ah."

"You'll see it yourself if you stay long enough. Every year, thousands of slaves freed and thousands of outsiders coming to Rome, expecting to walk under showers of gold. Like you did, didn't you?"

Ruso cleared his throat, hoping this was a rhetorical question.

"And when they don't," Balbus continued, "do they go home? No. They stay here, cluttering up the streets, looking for somewhere to live. And that's where I come in. I know what they say about some of my properties, and I wouldn't like to live in them either, but answer me this. Where else are those people going to go?"

"I don't know, sir."

"No. Nobody does. Not a lot of landlords are prepared to put up with what I put up with, especially for what my tenants are paying. And are they grateful? Of course not. You give most of those complainers somewhere decent and it'll be a midden within a week."

Perhaps seeing Ruso glance at the glittering fountain, Balbus continued. "Hard work, Doctor. Hard work. I've scrubbed floors and carried loads and tied scaffolding. You do whatever it takes."

"Yes."

"And now you're wondering what this has got to do with poisons."

"Yes."

Balbus shifted his weight on the bench. "I don't know what it's like out in the provinces," he said, "but here, there are men who don't like to see another man succeed. Men who think—wrongly—that I'm standing in their path." He paused, watching the bodyguard pacing the perimeter of the courtyard, half-hidden by rose bushes and trailing vines. "Latro is good. Very good. But he has his limits."

Wondering suddenly if the fountain—which worked much better than Accius's—was there to protect Balbus from eavesdroppers, Ruso turned the bottle on its side. "This is a theriac?"

Instead of answering, Balbus said, "A lot of people, Doctor, think the secret of success is getting rid of your enemies. They're wrong. The secret"—he raised a callused forefinger to emphasise his point—"is being one step ahead of them."

"Do you have a taster?"

"I can hardly take a taster out to dinner with me tomorrow. It's an insult to my host. Besides, they're no use against a slow-acting poison."

The bottle glinted in the sunlight. Ruso said, "Does this have a name?"

"Not one that I know."

"I'll check Kleitos's records, sir," he said, hoping some existed. A sole practitioner who saw the same patients week in, week out would work very differently from a legionary medic who was used to sharing information with a team. Kleitos probably had most of his patient records stored in his memory, and he had seen no sign of any hand-over notes. "You may have to wait until he gets back, though."

"I need my daily medicine, Doctor."

Ruso swallowed. He certainly wasn't about to start trying to mix up theriac himself. The universal antidote that had allegedly prevented King Mithridates from poisoning himself—even when he had wanted to—contained at least forty ingredients, several of them highly toxic and some only required in the sort of quantity you could scrape up under a fingernail. The recipe developed by Nero's doctor contained even more, including a large quantity of roasted and matured vipers' flesh. He supposed the patient would build up slowly to a full dose.

At the other end of the scale were the cheaper mixtures sold to nervous travelers venturing away from home. Ruso had no idea which recipe Balbus had been taking. The names Kleitos had given him were of simple herb sellers. Ruso didn't want to kill his new patient by accident before he found someone who could supply the correct mixture.

"So you can't help me?" Balbus prompted.

"Sir, if Kleitos hasn't left a record of the recipe, prescribing a different one could put you in just as much danger as the poison you're trying to avoid." Balbus responded with a cold stare that he had probably honed on tenants who were late with the rent. Ruso, who had spent years dealing with angry centurions, concentrated his gaze on the top of the man's bald head. "If I can't trace it," he continued, "I don't want to ask around and publicize the fact that you've run out."

Only Balbus's lips moved. "I was hoping you would be useful."

"If I can't find it, I can mix up something harmless that looks like it. That way you'll be seen taking your regular protection until Kleitos comes back."

Balbus's expression softened very slightly. "And nobody will get any clever ideas."

"Exactly, sir."

"And you'll keep this conversation to yourself."

"I will, sir."

Balbus shifted his position on the bench. "Deliver it to me in person at the building site on the Vicus Cuprius just before the tenth hour."

Ruso agreed, wondering whether Balbus really did have dangerous rivals around every corner, or whether he made enemies by insinuating that his hosts were trying to poison his dinner. Maybe gangs of angry tenants were plotting against him. Maybe he just had a vivid imagination.

"Two things for you to remember," Balbus added. "Don't tell anyone else you don't know much about poisons. And don't ever speak to my daughter again without my permission."

Firmicus appeared beside Ruso on the way out, eyebrows raised in query. "Everything all right, Doctor?"

"I'm delivering some medicine to your master just before the tenth hour at a building site on the Vicus Cuprius."

The steward showed no surprise at this complicated arrangement, saying only, "Make sure you get there on time. Horatius Balbus is a man who means what he says."

11

Ruso's pleasure at seeing his wife in a decent home—albeit a sparsely furnished one—was tempered by the news that he had missed several potential patients and that his choices for a late lunch were

    I. bread, kindly donated by the neighbor upstairs, or
   II. bread and fried onion, or
  III. bread and raw onion, or
  IV. bread with oil

"Or just onion," Tilla offered, putting the finishing touches to a pile of kindling under the grill. He went to shove Kleitos's document box back beneath the workbench after a quick and fruitless search. It was half full of battered scrolls, fragments of parchment, and writing tablets. He suspected someone in a hurry had picked out all the important items and thrown the rest back in the box.

Tilla called through from the kitchen, "I could fry it if you like."

"Onion soup?"

There were not enough sound onions for soup. There had been no time to buy anything else, and Tilla had very little money, because she had spent it all paying the porters.

He swatted at a fly before handing over a couple of sesterces without comment. She must already know she had been swindled, and the porters were long gone. So was the acquaintance of Accius's doorman, who had recommended them to him in exchange for an undeserved tip.

Tilla slid the coins into her purse. "Will you watch Mara while I fetch something from the bar?"

"Can't you take her with you? I'm working."

She said, "It is only next door!"

"Exactly!"

"I will not be gone long."

Ruso sighed. Ever since Mara had been weaned and the wet nurse had left for other duties, he and his wife had become the servants of a small and highly unreasonable mistress. It was ridiculous. Surely no man—certainly no former legionary officer— should have to participate in games of pass-the-baby like this? Tilla had been desperate for a child, but now that they had one, she did not seem anywhere near as desperate to look after her all the time, and she kept expecting him to help.

He weighed his purse in his palm. Most of it was copper, but presumably Balbus would pay him something for the theriac— genuine or otherwise—and Accius might be prepared to give him an advance now that he had work. It was clear from the emptiness of the apartment that Doctor Kleitos was expecting to be away for some time. "Tomorrow," he called, "I'm going to find us a slave."

Tilla paused in the doorway. "Sabella from the bar says if the debt collectors come, tell them the other doctor is gone away and everything here is ours, and if they don't believe you, to send them to her. She will frighten them off. And we must do something about that barrel out there."

He looked up from Mara's attempts to sink both her teeth into a fistful of bread crust. "What debt collectors?"

Tilla flapped a hand across her face to get rid of a fly. "They might not come."

Debt collectors. Ruso glanced around the half-empty living space with fresh understanding. The story about the sick father had been a polite fiction. The family had taken everything of value that they could carry and fled. Yet even in the midst of disaster Kleitos had remembered the needs of his patients, and of a colleague who was out of work. *Be careful who you trust* was probably a warning not to borrow money from people who would turn nasty if you couldn't pay them back. Best not to risk taking loans from strangers. If Accius didn't come up with the cash to buy a slave, Ruso would have to sell his army kit after all.

"I'll call you if she cries," he said, because it was important to establish the proper order of domestic life.

When his wife had gone, he propped the baby up on her sheepskin and cushions in the corner of the surgery where she could reach up to play with the dangling bandages. Then he tore off a chunk of bread for himself and began to work his way methodically around the room, starting with the left wall. He had bought himself some time with Balbus by suggesting a substitute, but he needed to find that medicine, or else some note of its name in Kleitos's records. The trouble was, while Kleitos had handed over his practice and his lodgings, there was no sign of any attempt to hand over any information about his patients.

The workbench creaked under his weight as he scrambled up to check the top shelf. The scatter of jars there held only dust and the shambolic corpses of spiders. Lower, the bowing of the shelves testified to a store of medicines far greater than the sparse collection of green glass bottles that now remained, not all of which were labeled.

A wail from the corner caused him to glance down. Two chubby feet were kicking from beneath a mound of white linen.

"Oh hell!" He leapt down, lifted off the tangle of bandages that should have been rolled and put away, and prized the end of one out of his daughter's hand. "You weren't supposed to pull them off the line," he told her. He piled them on the operating table, the white now soiled with dirt from the floor. Mara's chunk of bread had fallen on the floor and was filthy. He tossed it into the waste bucket and fetched her a fresh piece. That slave could not come soon enough.

Along the back of the bench, a perfect row of dust-free circles in diminishing sizes betrayed the absence of a set of bronze cupping vessels. Above and to one side was an empty hook exactly where he would have stored his own leather apron to protect his clothes during surgery.

Eyeing a tattered broom propped against a half-empty sack of sawdust—both of them cumbersome, low value, and not worth taking—Ruso thought about the number of hasty and desperate decisions Kleitos's family must have taken, and how much worse that same process would have been for his own ancestors.

Rome's Great Fire had been a catastrophe, but for Ruso's fore-bears it was a timely blessing. They never found out who had denounced them to Nero's brutal enforcers. It could have been a business rival. It could have been the couple next door, taking malicious revenge for the family's complaints about their noisy parties and drunken quarrels. It could have been a distant acquaintance, giving up a name that meant nothing to him in the hope of saving himself. The result had been the same.

The story went that, in a desperate attempt to protect his fleeing household, Ruso's great-grandfather had bequeathed all his nonhuman property to the emperor and was on the verge of taking his own life when the smell of burning wafted from the direction of the Palatine Hill. As the air filled with the crashes of falling buildings and the screams of fleeing humans and beasts, Great-grandfather slid his knife back into its sheath. He abandoned his best toga for a work tunic left behind by one of his slaves, and joined the crowds who were heading out of the city.

The family arrived in Gaul with only what they and the slaves could carry, less the items they had been forced to sell to buy their passage. One of the "items" was the children's much-loved tutor. Of all the sacrifices suffered by the ten-year-old who would later become Ruso's grandfather, that had been the greatest. Determined that his own family should never endure such a loss, Grandfather had grown up with an eye for a business opportunity and a horror of debt and waste. Unfortunately Ruso's father had inherited neither of them.

Ruso eyed the abandoned remains of another family's livelihood and wondered if Grandfather would have been disappointed in him too. Despite his best efforts, the family farm was still burdened with debt. And now here he was, a grown man, having to mind the baby while his wife went shopping, because he did not have the cash to buy even one slave.

"Somewhere," he informed Mara, not because she needed to know but because he suspected she never heard Latin unless he was in the house, "it's all gone very wrong."

Mara stared at him as if she were considering a wise and helpful reply, then busied herself with the bread. Ruso shooed a fly off the table, turned back to the shelves, and resumed the hunt for the medicine that would keep Horatius Balbus one step ahead of his real or imagined enemies.

Several minutes later he reported to Mara that he couldn't find it. "It might be labeled *Theriac*," he told her, "or *Mithridate*, or *Antidote*"—he turned his attention to the opposite side of the room—"or it might have *Balbus* written on it, or *Andromachus's Special Recipe* . . ." But the shelves here held only dusty boxes of bandages and dressings.

He bent down and wiped a lump of soggy crust from his daughter's cheek. "On the other hand," he told her, "it might just be labeled *Bloody Expensive*, which is why he's taken it with him."

Mara, pleased with the attention, laughed and waved her arms in the air. He grinned back. It was good to have an appreciative audience. His wife had been more than a little distracted lately. If she had even noticed the grazes on his sore knees, she had not bothered to comment.

"What is expensive?" Tilla's voice startled him.

"Rome." He flicked the soggy crust into the waste bucket, resisting the urge to tell her about Andromachus's Special Improved Theriac Recipe for Nero, a man who was justifiably afraid of being poisoned. The less Tilla knew about men like Nero, or indeed men like Horatius Balbus, the better.

Tilla held out a bowl of olives. He wiped his hands on a clean cloth. He was beginning to suspect that Kleitos had just bought the antidote mixture ready prepared whenever Balbus needed it. The gods alone knew who from. Always assuming, of course, that it was the genuine article and not just some concoction of his own that the little Greek brewed up in the kitchen when his wife wasn't frying onions.

She said, "That barrel outside, husband. Sabella at the bar is asking when we will move it."

He grunted his lack of interest and spat an olive stone into the bucket with satisfying accuracy.

"It belongs to the other doctor, and it is starting to bring flies. She says it will put their customers off."

From somewhere in the distance, he heard the ninth hour sounding. "I can't deal with it now," he told her. "I've got a patient waiting."

"Her husband says if we can't manage it, they can lend us a strong slave. I will ask—"

"I'm quite capable of moving it."

Tilla took the baby away into the kitchen and left the olives. He called, "Have you seen a bottle of medicine anywhere back there? Dark brown, thick, smells as if it's been scraped off the drains?"

She had not.

"Can you get that fire going, then? I need to make some."

He delved inside his medical case, brought out the jar of poppy and upended it into his palm. Nothing happened.

"Tilla?"

The sight of the jar brought a confession that she had used the last of it in a desperate attempt to get some sleep among the cockroaches.

If he found the name of the theriac supplier, he might be able to hurry there and still deliver in time. He reached below the bench and pulled out the documents box again, laying out the scrolls and tablets where they would catch the light from the door. The scrolls seemed to be a collection of scraps not unlike the note he had received earlier. They contained sections of medical textbooks that Kleitos had perhaps bought cheap. He recognized a section of Celsus on dislocations, which looked and smelled as if it had been salvaged from a bonfire, with missing words added near the ragged edges in an untidy scrawl. On the back was the note Kleitos had made during their conversation about the useful properties of dock leaves. He fortified himself with more olives before tackling the note tablets.

One or two tablets contained names that must have belonged to patients, but they were accounts for payment, not records of treatment, and Balbus's name was not among them. Neither, for that matter, was Accius's. Several more tablets in the same handwriting seemed to be detailed observations about anatomy. The delicate and complex bones of the wrist. How the main artery leading into the arm from the shoulder passes under the small pectoral muscle. Most of what Ruso could manage to make out seemed reassuringly sensible. He wished he had been able to spend more time with Kleitos. They could, he felt, have been friends. Perhaps one of the neighbors could suggest where to track him down so he could be asked where Balbus's medicine came from.

Setting the anatomy notes aside and swatting at another of the wretched flies, Ruso finally found a column of items and prices listed in quantities that could only mean he had found a record of supplies. This was more like it. Tipping the tablet toward the light from the door, he began to reread it more slowly, running a finger down each line and searching for any hint of a source for Balbus's precautionary antidote. He had just reached the last line without enlightenment, when a shadow fell across the writing and a nasal voice said, "I've come to see the doctor."

"I'm the doctor today. How can I—?"

"The other doctor," interrupted the man.

"He's not here. Can I help?"

"It's about my money."

Tilla's instant appearance from the kitchen suggested she had been listening for her cue. "The other doctor is gone away," she announced, "and all his things have gone with him."

"He was here yesterday."

"Ask at the bar next door: They will tell you the same."

"What about my money?"

"His debts are not ours."

The man craned to see past her, as if Kleitos might be hiding in the kitchen. "Where is he, then? When's he coming back?"

Still clutching the tablet, Ruso stepped in between them. "I've got his records here. What's your name?"

"Cash on delivery, it was."

"You'll be paid," Ruso promised, not wanting the practice to get a reputation for poor payment. "What was it you delivered?"

To his surprise the man retreated into the arcade. "I'll come back when he's here."

"Was it that barrel?" Tilla followed them both outside. "Because whatever it is, it has gone off. You can take it away again."

The man raised his hands. "Nothing to do with me, miss."

Ruso tried again. "If you give me your name, I'll give him a message."

But the man was already limping away down the arcade, the

lurch in his step exaggerated by the slanting shadows that the columns cast across the sunny paving.

Tilla said, "He was not much of a debt collector."

"No," Ruso agreed, privately congratulating himself on the ease with which he had seen the man off.

"Just as well. It is no good if I tell people we do not know where Kleitos is, and then you tell them you will give him a message. Husband, we must do something about that barrel. It is not—"

Seeing there would be no peace, he stepped past her, warning her to mind out as he tipped the barrel up onto its rim and maneuvered it awkwardly toward the door. Then he stopped. He recognized that smell. Tilla was right. He certainly did need to do something about it. But he had made a promise to meet Horatius Balbus before the tenth hour. Time was passing. He couldn't find the medicine or anywhere to buy some, and Horatius Balbus was a man who meant what he said. Whatever this was—and it was definitely not good—it would have to wait. He rolled it back to its former position.

"But, husband—"

"I'll see to it later," he said, stepping back indoors. "Stay away from it. Don't let anyone interfere with it, and don't breathe the air near it."

He put on the leather apron. He needed to concentrate on Balbus's medicine. He was lining up bottles on the table and wondering what sort of brown liquid burned onions mashed with black olives and dates would make, or if he should simply adulterate a mild cough mixture, when Tilla emerged from the kitchen clutching one of the fire irons. "I said I'll deal with it," he repeated, but she took no notice.

He hung the weighing scale from the hook Kleitos must have used for the same purpose, and surveyed the jars of potential ingredients his predecessor had left behind. Finally he checked the contents of a jar where most of the word POPPY was faintly visible in faded Greek on the outside, and was relieved to find that one dark lozenge of dried poppy tears remained inside. He sniffed it, then dropped it into the pan of the weighing scale, and licked his fingers, grimacing at the familiar bitter taste. Outside, he heard the sound of something scraping against wood and the screech of nails being prized out.

The next screech came not from the nails, but from his wife.

12

THE ONLY PERSON who was not disturbed by the opening of the barrel was the man inside it, because he must have been dead since sometime yesterday. Even Ruso, who was as accustomed to dealing with the end of life as Tilla was with the beginning, was shaken. Not that the sight was gory: The man's eyes were closed and the cropped blond head rested against the wooden staves as if he had crept in there for a sleep. But who curled up naked in a barrel and then nailed a lid on from the outside?

Tilla was gripping Ruso's arm as if she was afraid she might faint. He put his hand over hers and said, "It's all right," although if she had asked him exactly what was all right, he would not have been able to answer. "It's all right," he repeated. "Go and sit down."

Even as he said it, strangers drawn by her screams were gathering around the barrel and there were fresh cries of horror. He said, "Does anyone know who it is?" but nobody seemed to be listening. The crowd's exclamations drew new onlookers from the street, and now it seemed most of the drinkers from the bar on the corner were pushing their way forward to get a look so that they too could recoil in shock.

"Go and sit down," he urged Tilla, but instead she released her grip on his arm and bent to retrieve the lid.

"We must show respect!" She was trying to place the lid back in its original position, but the loosened nails snagged in the ends of the staves and other hands grabbed at it to hold it up.

Voices were demanding, "Let me see!" and "Is it anyone we know?" and "Ugh, these flies!" and then he heard the woman from the bar with "Let me through!"

He needed to take charge here before his new workplace became the center of a street show even more distasteful than the one he had witnessed this morning. "Stand back!" he ordered. "Back, everybody."

One or two people began to move but Sabella, who had forced her way to the front, placed both hands on the rim of the barrel and bent to peer at what could be seen of the man's face. "It's all right," she announced, straightening up. "It's nobody from 'round here."

"Stand back!" Ruso urged again, not for the first time frustrated by the inability of civilians to obey a simple order. To Sabella he added, "You shouldn't touch anything or breathe the air. You don't know what killed him."

Sabella let go of the barrel as if it were hot, and hid her hands behind her back. "You heard the doctor! Don't all stand there gawping. It's nobody we know anyway."

She would have made a promising centurion.

As the crowd shuffled back, Ruso squatted to position the lid over the nail holes. Then he retrieved the fire iron that Tilla had dropped, and used the end to hammer everything back into position.

"Nothing to see!" Sabella declared to the disappointed onlookers. "You can all go home!" To Ruso and Tilla, she said, "I'll get my husband. He'll have to see to it."

The crowd began to disperse, several of them pausing to point out the barrel to people who had arrived too late to see anything.

Suddenly realizing what they might be thinking, Ruso announced loudly to nobody in particular, "It was here when we got here!" One or two people turned to look, and he knew that nothing he said would make much difference: The doctor's emblem beside him on the wall, the stains on the leather apron, and the unlucky man in the barrel had combined to produce a very unfortunate first impression.

13

THE VICUS CUPRIUS was near the amphitheater, which was just as well. Ruso, as distracted as any man might be whose wife had just found a naked corpse inside a barrel, found it hard to concentrate on where he was going.

The site was barely more than leveled rubble crammed between two soaring apartment blocks. Someone was busy adding to a complicated web of twine that was pegged out on the ground. He was cautiously stepping backward over the existing lines. Two more men stood beside a wooden leveling instrument that had been placed upright in the rubble. A flimsy table had been unfolded in the middle of the site, and beyond it Ruso recognized the bald head of Horatius Balbus. His solid frame looked younger and slimmer inside a plain work tunic. Next to Balbus was a man wearing the same battered straw hat that Ruso had seen on the crane supervisor by the amphitheater this morning.

Balbus's bodyguard was leaning against the wall of the next apartment block, surveying the scene with his thumbs stuck in his belt and showing no interest in what the builders were doing.

Ruso approached and held out the bottle of thick brown liquid, wrapped in a cloth because it was still hot. "Horatius Balbus's medicine."

The man eyed him as if he were an interesting insect. "Delivery in person."

"I'm here in person," Ruso pointed out. "And I've got patients waiting." It sounded better than *I've left my wife in a new apartment with a screaming baby, a crowd of nosy neighbors, and a corpse.*

"Wait."

Out in the middle of the site, Balbus and the man in the straw hat peered at whatever was laid out on the desk. Then the man in the straw hat stepped across to the surveying instrument and squinted at the plumb lines dangling from the top. Ruso, who had watched military engineers doing this countless times and much faster, tapped one foot on the rubble, as there was the inevitable left-a-bit-right-a-bit exchange. Despite the girl's assertion earlier that "Pa always knows everything," his patient did not seem to have noticed that Ruso was here as requested. Ruso coughed as loudly as he dared. At least *delivery in person* meant he would be able to tell Balbus that a body had been delivered to his absent freedman.

Finally the man in the straw hat jabbed his forefinger downward. A boy dropped into a crouch at the feet of a workman holding a pole. The workman stepped back. The boy shrank away, leaving one outstretched hand holding a peg in position, and a second man swung a hammer down. The line of the future wall, or drain, or whatever it was, was set. The workmen moved away across the rubble, heads down, followed by the boy carrying a bag of supplies.

Balbus clapped the man in the straw hat around the shoulders as if they were old friends, and set off toward his doctor. The bodyguard said, "Go," and Ruso picked his way forward over the lines that crisscrossed the site like trip wires.

He was aware of the man in the straw hat calling, "Five thirteen to seven ten," and the measurement was echoed from somewhere across the site.

Balbus reached for the bottle in its cloth. "You look nervous, Doctor."

Ruso opened his mouth to explain, but before he could begin, Balbus said, "You haven't told anyone about our conversation?"

"No."

Balbus raised the bottle, tipped it sideways, and watched the liquid level itself out.

"Sir, about Doctor Kleitos—"

"No sign of him, I suppose?"

"No, sir. But there's a problem at the surgery. There was this barrel—"

"Talk to Firmicus." Balbus winced as his fingers met the hot glass, then he twisted out the stopper and sniffed. Ruso was struck by the absurd notion that he could be handing over a poison in the guise of medicine. His patient was right: He was nervous. Ever since he had realized what was in the barrel, *Be careful who you trust* had taken on a sinister new significance.

"As I said, my people will look after you. This smells disgusting. What's in it?"

Ruso forced himself to concentrate. "Not theriac," he admitted as Balbus wiped the neck of the bottle with the cloth and put the stopper back. "I couldn't get hold of any. It's mashed burned onions, wine, honey, and . . . some other things, thickened with flour." He could not remember what the other things were. It had been difficult to concentrate on boiling up medicine while Tilla fended off a crowd of neighbors, all of whom wanted to see the body for themselves.

"So is it any use at all?"

He remembered to explain that he had put poppy tears in there. "If you've been taking poppy daily, it's not wise to make a sudden change."

"So Kleitos told me."

That was reassuring. Repeating what he had inked on the wooden label tied around the neck, Ruso said, "One small spoonful every evening, and make sure you shake the bottle first."

Balbus nodded. "Firmicus will pay you."

He had almost escaped when a hand landed on his arm. "You said you didn't know anybody in the city?"

"Not really, sir."

"Come with me. I'll introduce you to Curtius Cossus. He's the man I'll be dining with tomorrow evening."

It was a sign of how distracted Ruso was that they were halfway across the building site before he realized that he had been ordered to deliver the medicine to the Vicus Cuprius at this hour precisely because Balbus had wanted Curtius Cossus to watch.

14

WHERE'S IT GONE?" Ruso shut the door behind him before peering around in the heavily scented dusk of the surgery.

Tilla's shrug indicated both ignorance and indifference, but he noticed she had the little carved horse from home still clutched in the hand that wasn't cradling Mara. "Sabella said her husband would tell someone to take it away," she told him. "And now it is gone. So you cannot look at it."

"Me? Why would I want to look at it?"

"You always want to look."

"Only when there's a problem," he told her. "Someone's bound to come asking questions. I might have been able to help."

But his wife was not interested. "I have told the neighbors, husband, and I told the slaves who came to fetch it, and now I am telling you. It has nothing to do with us, and I am tired of talking about it."

"But—"

"You do not have to deal with everyone's problems here. You are not in the Legion now. This filthy city has slaves to do everything. There is probably a Department of Dead Bodies with slaves who will bury it."

"They're called undertakers." He made his way toward the kitchen and sniffed. "Rose oil?"

Tilla lowered Mara onto her fleece. "I want to get that other smell out of my nose."

"We need to open the shutters," he told her, striding across the kitchen and matching the action to the words. "Why—"

The gaggle of children outside stepped back, looking as surprised as he was. Then a small voice piped up, "Are you the new doctor?"

"I am. Can I help?"

But they were already running away, shrieking and giggling.

"This is how it has been." Tilla reached past him to close the shutters again, but he held her back.

"I'm here now," he told her, hoping that would make a difference, "and we're not living in the dark. They'll get over it."

Before either of them could speak there was a knock at the door. "I'll go," he said, guessing the children had run 'round to the front.

The buxom woman on the threshold had her arms folded as if he had already insulted her. "You're this new doctor, are you?" He had barely opened his mouth to agree when she announced, "People are very upset."

He said, "Already?"

Her head receded into her neck in a manner that reminded him of a pigeon. Her two companions shifted closer, ready to support or possibly hide behind her if the new doctor turned nasty. She repeated, "Very upset!" and glanced at the other women for support. "Aren't they?"

"Very," said the woman on her left as the other gave a vigorous nod.

"Vibia's mother's had a funny turn and my neighbor's uncle fell on the stairs, and he's never done that before, even with knees like he has, and a dog 'round the corner just had two dead pups. If that isn't bad luck, I don't know what is!"

Ruso said, "Perhaps I can help—"

"This is a decent area," the talkative one continued. "People here make an effort. Not like down in the Subura."

"I see."

"We're not fussy," she said. "We don't mind Greeks and Syrians and Gauls, as long as they work, and we put up with followers of Christos, but this is too much."

"What is?"

"Her, keeping dead bodies!"

"Her?"

"Her!" She gestured toward the surgery. "That woman in there!"

That woman? Ruso took a deep breath and forced himself to unclench his fists while the visitor carried on talking. "It's disgusting, that's what it is. You're not in Germania now, you know. This is Rome. We honor the gods." She turned to her companions, who nodded eager confirmation but said nothing at all.

"I see."

"It's no use saying *I see*. What are you going to do about it?"

He said, "What needs to be done, exactly?"

The woman glanced at her companions, then back at him. He guessed she was summoning the courage to repeat whatever had been said between them. "At the very least," she said, as if it was a concession, "the whole place ought to be purified by a proper priest."

"Fair enough."

"And then we want the old doctor back. It's bad enough with that lot upstairs holding illegal meetings. We've nothing against you personally, but we can't have the place full of barbarians bringing bad luck with their filthy ways."

Ruso pulled the door closed behind him in the hope that Tilla might not be listening. "Is that so?" he asked, wondering what the woman would think if he shared his own suspicions about why the dead body was there. "You yourself—I don't recall you telling me your name—is that what you think?"

The woman bristled. "We're only telling you what everyone's saying. We've taken the trouble to come 'round and be helpful. If you don't want to listen, that's your problem."

"In that case," Ruso told her, tightening his grip on the door because he could feel Tilla tugging at the other side, "let me tell you some things, and perhaps you can pass them on to all these other people who are too afraid to talk to us." He could feel his voice getting louder despite himself. "Nobody in my family has ever been to Germania. Doctor Kleitos himself asked me to come here, and I've got the full approval of his patron, Horatius Balbus. My wife is a citizen of Rome by the emperor's personal decree, and nobody in these apartments has as much right to be upset as she has, arriving here with our baby to find a dead stranger outside the—"

"Doctor!"

Ruso twisted 'round, fully prepared to tackle a fresh complainant while keeping a grip on the door and ignoring the urgent whispers behind him and the pain from whatever his wife was poking into his back through the latch hole. To his relief, he recognized Balbus's steward.

"Ladies." Firmicus raised his remarkable eyebrows. "I see you've met our new doctor."

The women glanced at one another. The main complainant unfolded her arms and took a step back. "We were just talking, sir."

"Don't let me interrupt."

"They were telling me about a couple of patients," Ruso said, but nobody seemed to be listening.

The woman said, "Sir, about my cousin."

Tilla was *that woman*, but Firmicus was *sir*.

"Sir, is there any—"

"Three blocks north of the Forum of Augustus, opposite the bakers," Firmicus told her. "It's a nice room. She'll like it. Tell her to tell Felix I sent her."

Perhaps encouraged by this, one of the companions put in, "Sir, the balcony over the—"

"Didn't we get that fixed last month?"

"They came and did something, sir, but it's still loose."

"Talk to the caretaker."

"We did, but—"

"Am I the caretaker?"

The women hurried away. Ruso envied Firmicus his power. For some reason groups of angry women always seemed far more alarming than groups of angry men. Meanwhile Ruso's own angry woman had wrenched the door open behind him and was demanding to know why he had not let her out to deal with them.

"I didn't want to see a fight."

Tilla bristled. "I wanted to tell them all those things myself," she said. "And there is already a priest coming like they want. The magistrates will send one before sunset."

Before Ruso could reply, Firmicus turned to him. "We need to talk, Doctor."

"I was just coming to find you," Ruso assured him, ushering him indoors and closing the door on the outside world.

The steward repeated, "We need to talk, Doctor."

Tilla did not take the hint. Ruso said, "Thank you, wife."

Tilla gave him a look that said he would be sorry for this later, and retreated. She could have had no idea how cheered Ruso was by the way she shut the kitchen door: with a calculated firmness that said she was highly annoyed but was not going to make an exhibition of herself by slamming it. A couple of days ago she would have wandered out and barely noticed whether or not it was closed behind her.

15

FIRMICUS PLANTED BOTH hands on the operating table and leaned across to address Ruso in a low voice. "What did the master say to you back at the house?"

Ruso was aware of the clatter of crockery from the kitchen and Tilla's voice launching into one of her interminable songs about her ancestors. "Always stay one step ahead of your enemies."

Firmicus's attempt at a cold stare was almost as good as his owner's. "Don't try to be clever, Doctor."

A doctor who was trying to be clever was surely better than one who was resigned to being stupid, but pointing this out would only compound the offense, so Ruso said nothing.

"Tell me what's going on here."

"There was a barrel outside the door when I got here at midday," Ruso told him. "You must have walked past it when you came to fetch me."

"Go on."

"The neighbors told us it belonged to Kleitos. My wife opened it up and found a dead man inside. She says the caretaker's had him taken away. I was just coming to tell you."

Firmicus paused to assess this before saying, "The master told you that we would look after you."

"Yes."

"You should have told me straightaway. Let us deal with it. The master doesn't expect to hear this kind of thing from street gossip."

It was another version of *people are very upset,* and almost as annoying. "I tried to tell him," Ruso pointed out, "but he wasn't interested. If I find another body, you'll be the first to know. Meanwhile my wife was left here to manage on her own and she did what she thought was best."

Firmicus's "Hm" suggested that letting women think what was best was not a good idea. Out in the kitchen, the song was relating a tale of glorious victory for Tilla's tribe.

"Nobody seems to know who the man in the barrel was," Ruso said, assuming that at some point Firmicus would get around to asking. "I didn't get a very good look, but I'd say he was in his twenties or early thirties. Short fair hair, clean-shaven. Scar above the left eye. No clothes."

"So who put him there?"

It might have been the man with the limp who came asking for money. It might not. *It has nothing to do with us, husband.* He said, "We weren't here. You could try asking the neighbors."

"And you don't know why?"

"No," said Ruso, not wanting to voice his uncomfortable suspicion. "Maybe Kleitos upset somebody. Maybe it was put there to frighten him. Maybe it was just dumped."

Firmicus was looking around at the empty shelves. "And Kleitos has gone to visit his sick father."

"Yes."

The sudden grab at his tunic took Ruso by surprise. He was hauled forward across the edge of the table before he could back away. His attempt to resist died when he saw the knife.

Firmicus said, "That's a lie, isn't it?"

"I don't know."

"Kleitos's father has been dead for years. He's taken all his things with him. Who are you? What are you doing here?"

Straining his chin away from the knife, he said, "My name is Gaius Petreius Ruso. Until the start of last month I was medical officer with the Twentieth Legion. Publius Accius can vouch for me."

"Publius Accius has his own reasons for wanting to get close to my master."

Maybe it was time to call on Metellus after all. "And there's a man in the urban prefect's office who knows me."

"He can confirm that Kleitos invited you?"

"No." The blade of Firmicus's knife was pressing against his jugular vein.

"Where's Kleitos now?"

"I don't know," Ruso said. "He just left a note for me with Accius. I can show it to you."

"Why didn't you say that in the first place?" Firmicus released him as suddenly as he had lunged forward. "Give me the note."

Pulling his clothing straight, Ruso moved to place himself between Firmicus and the door to the kitchen, where Tilla's ancestors were enjoying some otherwise unrecorded victory over the invading legions. It seemed she had finally grasped that this wasn't Britannia, where women tended to think they could get involved in whatever they liked, and where men saw the look in their eyes and tended to let them.

He retrieved the little roll of parchment from his purse and placed it in the middle of the operating table. Still holding the knife, Firmicus took it across to where it caught the light filtering through the thick panes of glass above the door. He read the Latin aloud. "What's all this Greek about . . ." He paused, squinting at the lettering. "Death and being careful?"

"It's an old medical text," Ruso explained, realizing the light was too poor for Firmicus to see the difference in the ink between textbook medical advice and Kleitos's warning. Not inclined to enlighten him, he said, "He's reused it. Symptoms of quartan fever. You have to watch out which sort of herbs you use: Some of the usual fever treatments do more harm than good."

Firmicus squinted at the parchment for a moment, then tossed it back across the table.

"Always was a tightfisted bastard."

Ruso watched the knife slide back into the sheath at Firmicus's belt. "That's what Horatius Balbus's protection looks like?"

"That was me making sure you deserve it," said Firmicus, as if the explanation did away with any need for apology.

"I've no reason to lie," Ruso told him. "I don't know what's gone on here, but it's nothing to do with me. Now that you've done your job, perhaps you'd leave me to get on with mine."

Firmicus was already moving toward the exit when someone knocked on the door. As if it were an afterthought, he reached out and placed a handful of silver coins on the table. "The master sent payment for the medicine. And remember, if you get any more trouble—"

"You're the first person I'll come to."

The steward stepped out past a middle-aged couple. The woman was clutching her husband's arm. The man's voice was calm and measured, but the intensity of both their expressions suggested they would not breathe freely until Ruso told them whether or not the body that had been found was that of their missing son. When he told them about the hair color they looked relieved— and disappointed—and backed away, thanking him more than was necessary. Then they apologized for disturbing him.

To their retreating figures, Ruso said, "I'm sorry. I hope you find him soon." The man raised a hand in weary acknowledgment. The son had been missing for over a month, and so far no amount of pious hoping had done any good at all.

16

WHEN HE WENT back into the kitchen the Britons had finished chasing the Romans off the musical battlefield. Tilla said, "I hope that was not a debt collector."

"No," Ruso said. "He works for Kleitos's patron. He just came to make sure we were all right." Before she could ask why that had been confidential, he told her about the couple with the missing son. "Thank the gods for the fair hair," he said.

Tilla said, "Yes. He was probably only a dead barbarian."

It struck him that there was more color in her cheeks than he had seen for many days. "I meant," he said, "it'll make him easier to identify."

"The sort of barbarian who comes 'round to these nice apartments causing trouble and getting into fights. No wonder he was shut up in a barrel."

Realizing what this was about, he said, "I was trying to protect you from those women. The bit about not wanting to see a fight was a joke."

"You tell people I am a citizen of Rome but you make a joke about me being a fighting barbarian."

He perched himself on the stone counter of the kitchen and

contemplated the bare room, the blue curtain in the corner, and the cushions where Mara was busy examining the sole of her foot. Tilla had hung his cloak and her shawl on the back of the door. She had unpacked the red crockery and arranged it neatly on a shelf alongside a wooden platter, four spoons, two knives, and their one cooking pan. Unfortunately there was no sign of any of this display being used to prepare supper, and now that the initial shock had passed, he was hungry. He said, "Were there any patients while I was out?"

"No. Just more people being nosy and the slaves who took the body away and somebody looking for a lost brother." Tilla propped herself against the other end of the counter and folded her arms. "Sabella said it is unlucky to cook in here until the priest has been to purify the rooms."

"Sabella says?"

"Because that poor man's body was here and it is not buried yet."

Across the room, Mara put her toes in her mouth and sucked them.

He said, "The note offering me the job also said, *Be careful who you trust.*"

"You are only telling me this now?"

"I didn't want to worry you."

She wrapped her arms around her thin frame. "How will we ever be safe in this city? There is nobody in charge."

"There's a chap called the urban prefect, and there are departments for—"

"But it is not how a tribe should be," she insisted. "I thought before we came . . . But there is no tribe called the Romans."

"There are several different—"

"It is just lots of strangers all living in one place and fighting to get by."

"We'll get used to it," he promised, realizing this was not the time for a lecture on the benefits of civilization, literacy, and the rule of law. Especially since his first patient was convinced that malicious rivals were trying to poison him. "We'll make friends and find work, like we always do in a new place." He opened his fist to reveal two of the denarii Firmicus had left on the table. "Here's a start. I've had my first proper fee. Kleitos's patron is doing his best to put business our way. And it's obvious Kleitos won't be back in a hurry."

She picked up one of the little coins and clamped it between her teeth. Then she angled it toward the light of the window to check that there was no iron showing through the silver. "We can afford to eat from the bar tomorrow too."

Given the erratic nature of Tilla's cooking, this was good news. "And we have somewhere clean to sleep," he reminded her.

"And tomorrow we will buy a slave."

Only if Accius came up with the necessary loan, but he did not want to snuff out her flickering optimism by saying so.

"Perhaps the gods have taken pity on us. We will be—" She stopped. "What is that?"

Ruso tipped his head back, eyeing the joists and floorboards that separated them from the swelling noise of singing in the apartment above. "Who lives up there?"

"I thought just Phyllis and her husband, but . . ." As her voice trailed into silence, he saw her mouthing the words along with the tune.

"You know this song?"

She said, "I heard it in Gaul."

He was about to ask why he did not recognize it himself, when he realized. "Oh, holy Jupiter. Don't tell me our neighbors are followers of Christos." So that was what *illegal meetings* meant.

"Phyllis is very kind."

"Perhaps she would kindly tell her friends to go and sing hymns somewhere else."

"This is not a good building: The floor is very thin. She says they can hear what goes on in the surgery. Just imagine." She was swaying with the rhythm, mouthing more words.

He said, "Tilla, promise me you won't get involved with all that again. If we want to stay here, people have to trust us. It's bad enough starting with a dead body."

"They have some nice songs. I had forgotten this one."

"If you want songs," he told her, "Stick to the ones about your ancestors. They're much better. And longer."

A slow smile spread over her face. "You have never told me before how much you like the songs of my people."

"It's time Mara learned them," he assured her.

"Which one do you like best?"

He was saved by the sound of yet another caller at the door. "I don't think we'll be lonely here."

She followed him through the surgery. "Be careful who you trust. If it is the neighbors again, I will talk to them. If it is the debt collectors, remember—we do not know where he is."

It was neither. A man in a white toga was standing on the threshold. With him were two slaves. One was carrying a knife and a bundle of kindling, and the other a metal rattle and a basket containing some sort of bird that was unlikely to make it home again. It was the first time Ruso had ever been glad to see a priest.

17

R USO WOKE FROM a dream of falling off Kleitos's operating table to find himself hanging over one edge of a straw mattress that was too narrow for the bed frame. Careful investigation in the dark revealed that his wife was similarly marooned on the opposite side of the bed, while Mara lay spread-eagled and fast asleep across the middle. Not for the first time, he wondered if they could hire her out to patients who came seeking advice on contraception.

A voice whispered, "Don't wake her!"

He said, "We need a bigger mattress."

"Tomorrow I shall make a list of things we need. But it was very kind of Phyllis's friends to lend us this one."

"Hm."

"And the bench and table for the kitchen, and the two stools."

He said, "I'd rather have paid for them and not had to listen."

"You are very grumpy," she told him. "Christos has never done you any harm."

"I haven't got anything against Christos. It's the way his followers go on about him and turn their noses up at ordinary religion."

She said, "Sometimes I pray to him."

"Well, try not to."

"I always remember the other gods too."

"Mm." He had a feeling Christos's more ardent followers might have something to say about that. And also about the quarrel between husband and wife that had broken out upstairs after the hymn singers had clumped away into the night.

Lifting Mara's arm out of the way, he shifted himself off the rope supports that crisscrossed the bed frame and onto the relative comfort of the straw. Mara sighed, wriggled, and poked something—a foot, a knee?—into his back. He leaned against it, but instead of withdrawing, whatever it was pushed harder. Finally he eased himself out of range, pondering the unexpected intimacies of parenthood and wondering if he would be more comfortable on the floor. Or indeed on the operating table.

From the far side of the bed a voice said, "I keep seeing him when I shut my eyes."

"That will pass."

"He looked as if he was asleep in there. I am very sad for him and his family."

"We don't know he had a family. We don't know anything at all."

There was a moment where he could hear nothing but Mara's breathing and the distant squeak of a badly oiled wheel passing down the street. He was beginning to drift into sleep when he heard, "What if he is not buried yet?"

"He can't come back here," he mumbled, knowing what she was thinking. "The rooms have been cleansed."

"But if his spirit—"

"It won't. Your friend said they can smell incense and roast pigeon all the way up the stairs."

She sighed one of those you-do-not-understand sighs.

"Think about it," he whispered, annoyed at being awake despite the welcome muting of traffic noise and the absence of insect life. "If you believe in ghosts and Christos and the normal gods and all your gods from Britannia and—"

The hand groping across his face clamped over his mouth. "Sh, don't wake her!"

He lowered his voice, but he was determined to make his point. Propping himself up on one elbow to face his wife in the dark, he tried again. "If you believe in all these things," he said quietly, "then it's just as logical to believe that he's at rest because he's been properly buried and the sacrifice has dealt with anything that might be lingering here. You see?"

It appeared that she did not see.

"You have to be consistent," he urged.

The ropes creaked as she shifted in the bed. "It is the middle of the night," she reminded him, sounding farther away. "I do not have to be anything." It seemed like a satisfactory last word, but just when he thought that was the end of it, he heard, "I know I said it is nothing to do with us, but people think it is."

"They'll get over it."

"People think it is my fault because I come from a province a long way away."

If he was going to tell her, now was the time. "I think," he said, "they're more likely to think it's my fault."

When she did not answer, he continued very softly. "When you broke your arm, I didn't just guess where to join everything back together."

Any hope that she might understand was dashed by "What is that to do with it?"

So he made her whisper a promise into the darkness of the bedroom that she would say nothing of this to anyone. And then, wondering if he was making a big mistake, he told her about surgeons who were desperate to explore inside others' redundant bodies so that they could become better at their work.

The bed creaked as she rolled over to face him. "But surely—"

"That barrel was delivered here," he reminded her. "And someone wanted payment."

"You told me this Doctor Kleitos was a good man!"

They both fell silent as Mara snorted and shuffled about in the bed. Finally she seemed to drift back to sleep, and he said, "I think he's a good doctor." He had also thought Kleitos was a generous man, but he now was starting to wonder if he had been offered this practice because nobody else wanted it. "You know it's true," he urged. "There are patients we could help if we knew more about what's inside the human body instead of just inside animals."

"By cutting someone to pieces? What about respect?"

"Not a live someone, of course."

"What? A live— Husband, how could you even think of that?"

Trying to reconcile his wife to something she found disgusting by telling her about something even worse had definitely not been a good idea. "It was hundreds of years ago," he explained. "Across the sea in Alexandria. Their anatomists practiced on condemned criminals."

"Alive?"

"Apparently."

"And who said they were criminals?"

"It's appalling to think of," he told her, "but you and I probably benefit from the knowledge they handed down."

"Ugh. I think you are mad." She rolled away from him, and he heard her whisper fiercely to the opposite wall, "This whole city is mad. It is bad enough seeing the poor man in the barrel without imagining him being cut up into bits. Why did you have to tell me this?"

"Because it's true," he told her, wondering himself.

"And are you telling me that you—?"

"Me? Of course not!" He slipped into the denial before she could define the question. He had never done anything experimental, but there had been times when, left alone, he might have extended a postmortem examination just a little beyond what was strictly necessary. "It's not only immoral, it's illegal." Mercifully he had rarely been left alone with temptation. But his old colleague Valens, he was certain, possessed the right combination of curiosity and insensitivity to drive him further. Although not to the extreme of purchasing bodies to dissect. Once you went down that route, there was no telling where it would end. "At least this one was safely dead."

She said, "If you think that will make anything better, husband, you are insane. If this idea gets out, nobody will trust us to go near them."

"I know," he said. "That's why we need to make sure that it doesn't happen again, and that people know it's nothing to do with us."

"That is why," she told him, "we need to tell the neighbors a good story before they start guessing. Kleitos was in debt, and somebody put that poor man there to show him what would happen to him if he did not pay. That is why he ran away. Yes?"

"Yes," he said, seeing the sense of it. "That's exactly why." And for all he knew, perhaps it was.

18

ACCIUS LOOKED UP from his venerable desk. "Ruso! I was about to send for you. I've just had some very disturbing news." This was not a good start. Ruso, who had come hoping to discuss a loan, found himself having to respond to "What's all this about a body?"

"There was a dead man outside the doctor's rooms yesterday, sir," he said, wondering how Accius had heard. "But it's been dealt with."

"I know it's been dealt with," Accius snapped. "My men had him collected and taken out for cremation this morning. What the hell did you think you were doing? This is Rome, man. Surely you don't imagine you can hide a body in a barrel and dump it in a back street and get away with it?"

"We didn't dump him, sir. He was dumped on us. The care-taker's wife reported it, and he was taken away."

"Well, not far enough." The tribune glared at him for a moment, then said, "This is embarrassing, Ruso. The householder where the barrel was found this morning refused to move it, so my men threatened him with a fine for leaving rubbish in the street. He went to his patron, who happens to be a senator, and the senator's office put in a complaint about my men to me."

Accius paused, allowing the full extent of this complicated humiliation to sink in. "The senator's office then made some enquiries about where the thing had come from," he continued, "and they were told it was put there by some bartender just across the street from Trajan's baths. I sent my men to talk to him and he blamed the new doctor who's just moved in next door. There can't be two of you."

"No, sir. It is me. But I didn't—"

"Meanwhile the bartender has also complained to *his* patron about my men's attitude, and who do you think his patron turns out to be?"

Ruso suppressed a sigh. "Horatius Balbus, sir."

"Exactly. Horatius Balbus who gave you a job after I recommended you. Horatius Balbus upon whom I am attempting to make a good impression."

There was no choice but to apologize, even though it was hardly Ruso's fault if Sabella's husband had failed to deal with the body properly and Accius's men were rude to people.

"So now I've told him you can explain what's going on, but I'm buggered if I know how."

Ruso scratched one ear. "So am I, sir."

"Well, you must have some ideas. Try harder."

Ruso had spent the earlier part of the morning doing his best not to have any ideas at all, and to dismiss any that had popped up unbidden. Mara had been fractious and Tilla had barely spoken to him. She had not shut the bedroom door properly when she took the bowl in there to wash, and he had glimpsed her staring down at her scarred right arm as if it belonged to someone she did not much like. Then she shuddered and clamped it behind her back before dipping the cloth back in the bowl and wringing it out with one hand to wash her face.

Afterward, there'd been varicose veins to be examined and rebandaged. A small boy had needed a cobnut extracted from his nose, while the pregnant teenager Ruso had frightened the other day consulted Tilla about something so womanly that their discussion had to be conducted in whispers in the kitchen. Then Balbus had sent one of his plumbers to have a cut stitched. After that Ruso had needed to hurry across to one of the suppliers Kleitos had recommended to replenish his supplies of fleawort to make cooling plasters, and poppy tears, and sulfur for treating skin complaints. Now he needed to borrow some money and get down to the auctions before all the best slaves had been sold.

"Well?" Accius demanded. "How the hell did it come to this?"

Ruso summarized the story of the barrel and Tilla's discovery and the fact that the caretaker whose wife ran the bar next door had arranged to have it taken away. "That was the last we heard of it, sir. I'd assumed he'd called in some undertakers. I could follow it up if you like. In fact it would be useful to know if someone's identified him."

"Fortunately, that's not our problem."

"I know, sir. But relatives of missing people keep turning up at the door to ask."

"Send them out to the undertakers. They deal with unidentified bodies all the time. I believe they keep lists. If you worked in street cleaning you'd find it's not as uncommon as you seem to think."

Ruso was hoping they had come to the end of the subject when Accius added, "Although the barrel is rather odd."

"Yes, sir."

"Technically, it's up to you to keep the street tidy in front of your house. Not get your wife to ask somebody else to do it." He sighed. "We can hardly fine your landlord, either, because the landlord is . . ."

"Horatius Balbus, sir." The man who owned fourteen apartment blocks and upon whom a good impression needed to be made.

Accius turned to the clerk standing behind him. "Make a note that when we find out who left that barrel outside the doctor's rooms, we'll prosecute."

The clerk said, "Do you want someone to make enquiries, sir?"

"Absolutely not," Accius told him. "We've wasted enough time on this already." He returned his attention to Ruso. "Anything else?"

This was clearly not a good time to be asking for money. But he had promised Tilla some help around the house, and at least the first part of his speech would—he hoped—put Accius in a better mood. "Two things, sir. The first one concerns Horatius Balbus's daughter."

That made him sit up. "Horatia? What about her?"

"When I called to see her father yesterday she asked if you'd sent me with a message."

"You've seen her?"

Ruso was relieved to see the lines of Accius's perpetual scowl soften a little.

"What did you say?"

"I said no, sir."

The scowl returned. "Damn. If only I'd known. What else did she say?"

"She hopes you're well, and she's looking after the bracelet. She seemed very pleased with it."

Accius's face shifted into an unusual shape, and Ruso tried to remember if he had ever seen him look cheerful before. "Excellent. I bought it in Britannia, you know. If you see her again, tell her I'm enjoying the book. And don't forget to ask if there's any message back."

Ruso had been unaware of Accius's interest in reading until now, despite sharing a long sea voyage with him. He cleared his throat. "I'm not sure I'll be able to, sir. I was told by her father afterward that I wasn't supposed to speak to her."

The cheerful expression faded. "Quite right. Horatia is a respectable young lady. She can't be expected to talk to just anybody. What else?"

Ruso's rehearsal of this conversation had begun with Accius asking how things were going over at the surgery. Now, adrift from his imagined starting point, he needed to turn the tribune's mind to money without making it look as if he were asking for any. "Sir, I need your advice on something."

"If it's quick."

"Now that I'm covering a full practice, I need a slave or two to help out."

"Of course. Ask my housekeeper if she knows anyone she can recommend."

Ruso sounded the words "Thank you, sir," while desperately trying to imagine what Valens would have done to charm Accius into offering more cash than was needed, with no rush to repay it. But Valens was back in Britannia with the Legions, and Ruso was on his own.

"I'm a busy man, Ruso. I thought you only wanted two things?"

"It's the money, sir," he said, abandoning any attempt at subtlety. "I'm sure the practice brings in a decent income, but—"

"You're asking me for money?"

He braced himself. "A loan, sir."

"Why didn't you say so? You said you were asking for advice."

"I was working my way around to it, sir."

"I haven't got time to sit here while you work your way around to things. Horatius Balbus is expecting us at any moment."

He turned to his clerk, but before he could speak the clerk whispered, "A word, sir?" and Ruso was excluded from a muttered conversation.

When they had finished the clerk stepped back. Accius said, "You can't take on a temporary post and then use it as security for a loan, Ruso. Kleitos will be back before long, and then you won't have the income from the practice to repay me, will you?"

Accius knew nothing about money, but unfortunately it seemed he had the sense to listen to someone who did. Ruso cleared his throat. "I'm not sure that Doctor Kleitos will be coming back, sir."

"What? That wasn't him in the barrel, was it?"

"No, sir. But he's cleared everything of value out of his house, including most of the furniture. We think he may have been in debt."

Accius blinked. "He's gone for good? And did you tell Horatius Balbus that his man ran away just before somebody was found murdered outside?"

"His steward came and asked about it, sir, so he must know."

"But this alters everything! Surely you thought to warn him personally—and you should have told me—that his man was mixed up in some sort of unsavory goings-on?"

"I did try to tell him about the body, but—"

"Holy gods, Ruso! What do you think I invited you to Rome for?"

"I've been waiting to be told, sir," said Ruso, hoping he was at last about to find out what a Good Man did.

"I wanted you here," said Accius, as if he was talking to a small child, "to help me deal with delicate situations. I thought that was clear."

"Sorry, sir."

"And now you've landed in the middle of one and you didn't even notice it, let alone deal with it!"

Ruso cleared his throat. "I didn't want to get either of us involved in somebody else's difficulties, sir."

Accius sighed. "Well, we're involved in them now. We'd better find something sensible to say to Balbus. And if we see Horatia, leave the talking to me."

19

I T WAS LIKE being a small boy who had got into a fight. Adults asked for your account of the affair, and then sent you to wait outside while they discussed what should be done about it. Now Ruso was being called back in to Horatius Balbus's study to be told what had been decided by the adults, even though one of them was several years his junior.

"My young friend tells me," announced Balbus from behind his elaborately carved desk, "that you are a resourceful and intelligent man. When I met you, that was my impression too."

Ruso bowed his head in what he hoped looked like a respectful silence.

"Which leaves us both wondering," Balbus continued, "why you didn't notice that my freedman is in some sort of trouble. Or didn't you think it was important enough to mention?"

Ruso looked up. "I'm sorry, sir. I wasn't thinking clearly."

Accius said, "Horatius Balbus is very concerned for the welfare of Doctor Kleitos."

And doubtless Accius was concerned for the welfare of his courtship of Balbus's daughter, who was nowhere to be seen. On the walk over Ruso had wondered if he should ask Accius if he knew he had competition, but it hardly seemed the right time.

"My steward tells me Kleitos's father is long dead," put in Balbus. "And now it turns out the message saying he'd gone to visit him was delivered by some street brat that nobody can identify. I want to know what's going on."

"I don't know, sir."

"But I've promised that you'll find out," put in Accius, shooting a glance that Ruso interpreted as telling him to shut up.

"This all looks," said Balbus, "as if someone's trying to intimidate me."

Ruso, sworn to silence about the theriac, looked at Accius for a clue as to how to proceed.

"Well?" said Accius.

Apparently he was now expected to speak. "The neighbors suggested he might be in debt, sir. We thought perhaps he was the one who was being intimidated."

Balbus raised one hand and beckoned over his shoulder to the slave who was standing in the corner behind him clutching a note tablet. "Is Kleitos in debt?"

The man stepped forward and bowed. "The last time we checked, he was making a good living, sir."

"You see?" said Balbus, as if Ruso had accused him of negligence. "I would have known. My clerk helps with his accounts."

Accius said, "So if he isn't in debt, why has he run?"

"Because someone's threatened him, sir?" Ruso suggested, incurring a glare from Accius.

Balbus was running one hand over his bald head. "My man's gone," he mused. "If anybody knows where or why, they're not saying. And whoever sent that message was trying to stop me from looking for him." He leaned out over the desk and yelled, "Firmicus?"

"Perhaps he sent the message himself, sir," Ruso suggested, deliberately not looking at his patron. "The note he sent to me said the same thing—he was going away to visit his father. Your steward saw it. He can confirm the handwriting. Perhaps Kleitos doesn't want to be found."

The tone of "We've known each other twenty years! Why would he leave, after everything I've done for him?" took Ruso by surprise. Horatius Balbus sounded genuinely upset.

Accius's slave joined them outside and followed at a respectful distance. They were at least a hundred paces away from the house before Accius spoke. "Well, that was awkward."

Ruso said, "Sorry, sir."

"You should be. Up till now I was making a decent impression."

In the past few weeks Ruso had imagined all sorts of duties that a Good Man might be called upon to perform, but facilitating marriages had never been one of them.

Accius was still talking. "Balbus needs to know what's happened to his freedman. And don't tell me you don't have any ideas about what's going on, because I don't believe you."

For a brief moment Ruso considered asking for a private audience safely away from eavesdroppers, and confiding his suspicions about Kleitos's secret human dissections to Accius. But Accius was a politician, not a doctor. He would understand even less than Tilla had. "I think it's possible Kleitos managed to conceal the real state of his affairs from his patron, sir. The neighbors have mentioned debt collectors. And his note to me had a warning that I should be careful who to trust."

"Really? Why didn't you say so?"

Ruso cleared his throat. "I wasn't sure who I could trust to say it to, sir."

"Jupiter's bollocks!" Accius flung both hands into the air in exasperation. "This is ridiculous. I can't insist to Balbus that we know his own man's finances better than he does without some sort of proof. Why didn't you at least take a proper look at the body? We need to know exactly what we're involved in here." He paused. "You don't think Kleitos did away with him, do you?"

"Nobody's suggesting that, sir." At least, he hoped they weren't. It was even less plausible than the debt story, but if it spread it would destroy any remaining confidence in the practice. "I didn't examine the body because I would have been late for an appointment," he said, adding, "with Horatius Balbus. By the time I got back it had gone."

"And now it's been cremated," said Accius, stating this fact with considerably less approval than he had shown earlier this morning, although with no more concern for the deceased.

They turned a corner to find a slave in a familiar tunic hurrying toward them. Accius paused to read the message the slave handed over, then sent him home.

"It seems this bartender caretaker person has confessed about the disposal business," he said, snapping the tablet shut and handing it to the slave who was accompanying them. "He's Balbus's man, so I imagine Balbus will have plenty to say to him about it. As I could have told everyone myself if I'd been consulted, the undertakers aren't contractually obliged to collect stray bodies on the same day unless they're notified before the tenth hour. Which is rather annoying, since their headquarters is only just down the road outside the Praenestina gate. Apparently half the staff who would have fetched it were busy questioning somebody's slaves, and the rest were out of town organizing a crucifixion."

"Ah." Since questioning of slaves was routinely done under torture, the staff must have been very busy indeed.

"A deeply distasteful business, undertaking," Accius observed, voicing Ruso's own thoughts. "Not the sort of people one wants to mix with. Anyway, the bartender chap told his slaves to roll the barrel somewhere around the back and hide it with their own stores, but the slaves were so frightened of having it outside their bedroom overnight that they waited until it was getting dark and shifted it onto somebody else's patch, just to get rid of it. Unfortunately, they were seen."

This was starting to sound like the script of a bad comedy.

"Apparently the bartender chap was full of apologies. He's had the slaves soundly beaten, of course. Though frankly, one sometimes wonders if it's worth the effort."

They broke step to avoid a scatter of dung in the street. Accius ordered his man into the nearest shop to threaten the owner with a fine if it wasn't cleared up straightaway. "Street cleaning may not be much of a job," Accius observed as they waited, "but I need to be seen doing things properly."

"Yes, sir."

"As do you. Balbus was concerned that it's not in your interests to find Kleitos, but I told him you were a good man and you would want to help a colleague who'd supported you."

Ruso cleared his throat. "Sir, as I said, it's possible that being found is the last kind of help Kleitos wants."

"Never mind what Kleitos wants! The man's run off without a word to his patron. For all we know, he could have been kidnapped."

"With all his furniture, sir?"

"Don't be facetious, Ruso." The sound of raised voices caused Accius to glance into the shop. "Gods above, why is it so difficult to get the simplest thing done around here? Are you going to find Kleitos, or do I need to look for somebody else?"

"I'll do it, sir."

The slave emerged from the shop, followed by a scowling woman clutching a bucket and a shovel. They set off down the street again. As they passed a sundial, Ruso was unable to resist a glance.

"The auctions won't be finished yet," Accius informed him tartly and snapped his fingers. The slave stepped forward and handed him a leather purse. "My clerk will have drawn up the loan documents while we've been out. Go down there, get it over with, and then concentrate on sorting this mess out for Horatius Balbus. I want him to know I'm a man who gets things done."

20

SHOPPING WAS THE province of women. The purchase of items beyond the scope of shops—important items such as property, livestock, and household members—was man's work. Still, as Tilla had pointed out, they needed to choose a slave they could trust with Mara's life, and did he want to take responsibility for that all on his own?

Thus Kleitos's apartment was once again locked and deserted while its new occupants hurried across the city to catch the end of the auctions. One was clutching a baby. The other had Accius's cash concealed under his tunic. Apparently, having pointed out why lending the money was a bad idea, Accius's clerk had then warned his master that allowing Ruso to fall into the clutches of moneylenders would be even worse.

They arrived breathless after several wrong turns, rushing into an enclosed courtyard that smelled of stale bodies and fried food. Pigeons strutted about in the sunshine, pecking at scraps while the owners of the food stalls under the colonnades were already packing up. The remaining buyers clustered around the auction block were not as well dressed as the men already queueing at the payment tables and collection points. Ruso and his small family were joining the late bargain hunters, hoping to snap up the overlooked and underpriced.

At least, he hoped that was how it worked. Ruso had never actually purchased a slave at auction before. His father had owned a steward who dealt with all that, and later his brother had taken over the role along with managing the farm. His first marriage had been so brief that they were still relying on staff brought from their respective homes when it ended. Still, he had money, and he had common sense, and whoever he took home this afternoon would already have Tilla's approval. There should be enough left over to buy a clean mattress where whoever-it-was could sleep next to Mara while he and his wife enjoyed some uninterrupted nocturnal privacy.

Whoever-it-was would not be the current slave standing on the block: A sullen young woman with spear-throwing shoulder muscles was not what a family man wanted to face every morning over breakfast. Ignoring the babble of the auctioneer, Ruso turned his attention to the figures lined up in chains behind the temporary barrier. He had arrived too late for the advance viewing, but he was used to assessing physical fitness. He would run through the same points he usually considered for military recruits, leaving out the parts that didn't apply to women and letting Tilla deal with the extras that did. Physical fitness, however, was not all. How were they supposed to guess if someone would be a pleasure to live with or a scheming liar or a wet rag with no initiative? He had no idea. He was watching the young woman being led down from the block when someone cried, "Doctor!"

A portly figure he vaguely recognized was squeezing through a gap in the wooden barriers. "Simmias," the man reminded him, transferring the pastry to his left hand and holding out the other, which was slightly sticky to the touch. "Doctor with the second night watch. We met the other day."

"I remember." Simmias was a lot friendlier now than when Ruso had visited the fire brigade's headquarters last week on the hunt for work. He nodded toward the slaves as the auctioneer announced the next lot. "Are you buying?"

"Inspecting for a client," the man explained. "They tell me you're filling in for Kleitos. Glad to hear it."

"I've been asked to cover for him till he gets back. You don't happen to know how I can contact him, do you?"

Simmias shook his head before swallowing the last of the pastry. "Sorry. I hardly know him. Tell me, what's all this about a body?"

So. It was not friendliness, but curiosity. Ruso glanced up at the block to make sure he was not missing a suitable baby-minder, then gave a brief summary of the story. He tried to make it as unexciting as a body in a barrel could possibly be made to sound, and to his relief Simmias restrained any urge to speculate.

Instead he said, "It must have been a nasty shock for your wife."

"She didn't sleep too well last night," Ruso admitted.

"Not a good start for you, either."

"Apparently there's been some problem with debt collectors. I'm hoping people will realize it's nothing to do with me."

"Absolutely, brother." Simmias reached out and patted him on the shoulder. "Let's hope it's soon forgotten. Anything I can do to help you settle in, let me know."

"I'm very keen to track down Kleitos. If you hear anything—"

"I'll be in touch."

"And I'd welcome any recommendations about suppliers. I've got the basics, but I need to know about specialists."

"Ah, now there I can help you." But instead of offering names, Simmias broke off, his attention caught by something on the far side of the marketplace. A familiar female voice was calling out over the murmur of the crowd, demanding in a tongue that was wholly out of place at a Roman slave auction, "Is there anyone here of the Corionotatae?"

Tilla was standing on the high base of a column, clinging precariously to a marble pillar that was too broad to reach her arm around. With Mara clamped in the crook of the other arm, she was straining to see across the pen of unsold female slaves.

"Silly woman's going to fall off there," Simmias observed.

Ruso sighed. "That's my wife." It was hopeless to pretend otherwise.

"It's no good her shouting in—what is it, Germanic?" said Simmias. "Tell her to try some Latin."

"Anyone from the Brigantes?" Tilla cried, widening the net beyond her own obscure little tribe.

As Ruso shouldered his way through the crowd, someone who must have understood her shouted, "You're a couple of years too late, love—we've sold 'em all!"

It struck him that they must be standing where the surviving British rebels had ended up after being marched away in chains. Some of them, he supposed, must still be serving in households here in the city. The rest would be long gone. He doubted any would ever see their homelands again.

"I am searching for women of the Brigantes!"

More and more heads were turning away from the auction block to watch the barbarian woman making a spectacle of herself. "Wait for me!" Ruso shouted, hoping to silence her. Inside the pen, any dealer who grasped what was going on would be busy checking his stock for women he could pass off as Brigante at inflated prices.

"Do you a nice Thracian, miss!" someone offered.

Ruso reached up and lifted Mara to safety before she slipped out of Tilla's grasp and crashed onto the stone paving. "What the hell are you doing?" he whispered just as a gangly youth yelled from beyond the fence, "I am Dumnonii! I speak your tongue!"

"Brigante!" cried another. "I am of your people, sister!"

Tilla grabbed Ruso's shoulder for support and leapt down, almost overbalancing as she landed. "There is a man of the Brigantes over there!"

"We came for a baby-minder," he reminded her.

"And a boy of the Dumnonii!"

"The boy must be a criminal to be shipped as a slave, wife. They're a peaceful tribe."

"They are my people!"

The Brigante might have been one of her people: The Dumnonii were a tribe from the far southwest where, as far as he knew, there was nothing but sheep and a few tin mines run by contractors. He doubted Tilla would have any ties there. But it seemed any part of Britannia could look like home from this distance.

Ruso felt as uncomfortable as he always did about the idea of human beings standing to be assessed for sale like animals while desperately hoping they would be taken to a kind home. It was not ideal, but it was hard to see how else slaves could be distributed. "We came for a baby-minder," he reminded her. "Don't get their hopes up. It's not fair."

The look she gave him was not even one of reproach. It was the look of a woman who knew what it was to be bought and sold.

What she did not know, he reminded himself as he grasped her by the arm, was what it was like to be doing the buying.

The auction of a middle-aged weaver carried on above them while a smiling dealer stepped forward to bow to Tilla and offer her the two Britons at a special price. It would save her having to bid against some of those ruffians out there, who had no respect for decent people. He evidently did not expect her to be able to read the word RUNAWAY on the label tied around the neck of the skinny Brigante, nor to notice that the acne-sprinkled Dumnonii youth had the sullen expression of one not used to taking orders.

Ruso told the dealer they had come to buy a woman.

After more bowing and smiling, the Brigante woman they were promised turned out to be Catuvellauni. Tilla was not impressed. Evidently the solidarity of exiled Britons did not extend to the Catuvellauni. He could not remember why her tribe did not trust them, but it was bound to be a reason that went back generations and owed more to passion than logic.

"We don't have to have a Briton," he reminded her. "I'll see if there's a Greek. It would be good for Mara to learn another language." A proper, useful language.

"The Briton is fertile, sir," the dealer assured him. "And a hard worker."

"We do not want one that is fertile," Tilla told him. "We want one that is kind and knows her place and keeps her word. Who else do you have?"

The woman swayed slightly. Her face was pink from standing in the sun. Her hair had been dyed to make her look younger. For a moment the bloodshot gray eyes met Ruso's own. Then she squared her shoulders and looked away.

The Catuvellauni were longstanding allies of Rome. Whatever personal disaster had led her here, he had no doubt the woman understood everything they were saying about her. "Open your mouth for me," he urged, her obedience confirming her grasp of Latin. He checked her teeth and tongue and eyes and ears as he would any other recruit. "Now bend down and touch your toes."

"Husband, we do not want—"

"Does she look healthy to you?"

"She's in the prime of life, sir!"

"I wasn't asking you," he told the dealer. "Tilla?"

"She is Catuvellauni."

"We can wait for a Greek if you prefer." He turned to the slave and said in her own language, "Have you looked after small children?"

The woman brightened. "I cared for the farm manager's children back in Britannia."

"Can you cook?"

"I can cook, sir."

"Of course she will say that!" put in Tilla, who had once told him the exact same lie herself.

It was the cue for the dealer's practiced speech about his famous six-month guarantee.

"We'll see," said Ruso, taking his wife by the arm and leading her away. He was not going to buy the first slave they saw.

Half an hour later, the Catuvellauni woman became his legal property. Pointing out that the woman was nearer forty than the alleged twenty-five had got him a discount, and he had spent little more than half of the money Accius had lent him. He was hurrying across to collect the documents and pay the tax when Tilla said, "Nobody has bought the runaway Brigante. Or the Dumnonii boy."

He pretended not to hear.

"The Brigante will go to the mines."

He said, "He should have thought of that before he ran away."

"I ran away," she reminded him.

"That's not the same thing at all."

"Why?"

"We have the slave we want. We don't need a man."

"But they are my people!"

It was unfair. He drew her aside and hissed, "Wife, I have neither the time nor the money to buy every slave you feel sorry for! Even if I could, what will we feed them on? Where will they sleep?"

"If I might intervene," murmured a voice, "it's not advisable to have too many slaves from the same province under one roof. You never know what they're—"

"Simmias!" exclaimed Ruso before Tilla could say anything. "Simmias, this is my wife, Tilla. A renowned healer back in her native Britannia. If you have any patients needing a midwife, Tilla will be happy to help. Wife, our new friend is going to recommend some useful contacts for buying specialist medicines."

Perhaps seeing the expression on Tilla's face, Simmias swiftly handed over a battered wax tablet on which he had scrawled several names, and retreated.

"All from one province is only bad if you do not speak their tongue," Tilla insisted.

"We don't need extra slaves. Especially ones who can chat to each other all day and can't do anything useful. One of those is a runaway and the other one looks like a wet afternoon in winter. You have to think ahead when you buy people!"

"I am not talking about lots of extra slaves," she pointed out. "I am only talking about two, and I will see to it that they work to pay you back."

"Doing what?"

"They're both keen workers, sir!"

Ruso turned to glare at the dealer. "It's none of your business."

But it was, of course, precisely that: his business. Unabashed, the man named a price which was close to the remaining money in the purse, and doubtless far more than he would have got from anyone else.

At the same moment as Ruso said, "No," Tilla took him by the arm and said in a voice bright with innocence, "Oh, husband! Ask the nice man if he can take two hundred off, then you could afford them!"

The nice man gave Ruso a look that said he knew it was a game, and that he also knew he was much better at it than some newcomer who was fool enough to bring his wife to the slave auctions. Ruso gave him a deliberate stare of indifference. The dealer's face cracked into a grin, leaving Ruso's features stuck in the indifferent stare just a fraction longer than was appropriate. He had the distinct feeling that the man was laughing at them both.

"Just for you, mistress," oozed the dealer, "I'll go down to eight hundred." He gave a dramatic sigh. "I never could resist a beautiful lady, sir. You're very a lucky man."

21

TILLA SUPPOSED SHE must have once looked like two of their new slaves did on the long trudge back to Kleitos's lodgings. They were gazing up openmouthed at the gleaming temples and palaces that competing emperors had crammed into the center of the city. The Brigante was different. He shambled along, clutching his little bag of possessions with one of the new mattresses slung over his shoulder, and barely glanced up from his own bare feet. As if he had seen all of that marble splendor before and he did not care to see it again.

Tilla was not interested, either. It did not do to remind yourself all the time of how small you were and how little you mattered in this place, even if you were a citizen of Rome and a mother and an owner of three slaves when your husband had only wanted to buy one.

She swallowed. Three slaves. She would have felt terrible leaving these fellow Britons to their fate with the trader, but in truth Dumnonia was a very long way from her own people, and there might be a good reason why the boy had been sold. The woman was from a tribe that was not to be trusted, and now it turned out that the Brigante came from the other end of the territory and had never heard of anyone in her own family or even the name of the Corionotatae. She dared not look at her husband.

Buying the slaves had seemed the honorable thing to do. In their place, it was what she would have prayed for. She knew what it was to be a possession in someone else's homeland, doing her best to shut her thoughts away and forcing her body to endure through the long dreary seasons when no rescue came.

She knew, also, how little could be kept secret from a slave. Even if they did not speak, they would watch and listen. Then they would talk among themselves, because that was what slaves did, and if they were not loyal—as many slaves were not—they would talk to other people too.

She had made her husband invite these strangers to share their small lodgings, and suddenly she did not want them there herself.

They trudged up the hill beside the bathhouse. Several times she turned to check that the woman, Narina, was carrying Mara properly, and fought down an urge to snatch her back. Then the sight of the men with the mattresses and a glimpse of a girl crossing the street with a wicker chair balanced on her head brought on another worry. What would happen if they were wrong about Doctor Kleitos and his troubles, and the family decided to move back home again? Her own household would be crammed back into some horrible lodging house with three extra mouths to feed.

As they approached the Vicus Sabuci, an even worse fear gripped her. What if someone had left another barrel outside the door?

They turned the corner. A group of women with shopping baskets were strolling away along the arcade, blocking the view. Tilla held her breath. They passed the point where the barrel had been left, and she gave thanks out loud before she could stop herself. When her husband asked her what was the matter she said, "It is nothing," because indeed it was. Nothing! There was nothing there in the shade of the arcade.

The body had been taken away. The priest had purified the apartments. There was no new barrel, and there was no lost wandering spirit to haunt them. She must put all that behind her now. It occurred to her that there were no patients waiting, either. She hoped other people would also be able to put the body business behind them. It had not been a good start after all.

Phyllis was coming down the apartment steps as they passed. She pointed to the slaves in surprise and mouthed, "Three?"

Tilla gave a vague shrug and a smile as if it were a mystery to her too, and hurried indoors.

Her husband was already giving orders to the skinny Brigante. "I want you on duty just there, outside the door," he said. "Stand straight, take messages, and don't let anyone in unless my wife says so. If anyone tries to deliver a barrel, report it to her straightaway."

The man mumbled, "Yes, master," as though he were asked to watch out for barrels every day and had grown weary of it.

Tilla said, "Why? Where will you be?" but her husband was not listening.

"Look encouraging," he was saying, "and try not to put the patients off. If we don't get paid, you don't eat."

"Patients, master?" The Brigante seemed to have woken up at last and was eyeing the scarred surface of the operating table.

"We are both healers," Tilla explained.

Suddenly everything went dark. She staggered backward. Her husband shouted. She crashed into the table and hit the floor. There was something big and bulky on top of her. She could hear the frightened cries of her baby.

"Mara!"

Someone dragged the mattress off her.

"Mara!" She pulled herself to her feet.

"She is safe!" called the slave woman, bringing her forward. Mara's arms were outstretched toward her mother, who took her and quieted the crying. "It is all right, little one. Mam is fine. Nobody is going to hurt us."

The Dumnonii boy was standing in the corner clutching two mattresses and looking confused. The Brigante and her husband were gone. Tilla rubbed her bruised hip. "What happened?"

Narina said, "That Brigante threw his bed at you and ran away."

While Tilla was still digesting this, her husband reappeared from the street, breathless and shaking his head. "Lost him down an alleyway," he said. "I'll get a slave finder to pick him up." Then, glancing at the other two new arrivals, he said, "Anyone else frightened of doctors?"

The Dumnonii looked blank. The woman said, "No, master,"

but her gaze too was darting around the surgery like that of a nervous animal.

"We're not going to ask you to help with operations," her husband assured them.

The Dumnonii was still holding on to the mattresses and looking from one person to another. Tilla recognized that expression: the one where you hoped you would work out what was being said before it became obvious that you didn't understand or, worse, before you got into trouble because you had missed something important. She guessed the seller had trained him to answer the questions a buyer was likely to ask. "Narina," she said, "there is a jug of fresh water in the kitchen. Please pour us all a drink."

Moments later everyone was clutching a cup as if they were all at some sort of awkward party. Her husband was issuing orders. "Narina, my wife will tell you what your duties are. Esico, I want you to clear up in here. Roll up the loose bandages. Collect all the empty bottles and jars and boxes together and give them a good wash and a scrub clean, and wipe down all the shelves. Sweep the floor with damp sawdust, then fill as many lamps as we've got oil for. When you've finished that to my wife's satisfaction, she will give you enough money to go to the baths for a cleanup and a decent haircut and shave. And at some point you need to work out where you're going to fit your bed into the surgery tonight."

Tilla opened her mouth to point out that the dealer had surely made everyone wash before the sale and there was nothing wrong with Esico's hair, then realized that since there was not much for an unskilled helper to do, getting rid of him for a while was no bad thing.

"Back from the baths straightaway or there's no supper," he told him. "Got that?"

The lad looked puzzled. Tilla said, "His Latin is not good."

"You'll have to explain it to him. I've got to go out."

"But where—"

"I'll be back as soon as I can."

He almost rushed out without taking his medical bag: She had to call after him to remind him. She repeated the orders to Esico in a tongue he understood, adding, "When one of us tells you to do something, you answer, *Yes, master* or *Yes, mistress*."

Instead of obeying, Esico raised his chin. If they had not checked in the marketplace by speaking to him from behind, she might have thought he was deaf.

"Well?"

"These things are women's work."

"They are the tasks you have been given."

Esico squared his shoulders. He was a handspan taller than her, and she forced herself not to take a step backward. "In Dumnonia," he said, "I am the warrior son of an elder."

She felt something tighten inside her chest. "In Brigantia," she told him, "I was many things. But neither of us is at home now. I have done my best for you. If you don't do as you are told, my husband will send you back to the dealer. Now, what do you say?"

The pimply chin rose even farther. "I say I do not take orders from a traitor."

"Very well," she said, turning away so he could not see her face. She must not tell how she had slipped away from the Roman camp to tend Brigante warriors during the rebellion. The master and the mistress of the house must be united in front of the staff. "We have no use for a fool here."

"You can take your big mouth and your lazy arse somewhere else!" called Narina's voice from the kitchen. "When you have gone, there will be more food for the rest of us."

"And we have no use for a woman with too much to say!" Tilla snapped. There was silence from the kitchen.

This was not going well. One slave had run away, one was insubordinate, and the only one who might be useful thought she was running the house. For a moment Tilla wondered if they could send both of these back to the dealer. Then she felt the weight of Mara on her arm and reminded herself what it was like to manage alone. And then she remembered the terror of being a new slave in the control of strangers.

She put her head around the kitchen door. The bed had been neatly laid out in the corner. Narina paused from arranging kindling under the kitchen grill, clasped her hands together, and bowed her head. "I am sorry, mistress. I should not have said it."

Tilla knew she should remind her that a slave should speak only when spoken to. Instead she said, "Look at me."

Narina turned. The light from the window caught the track of a tear down one cheek. The woman had now spoken out of turn twice, but the first time was to take her new mistress's side against that big wrongheaded lump in the other room, and the second time was to apologize. Tilla said, "I am sorry also." That was probably the wrong thing to say to a slave too, but it was out before she thought about it.

"Thank you, mistress."

"You are a long way from your people, Narina."

"Yes, mistress." Narina sniffed, groped inside the folds of her tunic for a cloth, failed to find one, and wiped her nose on the back of her hand.

"Why are you in Rome?"

"My master brought me from Londinium to his home," she said, "but his wife does not want me in the house."

It had been a mistake to ask, of course. Everyone had a story. Even Esico, probably, although she was not going to let him tell it. Not yet.

"I will work hard, mistress."

"And can you really cook?"

"Yes, mistress. Can I ask something?"

Tilla held out a hand to receive the words.

Narina looked around the kitchen. "Where is the food?"

Tilla followed the woman's gaze. She had forgotten all about the shopping. Her spirits sank as she realized she would have to go to Sabella's again, and Sabella was bound to want to talk about what had happened to the barrel with the man inside. Then she saw the expression on Narina's face, and remembered: Standing in front of her was a servant who was waiting for orders. "Tomorrow, you will shop and cook," she announced as if she had planned it. "Today, when it is time, you can fetch us all something from the bar next door."

Out in the surgery, Esico added two more empty bottles to the snaking line of containers he had created on the workbench before stepping back and trying to melt into the wall at her approach.

"Very good," she said, looking at the bottles. "We will forget what happened before, because you are learning the Roman tongue and you did not understand." And because she knew that if it were one of her brothers standing there, he would have behaved in exactly the same way. It was no use asking for an apology: No honorable warrior would apologize to someone he saw as a traitor. "Here, when we ask a slave to do something, what does he say?"

He said, "Yes, mistress."

"Good. There is one more thing I need you to know. A healer's work is private. You will not speak to anyone of what you hear or see in this home or of any of our business." When he did not reply she said, "You know from your family about not saying things in front of the Romans. Around here, they are all Romans."

Esico cleared his throat. "Even the master?"

"The master is a Roman but he is one of us. Now you can get on with your work."

"Yes, mistress."

If it were her brother, he would be secretly lonely and afraid. "Esico?"

He looked up.

"In the house shrine there are some leaves from the oak tree at home. It is not Dumnonia, but it is the same island. You may pray to your own gods here."

Esico shifted awkwardly. "I do not think my gods can hear me over the din in this city, mistress."

She went into the kitchen, took Mara from her new minder, and held her very close, inhaling the soft baby smell of her and trying not to think about the goddess who protected mothers and babies being so far away across the sea and deaf to her calling. Then she said, "Something strange happened here yesterday, Narina, and I want to tell you myself before you hear any nonsense from the neighbors."

Narina said, "Was it the man in the barrel, mistress?"

Tilla blinked. "Who told you?"

"The slave dealer, mistress. He said if we misbehave, that is how we will end up."

22

PASSING SABELLA'S BAR, Ruso was startled by a cry of "Doctor!" from behind the counter. "I want a word with you!"

He could tell from the tone that the word was not going to be a friendly one. Heads turned to follow his progress between the tables, and he recognized the man from the amphitheater crowd again just as Sabella added, "About that body."

Until that moment, he had entertained a fond hope that he might escape being known as *the doctor whose wife found the body in the barrel.*

"How's your poor wife after her shock, Doctor?" A woman he didn't ever remember seeing before had raised her hand to attract his attention from three tables away.

He changed *very well* to "Recovering, thank you," just in time. It would have been even worse to be *the doctor whose wife found the body in the barrel and didn't mind a bit. Well, she is foreign.*

Finally reaching the refuge of the counter, he did his best to mollify Sabella with an order for spiced wine, and asked if they could talk somewhere quiet.

Sabella bristled. "Well I'm not going to say it in front of the whole bar, am I?" Clapping his cup down on the counter, she shoved open the door farther along and called to someone, "Come out and serve, will you? I've got the doctor here."

A younger and slimmer version of herself appeared, wiping sweat from her forehead with a corner of an apron. "Is my hair all right?"

"As it'll ever be," Sabella told her. "Make sure you count the change properly."

She stood back to allow Ruso into the sweltering atmosphere of the kitchen before pulling the door shut. Then she grabbed a cloth and shifted a couple of bubbling pans along the grill and away from the hot coals.

"The body," Ruso prompted, feeling the need to take some sort of charge here.

Sabella flung the cloth down onto a table. "My husband does you a favor getting rid of it," she said, "and what happens? Your posh friend goes right over our heads and complains about him."

"Accius? I don't think he meant—"

"We've had visits and inspections and I don't know what, the scribe's owner from two doors down is threatening to move him out of the shop, and now my husband's been told to explain himself. If he loses his job, you'll be sorry."

"I will," Ruso agreed, feeling a trickle of sweat slide down the small of his back. The atmosphere in here was like the steam room at the baths, only far less congenial. "To be honest, if I'd known what I was taking on here, we'd never have come. We've already had a visit from a debt collector."

"My husband's got enough to put up with in this place with the tenants. He doesn't need dead bodies cluttering up the place and he doesn't need the street cleaning department going over his head to Horatius Balbus."

"I'm as keen as you are to put an end to all this. I think we need to talk to Doctor Kleitos."

Sabella sniffed. "If I knew where he was, I'd be begging him to come back."

"My wife is saying the same thing." She wasn't, but it seemed like the right thing to say. "To be honest, I don't think he wants to be found. I can't say I blame him. He's probably afraid he'll end up in a barrel himself."

Sabella looked at him suspiciously. "He never had any bother before this."

"He seems to have covered up his debts very well," he agreed. "I expect he didn't want to upset his wife. Do you know if there's any family he might have gone to?"

Sabella supposed any of Kleitos's relatives would be back in Greece. "But he was a slave for years, and you know how it is. They don't really have family like us, do they? Anyway, he didn't know anything about that barrel. They were gone before it arrived."

Ruso blinked. "Were they?"

"Otherwise they would have answered the door, wouldn't they? And that old feller with the limp was there knocking for ages."

He raised both eyebrows and waited.

"Just as it was getting light," she said. "Him and a boy."

"Did he say anything?"

"'Delivery.'"

"Anything else?"

"He said he'd be back later."

"You don't know which side he limped on, do you?"

Sabella stared at him. "What's that got to do with anything?"

"Nothing really," Ruso admitted. "He can't have known what he was delivering, or he wouldn't have hung around." Recalling the sight of the man limping away under the arcade, he thought the weakness was on the left. That narrowed it down, but not a lot. There could be several hundred men like that across a city of a million people, and besides, if the limp had been caused by only a minor injury, it might have vanished by now.

The door opened, and Sabella paused to address another, smaller black-haired child who had staggered in with a rattling pile of crockery and a mercifully cool draft. "Only six high on the shelf!" she ordered. "How many times? And mind those cups!"

Turning back to Ruso, she said, "If I find out where Kleitos went, I'll tell him we all want him back. In the meantime, any more trouble and you're out. And if your patron goes running to Horatius Balbus with that, I'll tell him why myself."

Ruso was back in the street enjoying the fresh air when a small voice from behind him said, "They went on a vegetable cart, mister."

"The doctor?"

The small version of Sabella who had delivered the crockery nodded, and then glanced 'round and stepped back into a doorway where they could not be seen from the bar. "I looked out of the hole in the shutters when it was dark."

"If it was dark," he said, "how did you know it was a vegetable cart?"

The girl sniffed. "I could smell the cabbages," she said.

23

R USO STOPPED. THERE was a barrel protruding from a doorway not fifty paces ahead of him. He crossed the street and continued on the other side, relieved to see that the door belonged to a snack shop and not a medical practice. Even so, he made a mental note never to eat there. Then he strode out under the arch of the old Esquiline gate, past the grand gardens that someone had told him were built up over old burial grounds. The eccentric tomb of a baker still remained, an odd structure of concrete cylinders and circles that must have been in place before the city walls were expanded to enclose it. Beyond the nearby gate, he chose the left-hand fork and followed the Praenestina road past a series of competitively elaborate tombs whose occupants would never have wanted to sleep this close to the traffic when they were alive.

He wondered if this was the route Kleitos's family had followed in the dark.

Sabella's daughter had seen nothing that she could identify through the hole in the shutters: only shapes moving in the shadows. But along with the cabbage smell she remembered the whisper of voices and the scrape and heave of furniture and luggage being loaded up. She thought someone might have been crying. It was hard to tell. Then the squeak of wheels had faded into the night.

"My friend went away like that," she'd added. "Her pa said he would pay the rent next week, only they moved out instead. Ma said our pa was too soft."

It was not hard to imagine that conversation.

Following the girl's lead he had found the glum market superintendent at the local council office, and was surprised to recognize him as the priest who had purified Kleitos's rooms. According to the superintendent, the carts came in at night to deliver to the markets. Traffic regulations said they had to be gone by dawn, which made them a popular means of transport for anyone wishing to make a quick and quiet departure. Kleitos could have left with any one of twenty or thirty drivers. Many of them lived miles outside the city and would not turn up again for another seven days. That was always assuming, of course, that the driver in question had been delivering to the local market.

"And if he wasn't?"

"He could be any one of hundreds," said the superintendent.

Had he reported to Accius, Ruso knew he would have been ordered back to the apartment block to start questioning all the neighbors about the possible whereabouts of Kleitos. But he could think of very few doctors who would tell their patients where they went when they took time off. So instead he had chosen to deal with a matter of more personal interest: the business of the body in the barrel.

Undertakers might not be the sort of people Accius—or anyone else—wanted to mix with, which was why they were based out here and not in the city. Still, they performed a useful job that nobody else wanted to do. They also performed several jobs that not everybody wanted done, including the physical punishment of slaves. As a rule Ruso found that sort of thing deeply distasteful, but having seen his own money running away down a side street on British legs this afternoon, he was willing to concede that there were two sides to every question.

"Good afternoon, sir." The doorman's bow was respectful and the tone of "And how can my master be of assistance?" was suitably solemn.

"It's about a body," Ruso explained.

"Yes, sir. I'll have someone fetched right away."

A small boy was despatched and returned with a man who moved as though he were underwater and whose face had probably looked forty ever since he was four. "Sir." The man's eyes closed and his head drifted downward, then floated up again. "Lucius Virius, assistant head of funeral services."

Ruso introduced himself and was ushered through the entrance porch, around a courtyard with a couple of vehicles parked inside, and into a small room where a lamp was burning scented oil in a little shrine on the wall. Lucius Virius offered him a seat with his back to the window, but the sound of hammering still penetrated, as did the smell of pitch and freshly sawn pine and something less pleasant that they weren't quite managing to mask. Helping the departed to rest in peace provided a useful amount of work for the living.

Lucius Virius sank onto a seat on the opposite side of the table and peered at him over the top of a vase of dried flowers. "Allow me to offer my condolences, Doctor."

Ruso put his case on the floor. "Thank you, but it's not a relative."

"And how can we help, Doctor? We offer a comprehensive service from preparation of the deceased with a full parade with mourners and musicians to a simple farewell for a respected friend. We guarantee our personal and professional attention, and all equipment is supplied by our own craftsmen, so rest assured we have complete control."

The speech was delivered well, and Ruso was surprised to find himself suddenly recalling the voice of his uncle Theo. *Remember, boy—this may be the fifth case of the same thing you've seen today, but to the patient, it is new, and he expects to see that you care about it.*

"Special requests by arrangement," the man added.

"What sort of special requests?" Ruso was curious.

"Transport to the deceased's hometown, full burial for religious reasons— Is there something particular you had in mind, Doctor?"

"No," Ruso admitted, putting aside any thoughts of asking if any of the special requests ever involved a barrel. "It's about an unidentified body that was taken away this morning. I heard it was your people who picked it up."

"Sadly, it is a duty we are often called upon to perform."

Ruso explained the circumstances. The dried flowers wobbled as Lucius Virius placed his hands flat on the table. "I am familiar with the case. What is the nature of your enquiry, Doctor?"

"The doctor and his family who used to live in the apartment haven't been seen since, and his patron is very worried about them," Ruso explained, realizing as he said it that Balbus had never shown any concern for Kleitos's wife and children. "Also we've had people calling 'round to see if it was a missing relative. It's very upsetting for my wife."

"Please assure Horatius Balbus that the deceased wasn't Doctor Kleitos."

So Lucius Virius knew Kleitos well enough to know who his patron was. "I think he'd be doubly reassured if he could contact Kleitos for himself. You don't know where he went?"

"I don't know him well, I'm afraid. Purely a professional connection. I'm sure you understand."

Ruso nodded. "And the worried relatives? I've been sending them out here, but I thought if you had any idea who it was, I could save some of them a trip."

The dried flowers wobbled again as Lucius Virius's hands floated up off the table. "I can certainly help you there, Doctor. The deceased has been identified and the family have been informed. So if anyone else asks, perhaps you could tell them they need to search elsewhere."

"Can you tell me who it was?"

"I'm afraid not. The family have asked for privacy. Again, I'm sure you understand."

"It must be very distressing for them," Ruso agreed, shuddering inwardly at the thought of the bereaved relatives visiting the surgery to ask why their loved one had ended up outside the door of a man armed with scalpels and curiosity.

The tone of Lucius Virius's "Is there anything else we can help you with, Doctor?" was impeccably polite, but the implication was that he had spent enough time here, and there were genuinely bereaved clients who needed his attention. A fresh waft of pitch floated in, and Ruso guessed they were preparing torches for a funeral parade.

"One last thing," he said. "You deal with slave problems?"

"My colleagues can help you there, yes."

"I've just had a man run away."

Once more Lucius Virius managed to look genuinely sorry. "Our slave department can administer punishments and help with questioning to obtain evidence for court cases, Doctor, but I'm afraid you would have to hire a specialist to track down a missing man. As a first resort you might try asking the night watch—they don't take on searches, but they sometimes hold people they pick up."

Ruso, who had no intention of spending more money than he had already wasted on his missing slave, thanked him and got to his feet. He was on the verge of sending his condolences to the bereaved family, then decided that the less they connected the absence of their relative with the presence of doctors, the better.

Lucius Virius was escorting him out around the courtyard when a high voice called, "Doctor?" Ruso looked around, unable to see the youth who had spoken. Then the giant who was standing beside the cart repeated, "Doctor, a quick word before you go."

Ruso hoped his mistake had not been too obvious. "Of course."

Lucius Virius excused himself and slipped away, explaining that his colleague would see Ruso out.

The giant with the squeaky voice said, "You're the one who's taken over from Doctor Kleitos."

"I am."

"We liked him, me and my mates. He was a good doctor."

"So I gather." Ruso tried not to peer at the barrel loaded on the back of the cart, and became aware that the giant was waiting for an answer. "Sorry?"

"Doctor Kleitos. Where did he go?"

"I wish I knew."

"Well if you find out, can you send us a message?"

"I will." Ruso was about to ask the giant's name when he heard female laughter. Two people were making their way along the far side of the courtyard. The laughing woman was dressed in black and had the wildly dishevelled hair of a professional mourner, but it was her thinner male companion who drew Ruso's attention. Or rather, her companion's limp.

"Who's that?"

"Sorry about her, Doctor. The girls are supposed to change clothes when they're not on duty."

"Even mourners have to laugh," Ruso assured him. "The man. What's his name?"

The giant hesitated, as if he were not sure.

"I need a word with him." Ruso stepped across the courtyard. "Excuse me?"

The man spun 'round. The woman's amusement dropped away instantly, and she adopted a somber expression.

"Ruso," he said, introducing himself. "And you are?"

"Birna, sir," the man said.

"We've met," Ruso told him, recognizing the nasal voice. "You came to Doctor Kleitos's rooms yesterday."

Birna shook his head. "Not me, sir."

"You said you had some business with Kleitos."

Birna backed away, holding up his hands in exactly the same gesture he had used under the arcade. "Sorry, sir. You must be mistaken."

The giant came across. "Some problem, Doctor?"

"No," Ruso assured him, secretly relieved. He was not sure what he would have done if the man confessed. "I must be mixing up your colleague with somebody else."

But he knew he was not. This was the man who had come to Kleitos's door insisting that he had been promised cash on delivery, but keeping quiet about what he had delivered.

As he walked back past the grand tombs of the wealthy, Ruso mulled over his conversation with Lucius Virius. The undertaker might have been telling the truth when he said that the man in the barrel had been identified and that the family were requesting privacy. On the other hand, it was just the sort of thing you would say to fend off awkward questions about what your staff were up to and how much you knew about it.

24

TILLA HAD JUST found the abandoned head of a wooden doll under the bed when the tone of Narina's "Mistress!" made her drop it and run.

There were two of them this time. They were younger and bigger than the skinny man with the limp, and they had a better story. Instead of asking payment for something that had been delivered, they said they had been sent by Doctor Kleitos himself to collect all the bits and pieces he had left behind and sell them. It wouldn't take long, but they just needed to come in and—

"No."

The one who was doing all the talking shook his head sadly. "I know, miss. I'm a nuisance. They all tell me."

"Then you should go away," she said, not charmed by the lopsided grin. Once these men were inside, how could she stop them from taking whatever they wanted?

"They all tell him that too, miss," put in his friend, "but he just hangs around like a fart under the bedclothes. I'll keep him in order. I promise. If you just let us—"

"No." Tilla moved to close the door, but it juddered to a halt against a large boot.

"Miss," the first man said, his voice harder now, "we got sent here to do a job. We don't want bother any more than you do, but see . . ." He nodded toward the inside of the surgery. "Not all of that in there is your stuff, is it? And the man who owns it wants it paid for."

"This is our home." She wished her husband were here. Narina was good with babies, but she did not look as though she would be much use in a fight. "The other doctor has gone. The only things he left here were rubbish, and we threw them away. If you don't believe me, go and ask next door at the bar."

"We'll just come in and check, then."

"How will you check?" She drew herself up as tall as she could manage. "These things are ours. If Doctor Kleitos wants to argue, he can come here and do it himself." Although she hoped he would not.

So then they asked when her husband would be home, as she had known they would, and she waited until a couple of women with shopping baskets were walking past to say very loudly that she did not let strangers into the house when her husband was not here, and if they did not stop bothering her and leave, she would shout for help.

She never found out what would have happened next because a gangly figure appeared in the street behind the men. "Esico!" she said, adding in British, "These men are a nuisance, and I am not letting them in."

To the men she said, "He lives here. Let him past," and to her surprise they stepped back. She realized why when she almost gagged on the sickly waft of lavender.

"Nice hair oil, son," said the fart under the bedclothes, miming vomiting behind Esico's back.

Moments later she was pushed aside from behind and a stout stick was inches from the face of the no-longer-grinning man.

"Go," ordered Esico.

"We were only—"

"Go."

"You cannot reason with him," Tilla told them. "He does not speak Latin."

The no-longer-grinning man took a step back. "That's your husband?"

"Next time," Tilla told them, "bring a letter from Doctor Kleitos with his seal on it."

"Go."

And they did.

"Esico!" Tilla declared, waiting till the men were out of sight before taking the broomstick out of his grasp. "You are truly a warrior."

A blush spread over the angular features.

"But you do not smell like one."

The blush deepened, and as they walked through to the kitchen Esico rubbed his shorn head with both hands as if that might drive away the smell.

"Don't: You will make it worse."

Narina opened the door onto the courtyard and the window as well.

"The barber cut my hair," Esico explained, "and then I thought he was asking if I wanted a shave. So I said yes. Then he started pouring it on and I thought he was asking if I wanted him to stop. So I said yes again."

25

TILLA SENT ESICO to wash his head under the courtyard waterspout. On the way out she heard Narina tell him not to come back till he stopped smelling like a Roman whore.

When Ruso came home she would be able to tell him that although the runaway Brigante had been a waste of money, the other spare Briton was at least useful for something, although she was still not sure if he would be much help as a doorman when it came to getting messages straight. Not only was his Latin hopeless, but he was certain that when the master had rushed out this afternoon, he had only gone as far as the bar on the corner. Unable to believe it, Tilla had braved Sabella's curiosity and slipped out to buy some raisin cake they didn't need. After all, the slaves could not be allowed to suspect that their mistress was spying on their master.

When she got to the bar her husband was nowhere to be seen. Luckily, neither was Sabella, so she was spared any difficult questions. But where was he? And where had he been for the rest of the afternoon? She had no idea.

She was still pondering this back at home when there was another knock at the locked door. This time she motioned Narina to silence, crept up and squinted through a gap between the panels before letting Phyllis in.

"Do you swear not to speak of it?"

They were huddled close together on the bed in the only room where no slaves would be listening, but even so Phyllis was whispering.

"I swear."

"Timo says it is nobody else's business, and I know I should obey him, but I have to talk to somebody."

"Does he know you are here?"

"He is at work," Phyllis whispered, but she still glanced up at the rafters as if he might be lying in the upstairs apartment with one ear pressed against the floor.

"What work does he do?" Tilla asked, not because she wanted to know but because it was best to start with easy questions.

"He is a carpenter. He works for Curtius Cossus. The one who is building the new temple down by the amphitheater and wants to marry Horatius Balbus's daughter."

Everyone around here seemed to have some connection to Horatius Balbus. Tilla supposed that lots of men wanted to marry a rich man's daughter. "It is good to have a man with steady work," she said. "How long have you been married?"

Phyllis looked startled. "You can tell?"

"I can tell nothing," Tilla assured her, although the girl's reaction made it easy to guess. "How can I help?"

The girl's shoulders slumped. "It has been five years," she said, "and still it is just us."

"I am sorry."

"Everyone else . . . Timo says he is doing everything right."

"Do you think that is true?"

Phyllis shrugged. "It is as other women say it is. I have tried fasting and bathing and not fasting and not bathing, and celery seeds and burned pine and wine, but Timo would not go near me after the garlic, and everyone prays for me, but still nothing changes."

Tilla ran through the usual questions about bleeding and dates and diet and did an examination, pushing away any thoughts of how much more she might know if she had taken the terrible path followed by the doctor who had lived here before, and opened up dead bodies to see what was inside them.

It was useless to tell a follower of Christos to pray to any other gods, so she went into the surgery for the pot she had seen labeled CUMIN with some other writing in Greek. Instead of seeds, it held some sort of green powder. She put it to one end of the shelf to remind herself to ask her husband if he knew what it was and returned to the bedroom. "There are other medicines I can suggest," she said, remembering the ashes of hare's stomach and roast sparrow in wine back in Britannia that had been a waste of money and wildlife. "They are said to work for some women. But I have nothing here, and to be honest, none of them worked for me."

"But you have—"

"Mara is the daughter of a friend. She is adopted."

"Adopted?" Phyllis paused to think about this news. "And your husband was willing to adopt a girl?"

"He was willing to adopt a baby," said Tilla, knowing he had wanted a son.

"My husband says adopting would not be the same. But when I think of all the poor abandoned little babies we could bring home . . ."

"It is a different start on the same unknown path," Tilla assured her, but Phyllis had not finished.

"Sister Dorcas says it is because there is unforgiven sin."

"Unforgiven sin?" Tilla repeated, puzzled. This was a cause of barrenness that she had never considered. Then she thought of all the thousands of women who were not followers of Christos and had never confessed any of their sins to the One True God and yet who, like Sabella and her own sister-in-law, had more children than they knew what to do with.

"But I have repented of everything I can think of," Phyllis continued, "and Timo says he has too, and he is not doing any more."

No wonder he was reluctant to discuss their lack of offspring with anyone else.

Phyllis continued. "I told him last night he must stay away from me until he has confessed everything. But he said if he does that he will have lustful thoughts, and then we had a big argument, and now I don't know what to do."

"What does Sister Dorcas know about these things?" Tilla demanded. "Is she a medicus or a midwife?"

"She was given a word from the Lord."

"Then I shall pray that the Lord sends her a word to mind her own business," said Tilla, wondering if Sister Dorcas had designs on Phyllis's husband.

Phyllis squirmed. "But it is true. There is unforgiven sin."

"You have done something to offend Christos?"

"I try to change. But I keep failing."

Tilla wondered what this nervous young woman could possibly have done to offend her god, or indeed anyone else.

In a whisper, Phyllis confessed. "I do not love Sister Dorcas."

Tilla tried to hold back the laughter and could not. "Of course you do not love her! She is an interfering troublemaker! You think she loves you?"

"We are commanded to love our enemies."

"Well, you may have to love them," Tilla told her, "but I'm sure Christos never said you have to like them." At least, if he had, then he should not have. "And you don't have to listen to them, either."

"Timo's mother says—"

"It is no business of Timo's mother's."

But Phyllis was not that easily reassured. "She says if there is no hope, that if he will never gain the rights of a father, I am holding him back and he should find a new wife."

"I am sure Christos would not say that."

Phyllis stared at her lap. "I don't know what to do."

So much of a healer's work was not healing at all, but comforting. Tilla said, "Perhaps we could try a different way. If I have your leave to speak about this to my husband, he will perhaps meet yours by chance on the stairs, and they will talk about the things men talk about, and perhaps my husband will speak of his daughter with pride, and somehow your husband will find out that she is adopted."

"If he knows I have spoken of this . . ."

"He will not," Tilla promised. "But you must share his bed, or nothing any of us does will help."

Later, straightening the bedcover, Tilla pondered her own empty womb and wondered if unconfessed sin might be sealing the entrance. The gods sometimes made strange demands in return for their favors. At home they wanted gifts to the earth and the waters. Here, they wanted great stone temples and high arches that seemed to be trying to trap the heavens. And parades and dead animals and—no, it was the humans here who seemed to want to fill the arena with dead people. But what if Sister Dorcas was right, and her peculiar word from the Lord applied to other women as well as Phyllis?

There would be a long list to confess. It would include much that was half-forgotten, and things of which she was not proud.

She gave the last corner of the cover a sharp tug. The past was best left where it was: buried. She had Mara to look after now, and more important things to worry about.

26

As Ruso walked back toward the Vicus Sabuci, it struck him how provincial he had become. If this business had happened in Britannia, someone would have known someone who was a friend of the third cousin of the deceased's brother-in-law, and within a week everyone would know who had been in the barrel and be ready to offer some version of how he had got there. With enough persistence, it would be possible to find the link between the body and the man Birna at the undertakers', who had almost certainly delivered it. And also the whereabouts of a missing Greek doctor, who could surely not hide for long in a land largely populated by Britons and soldiers.

He inhaled deeply as he passed a bakery, trying to get the smell of the undertakers' out of his nose. In Rome, where it was impossible to know everyone, it was said that people could live on the same street and still be strangers. Small wonder that its inhabitants were eager to amass vast wealth, attach themselves to powerful men, form some sort of professional club, or get into a group like the night watch or the undertakers. The best you could hope for was to be part of something that was stronger than you were. Otherwise, it was every man for himself, and if you failed—well, Rome was a place where they genuinely needed a system for collecting the remains of the unwanted and unmissed. This was a place where a corrupt undertaker could deliver a dead man to someone's house and expect payment. A dead man who—if Lucius Virius was telling the truth—did have a family to mourn him after all.

He wriggled to unstick his tunic from the small of his back. It still felt clammy with sweat after that awkward encounter in Sabella's kitchen, which had added an unwelcome complication to a situation that was already disturbing and distasteful. Tilla was right, though: Whatever unsavory activity Kleitos had been up to, they were going to have to keep it quiet. Since anyone could call himself a doctor, a good reputation was all that distinguished the well-intentioned healer from the dangerous charlatan. Once his patients' trust was gone, a man might as well pack up and leave. So, he and Tilla must cling to their story and ignore any objections that Sabella might raise about the doctor moving out before the barrel arrived.

What they wanted everybody to believe was that the body had been put there because Kleitos was being intimidated by some very determined debt collectors. The truth, he supposed, was that the undertakers had been asked to deliver when they had a suitable body, and Kleitos had fled the city—for whatever reason—without remembering to cancel the order.

Back in the Vicus Sabuci, the British youth was standing outside the surgery door with his gangly arms folded and his head held high, as if he were daring any debt collectors to approach. Ruso sighed. The sight of him was enough to send all but the boldest patients scurrying in the opposite direction. Since there was no way to make him smaller, he would have to stand inside. Or Ruso would have to find something else he could usefully do. But not just yet. There was one more call to make.

Trajan's vast bathing complex was as magnificent inside as the soaring entrance porch had suggested. Ruso promised himself that one day he would make time to splash about in the swimming pool, take a long massage, and dawdle in the libraries under the marble gaze of poets and philosophers. Today was strictly utilitarian: He needed to find an attendant to guard his things, work up enough sweat to scrape off the dirt of the long walk, and dunk himself in the cold plunge before finding Simmias's poisons expert.

None of his fellow bathers knew how Doctor Kleitos might be contacted with an urgent message. The majority had never heard of him. Of those who had, several had heard of Ruso too. Wasn't he the one who had found the—

He tried to interrupt with "Yes," before the word *body* aroused more interest, and then took refuge in "It's all being dealt with by the officials." The mention of officials was enough to silence further questioning. Fortunately nobody asked exactly which officials those might be.

Ruso left the changing rooms feeling cleaner, but back in the same slightly clammy outfit. The poisons expert was called Xanthe, and she was somewhere in the row of shops that opened onto the far side of the exercise area, beyond a couple of noisy ball games and a scatter of grunting weight lifters.

He skirted the yard, envying several youths who were lolling about in the sun on the library steps. No doubt a library was a fine and respectable place for a young man to meet a young lady, which might explain Accius's newly acquired reading habit.

Meanwhile, the marble glare of the philosophers reminded him how quickly joy evaporated. Two days ago he had been convinced that he would be perfectly content if he had a job, a baby-minder, and a bedroom with no cockroaches in it. Now he had all of them. There had been brief moments of elation, it was true, and yet still he was dissatisfied and more than a little worried. Perhaps it was the fate of mankind to be forever searching. Perhaps he was just naturally miserable. Or perhaps the gods in whom he didn't quite believe were getting their revenge on him. How else could a man make sense of being offered a decent medical practice only to find a looming disaster in a barrel on the doorstep? Not to mention an all-powerful patient who wanted one of the few things he had no idea how to supply.

The first woman he asked looked insulted at the implication that she might be Xanthe. When he found the real Xanthe behind a curtain at the back of a bathing-oil shop four doors down, he understood why.

She could have been any age between fifty and ninety, with skin of creased leather and hands that reminded him of chicken's feet. When she reached up to draw him closer, the claws were cold on his forearm.

"Come by the lamp, where I can see you." The words were Greek: their edges softened by the absence of teeth.

Standing above her, he had a sensation not dissimilar to that of being inspected on parade.

"Who are you?"

He explained.

"Who sent you?"

He explained again.

"Simmias. Ah."

"Kleitos asked me to take over his patients while he's away."

He had hoped for, "Kleitos, ah!" as some sign of recognition, but instead she gestured toward his case. "Open it. Let me see."

Puzzled, he knelt in front of her and opened the case. Xanthe ran one claw along a probe and lifted a scalpel closer to the lamp for inspection. Pointing to an artery clamp, she demanded to be told what it was for. He told her. "And this?"

"Catheter."

"I am told that in Britannia there is a spiky hedge plant used to treat the heart."

"Hawthorn?" he guessed. "Don't use it with foxglove."

She nodded. "Good. You seem to be who you say you are."

Be careful who you trust seemed to be a general rule of conduct around here. He hoped this woman was as reliable as Simmias had said. He had no way of telling. In the past he had rarely needed to venture beyond the Legion's approved suppliers of antidotes for snakebites and scorpion stings. There had been the traveling snake tamers back in Nemausus, but they were regular visitors who had sold all manner of remedies in the street. This was very different. Still, Xanthe's caution was reassuring. A woman known to have expertise in poisons was walking very close to the edge of the law, and she was wise to make a show of being careful whom she supplied.

She picked out the theriac bottle, empty but for a brown smear in the bottom, and smelled it before asking him to identify the contents. "That's what I came here to ask you," he explained.

Keeping the bottle out, she gestured to him to close the case.

"I've taken over a patient who's had this prescribed by Kleitos," he told her. "I'm told it's theriac. But there's nothing on the bottle to say so."

"I would say it might be."

"I need to replace it. And to know if a day or two without will affect his protection."

The woman sniffed the bottle again. "A few days, no. A few weeks, yes." Then she clawed up a long feather from a pot on the table beside her, slid it into the bottle and gathered a touch of the medicine before painting it on her finger, sniffing again, and finally giving it a tentative lick.

The silence that followed was punctuated by shouts from the ball game.

"You are wise to come to me," she said. "There are people who mix up all kinds of concoctions and pretend to offer protection. Most of them know nothing. Some of them know a little. They are the worst. They are the ones who kill."

Glad that he had not attempted to guess the recipe, he said, "Did you supply Kleitos?"

"Leave the bottle and ten sesterces. Come back in two days."

"I'll be able to check with him when I see him," he said, annoyed by her refusal to give a straight answer. "I just need to know it's the same stuff."

"And will he be back within two days?"

"Possibly not." He handed over the coins.

"You are looking after his patients but you do not know this?"

"I don't know where he is. Do you?"

She did not. "Come in two days," she said, flapping a chicken's foot to shoo him back out past the curtain and into the dazzle of the exercise yard.

He was still blinking in the sunlight when a delightful young lady appeared by his side. Observing that he was looking weary, she claimed that her master had just the thing to restore his vigor.

"Really?"

"I take it every day myself, sir, and I'm always ready for anything. Come with me and let me show you."

Ruso declined the offer on the grounds that he had patients waiting. At least, he hoped he did. He needed to find a new job for the youth currently frightening everyone away from his door. Perhaps he could use him as a model for public lectures on anatomy. Others were keen to show off their expertise: why not someone who, after years of treating wounded men, genuinely had knowledge worth sharing?

The trouble was, educational demonstrations with no beautiful girls in peril, vanishing pig squeaks or exotic dead apes would appeal only to his competitors and the exceptionally studious. What he really needed was a miracle to attract patients. There was Tilla, of course, whose once-fractured right arm truly was a marvelous piece of work, but he doubted she would want to put it on display.

He glanced at the sweating weight lifters. He wondered how much he would need to pay one of them to swear that he owed his glowing health to his doctor. When competition was fierce, it was not hard to understand the temptation to cheat.

He pushed this unwelcome thought aside. His final errand here was to find Simmias's recommended supplier of medicinal wine.

He found the man next to a snack stall. The wine tasted acceptable, even if the seller did appear to have been sampling it himself. Ruso bought a small amphora and received along with it a torrent of unwanted information about customers who didn't "appreciate quality like you do, Doctor," and about the cost of renting a pitch in the bathhouse. No, he had no idea where Kleitos might have gone, but he didn't blame him. If he had the chance, he would get out of this place himself. Somewhere by the sea. Baiae—now that was a fine town. Or up in the mountains where the air was healthier. Instead he was stuck here heading into another cauldron of a Roman summer. When Ruso asked if it was likely to be hotter than the south of Gaul he offered a glum "You'll see."

Turning down a haircut and shave and the offer of the finest raisin pastries in Rome, Ruso finally escaped. As he nodded a farewell to the giant statue of the emperor Trajan in the entrance hall, he found himself wondering how his household of pale Britons would cope with a hot summer. Quite possibly he would be the only one left standing.

27

SEEING ESICO STILL guarding the surgery door, Ruso thought there must be a philosophical treatise somewhere on ambivalence. If there wasn't, there should be. It would explain exactly how a man could be glad that at least one of his unwanted slaves had not run away, while at the same time be annoyed to find that he was still bloody there.

As Ruso approached, a shabby middle-aged man detached himself carefully from the side of a nearby pillar and said, "Excuse me?"

"Can I help?"

"I've been here for hours. That useless boy doesn't seem to know anything, and the woman behind the bar is positively rude. When will Doctor Simmias be back?"

He definitely needed to take Esico off door duty. "Doctor Simmias doesn't work here," he explained.

"What? I've wasted half the afternoon!"

"I'm standing in for the doctor who does. Can I help?"

The potential patient glanced down at the wine amphora under one arm and the medical case in the other.

Ruso countered this impression by quoting his service with the Legion. The patient conceded that he might let him try, and lowered himself to grope for a bag of scrolls by holding on to the pillar with one hand and sliding downward, keeping a straight back and bending only at the knees.

Ruso resolved to place a bench outside so patients had somewhere to sit and wait without bothering Sabella. He ushered the man in past Esico and an unexpected smell of lavender. "Take a seat," he suggested. "I won't be a moment."

His return to the domestic hearth was acknowledged in very different ways. Mara shouted "Ah!" and waved her arms and legs in the air. Narina set aside whatever she was polishing and stood back with her head slightly bowed. To his surprise and pleasure, Tilla stepped forward and gave him a kiss. Here, at least, was a temporary respite from all his other worries. Perhaps it had been worth buying her those slaves.

He propped the amphora in the corner and rewarded his womenfolk with a warm smile. It was made warmer by the knowledge that soon, thanks to his investment in a baby-minder, he and his wife would be enjoying their first nocturnal privacy in many weeks.

Tilla glanced at the table, then sniffed his shoulder. "You have been to the baths."

"I didn't think you'd want a husband who smells worse than the staff."

"I have not been to the baths."

"Never mind," he assured her, pulling her close. "I like you the way you are."

She said, "I have been here dealing with the slaves and the patients and seeing off more debt collectors."

He tensed. "The one with the limp again?" While he was dallying at the bathhouse, Birna could have come straight here from the undertakers'.

"No, two new ones."

They could be some of Birna's cronies. "Did they say where they came from?"

"I do not care where they came from. Also there were patients. One for me, and two who wanted to talk to a man, but I could not tell them when you would be back, so one of them went somewhere else. The other one wants you to visit his father, but it is not urgent."

"There's a new one waiting in the surgery too."

She said, "Do not let him smell that strong wine on your breath."

Her tone seemed a little sharp, but no doubt she was tired. With no time to dwell on it, he went back into surgery and apologized for keeping his new patient waiting.

"I'm Tubero the Younger," the man announced. "You might not have heard of me."

"Ruso," said Ruso, who hadn't. "How can I help?"

The man snorted. "I'll bet you heard about that big crowd in the Forum of Peace last week, listening to the fine verses."

"No, I must have missed it."

"Well, you must be the only man in Rome who did. Spellbound, they were! You should have seen them. The woman next to me said, 'He's very good, isn't he?' And I said, 'He's very good at thieving.' Half of his lines were mine. But of course I couldn't get her to believe me. Nobody believes me. They'd rather listen to a pretty boy sponsored by a silly old man who thinks he's in love with him."

Recalling the debate about the content of arteries, and the crowds that had gathered to see the woman being dropped off the amphitheater, Ruso suggested, "If you object, you sound curmudgeonly."

"Exactly!" cried the poet, shooting out an arm to grab at Ruso while carefully keeping his torso still. "Exactly. It's such a relief to find someone who understands, Doctor."

Ruso lifted his patient's hand from his arm and recalled Tilla's warning about his breath. "So, how can I help?"

As expected, it was back trouble. Ruso performed the usual examinations on Tubero the Younger's flabby white torso. The man's effort to touch his toes was not a great success, and his attempt to squat was accompanied by a gasp of "I never have to do all this for the other doctor!" As Ruso noted the way the poet's head was permanently inclined to the right and his shoulder rose slightly to meet it, he was entertained by a monologue on the difficulties of earning a living as a man of letters.

There were the friends who borrowed a scroll and then had copies made by their own slaves rather than pay for one. "I donate to the libraries, of course—one has to do one's bit. And then they go and hide my work away in a corner where nobody can find it!"

"It must be a struggle," Ruso conceded, regretting his earlier sympathy. "Does the pain go down your legs at all?"

No, the pain did not go down his legs. "People don't appreciate the professional requirements of the job. I have to have my special desk, like you have your instruments. And my routine. The muse of poetry has to know where to find me. Although sometimes it must be very difficult for her. I get invited out a lot, you know."

"That's good."

"I used to think like that. But just because I recite in the Forum from time to time, people think I'll be happy to keep their whole dinner party entertained all evening for nothing. You'll meet new readers, they say. You can have some of the food, they say. Leftovers, they mean. But then, one of the guests might be a patron on the lookout for new talent. So I say, 'I'll come if you send me an escort,' and, you know, I never hear from most of them again. How's a man in my condition supposed to walk all the way across the city at night on his— What are you doing?"

"Testing your reflexes."

"Oh. Anyway, I'm not paying for transport to go and recite my poems. That's not how it's supposed to work at all."

Ruso, who was frequently expected to work for free himself, recognized the frustration. Still, it was hard to see exactly why anyone should pay for anything as pointless as poetry.

"A little respect is all I ask," insisted the poet.

"And payment. You can get down now."

Tubero the Younger grasped the scarred edge of the operating table with both hands and carefully lowered his feet to the floor. "Payment would be a token of respect. I'm thinking of going into funeral orations."

"That should be a steady trade." Ruso shoved the table aside to make more space. "Just turn and walk away from me, will you?"

The poet complied, announcing to the far wall, "Doctor Kleitos just gives me something to rub in."

"And back again, please. I thought you were looking for Doctor Simmias?"

"Only because I heard Kleitos is away."

"But Simmias doesn't—"

"Simmias covered for him last time he wasn't working," explained the poet, coming to a halt in front of Ruso. "If your doorman had had the sense to explain, I'd have gone straight over to the night watch barracks and asked to see Simmias there."

"He was working here?" So why, when they met at the slave market, had the portly doctor had claimed he and Kleitos barely knew each other?

"Only for a few weeks. Kleitos broke his arm—or leg—I can't remember. Are you going to give me some more of that rub?"

"Mm," said Ruso, pondering this new information. "Sit down somewhere here and write something." The new slave had left the workbench covered with clean, damp jars and bottles. He moved the stool across to the operating table.

The poet eyed the makeshift desk with distaste. "I can't just write to order, you know. People imagine I just scribble down the first thing that comes into my head. But a real poet has to consider every word."

"I don't mean compose something," said Ruso. "Just put your name on that tablet."

When the poet had finished slouching over the operating table the name appeared so deeply gouged through the wax that it was probably engraved in the wood underneath.

"You write very forcefully."

"I write with passion!"

Eventually Ruso prescribed light exercise, frequent breaks, and massage.

"No medicine?"

"I can give you something to help relax the muscles, but I think it's the way you sit," Ruso explained. "Maybe you could raise your special desk and stand instead."

"But I need to think!"

"Can't you walk up and down and think at the same time?"

"I have to think in the thinking position."

"You told me the pain and stiffness is interfering with your work. I'm telling you what you can do about it. Keep moving. Walk in the gardens. Go for a swim in Trajan's very splendid pool."

"Hmph. You military types are all the same. You'll have me sleeping in a tent next."

"You could write a poem about it," Ruso suggested as he

scooped some greasy white muscle rub from the main pot into a smaller one. "Rub that in morning and evening."

"I suppose you want to charge me?"

"I'll throw in the rub for free. Two sesterces for the consultation."

"I'm prepared to offer you and your friends a private dinner recital—"

"I don't give dinners," Ruso told him.

"I know!" The poet pulled a scroll from his bag and helped himself to the inkpot Ruso had set up for writing labels before turning back to the operating table. When he had finished he handed over the scroll. "Careful. The ink is still wet. Enjoy!"

With that, the patient disappeared into the arcade remarkably quickly for a man with crippling back pain.

Ruso gazed down at the scroll, where the crabbed handwriting suggested that Tubero the Younger was not a man to waste money on professional copyists. Above it glistened the letters, *To a fine Medicus, with thanks.* Neither Ruso's own name nor that of the poet, so it wasn't even any use as a recommendation. He sighed, shoved a few bottles aside, laid the scroll out on the workbench, and propped it open with a mixing bowl and a bleeding cup, and then went to find out what was for supper.

Ruso had hoped that buying a slave who could cook would make mealtimes easier, but evidently he had been mistaken. For reasons he could not understand, the cook had been sent to the bar next door to fetch the dinner, while his wife was worrying about where the slaves should eat.

"I am thinking they could eat with us," she said. She seemed to have forgiven the woman for being part of the Catuvellauni tribe. "Narina is a sensible woman, and Esico did well when those debt collectors came pretending to collect the other doctor's things. He says he was a warrior at home."

"I bet he didn't smell like that at home."

"It was worse before he washed."

Perhaps she was hoping that if she didn't mention the runaway, they could both forget he had ever existed.

The workbench was still covered with damp bottles and useless poetry. The operating table was the only other alternative to the borrowed kitchen furniture. It was less than ideal, even though the lad had done a fair job of cleaning up, and the waste bucket no longer held somebody else's teeth. Ruso said, "I think they should wait until we've finished."

"Then we will have to hurry up, or they will be watching their food get cold."

Ruso scratched one ear with his forefinger, pondering this modern dilemma. Things must have been so much easier in the old days, when an aristocrat like Cato could cheerfully assert that a farm slave only needed one new tunic and one pair of shoes every two years, and that anyone too old or ill to be productive should be sold off. But then, Cato's wife probably hadn't stocked his house with slaves who reminded her of home. And Cato's wife had surely never been a slave herself.

Tilla rarely spoke of that time. Assuming she wanted to forget, he did not ask. But it struck him now that you would never forget how it had felt to watch other people eat while you were hungry.

"They can eat at the operating table tonight," he announced. He was going to have to take charge here before his household became a little outpost of Britannia, full of barbarians all demanding the right to hot suppers. "Tomorrow we'll get Narina to cook, and they can both wait their turn."

"That is what I thought," said Tilla in a reassuring show of solidarity.

Finally the traditional domestic scene was in place. One lamp was casting a gentle glow over the two remaining barbarians as they dined at the operating table. The other illuminated the kitchen, where Mara was safely propped up on her sheepskin sucking her fingers, and his wife was free to tell him what she wanted him to do.

The first thing was to check what was actually in the jar labeled CUMIN and something in Greek on the end of the shelf, because it wasn't cumin at all. "And some of the other things are not right, either. I looked."

The second, for reasons he could not fathom, was to intercept the carpenter from upstairs and tell him how marvelous their daughter was.

"Just in passing," she added.

"What if he doesn't ask?"

"You will think of something."

"I don't want him thinking I might be interested in Christos."

"He is a carpenter. You could ask him about his work."

Unable to imagine how that conversation might unfold, he concentrated on tonight's stew, which tasted very much like last night's, although he was certain the portions were smaller.

She said, "You are very quiet."

"I'm eating." He wondered if he ought to tell her that his visit to the undertakers' had reinforced his suspicions about Kleitos—and raised new ones about the undertakers themselves—and that Sabella's order of events—which he doubted she would keep to herself—contradicted the cover story they wanted everyone to believe. Still, the visit from more debt collectors suggested that their story was partly true: Kleitos really did have money troubles. And if Ruso had learned anything from the charlatan at the amphitheater, it was that the most plausible lies were the ones that contained an element of truth.

Be careful who you trust.

He stirred the stew, watched the vegetables swirling around, and decided everything was bound to make more sense after a night's sleep. He would not burden Tilla with everything now. This would be their first uninterrupted night together in weeks and he was not going to spend it discussing the hunt for Kleitos, and still less the unsavory side of the undertaking trade.

Meanwhile, noticing her watching him, he said, "I'm not bothering to chase that runaway."

"I think you are wise."

Again, this unprecedented level of respect. It was almost worth the debt he had incurred. "But don't say that to those two out there," he added. "We don't want to lose any more."

"We must treat them well."

"Just be careful they don't take over. They're not visitors: They're here to work."

Tilla looked him in the eye, and he braced himself for her reply. But instead of arguing she said, "I heard something about Horatius Balbus's daughter today."

"She's much better company than her father," he said.

"Is she?"

"I met her over at the house. I'm supposed to be helping Accius make a good impression."

"Accius?"

"It makes sense. She'll have pots of money from her father's tenants, and he'll have the aristocratic background." Now that he thought about it, once Horatia inherited the properties all Accius had to do was appoint agents who would treat the tenants decently for a change, and he would have ready-made popular support. Some of them might even have votes.

Tilla said, "Perhaps, but Accius is not the name I heard."

"Oh?"

"I heard . . ." She paused. "Some names that both start the same. Curtius something. Phyllis's husband works for him."

"The carpenter?" He put down the spoon in which he had scooped up the last of the stew. "Not Curtius Cossus?"

"That is him."

"That can't be right," he told her, recalling the elaborate precautions Balbus had taken against being poisoned by Cossus's dinner. Not to mention Horatia's description of him as *that awful old builder.* "He's twice her age at least."

"You have met him too?"

"Balbus introduced us. It might lead to some work, but I doubt it." Cossus had acknowledged him with a nod and then politely excused himself to deal with a question from one of his men. He had not seemed particularly awful, but Ruso was not a teenage girl.

She said, "Phyllis seemed very sure. But Phyllis does not always think straight."

"Too much hymn singing." He mopped the bowl with a chunk of bread and stood up. "Where's the patient who wants a visit? I'll do it now."

His wife took the bowl, stacked it on top of hers, and dropped both spoons into it. "Whatever you think is right, husband."

"Tilla, are you feeling ill?"

"No."

"Then what's the matter with you?"

"There is nothing the matter with me," she told him, turning aside to put the dirty bowls on the tray.

He sat down again. "Perhaps I'd better stay. It's getting dark. If the debt collectors come back—"

"You will have to visit patients at night sooner or later, husband. I am not afraid of those men. We will bar the doors. If they try to break in, the neighbors will hear, and Sabella will frighten them off."

He leaned back out of range as she wiped the table with unusual vigor. Clearly there was some sort of problem, and he was supposed to guess what it was. "If you don't like it here, we can look for somewhere else." But here, apparently, was as good as anywhere else that was not Britannia. He stood again. "Well if there's nothing the matter and you're not worried about the debt collectors, I'll see you later."

"There might be robbers in the street," she told him. "You should take Esico."

Unable to decide whether this was a genuine suggestion or some sort of test, he chose to take her at her word. There might indeed be robbers in the street. Who knew? There was more of everything in Rome. He went into the bedroom, delved into the box under the bed, and strapped on his old army dagger. Then he stood beside the bed and listened until he was reassured by the sound of the neighbors moving about upstairs. Leaving Esico to wait at the foot of the steps, he ran up to explain to Timo and Phyllis that he was going out on an urgent call and that his wife was nervous about being on her own after dark—"But don't tell her I told you so." Otherwise he would be in even more trouble.

28

SINCE KLEITOS HAD left no covered lantern behind, and there was neither a torch nor any materials for assembling one, Ruso and Esico went without. The patient lived in an apartment block farther along Vicus Sabuci, and once Ruso's eyes adjusted to the dark he could see well enough. On the way, he tried asking Esico for more details of the debt collectors who had called this afternoon, but the slave had evidently understood Tilla's warning about nighttime robbers and was glancing around nervously, brandishing his broom handle in such a manner as to tell any lurking thief that something in Ruso's medical case was worth stealing. "Just walk boldly down the middle of the street," Ruso told him in British, deciding Esico must have been a very junior warrior and possibly not a well-practiced one. As far as he knew, most of the Dumnonii beyond the reach of the legionary base had adopted a policy of ignoring the soldiers and hoping they would go away.

"Yes, master," said Esico, obeying for a few paces and then carrying on exactly as before. Clearly Ruso would get no sense out of him until they were safely indoors.

The patient was a frail old man with the sort of cough that got worse at night, and since the whole family lived in one room that smelled of damp, nobody was getting much sleep. Ruso tried to find a tactful way of telling the weary and exasperated son and daughter-in-law that the father was not coughing on purpose. As he did so the father tried one of the cough-mixture lozenges Ruso had given him to suck and spat it out, declaring that everyone was trying to poison him and they would be glad when he was gone.

The son shot Ruso a glance that said, *You see?* and insisted on paying for the medicine anyway, saying the father might be willing to try it again later.

Ruso left with the feeling that he had been another in a long line of disappointments. Even if his medicine soothed the cough, he was powerless to treat the underlying problem: that eight people were living in a room suitable for only two. In addition, the flights of steps that he was leading Esico down were so steep that the old man would never be able to leave the apartment unless he were carried. He wondered how much they were paying in rent and to whom. *The property business is all about demand and supply.* It certainly wasn't about need.

On the way out he broke the news to Esico that they had another call to make. Esico managed to invest "Yes, master" with a sense of dread.

"It's not far," Ruso promised cheerfully.

This time, "Yes, master," was in the tone of a young man resigned to his fate.

Even indoors Esico still looked nervous, but to a man who had served in the Legions, the headquarters of the night watch on the Via Labicana felt comfortingly familiar. The dimly lit corridor where they were told to wait smelled of leather and beeswax and unwashed humanity. From somewhere deeper inside came the sound of whistling over the rhythmic swish of something being sharpened. Through the opposite doorway Ruso could see a couple of cloaks hanging on wooden pegs and a cupboard with a stack of documents on top.

Two men in uniform with fireman's axes strapped to their belts came out of a room farther up the corridor. Ignoring the visitors, they strode past with the confident air of trained professionals doing something that no civilian could possibly understand.

Esico was standing with his hands clamped behind his back. Ruso, unable to think of the British for *Stop chewing your lip* asked him again about the debt collectors, but it seemed Esico had concentrated on repelling rather than observing them.

Ruso said, "Thank you for looking after my family, Esico."

It was hard to tell in the dim light, but he was fairly sure the youth's angular face turned pink.

Esico went back to chewing his lip while Ruso gazed at the notices nailed to the board above the lone lamp.

A duty roster with scribbled alterations was followed in much larger writing by

NO MAN IS TO SWITCH DUTIES WITHOUT THE PERMISSION OF THE DUTY CENTURION.

BURIAL CLUB CONTRIBUTIONS NOW DUE.

ROOM TO RENT.

Ruso leaned back against the wall and stared down at the boots that had been tightly stitched and greased to keep out the British rain, wondering what was the matter with his wife, and if there was any chance she might have forgotten about it by the time he got back.

Thinking of Tilla reminded him that he needed to have a look at all the medicines Kleitos had left behind. If one of them was sloppily labeled, there might be others. He should throw them all away and start again. It was just as well he had smelled and tasted that poppy before dispensing it to Horatius Balbus.

A slave came hurrying along the corridor. Even in this light Ruso could make out the bloodstains on his tunic. The man bowed and announced, "The doctor will see you now, sir."

It was apparent from Esico's expression that he too had noticed the bloodstains, and Ruso's assurance in British that the man they were following into the dark was a healer's helper elicited only another glum "Yes, master." Leaving him outside the door to worry, Ruso followed the slave into the brighter light of the treatment room.

Last time he had been here, he had been sent away almost immediately with the news that the watch already had a full complement of four medics and a masseur. This time Simmias looked up from pouring something out of a jug into a glinting glass vial and greeted him with "Ruso! Sorry to keep you waiting, dear boy." He gestured toward the stool where a patient would have sat. "How can I help?"

Ruso glanced at the bloodstained slave. "It's a personal matter."

Simmias handed the vial to the slave and sent him to deliver it to somewhere else in the building. Taking up his own seat, he leaned forward with an expression of concerned interest that was really very impressive. "Tell me."

"I'm confused."

Simmias reached for a cloth and wiped his hands. Then he opened a cupboard and produced the sort of basin Ruso usually used when wounds needed to be washed. "Have a wine cake," he said, "and try to start from the beginning."

Ruso declined the cake. As Simmias helped himself and then put the basin away, Ruso said, "This afternoon I had a patient who told me that you took over in Kleitos's surgery when he was injured. So now that you've had a chance to think about it, I've come to ask if you've remembered where Kleitos might be or how I could contact him."

Simmias closed the cupboard door before replying, "I'm sorry. You've been misled."

"Also I see that his name's out there on the roster with yours as duty medic."

Simmias put his cake down next to a stack of bandages. "We work at different times. I don't know him well enough to know where he's gone."

"His patron's very worried about him. And I need to ask him about a patient."

"Can I help you with the patient?"

"No. Perhaps you have some idea why Kleitos has gone?"

But Simmias had nothing to offer on that subject, either. "I do hope you were out already this evening," he said, reaching for the cake, "because otherwise you've had a wasted trip."

"I had a house call," Ruso told him, "and, ah . . . I might want to report a missing slave."

The cake, which had begun its journey to Simmias's mouth, was lowered again. "Not one of your Britons?"

Ruso shook his head ruefully. "You were right. I should never have listened to my wife. The skinny one bolted as soon as we got him home. I'm not paying to get him back, but somebody told me to come and report him in case the watch picks him up. What's the procedure for that?"

"You'd need to talk to our centurion." Simmias was looking much happier now they were not discussing Kleitos. "I think he puts the name on a list, but after that I'm not sure what happens. If they find someone they suspect is a runaway, they usually hold on to him for a while in case he's claimed."

Ruso scratched one ear with his forefinger. "To be honest, I'm not sure I want him back. What happens if I don't report him?"

"Nothing, as far as I know." Simmias took a mouthful of cake and said 'round it, "If he gets picked up and refuses to say where he comes from, he'll be auctioned off."

"And if he doesn't get picked up by the watch?"

Simmias shrugged. "Who knows?"

Ruso pondered that for a moment. "I went to the undertakers' today," he said, "about that body in the barrel."

"I thought that was all dealt with?"

"It is. He's been identified, and the family have been informed."

Simmias, who had taken another bite, stopped chewing.

"I suppose," Ruso continued, "that we were all hoping it was some vagabond like my lost Briton—someone with nobody to mourn him. At least that way it would only be one man's tragedy."

"Absolutely." Simmias put the crumbling remains of the cake aside.

"Let's hope for the family's sake that he died of natural causes," Ruso added. "Otherwise they'll have the extra distress of deciding whether or not to investigate and prosecute."

The "Yes" sounded faintly strangled.

"But the undertakers won't divulge any details, so we'll never know."

"No," Simmias agreed.

Ruso said, "I'm hoping that was the end of it, and whoever arranged that delivery to Kleitos has realized it's a dangerous business and won't do anything like it ever again."

"I'm sure he won't, whoever he was."

"Even if he had the best of motives." Ruso was not enjoying

this. He had tried to heave himself up onto the moral high ground, but if he was honest, he felt sorry for Simmias.

"I can't imagine what his motives might be," said Simmias.

"I can," Ruso confessed, getting to his feet, "having listened to those idiots sharing their ignorance in the Forum. Anyway, thanks for your time. I'm sorry you couldn't help me find Kleitos, because that would have saved a lot of bother."

"I would have if I could—believe me."

He was almost at the door when Simmias called him back.

"Last time you were here you asked about a job. I'm sure if I put in a good word for you while Kleitos is away . . ."

"No, thanks," Ruso told him. "I'm busy at the moment, trying to find him and trying to keep clear of the mess he's left behind."

Simmias was on his feet now, leaning back against the cupboard, and gripping the top with both hands as if he was trying to hold it down. He said, "Did that man really have a family, Ruso?"

"So I'm told," Ruso said. He gestured toward the cupboard. "Enjoy your cake."

29

ON BEING TOLD that they were going home, Esico at last strode briskly down the middle of the street as he had been ordered. Ruso was reminded of a horse heading back to its stable.

He was pleasantly surprised by another kiss on his return, although Tilla seemed to sniff at him like a dog checking out a new friend. He hoped he hadn't picked up some sort of unpleasant smell.

"You were out a long time," she told him, unfastening his cloak and hanging it on the back of the surgery door before locking up. "I was worried."

"I had to wait at the night watch headquarters." He went through to the bedroom, unstrapped the dagger, and laid it safely back in the box under the bed, aware of his wife watching him.

At his instigation, the lamps were extinguished early. Mara was already settled to sleep on one side of Narina's mattress, and as he pointed out, everyone had had a busy day. But if Tilla noticed that this was their first night alone together for a very long time, she showed no sign of it, undressing in silence and shaking her golden hair loose in the lamplight before sliding under the covers.

He supposed she was tired. But he had spent a lot of borrowed money for this moment. A little intimacy did not seem much to ask in return. He licked his fingers and pinched out the flame, settling under the covers in the darkness and nuzzling her ear. "Finally," he said, "just us."

"Yes. Finally." The words were used like weapons.

It was one of those times where a man had to weigh up which would cause more resentment: asking—again—what was wrong, or making a risky guess. Or trying the tactic of surprise.

"Good night," he said, rolling away from her. "Sleep well."

The silence in the bedroom went on for so long that he began to wonder if his feigned indifference had been a failure. Then it occurred to him that if she were asleep, he would hear her breathing. Whereas all he could hear was the distant sound of a dog barking. And then, "I am doing my best, husband."

What was that supposed to mean? And more worryingly, what was he supposed to say in reply? Perhaps he could bluff. "I know."

"Do you?"

There was no way back now. "Yes."

"But I am not very good at it."

At what? Should he stumble on in the hope of enlightenment, or retreat? He could try taking hold of her hand and squeezing it. Would that help? If they did not sort this out soon, Mara would wake up and Tilla would be out of his reach once more, gone to snatch her away from the baby-minder. "Wife," he confessed to her back, "I need to tell you something."

She sniffed. "I know."

She knew? What did she think she knew? Or was she bluffing too?

He said, "I need to tell you that I haven't the faintest bloody idea what we're talking about."

And that was how he discovered that Tilla was doing her very best to be a Good Roman Wife while her husband went out to bars and bathhouses and met important people.

Recalling the kisses and the deference, he let the business of the slave auction pass. Even Tilla's best was not perfect.

Apparently one of the things Accius's housekeeper had told her on the journey over here—as well as how little she would like Rome—was that husbands were never as interested once there was a baby.

"And you believed her?" he demanded, torn between framing a

complaint to Accius and admitting that there might be some truth in it: All those broken nights and messy cloths were hard work.

Tilla said, "I told her when she had a husband she would know. But then you went out to the bar this afternoon, and then out to the baths, and then tonight—"

"Sabella wanted to complain about the mix-up over the body," he explained, wondering how she knew where he had gone. "And I wanted to see if she could tell me where Kleitos is."

"Why? We don't want him back."

"Ah, but his patron does." He saw now that in the rush of buying the slaves, he had shied away from breaking the unwelcome news that he was now actively seeking the man who might displace them from their new lodgings. "And I need to talk to him about a patient," he added.

Her "Oh" sounded baffled rather than angry.

He told her about buying supplies at the baths. Then he explained that he had been to visit Simmias at the night watch to try to make sure there would be no more bodies in barrels. When he had finished undermining tonight's main objective with all these unromantic complications, she said, "Is that everything?"

She did not need to know the details of Balbus and the theriac. "Yes."

"Good." And then, instead of worrying about all these things as he had expected, she slid one smooth thigh across his and murmured in his ear, "Welcome home, husband."

30

RUSO HAD NO idea what time it was, and he didn't care. He was a contented husband with a satisfied wife lying beside him.

They had a sleeping child and, it seemed, a loyal household.

The body in the barrel had gone, and he had seen to it that there would be no more of them. Soon he would track down his missing predecessor and get the recipe for bald Balbus's theriac, and everything would be all right. Because while he was out yesterday, Tilla had met some men who knew where Kleitos was.

He saw now how he and Tilla had been so anxious to allay any suspicion of Kleitos's performing human dissections that they had started to believe their own cover story. They had seized onto the arrival of anyone who came asking for money as proof that the man was in debt. But Balbus—who should know—had insisted Kleitos was solvent. And now that he thought about it, the man from the undertakers' had limped to the door only to request payment for a delivery. So it was very likely that the men Tilla said were "pretending to collect the other doctor's things" really had been. And if they were sent by Kleitos, they must have a way of contacting him to pass on the money from the sale.

It was all ridiculously simple. Now all he had to do was trace the men. It was a pity Tilla had sent them away, but they would surely be back, and they would want to talk to him. He had the perfect lure: money. If the remaining furniture and equipment here was for sale, who better to buy it than himself?

He was wondering if it was worth trying to have the runaway slave tracked so he could hand him over in exchange for Kleitos's abandoned possessions when he felt his wife move across the bed, and heard the soft shuffle of feet sliding into sandals.

"If you go in there and wake her," he said, "we'll all be sorry."

The bed creaked as she sat down again. She said, "Do you think Virana misses her?"

"I expect so."

"I am thinking we could send news."

"We'll do it tomorrow. Go to sleep."

"Where will we send it?"

"Albanus will know where she is," he told her, glad to turn his mind to happier times. He missed Albanus. The infatuation of his former clerk with a native girl who had no ambition beyond marrying a soldier had never made much sense to Ruso. Still, Albanus seemed to be flattered by the attention and Virana was delighted to have snared a real Roman at last. Meanwhile Tilla, desperate for a child of their own, had been happy to relieve her of the complication of Mara, who could have been fathered by any one of a number of Virana's former boyfriends. It was a good solution all 'round, as long as you didn't stop to wonder if Mara would grow up as feckless as her real parents.

"I will not tell Virana how horrible this city is," Tilla murmured. "Or about Narina being Catuvellauni. I will tell her we are in a nice home."

From beyond the bedroom door he caught the sound of someone moving about and then the trickle of urine going into the pot.

I am living, Ruso thought, *in a household full of stray barbarians.* More interesting was the thought that, at that particular moment, he really didn't mind. Tomorrow he would sort everything out. For now, sleep was holding out her welcoming arms toward him and . . .

"Master!" The thumping on the bedroom door echoed a distant banging from the street. "Master, wake up!"

His body rolled out of bed, leaving his mind somewhere else until it returned to remind him that the door would not open until he unjammed the latch. And that it would be a good idea to put some clothes on.

"Master, someone is at the—"

"I know. Shut up!" Dragging a tunic over his head, he stumbled across the kitchen in Esico's wake, urging, "Quiet!" but it was too late. The small wail from the mattress in the corner grew louder despite the whisper of "Hush!" from the woman slave, and then there was Tilla behind him saying, "What is happening? Mara? Is Mara all right?" and Narina was blundering about asking, "Where is the lamp?" and at the opposite end of the surgery someone was still banging on the door and Esico was shouting, "Yes, yes!" and then calling in British, "What is the Latin *for stop that racket— somebody is coming?*"

"Everyone shut up!" Ruso yelled, with limited effect. Mara carried on wailing and Tilla carried on shushing her and whoever was at the door carried on banging and shouting, "Doctor!"

"I'm coming!" Ruso called, groping for the lock in the dark. "Hold on."

"Doctor, Horatius Balbus needs you!"

The name hit him like a punch in the stomach. "What's the matter with him?"

Finally getting the door open, he recognized the man holding the torch as Balbus's bodyguard, Latro. "We can't wake him up!"

A cold shiver ran across Ruso's shoulders. *There are people who mix up all kinds of concoctions and pretend to offer protection. Most of them know nothing.*

"What happened?"

"He said he felt ill. Then he fell down, and we can't get him up."

Some of them know a little. They are the worst.

He should never have tried to imitate that antidote. He should have told Balbus to consult an expert. Someone who knew what he was doing. Someone who could prescribe something that worked, instead of poppy mixed with burnt onions and—holy gods, he still couldn't remember what else he had put in there. He had been too distracted to make notes. It had all seemed harmless at the time, but . . .

They are the ones who kill.

Like, presumably, the person who had first discovered that you shouldn't treat a patient with both hawthorn and foxglove at the same time.

Tilla was behind him, wanting to know who it was and what was happening.

He felt a sudden and shameful surge of hope at the thought that Balbus might have been poisoned by his dinner host, just as he had feared. But Xanthe had said a few days without his real medicine would not affect his protection . . .

. . . from the usual poisons.

Meanwhile, Ruso had knowingly dispensed something that he could not vouch for: a lozenge he had found in a jar faintly labeled POPPY. Put there by a man who had a jar labeled CUMIN on the shelf that contained something else entirely.

Fumbling with his belt, Ruso told himself to calm down. He was not a complete fool. He had smelled it. He had tasted it. It *was* . . .

It was stored by a man who reused old parchment that was only half-erased. A man who was fascinated by new medicines, and full of bold curiosity.

The strength of poppy varied from plant to plant: Everyone knew that, which was why he had used a conservative dose. But in a city that attracted exotic imports from all over the world, how could he be sure that this was not some especially powerful new strain? Worse—because it would be harder to check—what if it had been poppy *and something else?* It was the last letter of the word *poppy* that had been smudged off the jar. Only now did it occur to him that other letters, now vanished, might have followed. There was no way of finding out because all the empty containers had been scrubbed clean, at his own order.

Ruso fought down an urge to vomit. How could he have been so careless?

"Now, Doctor! Quick!"

He managed to say, "Let me get some shoes on." Maybe he could get the medicine back up before it was fatal.

Maybe.

Milk? Oil? Salt water? How could you know what would wash poison out, when you didn't know what you were doing?

His case was by the door where he had left it, ready to be grabbed at short notice. He had told the slaves not to touch it. At least he had got that right.

Gods above, I am ruined. And all these stray barbarians who depend upon me.

You could get a thousand small decisions right, but they would all be eclipsed by the one moment of stupidity when you had poisoned your chief patient.

Out in the street, Latro turned left.

"He's not in his house?"

"He's in the street, sir. He was on the way home from a dinner when it happened. Firmicus said not to move him."

"Right." So now he would be treating a poisoned man in the dark with nothing except what was in his case. Which meant more delay while somebody sent for the milk or the salt or whatever it was.

"We tried to wake him, sir, but he didn't hear us."

Ruso said, "Was he breathing?" but Latro did not know.

Ruso could feel his own heart pounding. His stomach seemed to be trying to crawl up behind his rib cage. He forced himself to keep walking. He was about to ask, "How much farther?" when they turned another corner and he was dazzled by several torches illuminating a cluster of figures. They were gathered around something on the ground. Above them, pale faces were peering down from apartment windows.

"The doctor's here!" shouted Latro. Other voices repeated, "The doctor!" and the figures in the street parted to let Ruso through to his fate.

31

THE WHITE TOGA draped around the collapsed figure already made him look like a ghost. Ruso tightened his grip on his case and stepped forward. As he knelt by the head of his patient, Latro shouted at the onlookers to get out of the way. He was aware of people shuffling back. Now it was just him and Horatius Balbus. Or rather, just him between Horatius Balbus and death, because as he placed a hand on the chest the patient made a ragged inhalation. *Thank you, Jupiter, Aesculapius, Christos—anybody.* It might not be too late.

Aloud, he called, "Lights! I need more light!"

Latro announced, "The doctor can't see!"

Firmicus was beside him, arranging the lights and calling for a fresh torch.

Latro again: "Get them torches in here!"

There were echoes of "Lights! Where've the lights gone? Bring a lantern!" and suggestions to "Give him wine!" from among the onlookers, several of them sounding seriously drunk. Ruso was in the middle of his own show in the street.

Feet shuffled forward again, and the side of Horatius Balbus's head became clearer. Ruso leaned closer, bending at an awkward angle so as not to obstruct the light. The bald scalp seemed to ripple with the movement of the flames.

"Balbus? Balbus, it's Ruso. The doctor. Can you hear me?"

He was vaguely aware of more shouts of "Bring a torch!" and "Man down!" and Latro yelling at people to shut up and piss off. From Balbus himself there was nothing.

He reached down between the neck and shoulder to pinch the trapezius muscle, but to no effect.

"We didn't know if we should move him." The shadows wavered as Firmicus knelt on the opposite side of his master, holding the light above him.

"You did the right thing," Ruso told him, surprised at the calmness of his own voice. It was as if someone else were speaking through him. Someone competent and unflustered. "But we need to get him home now." As he said it, he remembered there was no stretcher at the surgery.

"There's a light!" slurred a drunken voice behind him. "He's got a light, look!"

There was a commotion, followed by cries of "Leave him alone!" and "He was only trying to help!"

"Latro!" The competent medic using Ruso's voice wanted to distract the bodyguard before a street fight broke out around them.

"Doctor?"

"Send someone sober to call the watch," said the competent medic, willing his patient to breathe again.

"It's done, Doctor."

"And ask someone to take a door panel out. We can carry him home on that with a cloak around it." Searching for a pulse, he said, "What happened?"

"He was fine," Firmicus insisted. "We were walking home, and he was talking about getting some work done on the building across the street . . . We just got past the corner and . . ." Firmicus shook his head, as if he could hardly believe what he was about to say. "He just said something I couldn't make out, made a sort of choking noise, and he was down. So fast we couldn't catch him."

"How much had he drunk?" asked the competent medic.

"Not much. He likes to keep his wits about him."

"Does he ever have fits or fainting?"

"Never. What's the matter with him, Doctor?"

The competent medic asked what the patient had eaten this evening. Firmicus, who clearly understood the reason for the question, said as far as he knew it was the same as everyone else, "And we had some of it in the kitchen."

The competent medic beat back a fresh wave of panic and remembered to check for injuries. "Move the light across—ah!" He held his fingers up and sniffed the dark liquid. *Head injury. You know what to do for a head injury. Now check the rest. Never assume the first thing you see is the main problem.*

"Don't move him," said the competent medic. "Just help me lift his clothes out of the way . . ." But there was no sign of any other injuries. They were replacing the warm wool of the toga when he heard the approaching tramp of the night watch. The marching boots fell silent and over the sound of Latro banging on the nearest shop door, a voice demanded, "What's all this?" in a tone that suggested he did not expect to like the answer.

Several people all tried to tell him at once. "One at a time!" the watchman ordered, picking on the nearest onlooker. "You. What's your name?"

Leaving the watch to it, Ruso placed a soft wad of wool wrapped in linen against Balbus's temple, where it seemed the blood was coming from. Farther up the street Latro was shouting, "Open up for Horatius Balbus!"

"Horatius Balbus, the landlord?" demanded the watchman. "Is he here?"

"This is him," Firmicus said. "My master. He just collapsed."

The watchman used Ruso's shoulder for support as he leaned down to examine what could be seen of the patient's face. "So that's what he looks like."

Firmicus said, "We don't know what happened."

The watchman straightened up. "Nobody leaves!" He ordered one of his men to look for anything that might have fallen from the buildings above. Turning back to Firmicus, he said, "Is he dead?"

"No," said Ruso, hoping it was true. "We need—"

"Then what's he doing lying in the street? Get him home! And get away from that bloody door, you!"

Ignoring him, Latro gave the door a kick. "I'm not drunk!" he shouted in reply to someone behind it, "and I'm not going away!"

Ruso said, "Have you got a ladder? We need something to carry him on."

"We don't carry them around just in case, mate," said the watchman.

"Then let him get a door panel."

The watchman nodded and stepped across to the front of the closed shop. "I told you to get away from that door!" Ruso was vaguely aware of some confused pushing and shoving, followed by "You in there, listen to me. This is the night watch. It's an emergency. Open the door."

When there was no response he called, "Victor, get over here with that axe."

But before Victor could do anything with the axe there was a screech of metal hinge on stone, and the door opened.

Finally the makeshift stretcher arrived, along with the news that no fallen object had been found. "We're going to take you home, sir," the competent medic told his patient. "We'll just have to lift you up for a moment." If Balbus had heard, he showed no sign.

"Gently!" the medic urged, placing a second dressing against the injured head and holding it there as they counted to three and then rolled Balbus sideways to get the support underneath him. "We're taking you home now," he said again, taking hold of the wrist and feeling in vain for a pulse. "Not long and you'll be in your own bed."

But he was speaking for the benefit of the onlookers, not of the patient. Horatius Balbus, he was fairly certain, was already dead.

32

RUSO INSISTED ON tidying up alone after Balbus had been carried out of the bedroom. The silence was a chance to regain his balance: to distance himself from the horror and desperation of a household thrown into chaos in the middle of the night.

The far-off sound of wailing told him the body had been laid on the couch in the entrance hall. He bent down to retrieve something glinting on the floor in the lamplight: a scalpel he must remember to check, lest the fall onto the tiles had damaged the blade. For now, he wiped it and put it back in the case. One by one, he restored the probes and the tweezers to their places. Once all the instruments were safely accounted for, he collected up all the used dressings and stuffed them into an old flour sack. The staff would have to deal with the bedding later. There was nothing more he could do here now. He had spent longer than he normally would with his patient, trying to revive him. Trying and failing to find conclusive proof either that the death had been accidental or that the man had died of natural causes. He had scrutinized the hands and the elbows, but there was no sign that Balbus had tried to save himself. There was nothing to explain the fall or the death, beyond the obvious skull fracture, and his own presence here now was an intrusion.

The fountain was still trickling outside in the dark garden. He passed between rose-entwined columns lit by a couple of wavering torches. The wailing grew louder as he entered the next courtyard, and the air was heavy with frankincense. He jumped at the sight of a hooded figure loitering in the shadows of the colonnade, then realized it was just one of Balbus's statues, no more alive than its owner. Farther down, a new statue crouched with its head in its hands, and looked up as he passed.

"You couldn't have done anything to save him, Latro," he told it.

The head slumped into the hands again. Ruso moved on into the entrance hall, and the sounds and smells engulfed him like a warm bath.

Horatius Balbus had been laid with his feet toward the door in the traditional manner. The lampstands at the head and foot of the couch illuminated the purple-stripe toga he had been dressed in by the staff and the pale faces of the household standing around the master. Horatia, her hair gray with the ashes of mourning, was still rocking backward and forward in a creaking wicker chair in the corner, weeping and clinging onto her serving maids for support. Beyond flinging her arms in the air and screaming out her father's name, she had been too upset to help with any of the preparations. The calming concoction Ruso had recommended—her slaves had asked, and he could not refuse—sat untouched on the table beside her. It hardly mattered. A man who now dared to prescribe nothing more powerful than boiled lettuce might as well not bother.

He paused and bowed his head as a last mark of respect to the patient he had known all too briefly, then tried to make his way past the couch as unobtrusively as possible. He was almost at the street door when he felt a hand on his arm. He turned to see Firmicus, who mouthed, "Thank you."

He was glad for Horatia's sake that there was someone as capable as Firmicus to take charge. "I'm sorry."

"You did all you could, Doctor." The steward shook his head, dislodging his own fine shower of ash. "Something's not right about this. He was a healthy man."

Ruso was saved from replying by the sight of Lucius Virius floating in through the entrance hall. The undertakers might be slow to pick up an unclaimed body, but they had lost no time responding to a wealthy household in the late hours of the night.

The doorkeeper let Ruso out in silence, head bowed. The heavy oak door clunked into place behind him, and he surveyed the outlines of the predawn street. Everything was gray, mirroring the numbness of his mind. His senses registered that the aroma of frankincense had faded and been replaced by baking bread and fresh ox dung, but it was as if everything were taking place behind a thick pane of glass. A cart rumbled past. He turned left, walking in the direction of Accius's house. He had one last duty to perform before he had to stop acting the competent medic and face up to whatever it was he might have become.

33

THE PATIENT HAD collapsed on the way home from a dinner party, as middle-aged men who ate and drank too much sometimes did. There was rarely anything anyone could do to save them. While the rest of Rome was waking up, washing its face, and preparing to deal with the new day, the family would be mourning their loss. The doctor who had been called from his bed in a hopeless attempt to hold the patient back from the next world should have been catching up on some sleep.

Instead, he was blundering around the surgery picking up containers and examining them, and opening half-empty bottles of medicine to sniff what was inside.

"Have you lost something?"

Tilla had to repeat the question before he noticed she was there.

"It's all old," he muttered, not looking up. "Useless." He upended a jar. Several black lumps thudded into the waste bucket.

"What are you doing? Is that the cyclamen root?"

"It needs replacing." He picked up another jar. Its contents too ended up in the bucket.

When he reached for a third she stepped forward and seized his hand. "Husband, what are you doing?"

He shrugged. "Having a clearout. Might as well do it sometime."

She wrested it out of his hand and put it back on the shelf. "You should sleep."

"I'm not tired."

She peered at him, reaching up to push a strand of hair off his forehead. "Either you are very tired, or some god has made you ten years older during the night. Go and rest. I will call you if we need you."

He opened his mouth as if he was about to argue, but then seemed to change his mind and put his arms around her, resting his chin on her shoulder. She felt rather than heard the depth of his sigh.

Just at the wrong moment, Esico wandered in from the kitchen with a jug of water. Behind her husband's back, she gestured frantically to him to go away. The door closed again and they were alone. "You did your best," she said softly.

"It looked as though he hit his head on the curb."

"Then what could you do?" she asked, surprised at how upset he seemed. Of course it was always bad to lose a patient, but he had met this one only two days ago, and the man was not young. It was not like her husband to mourn the loss of someone just because he was rich and powerful. "I know he was very important," she continued, "but I am sure nobody could have done any more for him. Not even Doctor Kleitos."

The grunt could have meant *yes*, or *no*, or *stop talking—it is not helping*.

"We will manage without him," she promised. "We know lots of people here now."

He said, "I've been to tell Accius. I'm not sure what'll happen now."

"What did he say?" If it was Accius who had upset him, she would go over there and tell him what she thought. She had given up trying to be a Good Roman Wife now. It was very confusing having to say one thing and mean another all the time.

"He's gone straight over to see Horatia."

"That is very good of him."

He released her and leaned back against the bench. "Did I tell you he brought her a birthday present back from Britannia?" he said. "One of those jet bracelets they make over on the east coast."

"Did she like it?"

"I should never have left the Legion."

She had always thought that when he finally admitted it, she would say, *I told you so.* But now she took him by the arm and steered him toward the back rooms of the apartment. "Just sleep. I will see the patients and call you if we need you."

"Don't use any of those medicines. Only use what we brought with us."

"Husband, what is the matter?"

"Nothing."

When she got him to bed she said, "Do you want herbs to help you sleep?"

"No!"

She sat beside him on the bed. "What happened out there?"

"Nothing. I lost a patient. That's all."

When she lifted her hand from his shoulder, he rolled over and curled up like a small child.

"We will talk about it when you wake up."

"Yes."

"It will be all right," she promised, but she had no idea if it would be, because she had never seen him like this before. She had seen him exhausted and anxious and sad and confused, but never like this. Despondency was a new enemy, and most of the gods who might have been persuaded to help them were a very long way away.

34

H E L O O K E D M U C H better when he wandered out of the
bedroom. Still rumpled, but some of the bleariness in his
eyes had gone. In response to Mara's greeting of "Ah!" he crouched
in front of the fleece and bent to kiss her on the forehead. Mara
rewarded him with a smack on the ear and a giggle.

"There is porridge," Tilla told him. "Or if you wait, Narina has
gone out for bread."

"I'll wait." He picked up a towel that had been slung over the blue
curtain, crossed the room, and stopped with his hand on the back
door. "Has anyone called?"

"The woman with the bad veins came again. I said does she
want to think about surgery but she said no, so I showed her how
to do the bandaging herself."

"Did you tell her not to make ridges?"

"Of course. Then I talked to the pregnant girl from across the
court, and cleaned and dressed a dog bite."

"Serious?"

"He was lucky. The dog ought to be got rid of: They said it was
not the first delivery boy he has bitten, but he belongs to a rich

man so nobody dares. Oh, and Sabella and lots of other people wanted to know if it is true about Horatius Balbus."

"Uh."

Moments later he was back from the courtyard, rubbing his wet hair.

She said, "I said you would go and see Accius when you wake up."

He stopped rubbing and looked up from under the towel. "He came here?"

"It was only a message. Have something to eat first. He does not know you are awake."

She had thought he might rush off anyway, but instead he sat down at the kitchen table and said, "I must find Kleitos."

She went to check that Esico was standing out by the front door. Narina was still not back with the bread. Certain they were alone, Tilla sat opposite her husband and said softly, "Are you worried about that medicine you made?"

"You think I should be?"

"You did boil it up very quickly," she said, "And there was all that fuss going on outside about the body." Catching the stricken expression on his face, she reached for his hand. "But there was nothing in there to cause harm."

"I'm sure it was fine," he agreed, patting her hand as if he were the one offering reassurance.

When people really were certain about something, they just said it. They did not bother to tell you how sure they were. Nor did they say, "Don't say anything about it to anybody, will you?"

"Of course not." What did he think she might say? *My husband is afraid he might have poisoned one of his patients?* "I am sure there is nothing to worry about." There: She was doing it herself now.

"The jar definitely said *poppy* on the outside."

"You always check."

"I tried some. It tasted right."

She said, "I will try it myself."

"You can't," he said. "I used the last of it. Then I told Esico to scrub all the empty containers clean. None of them has any writing. I've looked."

She took a breath. "Lots of men that age fall down and die, husband. What were you treating him for?"

Instead of answering, he got to his feet. "I'll go and see what Accius wants," he said. "Might as well get it over with."

He was halfway to the door when he paused to say, "Those men who wanted to sell Kleitos's things might have been telling the truth. If they come back, ask them in and tell them they need to wait and talk to me. I need to track him down. He'll know what was in that jar."

35

ACCIUS, AS FAR as his doorman was aware, was still at the house of Horatius Balbus. As he set off in search of him, Ruso realized he was feeling calmer. Tilla had been right: The sleep had done him good, and a brisk walk through the sunny streets was helping him put the night in perspective. He could now see that he had overreacted. Somehow in the darkness and the panic, his mind had pulled together the body in the barrel, his hasty inclusion of an ingredient he couldn't vouch for, Balbus's odd fear of being poisoned, and that conversation with the old woman in the bathhouse. Now that he thought about it, she was bound to try to surround her knowledge with mystique and issue dire warnings about the dangers of amateur dabbling. Poisons and antidotes were sold by fear. There had been nothing dangerous in that mixture.

Probably.

By the time Ruso could hear the sound of mourning drifting out from the courtyard of Horatius Balbus's house, he had decided that the chance of the death being caused by his own concoction was very small indeed. Firmicus seemed eager to blame someone— hopefully someone other than Ruso—but in truth Balbus could have collapsed from natural causes. A sudden failure of the heart.

A seizure or even a simple faint. In the darkness he might have tripped up without his companions realizing what had happened. There were any number of reasons for a man to fall, but only one result if he was unlucky enough to crash heavily onto the thin bone at the temple as he hit the ground.

Accius responded to his message by leaving the mourners and steering Ruso to the nearest bar, where he requested a private room. "I can't be seen hanging around a cheap drinking hole dressed like this," he explained, grabbing fistfuls of his dark mourning clothes to avoid tripping over them on the stairs. "It's disrespectful."

The room was not especially clean and was equipped for private meetings of an entirely different kind. Accius surveyed it with a faint expression of disgust, said, "It'll have to do," and sat on the bed. "I need your help, Ruso."

Ruso tweaked the curtain aside to check that Accius's slave was stationed at the top of the stairs, and then perched farther along the grubby bedspread.

"You wouldn't believe the chaos back there," Accius told him. "Poor Balbus is hardly cold and every friend and relation who might possibly be in the will has rushed to offer condolences. The staff are drooping about all over the place, the official mourners are making an appalling racket, and there's a whole crowd of hangers-on who are just there to gawp. It's outrageous. I'm sure some people just wander the city looking out for a door with cypress over the top and then call in to see if there's anything to eat. I've told Firmicus he's got to get a grip for Horatia's sake, but I don't think any of them is in a fit state to listen."

"He's been up all night, sir." Ruso scratched an itch on the back of his leg and tried not to think about bedbugs.

"Well, we need to do something about it. I've been blind, Ruso. Horatia needs protection. The vultures are circling." Accius shifted closer on the bed and lowered his voice. "Horatius Balbus is—was—a shrewd businessman and a devoted father, even if he did have terrible taste in statues. But to be honest I always thought he was a little odd."

"In what way, sir?"

"He was convinced there were people out to kill him. Did you know he took antidotes?"

"He seems to have fallen and hit his head, sir," Ruso insisted, trying to ignore the sudden churn of his stomach as he remembered the very public handover of the imitation medicine. "His own men were there at the time."

"Ah, but why did he fall?"

He must tell Accius about that medicine. "Sir—"

"Who had he just been dining with?"

Ruso could see where this was going. What he could not see was a way to stop it. "I believe it was Curtius Cossus, sir."

"And who exactly is Curtius Cossus? Eh?"

Ruso was not in the mood for rhetorical questions. "He's a builder, sir. Balbus introduced me to him in case he ever needed a doctor."

"Really? Well, I imagine he soon will, at his age. He's not just a builder, Ruso, he's an entrepreneur who buys up cheap apartment blocks on decent plots and pulls them down to make space for clients who want expensive houses. Only last month Balbus outbid him on a block in the Aventine that has some very fine views."

"Then why was Balbus dining with him, sir?" The medicine business would have to wait: Accius was leading on a different trail altogether.

"I imagine they were going to discuss some sort of deal. But Cossus wants more than property. He's had the nerve to turn up and offer to look after Horatia with some mad tale about being betrothed to her!"

"I believe he's been telling other people the same thing, sir."

"That he's betrothed to them too?"

"That he's going to marry Horatia, sir."

"What? Why didn't you tell me?"

"It was just thirdhand gossip, sir. I told them he wasn't."

"Well, it would have helped to know." Accius shifted position on the thin mattress. "He's obviously been plotting this for some time. It all makes sense, once you see it. He invites Balbus to dinner, has a conversation with him that none of Balbus's people overhear. Balbus conveniently drops dead on the way home, and Curtius Cossus has his own witnesses to say that Balbus has promised him Horatia in marriage."

Ruso blinked. "Why?"

"To get his wrinkly fingers on all of Balbus's properties, of course! And on Horatia—the bastard. The poor girl's not in a fit state to deny it: She can hardly speak. He's got to be stopped. In fact—" Accius paused, as if listening to another wild idea being announced inside his head. "Don't you see? He must have found some way to get rid of Kleitos!"

"But, sir—"

"Listen to me, Ruso. He's got to be stopped."

"You're saying Curtius Cossus got rid of Balbus's doctor so he could murder Balbus?"

"Of course that's what I'm saying! So he could poison him."

Ruso took a deep breath. "Sir, I need to explain to you about—"

"You were with him at the end. Did he say anything?"

"He was already unconscious when I got there, sir." No point in adding that Firmicus hadn't understood his master's last words, or that Latro thought he had said he felt ill. Latro might have misheard. It might have been indigestion.

"Well, never mind. You're a medical man. I want you to find out how Cossus did it."

Deliberately calm, Ruso said, "I don't think he did, sir. Why would he get rid of Balbus before he'd got a proper betrothal agreed?"

Accius sighed. "Do wake up, Ruso. Because he would never *get* a proper betrothal, would he? Between you and me, Horatia was certain it was only a matter of time before Balbus accepted my offer for her."

It all made some kind of horrible sense. It also had the dubious merit of casting the blame a long way from Ruso.

Accius had not finished. "Now apparently the poor girl will be under the guardianship of some cousin she hardly knows, and if Cossus can convince this cousin that he's the one Balbus wanted her to marry . . ."

"But if you could convince the cousin she was supposed to marry you, sir—"

"Horatia will back me up, of course, but we don't know if he'll listen. For all we know, Cossus has been working on him already. Anyway, I've told her not to worry. I'll find a way to sort this out. Meanwhile I've told Firmicus to tell the cousin not to listen to a word Cossus tells him, and to make sure he knows my men are looking into it."

"Men, sir?" As far as Ruso was aware he was Accius's only man when it came to investigating suspicious circumstances. All the others were domestic staff or workers on some distant agricultural estate.

"I'm not saying you're not up to the job, Ruso. But everyone knows you're my man, so you're not going to get anything out of Cossus's household without help. And besides, you've got patients to look after. Luckily, I know just the chap. With your medical skills and Metellus's—"

"Metellus?"

"Yes. You must remember him from Britannia. Did you know he's here now? He's always remarkably well-informed. You'll have to keep it quiet that he's working for me, of course."

Ruso was groping for words. "Sir, Metellus is . . . Well, his methods are—"

"I'm not asking you to marry him, Ruso. I'm just asking you to work with him. And frankly, given the methods of the man we're up against, I don't think we can afford to be too fussy. There's a lot of property at stake here. Cossus may try to poison me too if I get in his way."

"But, sir—"

"Metellus doesn't feel the same way about you. In fact, his note said he was looking forward to seeing you again."

Unable to say anything positive, Ruso was silent.

"You're not sulking, are you?"

"No, sir."

"I wouldn't like you to think I've lost faith in you after you left that body to be dumped in the street. Did you buy a slave, by the way?"

Ruso felt his spirits sink even farther as he recalled his houseful of barbarians. "Yes, sir."

"Good. I don't want you distracted. Anyway, I've canceled all my meetings today. I'm not leaving Horatia on her own with that murderer Cossus around."

"I don't think she's in immediate danger, sir. It sounds as though he plans to marry her." Ruso stopped short of *before he murders her.*

"Exactly!" His former senior officer reached across the stained bedcover, gripped him by the arm, and informed him with an intensity he had never shown before, "You must help me save her, Ruso. She deserves better. She deserves me."

Accius was right, of course. Metellus was just the chap, as he had demonstrated many times back in Britannia on behalf of the Imperial cause. If Ruso had been asked to write a list of all the people he disliked and rank them in order of deviousness, Metellus's name would have come so far ahead that everyone else's would have been written on a different sheet altogether. But as Accius said, he was remarkably well-informed. Metellus was the kind of man who knew what people were thinking—usually because they were too frightened not to tell him. Back in Britannia he had placed Tilla on a list of potentially treacherous natives, and even though he was probably right, Ruso had never forgiven him.

Still, that was a long time ago. Tilla was now a somewhat ambivalent citizen of Rome, Ruso's chief patient was dead, and Accius was in love. The world had changed, and he and Metellus were going to have to find a way to work together.

36

THE MAN WHO came to the gate of the auctioneer's yard was neither of the ones Tilla now regretted chasing away from Kleitos's house. He had greasy hair and a quick glance that seemed to assess visitors' worth before he invited them in. As soon as Tilla, Mara, and Narina were through the gate, he slammed it shut behind them.

There was a smell here that Tilla did not like. She gazed 'round at a covered area crammed with the insides of other people's homes. A dozen upright bedframes leaned like a row of drunks. Two cupboards glared at each other, so close that the drawers of neither could be opened. The lumpy yellow cushion on the couch beside her bore the marks of dried puddles.

"What can I do for you, lady?"

Those quick dark eyes, the hair slicked back behind pink ears, the way the teeth reached forward as if they were racing to get ahead of the nose—Tilla pressed her feet against each other and tried not to think about rats. If finding Kleitos would restore her husband's spirits, then she must find him. "My family have moved into the rooms of Doctor Kleitos in the Vicus Sabuci," she told the man, "and we would like to make him an offer for the things he left behind."

"You want me to value them for you?"

"I need to find the men he sent to ask about them. I want to tell those men we have changed our minds."

"It wasn't me, lady."

"I know it was not you," she agreed, "but I do not know who they were, and they did not leave a name."

The man dislodged a few clumps of hair with one finger, then tucked them back behind his ear. "Let me get this right," he said. "You've got the furniture somebody else left behind when he moved out. He sent a man to ask you to pay for it, and you said no."

"Two men."

"And these two men went away, leaving you with the stuff."

"Yes."

"And they haven't come back to ask for money."

"Not yet."

The man glanced at Narina, as if wondering if she might take her mistress home for a quiet lie-down. "But you're trying to find them so you can pay anyway," he said.

"Yes." Put like that, she had to admit that it did not make a great deal of sense. She lowered her head and looked up at him from under the wisps of hair that always escaped no matter what she did to tame them. "My husband was not at home when they came," she told him. "I didn't want to let strangers into the house, so I sent them away. But now I am afraid Doctor Kleitos will sell it all to somebody else and then they will send the men to collect it and we will lose it and I will be in trouble."

"Ah."

"So that is why I am trying to find the men who are dealing with it." She tugged at a strand of hair in a way that she hoped would look nervous. "I was thinking if you can find them for us, you could have a commission or something." She was not sure if that made any sense at all, but at least the man did not laugh at the idea.

He held out one dirty hand as if he would have liked to touch her but did not quite dare. "I'll put the word out, miss," he promised. "Don't you worry. I'll see you're all right."

"I hope so." She gave him her very best silly-wife smile and said, "You are very kind."

"And if I can't find them," he said, "You come back with your husband and I'll do you a good deal on a few things here."

37

"OUT?" RUSO DEMANDED. "Out where?"

Esico didn't know. The mistress had only said she would not be long.

"What are you supposed to do if patients come?"

"I ask them to wait." Esico pushed open the door and announced proudly in Latin, "There he is."

He was, but the man standing examining the contents of the shelves was not a patient.

"Ruso!"

"Hello, Metellus."

"I seem to have come at an awkward time."

"Sorry you've had to wait. I think Tilla's been called to an emergency."

"Of course," said Metellus, who probably understood enough British to know what had been said at the door. "Good to see you've found a place, although I was sorry to hear about your difficult start."

"It's all sorted out now," Ruso assured him, wondering if he had been here long enough to search the whole apartment or just the surgery.

"A body. It must have been very unpleasant. Someone playing some sort of practical joke, do you think?"

Ruso hitched himself up to sit on the table and indicated a seat to Metellus. "We suspect my predecessor was in debt." Having started this story, he was going to have to stick to it.

Metellus swung a leg over the patients' stool. "I could help you find out."

"I think we have more urgent things to deal with."

"Sadly, yes. The murder of your very important patient."

"He hit his head on the pavement. We don't know he was murdered."

"Yes we do, Ruso. We're working for Publius Accius, and that's what we have been hired to prove."

Ruso let out a long breath. "I'm surprised you were prepared to take this on, given your view of Accius."

"I have no particular view of Accius. I merely told you you'd need better connections to get on here. He's a young man with very limited influence, not because he's an opponent of Hadrian—I don't think he is—but because ever since some of Hadrian's rather overeager supporters executed one of his relations, people haven't trusted him."

"That hardly seems fair."

"I agree. He was a good officer when we were in Britannia, and he needs help."

"And the urban prefect's office is happy for you to do that?"

"The urban prefect is always keen to maintain good order. The murder of a successful businessman by one of the emperor's building contractors could lead to all sorts of difficulties."

"What is it you do for the prefect's office, exactly?"

But before Metellus could slide around the question they were interrupted by a call of "We are back!" from Tilla, who had evidently been warned that he was with a patient.

"Metellus is here, wife!" Ruso named the visitor in a cheery tone, as if their visitor were someone she might be pleased to meet.

A face appeared around the door. "What did you—?" She stopped.

Metellus got to his feet and bowed.

After a moment Tilla remembered to close her mouth. Then she said, "What is he doing here?"

"Darlughdacha of the Corionotatae. A pleasure to see you again after so long."

"Is it?"

As far as Ruso knew, this was the first time anyone had addressed Tilla by her proper name since they had said their farewells to her family in Britannia.

"It must be—how long since Eboracum?" Metellus ventured. "A year?"

Instead of replying, Tilla urged Narina to hurry through to the kitchen and take the baby with her. It seemed she did not even want their visitor to hear Mara's name.

"Metellus is working for Publius Accius too," Ruso told her, trying to convey as much information as possible before she said something they would both regret. "We're going to be investigating the death of Balbus."

She said, "Why?"

"Accius is concerned that—"

"I think what she means is," Metellus put in, "why me?"

"That is what I mean."

Metellus stepped aside, offering her the stool he had been sitting on. Tilla glanced at her husband, then brushed invisible dirt from the seat before using it. "Well?" she demanded, looking from one to the other of them.

Metellus gestured to Ruso, inviting him to speak.

"You try," Ruso offered. "It's beyond me."

"Publius Accius," Metellus began, "believes Balbus was poisoned by a builder who wants to marry Horatia. He believes that by combining your husband's skills as a medicus with my skills in obtaining information, we can reveal the truth."

"In Britannia, you tortured people."

Metellus nodded. "Britannia is a difficult province," he said. "I won't deny it: There were things that had to be done. But your people did them too."

Having accepted the offer of the seat, Tilla was obliged to look up to see their visitor's face.

"Britannia is also a long way away," he continued. "You have no tribe to defend here, Darlughdacha. You are a citizen of Rome called Tilla, and the wife of a citizen who served the emperor in the Twentieth Legion." He held out his hand. "None of us can forget what happened in Britannia, but now that I am working with your husband, perhaps we can agree to put the past behind us."

Very slowly, Tilla got to her feet. Leaving the outstretched hand untouched, she said, "This is my home for now, and the people who live here are my people. You will swear to respect us all. You will speak only the truth to us, and about us, and you will defend my daughter to the last drop of your blood."

It was not until Metellus said, "I swear," that she took his hand.

38

Ruso and Metellus crossed the street and went up the steps into the walled gardens of Livia to conduct their discussion. Anyone watching them would have seen two friends chatting as they strolled past the statues and fountains in the dappled shade of the elegant vine-covered portico. There would be no way of confirming this, however, because while the men kept walking there was no way for anyone to eavesdrop. Which was precisely why they were there. Given the complicated personal life of the emperor Augustus's wife—the Livia after whom Ruso supposed the venue was named—it seemed very appropriate.

"I'm trying to get the sequence of events straight in my mind, Ruso. Perhaps you could help."

Ruso glanced at a remarkably lifelike statue of a hunting hound and knew he must set aside his reluctance to tell Metellus anything at all. "Where do I start?"

"Tell me how you came to be Balbus's doctor."

Metellus often asked seemingly irrelevant questions to see what response they provoked, rather like a doctor prodding to find out where it hurt. Querying the subject would only make it look as though he had something to hide. "I'm looking after Doctor Kleitos's patients while he's away," he said. "Balbus was one of them."

"Ah. So when I saw you at the amphitheater, and you told me there was an opportunity coming up that you couldn't reveal—"

"That was a lie," Ruso admitted. The closer he could stick to the real story, the less suspicion he would arouse. "I didn't want to tell you that I was short of work. But when I went to see Accius later, I got a note asking me to take over Kleitos's practice."

"That same day? The note came from Accius?"

"No, from Kleitos via Accius. Accius was the one who introduced us. Kleitos is his doctor too." And none of this was relevant.

Metellus said, "I thought you were Accius's doctor?"

"Kleitos has looked after the family for years."

"So why did Accius bring you here?"

Ruso shook his head. "I think he thought he was doing me a favor. People who come from Rome tend to assume everyone else is desperate to live here."

"And it seems you were."

"I was flattered to be invited," Ruso confessed, voicing it for the first time. "Weren't you?"

"This is my home. Britannia is a fine province to make one's name, but only if one has a chance to return to Rome and reap the benefits of all that mud and fog. Tell me what happened after you got the note."

Metellus had probably been given half of this story by Accius already. He would be checking to see if Ruso's version tallied with what he had already been told.

"I went straight to Kleitos's rooms. I was hardly through the door when I got called to see Balbus."

"He was ill?"

"His medicine had run out," Ruso explained, wishing he had told Accius the whole story straightaway. Now it looked as though he was concealing something. "Kleitos was supplying him with a theriac. He seemed to think he was under threat."

"Did he say who from?"

"His competitors, he said. He'd trodden on a few toes." Ruso made a mental note to ask Firmicus if the injured toes included those of Curtius Cossus. "He wasn't popular with his tenants either, but I'd imagine most of them fantasize about murdering the caretakers or Firmicus first."

Metellus reached up and pulled a dead leaf from the vine. "Interesting that Balbus's doctor vanishes on the day his medicine runs out, no?"

"He wasn't pleased."

"And the body in the barrel?"

The switch of topic caught Ruso off guard. "That had nothing to do with it."

"So you gave Balbus some more medicine, and he took it?"

Breathe normally. You are telling the truth. "I didn't have the recipe, so I gave him something harmless that looked like it. I didn't see him take it." Before Metellus could ask more about the medicine itself, Ruso explained the circumstances of the handover in front of Curtius Cossus.

"Hm. It would be interesting to know exactly how Balbus achieved his own rise in fortunes."

Ruso, who had never considered until now that Balbus might have something worse than cockroaches to hide, said, "What I don't understand was why he would want to do business with a man he thought might poison him."

It was a moment before he realized the sound from his companion's throat was a chuckle. "Ah, Ruso. Still the man of principle. I'd forgotten how refreshing that is. You'd be surprised what men are prepared to do when large sums of money are involved."

Be careful who you trust. He was beginning to wonder if anyone in this place had clean hands. "For all we know," he said, "Balbus could have died of natural causes. Or been murdered by angry tenants." *Or accidentally poisoned by his doctor.* "But here we are, talking about finding ways to have Cossus tried for murder."

Metellus paused. "Dear me, that's very dramatic. I don't think anyone has suggested actually prosecuting anybody."

Ruso stared at him. "Then what are we doing this for?"

"Just so that Cossus will understand what might happen if he doesn't back off and let Accius marry the lovely Horatia."

"Holy gods." Ruso shook his head. Evidently the question of who or what really had caused the death of Horatius Balbus was of no interest. He felt a sneaking sense of relief, swiftly followed by shame.

"Let's come back to this body in the barrel."

"If you like." He wasn't going to insist yet again that it wasn't relevant.

"What was that all about?"

"We think somebody was trying to frighten Kleitos into paying his debts."

"That's your story?"

"It makes sense. He's cleared off and taken most of his stuff with him."

"He would have done that if he'd murdered the man in the barrel himself," Metellus pointed out.

"If he'd killed the man himself," said Ruso, scrambling to plug a hole in the story that he and Tilla had not considered, "he wouldn't have left the body outside the surgery. He'd have found a way to get rid of it."

"Let's not waste time on this." Metellus's tone was suddenly sharp. "You know why it was there. You've made enquiries."

"You've been making enquiries about my enquiries?"

"I don't need to. I know you. You know exactly who the dead man was and why he was there, or you'd be making more fuss about it."

"Then trust me when I tell you it's not relevant."

This time the chuckle was more of a laugh. Metellus had never been this jolly in Britannia. Perhaps his sense of humor had been repressed by the mud and fog. "So I did manage to teach you something about discretion after all. I assume you're afraid Kleitos was collecting bodies to dissect, and since you're his chosen successor, you're worried the dirt will land on you too."

"If he was—"

"You're right. Much wiser to go with the debt-collection story. After all, whatever he was up to isn't your fault, is it?"

Ruso glanced across at the slaves who were scrubbing out the fountain and sweeping the stray gravel from the paving back into the central area, and decided there was much to be said for a job where you were not required to think about anything. "You know what Kleitos wrote on the end of his note?"

"This may surprise you, but I don't know everything."

"He wrote, *Be careful who you trust.*"

"Very good," Metellus said. "Now tell me what really killed Horatius Balbus."

"He hit his head," said Ruso, both answering and not answering the question.

39

THE ARGUMENT WITH Tilla was as predictable as it was inevitable, their tempers heated further by each of them telling the other to "Keep your voice down. Do you want the neighbors to hear?" Ruso already knew all the reasons why Metellus was not to be trusted. What he did not know was why his wife insisted on making an enemy of him.

"I have not! I have made an agreement with him! Did you not see me take his treacherous hand?"

"I saw you making him swear to things, but I notice he didn't get any promises out of you."

"I would not make them."

"And you don't think he noticed?"

"I am not the one who is working with— Oh, not now!"

The new arrival was a woman trailing three small children. All peered out through pink bloodshot eyes. Ruso could not remember a time when he had been happier to see a patient.

"It creeps," the mother complained, rubbing her itchy eyelids and wiping her hand on her skirts. "It's creeping up the building. First the children downstairs, now mine. We're all using the ointment but it's no good."

"I'm afraid where there's one case, there are always others," Ruso told her.

"Like rats."

"At least this usually goes away of its own accord."

"I want it to go away now," she told him. "It's driving us all mad."

He lined the children up outside where the light was better, and crouched in front of the tallest one to reassure himself that it was a simple case of pinkeye and nothing more sinister. The boy said in a very small voice, "Will I go blind?"

"No, you'll get better soon."

"My friend's cousin had it and he went blind."

"Your friend's cousin must have had something different," Ruso assured him.

"I been practicing walking around with my eyes shut."

"I told you to stop that!" his mother put in. "You'll fall over and break your neck. Then you'll be sorry."

He moved to the next one in the line. "That looks sore. Can you open your eyes and look at me?"

The child squeezed her eyes tight shut and shook her dark curls from side to side.

"Probably best to keep them shut," he agreed. "Otherwise you might see what I'm doing."

Moments later the eyes were shut again, but he had seen all he needed to see.

The final child squinted at him and said, "Can we look at the man in the barrel?"

The mother grabbed the child by the shoulder. "What did I tell you? Say sorry to the doctor!"

"It's all right," Ruso said, wishing it was, and aware that his cover story was not suitable for children. "Somebody put him outside to play a trick on the doctor who lived here before, but he's gone now. Tell me, is there a fountain near where you live?"

The boy nodded, while his mother pointed out that it was down four flights of stairs.

"I want you all to splash your eyes every morning and evening with cold water. It'll help to relieve the itching. Make sure it's fresh out of the fountain so it's as cold as you can get it. And try not to rub. It just makes the soreness worse."

"Do we do the water before or after we use the ointment?" asked the mother.

"What ointment is it?"

She groped inside the folds of her tunic. Ruso had been hoping for something with an identifiable oculist's stamp on it. Instead she produced a round lump of something that looked like lard. It was covered with dust and wool fibres.

"I wouldn't use that at all," he told her.

"I paid the other doctor good money for it!"

"Then you need to keep it clean inside its own pot," he explained. "Otherwise you're just adding to the problem. I'd stick with the cold water. Lots of illnesses aren't helped by medicines. You should all be clear in a couple of weeks, but if not bring them back and we'll try something else."

"Just cold water?" The woman sounded offended.

"As often as you like, but at least morning and evening."

She shrugged. "Ah well. At least it's free. Come on, you lot."

He said, "I'll count you all as one consultation, so that'll be one sesterce."

"What for?"

"For the examination and the advice."

"But you didn't give me any medicine," she pointed out. "Doctor Kleitos always gives me medicine."

"Do you know where Doctor Kleitos is?"

She bridled even further. "There's no need to be like that about it. You should be glad we came here. A lot of people wouldn't have, after what we've heard."

"I didn't mean it that way," he said, wondering what she had heard. "All I meant was—"

But she was gone, trailing her pinkeyed offspring behind her. He washed his hands and searched out a blank tablet to write a brief and pointless note about the children. Having left owing money, the family would not be back. He pushed aside a wave of nostalgia for the Legion, where the doctors were protected from time wasters by centurions with short tempers and large sticks, and where nobody had to extract his salary from his patients one coin at a time.

The Britons were singing another war song in the kitchen, Tilla comforting herself with tales of past glories. He suspected that the quarrel about Metellus had left her just as drained and anxious as he was himself. Already he regretted his anger. The truth was, she was voicing his own fears.

Be careful who you trust was good advice, but following it was exhausting. Especially when one of the people you weren't sure you could trust was yourself. If Curtius Cossus did not take kindly to being threatened—and who would, especially with a lot of money at stake?—he might well strike back, and before long someone was going to ask exactly what had been in that bottle of medicine.

He needed to know what really had happened to Horatius Balbus.

He needed to know exactly what that black lozenge had contained.

He needed to find Kleitos.

The men who had tried to collect the absent family's furniture had not returned. Tilla had apparently been out trying to trace them when Metellus arrived. Maybe her efforts would be more successful than his own. Maybe he should enquire which god, from the many on offer here, might be willing to help for a reasonable fee. Maybe he should have been politer about Christos.

He dropped the pointless note into the chaos of Kleitos's records box. The war song fell silent as he entered the kitchen to find Narina scattering olives across a bowl of lettuce and his wife slapping an unappetizing lump of grease around a mixing bowl.

"Linseed in oil and goose fat," she said, answering his unasked question.

If this was some obscure dish she and Narina had dredged up to remind them of home, he would buy a snack while he was out. "Supper?"

"Suppositories. For women's monthly pains." She nodded toward the shelf, where he was relieved to see a basket of eggs. "*That* is supper."

"Ah. Do we need anything fetched while I'm out?"

The slapping stopped. "You are going out again?"

"There aren't any patients waiting."

"They must have heard that the new doctor is never here."

He said, "Can I put in a request to have the Roman wife back?"

On the way out he told Esico that the mistress would be at home to deal with visitors. Esico nodded, and said in Latin, "There are not many . . ." He searched for a word. "Sick people."

"No," Ruso agreed. "Evidently we've cured them all."

40

METELLUS WAS TO make discreet enquiries about what had happened during the dinner at Cossus's house. Ruso took this to mean that he would pick out a vulnerable member of Cossus's staff and then decide whether to use bribery or threats. Meanwhile, since Balbus's body had showed no obvious sign of being poisoned (a fact Ruso found far less disappointing than did Metellus) Ruso had offered to see what else he could discover about the death. If Metellus had sensed his anxiety, he'd pretended not to.

The scene of last night's tragedy took longer to find than he expected, because even when he thought he was in the right place, he recognized very little in daylight. All the shops that had been shuttered were now open with their wares spilling onto the pavement. Weaving his way around a few shoppers and a couple of heavily laden mules, he passed displays of cabbages and onions, cooking pots and wooden spoons, sandals and children's toys, painted clay gods, and billowing festoons of fabric. One doorway seemed to offer nothing but strings of sausages.

Higher up, apartment windows and balconies stared at one another across the narrow street. He paused, wondering what the people who lived in those rooms thought of Horatius Balbus. And whether it would have been possible to act upon those thoughts if they'd seen him passing along the street below.

Ruso walked all the way around the block and then back past the same displays again. He paused in front of the toys.

A voice said, "Boy or girl?"

He wondered if Mara would appreciate a wooden doll, then decided she would only chew it and give herself splinters or use it as a weapon. "She's not old enough yet."

"She soon will be."

"I'll bear it in mind," Ruso said, looking 'round. "Is this the place where there was the disturbance last night?"

The man finished painting a smile on a jovial-looking wooden dog, and placed it on the display. "Disturbance here every bloody night," he observed, rinsing the paintbrush before wiping it on a rag and upending it in a pot. "Drunks singing and fighting and pissing in the doorways. Traffic. Animals. Take your pick."

Evidently the painting of smiles did not cheer the heart. "Someone was injured."

"He's not injured. He's dead." The man leaned out and called to his neighbor, "Oi! Someone here about last night!"

The strings of sausages parted to reveal a small wrinkled man with greasy hair. "Where is it, then?" he demanded, looking Ruso up and down.

"Where's what?"

"Somebody's supposed to bring back my door."

"I'll tell them."

"They've been told twice already. You tell them I want it done tonight. I'm not going on some waiting list. I did old Balbus a favor, which is more than he ever did for me. You tell them I'm not having some cheap bodge. It's got to fit."

"I will," Ruso promised. He had last seen the door propped against the garish paintwork of Balbus's bedroom wall. "Does he own all of this block?"

"And the one across the street," said the sausage man.

The toy seller said, "Not anymore."

"Tonight," the sausage man repeated. "I can't be up another night guarding my stock."

"I'll tell them." Now that he had a fixed point he scanned the street again, getting his bearings. Balbus's last steps in this world had taken him past that weaver's workshop on the corner. A shoemaker's bench now looked out across the pavement where the injured man had lain while Ruso shouted for light and made frantic and hopeless efforts to save him.

"Did you see what happened last night?" he asked.

"Hard not to, with no door."

"Before that," he said. "I'm trying to find out what happened to Horatius Balbus."

The toy seller and the sausage man exchanged a glance. The sausage man ventured the opinion that their visitor wasn't from around here.

"What happens around here?" Ruso asked.

The toy seller said, "around here, when the sun's down, you bar the door and mind your own business."

"There were people looking out of their windows," Ruso told them. "Up there." He pointed at the apartments above the shoemaker's workshop. "And up there." He indicated the balcony directly overhead. Many of the higher windows had no grilles or glass: Instead there were shutters that could be opened wide enough for someone to lean out and fling a missile.

"If you were here," the sausage man pointed out, "then why ask?"

"I came later," Ruso explained. "The staff want to know if there was anything more they could have done."

"You mean the family want to know whether to have them flogged."

Ruso shrugged. "You know how it is." It was a statement that he had found to be both meaningless and useful. People rarely admitted that they didn't know how it was.

"He got what was coming to him," observed the sausage man. "That's how it is. But you didn't hear it from me."

"Or me." The toy seller wished him luck in a tone that suggested luck was in short supply around here.

The caretaker of the block was busy introducing a scantily clad young woman to a large jug of wine, and their brief conversation left Ruso none the wiser. Tramping up and down smelly stairs and corridors taught him three things: that nobody who was prepared to speak to him had seen anything at all, that nobody knew anyone else who had seen anything, and that a surprising number of apartments were occupied not by people but by angry dogs who, fortunately, did not know how to open the door.

The shoemaker—another potential witness who had seen nothing—agreed that one of his boys had indeed washed the pavement this morning. "And every morning," he added. "You're not from the street cleaning people, are you?"

Ruso assured him he was not. The boy in question was fetched. He pointed to the sharp edge of the curb where he had washed away blood.

"Right on the edge?"

"There," the boy said, pointing again. Asked if he had cleared away any sort of unexpected stone or heavy object, he looked blank and then scuttled back into the safety of the shop.

Ruso surveyed the big flat cobbles that had been fitted together to make up the surface of the street. There was nothing obvious to trip over. He waited until there was no one coming and said "Excuse me" to the shoemaker before lying down where the boy had indicated. The stone was warm and smooth against the skin of his temple.

"You all right, mate?" demanded a voice from behind the counter.

"Oi!" called the toy seller. "You can't lie there!"

"What about my door?"

Somewhere behind him, a small child announced to her mother that the man had had too much wine.

Ruso lifted his head from the edge of the curb. Then he turned and lay at a different angle, still facing the same way with the side of his head on the curb, and a couple of old cabbage leaves and a squashed cockroach a few inches from his nose.

If Balbus had hit his head on the curb, he had fallen at a very unlucky angle. But in the absence of any sign that he tried to save himself, perhaps the blow had come before he fell, not after. A bald head would have made a clear target in torchlight. The two men with him might never have seen a missile flying toward them from the surrounding dark.

When he had gathered enough of a crowd he got up again, dusted off the worst of the grime, and surveyed his audience. There were two or three men who might be military veterans. A stone was not a glamorous weapon, but any recruit who had survived basic training would know that in the right hands it could be both accurate and deadly.

"I'm the doctor from the Vicus Sabuci, outside the entrance to Trajan's baths," he told them. "I treated a man who fell here last night. I'm trying to find somebody who saw what happened."

He was expecting the silence but with luck, behind the blank faces, the neighbors would not be as united as they appeared. His hope was that if there was something to tell, someone would contact him privately later in search of a reward. What he was not expecting was, "I know you."

He spun 'round to see the man with the bad haircut who had baited him outside Sabella's bar.

"He's the one who started that trouble down at the amphitheater," the man informed his neighbors. "Pushing women and kids out of the way to get to the front."

Later, he would rationalize his denial. He had meant, *It wasn't like that. I am not a man who would start trouble and push women and children.* But what came out was, "Not me." And then it was too late to explain.

"He got that other doctor run out of Rome. Then he couldn't save old Balbus. Now he's looking for somebody to blame."

"I didn't—"

"He said he served in the Legions," put in somebody else.

"It's him all right," insisted the man with the bad haircut.

"But I didn't—"

"You didn't serve in the Legions?"

"No, I meant—"

"Bloody veterans! Always picking fights."

"Coming 'round here making trouble," put in a voice behind him. "Time you learned some manners."

They were closing in now, fists at the ready. The shoemaker was clutching a hammer. Another man was drawing something from the back of his belt.

He held his hands up in surrender. "I was just trying to find out what happened."

To his relief a couple of women moved aside to let him escape.

As he forced himself to walk rather than run away, a voice called after him, "So what sort of a doctor are you, then?"

It was a good question.

He reached the main road and turned to look back. His accusers had dispersed into the long shadows of the street, making their way home to eat their meals, bar their doors, and mind their own business for another night. With luck, they would forget about him when the next victim came along. Nobody would remember as clearly as he would the exact moment when Gaius Petreius Ruso, former military surgeon, had decided he would rather be somebody else.

41

PASSING THE MASSIVE porch of Trajan's baths, Ruso wanted
to stride in across the polished marble and fling himself into
the cold plunge. The shock would wash away all memories of the
incident at the amphitheater, of Horatius Balbus and his wretched
medicine, of the body in the barrel, and of an afternoon that had
got worse as it went on. Unfortunately there was one last mission
to complete.

The eerie wails of the women mourning for Balbus were audible
from the street outside his house, and the air inside the entrance
hall was still heavy with incense.

Beneath the heavy brows, Firmicus's eyes were creased with
fatigue. Reminded about the borrowed door, he observed that the
man should be grateful the night watch hadn't smashed it down.

"He said he needs it put back before dark."

"You'd think they'd show some respect."

"It's in your master's bedroom."

Firmicus sighed and beckoned over a junior slave to fetch one of
the carpenters. "Latro can show him where to take it. Tell him I
said it's urgent."

When the slave was gone Ruso said, "How's Horatia?"

"The lettuce hasn't helped."

Seeing Firmicus trying to stifle a yawn, Ruso found himself yawning in echo. "Sorry. I know this isn't the moment, but I'd like to talk to you sometime about last night."

"You're one of the men Publius Accius is sending to help?" Firmicus sounded resigned rather than grateful. Before the steward could ask whether Accius had the permission of the family to interfere, Ruso added, "I need to talk to Latro as well."

Firmicus massaged the inner corners of his eyes with the tips of his fingers. "Now is as good a time as any. The undertakers seem to know what they're doing." He led Ruso down a narrow service corridor. "You won't get any sense out of Latro. I've been finding him things to do all day. He's afraid he'll be sent to the mines for not saving his master." He pushed open a door. "I'd take you up to my office, but this is farther away from the racket. Those women's throats must be raw. The things people do for money."

The light from the barred window above their heads showed a jumble of furniture and a priapic satyr with a missing nose and one arm broken off. Firmicus said, "Shall I have Publius Accius called?"

"No, thanks. Who else is out there?"

"Who isn't?" Firmicus shut the door and leaned back against it, gazing around the abandoned furniture. "I can remember my father buying some of this."

"You were brought up here?"

"Pa was steward to the old master. Balbus kept most of us when he bought the property."

"That must have been strange. Wasn't he a slave here once himself?"

The steward's drawn face eased into half-smile. "Pa used to send him to run errands. I was there when he got his freedom. I can see the look on his face now."

"How did that happen?"

"Reward for catching one of the clerks dipping into the master's money chest." He looked up. "People said he was a hard bastard, and he was, but he wasn't bad to work for. To be honest the old master let things go a bit. Wouldn't make decisions, wouldn't let anyone else do it, either. Balbus got the place for a fraction of what it was worth and turned everything around. We've done very—" He stopped. "Up till now, we've done very well. The gods alone know what'll happen after this. The cousin is the nearest male relative. He runs a butcher's shop out in Fidenae. Hasn't a clue about the business."

"But won't all the property go to Horatia?"

Firmicus sniffed. "She'll have to learn fast if she's going to manage it. There's not much call for Greek poetry in the rented property business." He folded his arms. "Between you and me, Doctor, right now I think I'm the only one who realizes how much of a disaster this is."

"Could you manage the business for her?"

"I'd do my best, if the cousin agrees. I'm guessing he'll want to hand her over to a husband and get rid of the responsibility. Which brings us to why you're here, doesn't it? Publius Accius wants us to tell you that the master was poisoned by Curtius Cossus."

He hoped Accius had been more discreet outside the household. "Would Cossus have any reason to want him dead?"

"A lot of his competitors wanted him . . ." Firmicus paused, searching for the right word. "Under control." Before Ruso could ask what that meant, he went on, "I keep going over what happened. Trying to work out what the boss was trying to tell us."

Ruso was not going to tell him that Latro thought Balbus had said he felt ill. "Would you mind going over it again?"

Firmicus had not heard or seen a missile, but he agreed that such an attack was possible. The street, too narrow for traffic, had been quiet and there was a chance someone could have identified Balbus's voice from above. He had no doubt the caretaker of the building could name tenants who thought they may have had a grievance, but as to murder . . . "Aren't you supposed to be asking about poisoning?"

"I'm considering the possibilities."

"The boss spent a fortune on that medicine."

"I need to talk to Kleitos. He would know better than me."

"Any sign of him?"

"There's a possible connection I'm going to follow up tomorrow."

Firmicus sighed. "Poor old boss."

Ruso said, "I'm sorry."

"Maybe he was right after all: Someone was out to get him."

"Perhaps it was an accident," said Ruso, forgetting he was supposed to be proving that it wasn't. "Or natural causes."

"You and I might want to believe that," Firmicus told him, "but they won't. With all Horatia's money up for grabs, they'd rather pick over the carcass and fight."

Ruso walked back through the darkening streets without paying much attention to his surroundings, which was probably why he missed the right turn to the Vicus Sabuci and ended up making a circle of the block.

Firmicus had told him nothing new about the death, but he had learned something completely unexpected about the circumstances. In response to, "Is it true Curtius Cossus made an offer for Horatia?" the man had replied without hesitation, "As far as I know, it was the boss who made the approach."

"But what about Accius?" And what about Horatia, who clearly had her heart set upon him?

"I'd guess Accius was being kept in reserve in case Cossus wasn't interested. The boss wasn't known for being sentimental. And to be honest, your patron's name isn't the best in the city."

"It's still a big step up for a freedman's daughter," Ruso pointed out, feeling aggrieved on Accius's behalf. "And Balbus didn't trust Cossus."

"You mean he wanted it to be obvious that he was taking an antidote in case Cossus was thinking of poisoning him," said Firmicus, as if this were a normal way of going about things.

Always stay one step ahead of your enemies. Ruso was beginning to feel like a country bumpkin. "But why in the gods' name would anyone offer his daughter to a man he thought was capable of murdering people?"

Firmicus yawned. "The boss wanted to play with the big boys. And Cossus has no living children."

Ruso said, "I'm a simple medic. You'll have to explain. Some other time, if you'd rather."

"I'd rather stay here than go out there," Firmicus said. "How much do you know about the building trade?"

"Nothing." Nothing good, at least. This was not the time to talk about the temple his father had decided to donate to his hometown in Gaul, which had practically bankrupted him and driven him to an early grave.

"Getting a building project funded is a complicated business,"

Firmicus explained. "Past a certain point, unless you're the emperor, you need other people to split the costs. They share the risk in exchange for a cut of the profits. Are you with me so far?"

"Yes." It was a pity nobody had told his father that.

"The boss is—was—keen to expand, but we don't have the right connections with investors. Cossus does. He's got a lot of money in property himself and he's already got the contract to clear that massive site for the emperor's new temple down by the amphitheater. The boss got the attention of Cossus and his cronies by buying a property he knew they wanted over on the Aventine. That gave him the chance to tell Cossus about all the other development opportunities he could get his hands on if they pooled their resources."

"Through a marriage with Horatia."

"Yes."

Poor Accius. It seemed he too had no idea what men were prepared to do if there were large sums of money involved. When he said of the dinner that *I imagine they were going to discuss some sort of deal* he could have had no idea that Balbus would be offering Horatia as part of it.

"If the gamble paid off," Firmicus explained, "any future grandson could climb way beyond rent collecting. He'd inherit a substantial and respectable business. From slave to top man in two generations."

"And if Cossus and his associates didn't want to let Balbus in?"

"Balbus would carry on as a competitor, still watching his back, and use the other route to the top. Accius is from a reasonably good family. With the boss's money behind him, the grandson could be making speeches in the Senate."

And Balbus would have pleased his daughter, although that did not seem to have been a priority.

Firmicus had no idea what had been discussed at the dinner, or indeed if the match had even been mentioned. The visiting staff had been sent to the kitchen to sample the leftovers.

"Whoever else was there will know," Ruso suggested.

"It wasn't a big affair. Just a couple of Cossus's cronies."

"Names?" Metellus would no doubt find them out, but it would do no harm to have confirmation.

Firmicus reached for the writing pad tucked into his belt and flipped it open. "You're welcome to try," he said, scratching in the wax, "but you're wasting your time." He tapped the first name. "That one's a shipping insurer." He wrote again. "This one's a junior politician. Both of them are Cossus's backers for the work on the temple site. They'll say whatever he wants them to."

Publius Accius had seemed far less happy than Firmicus to be called away from the mourners to hold a conversation in a store-room. He was even less pleased when he heard what Ruso had to tell him. But as Ruso pointed out, Firmicus had no reason to lie about Horatia's suitors. And if Balbus had offered his daughter to Curtius Cossus, then Cossus had no reason to murder him. "This investigation has to stop, sir. You need to find some other way of winning the lady. You're in danger of making some powerful enemies."

"So Cossus has paid off Firmicus."

It was not the response Ruso was hoping for. "Sir, what if Firmicus is telling the truth?"

Accius snorted. "He's got you fooled too."

Ruso lowered his voice to whisper, "Sir, this is Horatius Balbus we're talking about. You know what his business methods were like. If he saw some advantage in allying his own family with Cossus's, are you certain he would pass it up for the sake of his daughter's happiness?"

But Accius did not even draw breath before telling him the idea of Balbus offering Horatia to another man was ridiculous, adding, "I've known him and his daughter far longer than you have."

"I'm advising you to stop and think, sir."

Accius drew himself up to his full height in the gloom of the storeroom. "And I'm advising you, Doctor, not to offer opinions on matters about which you know nothing. Just trust me and continue with the investigation."

"It's not that I don't trust you, sir, but—"

"But what?"

Ruso took a deep breath. "I think we're all shocked by the death, sir, and—"

"You're questioning my judgment."

"Yes."

"In that case, get out. I'll leave it to Metellus."

"Sir—"

"Out!"

Ruso paused in the corridor to smack one fist against his head. He should have left Accius to come to his senses slowly, instead of pushing a man who was so irrational that he seemed to have mistaken a junk room for his personal office. He strode away, slapping his feet onto the concrete floor to make as much sound as possible, so that Accius would know it was safe to come out of the room—in which he had just marooned himself—with some shred of his dignity intact.

42

B Y THE TIME Ruso got back to the Vicus Sabuci the glazed windows of the occupied rooms above him had become dull orange shapes against black. Elsewhere, pale streaks outlined ill-fitting doors and shutters. Announcing, "Esico? It's me!" he groped for the latch and plunged into the surgery only to find himself in utter darkness. Not in silence, though. The followers of Christos were flouting the law again upstairs.

"Master!" Light spilled in from the kitchen and Esico's silhouette appeared in the doorway. "Food is here."

Food was indeed there, although not a great deal of it. There was a salad, a chunk of bread, and two hard-boiled eggs. Tilla was absent. So were his daughter and his baby-minder. "Where is everyone?"

Esico raised a forefinger toward the sound of the singing.

"All of them?"

"Yes, master."

The singing had stopped by the time he got there. From the other side of the door he could hear a lone male voice raised in prayer. Ruso hesitated, not keen to interrupt. The lord was being implored to remove the demon that cast Brother Justus's boy down in fits, to rise up against the evil of the Games that would be upon them at the end of the month, to comfort the family of Horatius Balbus and bring fairness and justice to his tenants, and to bring healing to Sister Phyllis, because the lord knew what a heavy burden she carried. Apparently so did everyone else, because her name brought a chorus of "Amen!" from others in the room.

Ruso's limited experience with the followers of Christos back in Gaul—the neighbor's farm was infested with them—suggested that this could go on for ages. Besides, he had specifically asked Tilla not to get involved with these people. Perhaps that was why his fist hit the door more forcefully than he had intended, and more than once.

The praying stopped. There was a frantic whispering instead, and then a woman called out, "Christos is with us! We are not afraid!"

Deciding that *Tell Christos I want my women back!* might not go down well, he tried, "It's the doctor. Is my wife in there?"

Moments later he found himself looking 'round at a surprising number of alarmed faces. Figures were crammed together on the floor, sitting cross-legged or hugging their knees. Others were perched on the couch, and more were standing against the walls. The two youths lolling on the windowsill were probably the only ones breathing fresh air.

Two figures rose from the crush on the floor: Tilla and Narina. Narina stood where she was, looking anxious. Tilla stepped carefully over the legs of strangers to reach him, and he could not help thinking that she was holding Mara in front of her as a form of shield. The bright "What is the matter, husband?" had undertones of, *Why are you embarrassing me like this?*

"There's nobody downstairs," he said, still clutching the lamp he had used to light his way up the dark steps and aware that he sounded like a small boy who was missing his mother.

Instead of apologizing, Tilla frowned. "No? Esico should be there."

"I mean, apart from—"

"Did he not give you the message?"

He was saved from replying by a cry of "Come in, Doctor! Come and say hello!" from Phyllis, who scrambled up from somewhere on the floor to stand beside him. Tilla gave him a look that said it would be churlish not to comply. "Everybody!" Phyllis announced, "This is our new neighbor, the doctor. Tilla's husband, Mara's papa, Narina's master."

"Ruso," he announced to all the resolutely cheerful faces. Sensing that more was required, he gave his "Doctor Kleitos asked me to help out" speech, but it appeared everyone knew this already. Then he remembered that his family had been the subject of an appeal for spare furniture.

From the couch, a beaming woman with frizzy hair poking out from under her head covering declared, "We have just been praying for you, Doctor!"

"Really?"

"We have been asking the Lord to help you find Doctor Kleitos."

"Oh," he said, taken aback. "Well, let's hope the Lord knows where he is."

"I'm sure he does," the woman assured him as Tilla's foot moved to press on his toe. "And we have been giving thanks for—"

Tilla's "Have you eaten, husband?" cut across whatever was coming next.

"Oh, yes!" Phyllis leapt back to her feet and indicated the scattered remains of food on the table. "We should have offered, Doctor. I am so sorry."

He held out one hand in refusal, making a retreat toward the cooler air of the corridor. "My wife left my supper downstairs for me."

"We were so sorry to hear about your difficulties," put in the woman with the frizzy hair. "First no furniture, then the man in the barrel, and all that trouble with the neighbors, then your slave running away, and—"

Phyllis tried to interrupt with, "Sister Dorcas, he already knows—"

"And now poor Horatius Balbus," continued Sister Dorcas, unabashed. "Your wife has told us all about it."

Tilla had the grace to look embarrassed.

"You're welcome to stay and pray with us," put in the man he recognized as Phyllis's husband, Timo the carpenter.

Ruso shook his head. "It's not really my area, I'm afraid." He turned to his wife. "Tilla? Narina, it's time to go."

Narina moved toward the door immediately, as ordered. To his surprise, so did Tilla. Perhaps the Roman wife had remembered her duties after all.

There was a jolly chorus of good-byes and then they were squinting into the dark of the corridor, with only the swaying lamp flame to guide them.

"What the hell have you been saying to them?" Ruso hissed.

"Nothing!"

"Nothing?"

"They asked everyone to share needs for prayer. I said you would like to talk to Doctor Kleitos so that you could treat his patients better."

"What?"

"I am trying to help! One of them might know where he is!"

It was a good idea, but he was not in the mood to say so. "What about all the other things she knew?"

"I don't know! People hear gossip and then they want to talk to you about it. Do you want me to say it is not true?"

"I want you not to mix with them." The lamp picked out the shape of the next door: a room occupied by strangers. When they were past he took her by the arm to murmur in her ear, "If word gets around that you're part of a group that prays against the emperor's Games . . ."

"But it is true, husband. The Games are evil. You know what goes on."

The singing had started up again. He wanted to go and strangle them. Especially Sister Dorcas. "I also know," he hissed, "that if you pray against the Games in front of the wrong people, you're liable to end up starring in them."

They broke off the conversation at the end of the corridor: negotiating a steep flight of concrete steps with only one lamp between them required concentration. That was why, even when they heard the crash from downstairs and Esico shouting, they could not fling themselves down the steps to find out what was happening. Grabbing at the wall to steady himself as he reached a foot out into the dark, Ruso yelled, "Esico! What's going on?"

The only response they could hear above the singing was another shout and the smash and tinkle of breaking glass.

43

R USO GOT THERE first, swinging the door back so hard that it crashed against the wall of the surgery. "What's going on?" he demanded. "Where's my slave?"

Even in the lamplight the squeaky-voiced giant from the undertakers' yard was unmistakable. The muscular stranger standing beside him was not much smaller. Each had a knife at his belt and together they seemed to fill the room. Ruso was unarmed, because who took a weapon to a prayer meeting?

The followers of Christos launched into a new tune as Squeaky slid down from his seat on the operating table. "We've come for a talk."

"What have you done with Esico?" demanded Tilla, trying to push aside the arm that Ruso had put out to protect her. "What is happening?"

Ruso moved to block the space between her and the men, but Squeaky reached out and hauled him aside. His companion seized Tilla and dragged her in, almost jerking Mara out of her arms. The door was slammed shut behind her. There was no sign of Narina.

Squeaky nodded to his companion, who moved to guard the exit.

"Where is Esico?" Tilla demanded again, cradling Mara's head in her hand.

"Shut up, bitch!" squeaked the boy's voice from the man's body. "We're talking to the doctor."

"You shut up!" snapped Tilla. "This is my home."

Ruso tried to mouth "No!" at her. Doubtless she thought she could say what she liked from behind the protection of the baby. But the undertakers were professional inflictors of pain. He had no idea where they would stop. As calmly as he could manage, he said, "How can I help?"

Squeaky said, "We're here for a private consultation."

"Where's my slave?"

Squeaky shook his head. "So many questions."

"Too many," said the companion.

Glancing around, Ruso saw that several bandages had unravelled across the floor like long white ribbons. One was draped over what seemed to be the shattered remains of the broom handle, and nearby he saw a glint of broken glass. He called, "Esico!"

There was no reply.

A third, smaller man came wandering in from the kitchen. "Not enough to keep a flea alive back there," he observed, putting what looked like a quarter of hard-boiled egg into his mouth.

"Let me see the slave," Ruso urged. Instead of replying, the big men seized him under his arms and lifted him up like a child to sit on the table between them

"Don't hurt him!" cried Tilla. The third man strolled toward her. She gave a little cry: Ruso craned around his captor's shoulder to see the knife pointing at the curl of Mara's ear. To his horror Mara wriggled 'round and stretched her chubby fingers toward the blade. Tilla grabbed her hand and the man withdrew the knife, but not far.

"Be a good girl and keep quiet," the man said. "Otherwise my friends might get annoyed. And when my friends get annoyed, accidents happen."

Deliberately lowering his voice in an effort to keep it steady, Ruso said, "We can't do business until he puts that knife away."

Squeaky nodded to his man, who made a show of offering Mara the blade once more before he stepped back.

Ruso said, "Tell me what it is you want."

Squeaky put his face close to Ruso's ear. His breath smelled of fish sauce. "We hear," he said, "that you're poking your nose into other people's business."

"What business?"

Squeaky sighed. "There you go again, see?"

"Too many questions," agreed his companion.

"You want to stick to doctoring." Squeaky reached up and took a bottle down from the shelf. "What's this?"

"Medicine," Ruso told him, unable to see in the poor light and hoping Squeaky would not turn his attention to something really expensive and delicate like the weighing scales.

The giant extended one arm, twisted the wrist, and let the contents of the bottle dribble onto the floor. He sniffed. "Mm. What does that smell like to you?"

It was what was left of the rose oil. "It smells like a waste of money. What is it you want?"

"I want you to stop making complaints to people about our service. Complaints and accusations that undermine the boss's good name just when the city's about to renew his contract."

"Which people? What service? I've never said anything about you to anybody."

"Doctor Kleitos never complained," Squeaky observed. "We liked Doctor Kleitos. We want him back."

"You won't find him here."

"We know," Squeaky agreed. "We've looked."

Upstairs, the singing fell silent.

"I don't know where he is."

Squeaky turned to his friend. "You know," he observed, "old Birna was right. The woman's the clever one."

"Kleitos cleared the place out days ago," Ruso insisted. "Ask anybody. We've had to borrow furniture."

"And he went to—?"

"Nobody knows."

Squeaky let out a long, odorous breath. The bottle glinted in his fleshy grasp. Holding it between finger and thumb, he raised it in the air.

Above them, the followers of Christos were clumping across the floorboards on their way home.

"I told you yesterday," Ruso said. "I don't know where he is. I want to talk to him myself. I've been asking all over the place."

The large hand opened. The bottle fell, hit the tiles, and shattered. Mara began to cry. Squeaky said, "Whoops. That was clumsy."

Tilla tried to shush Mara as a cloying smell of roses drifted up from the floor. Ruso said, "I can't tell you what I don't—"

He stopped, startled by a loud bang from above. Dust pattered down from the rafters as Phyllis called, "Are you all right down there, neighbors?"

Squeaky glanced at his companion. "We're just having a chat," he told Ruso. "Tell her."

"Sorry!" Ruso shouted back.

"We heard something break."

The giant raised his eyebrows and looked at Ruso, who called, "I dropped a bottle!"

For a moment he thought the followers of Christos might have realized something was going on. Then came, "Is Tilla all right?"

They had seen the tension between him and his wife in the prayer meeting. Now they thought they were hearing a fight.

Tilla called, "It is all right, Phyllis!" and Phyllis wished her good night.

"Nice lady," observed Squeaky. "Always good to have friendly neighbors. Perhaps she can tell us where Kleitos is."

"None of them knows. I've asked."

Squeaky was towering over him once more. He could feel the warm flesh of the other man pressing against him from the other side.

"See, Doctor, here's my problem. When you say you don't know where he is, you sound like you mean it. But when our friend Birna was here the other day you were singing a different song."

"The man with the limp?"

"It's coming back to you now, is it? You chased him off."

"We thought he was a debt collector."

"So he was," Squeaky agreed. "For a delivery that wasn't paid for."

"It's not my debt."

"You offered to send Kleitos a message for him."

"That was before I knew Kleitos had vanished."

"Your woman, see, she was a bit more clever. She said straightaway that he'd cleared off."

"I swear I don't know!" Ruso insisted, looking up at them. "Why would I hide him? Horatius Balbus wanted me to find him, but I couldn't."

"Horatius Balbus." The large head nodded. "Ah, yes. Shame about him."

It certainly was a shame. If ever Ruso had needed looking after, this was the hour. But Balbus's people were all gathered around his dead body, and Firmicus, who might have done something to help if he were summoned, was busy trying to pull together the devastated household.

"Tragic," said his companion.

Ruso sighed. "Just go. Please. I haven't said anything about you to anybody. You're upsetting my family and my neighbors and you're wasting your time."

"We'd like to," said Squeaky. "Believe me, my friend. We got better things to do. We've got two floggings to get through before bedtime."

"If I find Kleitos, I'll tell him you were asking."

The head nodded again slowly, as if he were assimilating this offer. "Meantime," he said, "somebody needs to pay what he owes us."

So in a way the story they'd wanted everyone to believe had been right all along: This was about money. The real debt collectors had arrived. Except the body hadn't been put there as a threat: the body itself was the item that had to be paid for.

"Someone needs to pay what Kleitos owes, and we think you're the man."

Ruso was silent, desperately casting about for a reason not to be the man.

"You don't want it put out that you've been . . . experimenting, do you?"

"Anything that's happened here in the past has nothing to do with me," Ruso insisted.

"I think you might have a hard time making that clear when word gets around."

"If you put out lies about me," he tried, "people are going to ask how you know."

Squeaky sighed. "There you go again with the threats, Doctor. See, when Kleitos pushed off and everything was quiet, we were prepared to be patient. We didn't mind you coming to ask about the dead man. Very commendable. But now we hear you've been threatening to talk about us to your fancy friends in high places, and we think it's only fair to have some compensation."

"I haven't been threatening anything!" Ruso insisted. "I haven't—"

"How much?" Tilla asked

Squeaky's face cracked into a smile. "You see? That, my friend, is the right question. You should listen to your wife. Six hundred sesterces."

Ruso opened his mouth to say how ridiculous that was, caught sight of his wife and baby, and closed it again.

Something was happening in the back room. There was someone—several people—moving about out there. There were voices. The undertakers stepped away from Ruso just as the kitchen door opened, and Esico said, "Visitors, master."

"We heard you had a bit of an accident, Doctor," said the carpenter, stepping into the surgery. "Some of us thought you might want a bit of help clearing up."

44

IT WAS A very polite eviction.

As soon as the big man with the child's voice saw that more and more people were crowding in from the kitchen, he began to edge away. "We were just leaving," he said, as if they had dropped in for a drink and a chat. Then he said, "Mind the glass, friends. The doctor's broken a medicine bottle."

Tilla wanted to spit in his face, but instead she pointed at the floor, still clutching Mara's soft hand in her own. "There," she said. "And in front of the bench."

The man's arm was around her husband's shoulder. "We must do this again, Doctor. Don't leave it too long, eh? We'll drop by in, say, three days?"

He said, "I'll look forward to it," and she was proud of him, because she knew he was afraid but he did not sound it.

The big man's horrible friends were already outside when the man himself turned to add, "By the way, Doctor, if you're short of cash I hear there's a vacancy with the second night watch." He bent to avoid banging his head, and was gone into the night. The door swung open again behind him, and she saw for the first time that the lock had been smashed off.

Now everyone was crowding forward and telling one another to mind the glass and fetch a broom and "What about some sawdust?" and "Are you all right, sister? Are you quite sure you're all right? Who were those men?"

"I don't know," she said, leaning back against the bench and holding Mara very close so she could feel warm baby breath on her neck. "Thank you, all. Thank you so much." Then Mara was wriggling to get free, and she could hear her husband calling, "Esico, sit down and let me take a look at that cut on your head," and "Narina, pass me that lamp" and then she heard Sabella at the door, saying her husband wanted to know what was going on here. That made Tilla laugh, because it meant Sabella herself wanted to know, and for once she was the last to find out.

"Tell her to come in," she urged Phyllis, but Sabella would not, insisting that there was no room and were all this lot the people who had been making that racket upstairs?

"They came to save us," Tilla called.

"Don't listen to them. You don't know what you're getting into."

"No, no, from—" Tilla stopped, not knowing how to describe the men. "There were three of them. They broke in. They hurt our slave." She swallowed. "They held a knife at Mara." She bent and kissed the soft little fingers she was still holding. Mara pulled them free and gave her a cheerful smack on the head.

Sabella's husband appeared at his wife's shoulder. "Now what's going on?"

"Three burglars," Sabella told him. "Beat up the slave, threatened the baby."

"Shall I call the watch?" he asked her.

"They are gone," Tilla told him. "But the door is broken."

Behind her was the tinkle of broken glass being swept up and the excited chatter of people whose hearts were still roused for action even though the danger was gone. Sabella's husband was muttering about not being able to get the lock fixed at this time of night, and tomorrow being the boss's funeral, and—

"Don't worry!" she heard Phyllis say. "Timo can patch the door up in the morning."

Tilla closed her eyes and leaned back against the wall. Whatever her husband might think of the followers of Christos, and no matter how much she herself might want to gag Sister Dorcas, the man with the child's voice had been right about one thing. It was good to have friendly neighbors.

45

RUSO ROLLED OVER, punched a lump in the mattress, and wondered how a reasonable man such as himself could have let things come to this. Now even sleep was beyond his control. The medicinal wine he had prescribed for himself on top of an empty stomach—that bastard had stolen his supper, and the bar was closed—had certainly made him drowsy, but it did nothing to answer the principal question that was keeping him awake: How could he get them all out of this mess?

Tilla's only suggestion after all the fuss had died down and everyone had gone away was, "We should go home to my people."

To which, rather than say, *It's not that simple,* he had answered, "We'll talk about it in the morning."

Then she put her hand on his arm and said with an air of quiet concern that warmed him inside, "Are you all right?"

He assured her that he was, but he was glad when she didn't believe him. Being worried about was the best thing that had happened to him all day.

"Are you sure? You look pale."

"So do you," he said, putting his own hand over hers in what he hoped was a reassuring manner. "It's been a difficult day." The last thing his wife needed to hear was that he was exhausted and angry and confused. That he felt humiliated. That he had fallen out with his patron, he didn't know what to do, and he was afraid of what might happen next. That he too wanted to run back to Britannia where they both had friends, and where her family really weren't that bad.

He did not want to tell her any of these things. What he wanted was to take her to bed and for a few brief moments, to forget he had ever been unwise enough to bring them here. He said, "I think we should all try and get some rest."

"Yes," she said, gently lifting his hand away. "I am thinking, if you are sure you are all right, perhaps Narina and Mara should come in the bedroom with me and you can be in the kitchen to guard the door."

"What?"

She cuddled Mara closer. "I keep thinking about that man with the knife."

"She's safe now," he assured her, bending to kiss the top of Mara's head and not sure whether he was doing that because he was fond of the baby, or because it seemed the easiest way to retain the attention of his wife.

So that was how they had ended up as they were now: Esico with a bandaged head, lying on a straw mattress in the surgery, secure behind a street door that had the operating table pushed up against it until Christos's carpenter could fix it tomorrow. Ruso had the mattress on the kitchen floor, guarding the back door even though it was already securely barred and he was certain that the undertakers would not be back tonight.

He had spent all that money on a baby-minder and instead of the baby being moved out of the bedroom, the baby-minder had been moved in.

A dog was barking in a nearby apartment. There was that cry again from somewhere around the courtyard: the third or fourth time since he had become aware of it. A woman giving birth. He hoped Tilla wasn't awake to be counting the gaps and wondering if she should go and see if she was needed. She would be mustering the courage to venture out in the dark, and doubtless wishing she were on a damp and windy island a long way from Rome.

She was right, of course. They should never have come here.

But leaving was not as simple as she seemed to think. Tomorrow, he would have to explain to her why a doctor could not flee the city while the death of his chief patient was under investigation. Especially when that investigation was being carried out by Metellus, who had contacts all over Britannia and access to the official postal service.

So, if leaving was not an option, he was back to the question: How to get out of this mess?

He must think logically. *First, define the problem.*

Where to start?

One: the body in the barrel. His own attempts to distance himself from whatever Kleitos and Simmias had been up to had been a spectacular misfire. It had never crossed his mind that Simmias—it must be Simmias—would go to the undertakers after what had been meant as a friendly warning. He could only assume that there was some sort of regular order for bodies that had to be canceled, and Simmias was so frightened of Squeaky that when he went to cancel it, he had trotted out some excuse about Ruso threatening to call in the authorities. So now Ruso had a bunch of professional torturers demanding six hundred sesterces in three days' time, and even with the money he was holding back to pay Xanthe for the theriac that Balbus no longer needed, he could not muster more than a hundred and thirty-five to pay them.

No wonder Kleitos had run away from these people. *Be careful who you trust* indeed! Ruso was feeling less and less kindly inclined to the little Greek and his masterly grasp of understatement with each hour that passed.

Two: Accius, his only friend in moderately high places, had been driven away by another of Ruso's attempts to offer helpful advice. He should have learned the first time.

Three: the death of Balbus. Even thinking about that medicine made him feel nauseous. Nauseous and ashamed of how desperate he was to cover up his carelessness. Balbus's tenants had been right to be suspicious: Ruso had spent much of the afternoon trying to find a way to blame them for their landlord's death.

Meanwhile Accius, instead of abandoning his misguided attempt to chase Cossus away from Horatia, had now put Metellus in sole charge of it. If Cossus were to retaliate by making his own enquiries, someone would surely ask why a doctor who admitted to knowing very little about poisons had been mixing up something that he had apparently presented to his patient as theriac. *And if it wasn't theriac, Doctor, then what exactly was it?*

If only he had thought to keep some of the mixture back instead of filling the bottle. The only sample must be somewhere in Balbus's house. It was hard to see how he could get hold of it without arousing suspicion. Anyway, what would he do with it? Tip it down the nearest drain? Replace it with something definitely safe, in case anyone asked? Ask Xanthe what she thought of it? No: She might talk. The only way to find out in secret was to drink it and see what happened.

Ruso squeezed his eyes tight shut and tried to silence the echoes of Xanthe's dramatic warnings, but telling himself that he very probably hadn't poisoned his chief patient did not provide a great deal of comfort in the lonely dark of the kitchen.

The patient trusted you, Doctor. And where is the patient now?

Dead, sir.

The woman cried out again.

Everything depended on finding Kleitos. Kleitos could reassure him that what was in that pot was simply normal-strength poppy. Kleitos could sell some of the possessions he'd taken away with him on that vegetable cart and pay off the undertakers for their unwanted and illegal delivery.

Christos had already been roped in to join the hunt. Perhaps they should try a wider appeal for divine help. It could do no harm. He had met people who were sure they had been healed after presenting some god with a clay replica of the affected part of the body. The priests in the temple over on Tiber Island asked the patients to do little more than lie down and sleep and think good thoughts, and their eager scribblings on the walls testified to the cures that had come to them in dreams.

He turned to face the little shrine on the wall where Tilla had put the oak leaves and the little horse and the statue of Mercury. "The gods who lived here before you," he whispered to the dark, "where has Kleitos taken them?" But the oak leaves and little horse and the statue of Mercury remained stubbornly silent: only the woman cried out.

Why was he even thinking like this? It was insane. The gods

were the invention of storytellers: the product of collective imag-
inings that only existed because people agreed to believe in them.

He yawned, punched the wretched lump in the mattress again,
and had just closed his eyes when he heard Esico moving about in
the surgery. Moments later the door was pushed open and someone
was shuffling across the kitchen, feeling his way around the
furniture.

Ruso spoke in British. "How's the head, Esico?"

The slave gasped in fright and crashed into something.

"Sorry."

"The head hurts, master. And now my foot."

"Do you feel sick? See flashing lights or seeing double?"

"No, master."

He heard the rustle of the curtain being pushed back and a sigh
as Esico sat on the pot. The slave had not had the best of evenings,
either. His new family's home had come under threat for the second
time in two days, and in trying to defend it he had practically been
knocked senseless. He had managed to blunder out into the courtyard and tried to explain to a passing neighbor but it was not until
Narina arrived to translate that help had been summoned.

"You see," Tilla had observed, tucking in the knot on the
bandage around Esico's freshly stitched forehead, "It is good to
have slaves who speak the same tongue."

The curtain was pulled back into place. Esico said into the darkness, "Will you sell me, master?"

"Why do you ask?"

"Narina says those men want money."

Ruso was not proud of imagining a torrent of coins rolling
toward him in exchange for a loyal and healthy slave who was
bound to get a grip on Latin before long. "Go back to bed, Esico."

Esico shuffled out. The woman shrieked.

Ruso lay down, closed his eyes, and put his fingers in his ears. If
the boy had to go, he deserved to go to a good home. That was
what any decent man did when disposing of loyal members of his
household. But the trouble was, Esico would be sold only if things
were desperate, and that very desperation might mean he had to go
to whoever would pay. Once that happened, his former owners
would have no more control over how he was treated than they
would if they had sold a dog.

He needed to find Kleitos. He needed reassurance and information and he needed hard cash.

It was impossible to get comfortable with his fingers in his ears. As he removed them he heard a bloodcurdling scream. Then a silence, followed by the scratchy and irritable wail of a new soul forced out to cope in a messy world.

46

EVERYONE WAS UP early. Narina was making proper porridge with milk. Esico's head was still sore and the first shadows of a black eye were showing, but he seemed keen to work. He even took on a woman's job, going out to the fountain for water.

While the slaves were busy Tilla joined her husband in the surgery. As she had feared, he refused to think about going back to Britannia. He looked so tired that she decided to leave that argument for later, but as she told him, if they were to stay, they needed a plan. Or six hundred sesterces. Or some way of earning in two days what an ordinary person might hope to earn in many months.

"As rich men say," he told her, "it's only money. Careful!" He reached out to hold her back, then crouched to pick up a tiny sliver of glass and wipe it off his finger into the bucket.

"If we do not leave today," she said, "we must find Kleitos, or some new patients who are very rich, and you must go to Accius."

"I don't want to involve Accius."

"But you must! He needs to know. Someone is threatening his man. It is an insult to him."

"I'm not sure I am his man anymore. Besides, I can't go today. It's the funeral."

She had forgotten the funeral. She needed to find something dark to wrap around Mara, and she must remember to take the gray cloak and her own night blue tunic out of the trunk and hang them to get rid of the creases. She would tell the slaves to stand on either side of them. The household needed to look respectful for her husband's sake, even if the dead man had allowed people to live in homes overrun with cockroaches.

"You can see him tomorrow, then," she said. "He must be able to do something. Can he not talk to somebody?"

"It was talking to people that got us into this." He lowered his voice. "I can't explain why Squeaky wants money without telling Accius what was going on here, and once he knows, he's implicated in covering it up. I'm supposed to help his career, not drag him into scandal."

"Tell him something else. Tell him you need money because one of our slaves ran away and—wait!"

For a moment he looked hopeful. Then when she told him her idea, and he explained why it would not work, she felt foolish. Of course the dealer's famous six-month money-back guarantee was only a promise that the slave was *as described*. You could not complain when someone who bore the label *runaway* ran away. "Tell Accius one of them died and we need to buy another one," she suggested. "He is a rich man with a big house—he will hardly notice it."

"He's not as rich as you imagine. And I already owe him for the slaves we still have."

She swallowed. It was her fault, so she should be the first to say it. "If you want to sell them . . ."

"I don't. Yet."

"I will tell everyone I am taking on patients now we have Narina. And you could earn some money with the night watch. Those men said there was a job."

"They know that because it was one of the watch's doctors who brought them down on us. Besides, I'm not leaving you here overnight."

She wanted to shout, *Then what* are *you going to do?* but as the words formed in her mind she heard an echo of them in her mother's voice. "This is what bullies do," she said, remembering the raised voices around the fire night after night while she and her brothers were supposed to be sleeping. "This is what my people did when the Legions came. Nobody knew what to do." And then, something she had never spoken aloud before. "It was not the soldiers who broke us," she said. "It was we ourselves with our quarreling."

"We're not quarreling. We're having a discussion."

"No," she told him, even more annoyed now. "I am having ideas and you are saying no to them. You have been like this ever since that patient died, and he was not a nice man anyway. I am going to stop talking to you until you have an idea of your own."

She leaned back against the workbench and folded her arms. He did the same. She wondered if he had thought about the box of soldiers' kit under the bed: the valuable kit that he would need if they were to go back to Britannia. Soldiers always needed doctors. If Accius could get him out of the Legion, Accius could surely get him back in. She knew she could suggest selling it, and she knew she was not going to. Not yet.

Nor, it seemed, was he. "We're talking as if they're coming back this morning. We still have two days. We could ask Metellus."

"Metellus? Husband, are you losing your mind?"

"Possibly," he said. "But if anyone can find Kleitos, he can."

She took a deep breath. "I am sorry," she said. "I thought you meant you would ask Metellus for money."

"Mm. We could try that too if Kleitos won't pay up."

"Tell me you are teasing me."

He shrugged. "You complain when I turn down all your ideas."

"Perhaps the men will come back today to fetch Kleitos's things," she said, trying to find something hopeful to say. "Then we will find him and he can sort everything out and we will have no need to do anything."

"Perhaps."

It was as near an apology as she was going to get. She reached up to flatten a spike of hair that was sticking out above his ear. "You must comb this before you see anyone. You look like a man who has slept with his head on upside down. Did I tell you what Narina said about the followers of Christos?"

This time he made the effort to grasp her peace offering. "Tell me."

"She said, 'If he is a powerful god, why does he put up with that Sister Dorcas?'"

The smile was not broad, but it was there. And that was when he told her the other thing that was worrying him: how Accius had fallen out with him because Ruso was refusing to help prove that Curtius Cossus the builder was a murderer.

She was saying, "He wanted you to prove *what*? What is the matter with him?" when they both heard the scrape of boots on stone very close by. Then something scratching at the door, as if someone were trying to work out a way of getting in.

She put her hand on his arm. He nodded, and she ran to the kitchen to warn Narina, who grabbed a cloth and moved the porridge pan off the heat. The one thing they had all agreed on this morning was a plan. If there was danger, Narina would snatch up the baby and run—in the daytime, to the baths, where there would be plenty of people. At night, she would try to get up the steps to Phyllis, or knock on any door where there was a light showing, or . . . The nighttime plan needed more thought. But not right now, because her husband called through to say it was only Timotheus measuring up the door. Cossus had told all his workers to take the morning off and line the streets for Horatius Balbus's funeral procession.

Out in the courtyard, Tilla took a great lungful of the nearest thing this city had to fresh air, and told her heart to slow down again.

She hoped her husband had remembered what he was supposed to say. With Timo standing there, it was the ideal chance to work the conversation around to family life and babies. Slipping back inside to listen, she heard him thanking Timo for everyone's help last night— but as far as she could tell, the chance to say how precious Mara was went by unused. Timo said he hoped those men wouldn't be back, and her husband agreed, and then there was a silence.

"Two six," said Timo. There was a pause, then, "Six four." When she looked, he was holding a wooden rule up against the door. "Top, three and a quarter inches." He clamped the rule between his teeth and the little slave boy beside him held out a tablet and stylus so he could write the numbers down.

Her husband went back to work, sorting through the jumble of documents in the box under the workbench.

"Done," said Timo, handing the rule back to the boy, who knelt to put it in the battered leather tool bag. "If I can get that sawn this afternoon, I'll do it tonight."

Her husband said it was very good of him, and Timo grunted that the wife had told him to do it. No, he didn't need money in advance for the timber.

"We'll pay you when it's sorted, then. Thanks."

At this rate the ideal moment would be wasted. And so would the chance to repeat the other story that needed to be passed on to the neighbors at every opportunity. Tilla stepped forward, greeted Timo, and said, "You and Phyllis have been very kind. We are so sorry that Kleitos's debts have caused so much trouble. If we had known what a bother it would all be for everyone, we would never have come here."

Timo seemed just as surprised as everyone else had been at the news that Kleitos had debt problems. Tilla could hear the disbelief in his tone. She supposed this was how it was going to be, even with people she had begun to look on as friends. Everybody would think they had brought trouble to this place themselves, and now they were trying to blame somebody else.

"I have work to do," she told him, retreating toward the kitchen. "But if there is anything we can do to help you in return, you must say so. And please tell Phyllis you are both welcome here at any time."

Her interruption had made the men talk to each other, but not in the way she had hoped. As she retreated she heard Timo telling her husband he was sorry if they had troubles, but he had told Phyllis she was to stay away from here in the future. "I can't have my wife near men like that," he said. "Not with her on her own and me out at work all day."

With one ear pressed up against the crack in the door she heard her husband say, "Of course not," and "Absolutely," and "We're very grateful to you," because there was nothing else he could say, and then Timo went through his reasons all over again, perhaps because he was embarrassed or perhaps because he was enjoying being seen protecting his wife. So there was some more "Absolutely" and "Yes, I understand," and now instead of willing their visitor to stay, she was willing him to go.

At last he seemed about to leave, when she heard her own husband say, "While you're here, I'm sure there was something I had to say to you."

"It was nothing!" she called, hurrying out to join him and hooking one arm through his. The whole point of telling Timo how happy they were with their adopted daughter was that her husband had to slip it in casually and pretend that it was his own idea. That nobody had asked him to say it and certainly no one—least of all Phyllis—had ever mentioned the barrenness of Timo's marriage. "Husband, our neighbor is a busy man. He does not want to spend all morning here talking to you."

But instead of agreeing he said, "Ah, I've got it!" and turned back to the carpenter.

She tightened her arm around his. "There is a funeral procession to dress for, husband!"

"Sawdust," he said. "Could you let us have a sack for sweeping up? We've run out."

"Sawdust," repeated Timo, bending to pick up his toolbag. Then, as if he too had remembered something, "The wife said to ask you about Paullus. A good friend of yours, is he?"

"Paullus?" Her husband shook his head. "I don't know him."

"She saw you in the gardens with him yesterday."

Metellus, the man who could look like no one and anyone. And no better to have around than the undertakers. Tilla said, "She is mistaken. That was a man we know from Britannia."

"That's him, then," said Timotheus. "Clerk in the urban prefect's office?"

Her husband said, "Something like that."

"That's the one," said Timo. "Metellus Paullus. Next time he's around, tell him to drop in. We haven't seen him for a while."

Tilla could not believe it. "Metellus is a friend of yours?"

Timo glanced sideways at the steps to his apartment, as if he was wishing he had not started this. "Sort of."

"Surely he is not a follower of Christos?"

Timo sniffed and rubbed his nose with his free hand. "Don't say anything. It might not go well for him at work. But he's on our side."

"We will keep it quiet," Tilla promised. Not because she wanted to save Metellus from embarrassment at the prefect's office, but because she was certain he was never on anyone's side but his own.

47

THE FIRST PATIENT of the day arrived at the back door. Tilla was surprised to see the girl from upstairs, now no longer pregnant but carrying a very small and angry baby and a water jug.

"Oh, what a clever girl you are! Let me see!"

The girl was on the verge of tears. "It won't feed," she said, waving the water jug in frustration. "And Ma says I've got to get rid of it."

Remarking that it sounded healthy enough, Tilla fetched a chair into the surgery and gestured to her husband and Esico to get out of the way. The girl sank gratefully onto the cushion.

"Why did you not call me when you were in labor?"

"Ma said she could manage."

Assuring her she had done very well, Tilla checked the baby, who was a boy, and congratulated the mother again. Somebody had to. She bit back a question about the name: If a child was not to be kept, it was best not to think of one. "I'd have come if I'd known."

"I thought I was going to die," the girl told her. "I was hoping you would hear me."

"I am sorry to have missed it." Tilla wrapped the protesting baby in a blanket while she examined the mother.

"Ma said I wasn't to come here," the girl told the ceiling. "She says you'll take it away and give it to the followers of Christos."

Since the grandmother wanted to get rid of the baby anyway, this did not seem to make much sense. "You have done very well indeed," Tilla said, changing the girl's cloth for a clean one. "You and your ma. You can sit up now, and I will help you feed him."

With the baby finally settled at the breast, the girl visibly relaxed. "I was thinking," she said, "if it stops crying, somebody might want it."

It was one of those moments when it was best to say nothing, because it was not fair to raise false hopes.

"At least it's a boy. People want boys, don't they? Perhaps somebody might buy him to bring up."

There was no point in telling her this was unlikely: no doubt her own mother would be quick to inform her that households who wanted newborn slaves usually bred their own. At least that way you knew what you were getting.

"I just don't want him to go to no followers of Christos."

"Why is that?"

"They meet in secret and kill babies and eat them, Ma says."

"Your ma has been misinformed," said Tilla, because that sounded better than *Your ma is an ignorant gossip.* "And I would never do anything with your baby if you didn't want me to." *So you can tell her that from me.*

The girl did not stay long: She had only slipped out with the excuse of fetching water. Tilla watched her go, heavyhearted.

48

A RICH MAN'S FUNERAL procession was a fine excuse to abandon work, and there were already plenty of people lining the street by the time Ruso and his household went out to join their neighbors on the Vicus Sabuci. The tables at Sabella's were packed and many of those standing on the pavement were clutching drinks. Timo and Phyllis must have got there early: They had places at the front. Ruso noticed that Tilla made no attempt to approach them. She must have overheard the carpenter's complaints about the company they kept.

He was glad she had not seen the anonymous sliver of wood Esico had found pushed under the surgery door just after dawn. He had slipped it into the kitchen fire before she could read the simple message scratched across the grain: GO HOME.

"It's a good turnout," observed a spectator somewhere to his left.

"Come to make sure he's really dead," said somebody else.

There followed a frank exchange about Horatius Balbus's shortcomings as a landlord, ending with the glum reflection that at least they knew what to expect with the old man, whereas with the girl . . .

"She won't be in charge. They reckon it'll be Curtius Cossus."

"Who?"

"The one who's building the emperor's new temple down the hill."

"No? Well! I'll have a mosaic in the dining room and columns 'round the front door, then."

The conversation became a debate on what pictures the tenants would like painted around the cracks in their wall plaster and how much rents might rise as a consequence, all of which kept Ruso moderately entertained until he heard the distant blare of horns and trumpets. All heads were turned in the direction of the baths. A couple of black-clad slaves appeared first, herding the onlookers back onto the pavement. Then came the musicians. The lighter notes of the flutes were audible now, and the sound of wailing. As the procession rounded the corner three wild-haired women appeared, flinging their hands in the air and beating themselves on the chest in a dramatic and professional show of grief. Just as Ruso recognized one of them as the woman from the undertaker's yard, another let out a particularly bloodcurdling howl. It frightened Mara so much that Narina had to take her away to recover.

Standing on tiptoe to see over the people in front, Tilla said, "That is the man who came to the house!"

"Firmicus," Ruso agreed over the din. "Balbus's steward. He must have been freed in the will." Glancing along the line of oddly matched pallbearers, he saw several more wearing the caps of newly freed slaves. "Some of the other household staff have been freed too."

"Not the one with the eyebrows," she corrected him. "The one waving the incense thing."

Some other man who had come to the house? Squeaky was nowhere in sight. Hopes raised, he stood on tiptoe, and leaned sideways to peer over the shoulder of the man in front. To his disappointment the figure swinging the incense was not the auctioneer who might give them a link to Doctor Kleitos, but Birna, the skinny man with the limp who had come to collect payment for the barrel. Ruso shifted one elbow to dig into his wife's ribs. The last thing they needed was any further association in the neighbors' minds between themselves and the undertakers.

Behind them someone was telling her friend that this bier was not as smart as the senator's last week. "His had ivory panels and brass handles."

Tilla said, "Do they have a long walk to the cremation?"

He said, "I suppose so." It must be a good way outside the city gates.

"Good," she said in British, raising her fist at Birna. "May your foot hurt every step of the way, you wicked, slimy . . ."

He was not sure what the last word meant, but doubtless it was graphic. Fortunately she had had the sense to stay in her native tongue for the curse. Glancing at the fist, he saw the head of the little wooden horse poking out between her finger and thumb, lending power to the words. If the followers of Christos ever decided to expand into Britannia, they were going to find it an interesting challenge.

"Gently, wife," he murmured.

Mercifully Tilla's attention was drawn to another part of the procession. "Is that the daughter? Next to the man with the skull face?"

"Horatia," he agreed.

"She looks lost. Has she no mother to walk with her?"

"Died years ago, love," put in someone behind them.

Horatia was drifting along as if she were in a trance. He guessed the man at her elbow must be the butcher cousin from out of town who would now become her guardian. The face beneath the hood reminded him of those macabre pictures of skeletons that people sometimes had installed in their dining rooms—allegedly to urge their guests to eat, drink, and make the most of the time that Fate had allotted to them.

Tilla hissed in his ear, "Tell me who they all are!"

"Only if you promise not to curse them."

"Not all of them."

"The older man on the opposite side of the street from Accius is Curtius Cossus, the builder."

"The one who wants to marry Horatia?" Tilla put a hand on his shoulder for balance as she stood on tiptoe. He was ready to interrupt, but to his relief she said nothing about Accius's foolhardy plans to thwart Cossus with a murder charge.

"Are you sure?" she said. "He could be her grandfather!"

"Marry him quick, love!" called the woman in front. "Tell him I want the roof fixed!"

Accius and Cossus had been tactfully positioned an equal distance behind Horatia. Each of them, he noted, had draped himself in black and covered his head as if he were already the son of the deceased.

"What she ought to do," speculated one of their neighbors, "is marry the builder first and save the handsome one for later."

"If she don't want the handsome one, I'll have him."

"You wouldn't have him long. She'd finish the old boy off within the year. Oh look—whats-his-name from the council! The one whose wife ran off with the gladiator."

The councillors were of little interest to Tilla, but the household staff were a different matter. "So many servants for one man! What do they all do?"

Ruso had no idea what anyone would do with forty-three domestic slaves. "The one in the second row with the walking stick is the doorman," he told her, scanning the group of black-clad slaves in search of Latro the bodyguard, but failing to find him. "The rest are—I don't know." The round-faced girl he had seen carrying linen in the courtyard was sobbing uncontrollably, leaning on the small woman who had tried to stop him from talking to Horatia at their first meeting.

There was a figure wandering along behind the household staff. One hand was clutching a scroll and the other was attempting to control the wayward drapery of a murky-colored toga that might once have been black. Tubero the Younger seemed to be looking for someone in the crowd. When he spotted Ruso the poet waved the scroll in an inappropriately jaunty manner, mouthed something, and then waved it again to make sure his meaning was clear. Evidently his expansion into the funeral oration market was proving a success. Ruso was even happier than before that he would not have to listen to the speeches around the pyre.

"I said," Tilla repeated, "Who is the pregnant one?"

He frowned. "Is one of them pregnant?"

"The very weepy one holding the short woman's arm. Did you not notice?"

"I wasn't looking," he told her, scanning the crowd for Metellus. He couldn't see him, but it was a long route and he could be anywhere. Probably hanging around Curtius Cossus's people, listening for incriminating gossip.

That had been an odd conversation with the carpenter. Metellus, a follower of Christos? They would be claiming the emperor himself next.

The domestic staff were followed by a shambling collection of men whose attempts to stay in line would have made a centurion weep. These must be Balbus's caretakers: He spotted not only Sabella's husband and the seducer from the block where the toy seller lived, but the man who had tried to convince them that their cockroach problem was nothing to worry about. Fortunately Tilla's attention was elsewhere. Two cursings in one morning would not impress the neighbors.

Finally a couple of grinning boys who had decided to strut along behind the procession in exaggerated military step were sent packing by the undertaker's slaves, and the crowd began to disperse. Tilla went inside to see how Mara had recovered from the mourners.

Ruso was about to follow her when a heavy hand landed on his shoulder. "So sorry to hear about Balbus, dear boy. Terrible shock."

Ruso's mouth offered "Yes," while his mind was searching for reasons why this man might dare to approach him.

"I was thinking of having a spot of lunch," Simmias continued. "Would you care to join me?"

49

PRESSING A HAND into the small of Ruso's back, Simmias attempted to steer him toward the only empty table at Sabella's. Ruso stood his ground. "You can buy something here and eat across the road in the gardens," he said. The only conversation he wanted to have with Simmias was not one he wanted anybody else to hear.

The bar was still busy, and it seemed everyone else was going to get served before them. When Sabella finally acknowledged Ruso's presence it was with "You. My husband wants a word with you."

"I'll be around later," he promised, leaving Simmias to hand over the cash for a couple of pastries. As they made their way across the street toward the gardens of Livia, Simmias said, "The service in that place is getting worse."

Ruso could not bring himself to reply.

"I expect you're wondering why I'm here."

They paused to allow a group of weather-beaten and muscular men to swarm down the steps, laughing and joking with each other. Evidently some of Cossus's builders had decided to make the most of their morning off. "I was hoping," Simmias said, "you might reconsider joining us over at the night watch. We really could use a man with your experience."

Again Ruso said nothing.

"We take turns on night duty. One in four." Only half a dozen steps up, and already the man's speech was reduced to short phrases with a pause for breath between each one. "I covered for . . . Kleitos last night. I was very much hoping . . . perhaps tonight . . ."

They stepped through the gateway and turned right under the same shaded colonnade that he had paced yesterday with Metellus.

Ruso said, "Tonight?"

"Short notice. Yes . . . of course. Sorry." Simmias glanced down at the food in his hand as if assessing whether he was prepared to risk asphyxiation for another mouthful of lunch. He held the other pastry out to Ruso, who declined the offer.

"Tomorrow, perhaps. I'm sure you'd find the work . . . interesting. It's not all burns and . . . smoke inhalation. We get injuries from falling . . . debris, men coming off ladders . . . that sort of thing. And some street fights." Simmias succumbed to the pastry and fell silent.

Ruso glanced across at the maintenance slaves raking the gravel. Despite his lack of response, Simmias seemed determined not to give up. "It's a good position, dear boy. Salaried. Obviously the men don't pay personally for treatment, so . . . that's one less thing to bother about." He was saying something about supplies. "Anything you ask for . . . never any quibbling."

Any minute now the man would be on his knees begging. Ruso wished he would either admit what he had done and apologize for it, or shut up. Unable to stand it any longer, he said, "I had a visit from your friends last night."

"My friends?"

"Well they certainly weren't mine."

"I'm afraid I don't quite know what you—"

"What did you think they would do?" Ruso demanded, coming to a halt. "Offer me a cut of the business?"

"Friends? Business? My dear boy—"

"What harm have I ever done to you?"

"None!" Simmias tried to back away and collided with a pillar. "I'm offering you work!"

Ruso grabbed the front of his tunic. "I came to you in good faith," he hissed. "I didn't like what you and Kleitos were doing. I didn't want to be involved with it, and I said so. To your face.

Then I went away and kept quiet. And that's where it should have ended."

"It did!"

Ruso pushed harder. "What did you say to them about me?"

He was aware of a woman hurrying toward them, calling her children away from him. Of someone shouting, "Are you all right there, sir?"

"What did you say? Who did you tell them I'd report them to? Did you drag my patron into this as well?"

Simmias's double chin wobbled as he gulped. Ruso saw genuine fear in his eyes and, at that moment, saw himself as the other man must see him. An angry, violent ex-soldier seeking revenge. As the woman must see him: a threat to her children. As the slaves striding toward them brandishing their rakes must see him: a bully threatening a weaker man in the peace of a public garden.

He stepped back and took a long, deep breath. Simmias was leaning against the pillar, his chest heaving and his head sagging. For a few dreadful moments Ruso thought his heart might be failing. Then he realized the man was sizing up the pastry he had dropped onto the paving stones.

"I'm sorry," he said. "I shouldn't have done that."

The slaves had stationed themselves on either side of Simmias now. "Are you all right, sir?"

He nodded. "Quite all right. Thank you. Yes. Quite all right."

While one of them was asking if he was sure, the other was eyeing Ruso as if daring him to try that again.

"Very good of you both to be concerned." Simmias wiped his fingers on his tunic. Then he reached into his purse, and the slaves went away happy. But not, Ruso noted, very far away.

"They broke in and attacked my slave," he said quietly. "They frightened my wife and they threatened our baby with a knife."

Simmias's eyes widened. "Dear boy! I had no idea. Truly. Do you mind if we sit down?"

Ruso would have been more convinced of Simmias's innocence if he had needed to explain who "they" were. Now, seated at the opposite end of a stone bench from a visibly flustered colleague, he watched a couple of sparrows flitting around the vine leaves for a moment before he said, "What did you say to them?"

Simmias was fiddling with the drawstring on his purse. "This is about, ah—"

"Of course it's about *ah*. What else would it be about?"

"I did say to my contact that I'd like to suspend our arrangement for a while. Perhaps for good. But believe me, I never mentioned your name."

"You didn't need to."

"I never said anything about reporting them to anybody. Why would I do that? Whoever I went to would ask how I knew!"

"You said I was going to report them, not you."

"No! Never. Someone's lying to you."

"Perhaps it's you."

"To be honest, Doctor, after our last discussion . . ." Simmias scratched his head. "I found what you said very upsetting. I've been uncomfortable about the—ah, the origins, so to speak, for a long time. But the suppliers had promised us that their source was above reproach."

"And you believed them?"

"Kleitos was so very keen, you see. Eager to learn."

It's not my fault. Another boy made me do it and then he ran away.

"He kept saying, 'There's so much we could do if we knew more.' It's true, isn't it? You must agree. You've seen the ignorance on display yourself. It's the patients who suffer."

The sparrows had come down from the vine now and were making cautious hops in the direction of the ruined pastry.

"And even the best of us . . . Take Aristotle's claim that the right kidney is always higher than the left. Well perhaps in animals, but did you know that in humans—"

"It's too high a price to pay for knowledge."

Simmias sighed. "The suppliers took the subjects away and had them respectfully cremated afterward, you know. I specifically asked for reassurances."

Ruso said, "That's what they told you?" When he looked up, Simmias was staring in the direction of the sparrows, but his gaze was not following them.

"In two days' time," Ruso told him, "your suppliers will be calling on me to collect what Kleitos owes them."

"Kleitos owes them money?" Simmias's head lifted. "Oh, dear. I do wish you hadn't managed to annoy them, dear boy."

"I just wanted them to stop!"

"I'm sure you thought you were being helpful getting involved, but you need to understand how things are done around here. This business about money is totally unexpected."

"You must have known there was cash changing hands."

"Well, of course, but Kleitos dealt with all that."

"And he let you join in his explorations out of generosity?"

Simmias cleared his throat. "I made a contribution."

"Make a contribution now," Ruso suggested. "Any part of six hundred sesterces will be very welcome."

"Dear gods! It was never that much!"

"They didn't seem open to negotiation."

"I have very meager savings."

"I have none at all," Ruso told him. "And it's not my debt. Kleitos is your friend. When he turns up you can ask for it back."

"But I don't know where he is!"

"Neither do I," Ruso agreed. "But if I haven't got either Kleitos or the money by the time your suppliers come back, I'm going to send them over to you." He got to his feet, causing the sparrows to flutter up in alarm. "So now we both need to find him."

50

W HILE HER HUSBAND was out somewhere with the fat doctor they had met at the slave market, Tilla considered asking Esico to throw out all the remaining medicines left by Kleitos. Then she decided it would be wise to leave something useless for Squeaky and his friends to destroy. So instead she sent her bandaged and black-eyed slave to refill all the lamps while she sat at the work-bench and finished rolling myrrh-and-pepper pills to treat coughs.

Having slaves made work for the owners too. She was wondering what job to give Esico next when a figure she remembered only too well appeared and announced that he had come to talk to the doctor.

"The doctor is out."

The caretaker from the cockroach-riddled apartments leaned in and displayed his scummy teeth. "Nice to see you again, miss. Perhaps you can help instead."

She tipped the finished pills into a box before answering. "I mostly help women. Are you suffering from something a woman might have?"

"Ah, it's not for me. My friends here want to value some items from the last tenant, so I thought I'd pop along to say hello."

The two men had come back to fetch Kleitos's things! Her prayers were answered. "Should you not be at Horatius Balbus's funeral?"

"Family only at the cremation, miss."

"There is not room for everyone in here," she told him. "You can wait outside."

Two others trooped in. She recognized the porter with the stylus tucked behind one ear, and the youth whose gaze seemed to be moving between his boss and Esico, as if he were deciding which of them to back if it should come to a fight.

Esico, meanwhile, was clutching the oil jar like a weapon and warning her in British that he did not like the look of these men.

"I know," she told him, wishing she had sent him out earlier to buy a new broomstick. "But they might know something we need to find out."

The trouble with going to ask the other auctioneer for help, she now saw, was that anyone who heard the story could turn up in the hope of being paid for nothing. Already the porter was taking in all the contents of the room with the eye of a man who knew exactly what he could sell them for.

"Many of these things are ours," she told him, moving between him and the case containing her husband's surgical instruments: by far the most valuable thing in the room. "And some of the medicines the other doctor left are worthless." No sooner were the words spoken than she was struck by the fear that he might repeat what she had said to someone who would then ask if her husband had ever used any of them.

That wretched secret. It kept spreading like a crack under the floor, undermining every thought.

The porter suggested politely that she should just take him through the apartment and show him what he had to value.

"We may want to buy the things ourselves," she told him. "But you will have to talk to my husband about a price. He might want someone else to confirm what you say."

"Very wise, miss," put in the caretaker, who was blocking the doorway. "You tell the doctor to do that. He won't get a better deal, what with the discount the boys'll give him for being a customer already. And with what the other lot'll charge for the valuation. But you tell him to go ahead."

"You need to move," she told him. "You are making it dark in here."

He stepped aside, running his fingers over the broken lock. "Had a bit of trouble here, have you, Blondie?"

She turned to the porter. "I will need someone to confirm that you have the doctor's permission to sell his things."

The porter agreed. You couldn't be too careful these days. Especially when you were new in town. "You'd be amazed what goes on, miss," he assured her, as if he were proud of it. "Full of crooks, this city." He pulled out the writing tablet that was tucked into his belt and groped behind his ear for the stylus. "Do you want me to start in here or somewhere else?"

She did not want him to start at all, but if she told him that, he might go away and not come back, and there was a chance he really might be able to lead them to Kleitos. "I need to tell my housekeeper." She picked up the case and handed it to Esico, saying in her own tongue, "Put that a long way in under the bed, and tell Narina there will be Romans looking through the rooms. Then come straight back."

As Esico went, the porter was giving orders to the youth. "Stand there," he said. "No touching, no talking. Like I told you. Respect for the customer." To Tilla he said, "Sorry, miss. He's got to learn. Only bought him last month."

In another time and place and in different company, Tilla might have said she too had new slaves to train, and that would have been an interesting thing to talk about. But it was bad enough having these men sniffing around her home. She was not going to tell them anything more than they could see for themselves.

The caretaker was still peering in and the porter was lolling against the table in a pose that did not show any respect for the customer at all. He patted the surface with one hand. "This table, miss?"

Tilla clutched a fistful of skirt. "Perhaps I should not be doing this without my husband here."

"You don't have to worry about the boys, Blondie," offered the caretaker from the doorway. He gestured toward the porter. "I know he's an ugly sight, but he managed your things all right, didn't he? Was anything broken?"

"No," she admitted, clutching the skirt tighter.

"There's a good girl," said the porter. "We'll start with the easy ones, like. My lads didn't bring the table, so I'll put that down as belonging to Kleitos."

"Oh, dear!" Tilla put her other hand on the table as if to hold it down. "I don't want to make a fuss, but my husband has gone out to see his patients and he will be so cross if I do this without his permission."

"Don't you worry, miss. We'll talk to him when we come back for the money."

"If you could just tell me where the other doctor went, then perhaps I could send one of our slaves to him with a message to check that this is all right."

"The other doctor?"

"Then as soon as the message comes back you can get on with your work. I don't want to cause you any bother, but I think I should take your advice and be careful." She twisted the handful of skirt. "We haven't been in Rome very long and I'm all on my own here with the slaves."

The porter let out a sigh that said she was, indeed, making a fuss.

From the doorway, the caretaker offered, "His boss didn't like it much when you sent the other lads away, miss. They got into a lot of trouble."

"Oh, dear!" Tilla looked wildly around the surgery, as if she was hoping for some sort of answer to appear. "I don't know what to do. My husband was cross about that too, but now you tell me Rome is full of crooks and I should be careful."

"Lucky you've got us, miss," said the porter.

From the doorway: "You know us."

"Yes. Yes, you're being very patient."

This whiny-woman behavior was surprisingly easy: You just had to look cowed and say no by pretending to be too frightened to say yes. Then unless the people asking you to do something were very stupid, they would realize that the harder they pushed, the more stubborn your no would become.

"I'm sure you understand why I just need to make sure," she said. "There is a saying amongst my people in Britannia, *No man minds being proved honest.*"

The porter gave a sickly smile. "You send your message if you like, miss. But I'm not sure the doctor's going to be there in the afternoon, not with day being as night over there, like."

So Doctor Kleitos was nearby after all! It was that easy! "I don't like to make you wait," she said, trying to keep the eagerness out of her voice. "Perhaps if you tell me where to send the message, and then when my husband is home to talk to you we will send our slave to fetch you. I will ask my husband to have plenty of money ready and you can do everything with one visit this afternoon." She looked the porter in the eye, gave him her best smile, and held his gaze until the stylus went up behind his ear again.

"He's over at the second night watch station on the Via Labicana," he said.

"Doctor Kleitos is with the night watch?"

"No, miss," he said, explaining as if he were talking to a child. "Doctor Kleitos is the one who's gone away. Doctor Simmias is looking after his things for him. We've been sent by Doctor Simmias."

51

THE EDGES OF the glass glinted in the lamp that lit the gloom behind the curtain. Ruso's hand brushed against one of the chicken feet as he took the empty bottle from Xanthe.

"That one would not be my choice," she told him, gesturing at the residue of Balbus's original theriac. "There are better recipes. But it is the work of a man whom many people trust."

Feeling his stomach sink, he stashed the bottle in Kleitos's old satchel. "So a person taking it might still be vulnerable?"

"I could sell you something much better," she told him, now groping behind her and placing a full bottle on the table. "But since your patient is dead, and I have bought this nonsense for you specially and cannot sell it to anybody else, that will be one hundred sesterces."

Desperation told him to grab that stringy throat and demand to know whether this stuff really did work or whether he might have poisoned Balbus. Cowardice wanted him to run away with his hands clamped over his head in terror. Reason reminded him that she was bound to disparage a competitor's product. He said, "That's more than the patient usually pays."

"Then I have been swindled," she told him. "That is what I gave for it."

She was probably lying about the price she had paid. If he bought it, he would be seriously out of pocket. If he didn't, he would be making an enemy of a supplier.

He paid. He was already in trouble with a professional torturer: He did not want to upset a poisons expert as well. Now he only had thirty-five sesterces to fend off Squeaky.

When she said, "You can always sell it to someone else," he pretended not to hear. The last thing he would give any patient now was a medicine full of ingredients that his supplier refused to vouch for.

Instead of going straight back home, he tramped across to the Praetorian guard camp outside the city walls and had a conversation with a watch captain and an armorer that made him feel homesick for the Legion. Then, since he was passing that way, he called in at the tenement block to see if the old man with the cough was still alive.

Ruso was surprised to leave the apartment greatly cheered. He was, apparently, a marvelous doctor. Not because he had offered any relief to the family or done anything useful to ease his patient's suffering—he had not, and the old man was unlikely to last beyond the night—but because he had bothered to turn up and shown some interest.

The irony was compounded by the concern of the old man's son, who followed him into the hallway to tell him he wasn't looking too good himself, and he ought to take it easy. "I bet you'll be glad when Doctor Kleitos is back."

"I will," Ruso assured him. "You don't know where he might be, do you?"

But of course the man had no idea.

52

O N T H E W A Y across to the night watch Narina said, "May I
speak, mistress?"

"Do."

"The saying that *No man minds being proved honest*— it is very
good. I never heard it amongst the Catuvellauni."

Not even tempted to offer the obvious insult to the Catuvellauni,
Tilla said, "Nor I amongst the Brigantes. But when you are foreign
you can tell people whatever nonsense you want about your homeland, and they will believe you." She peered past an old man on a
donkey at a tall brick-fronted building farther down the street. "I
think that must be it. Give me Mara now."

Narina offered to help her tie the shawl, but Tilla told her to
carry it. "I want them to be able to see her face," she explained,
pausing as they approached the open gates. There was an engraved
plaque on the wall outside, but after working her way through the
lines of pompous blather about emperors and consuls and being
none the wiser, she gave up and did what any sensible person at
home would do: ask. The girl who was leading a brown spotted
goat along the street said that, yes, this was indeed the home of the
second cohort of the night watch.

She drew Narina aside to stand beside her under the high wall.
"I have dealt with soldiers many times," she said, "and I think
these men may be the same. The trick is to make them think you
belong to one of them. And if they make ignorant remarks, pretend
you have not heard."

Narina's nervous "Yes, mistress," reminded her that this woman
was not a new friend but a slave. It was not wise or even fair to
explain everything to a slave. But with Phyllis banned from visiting
and Sabella threatening to evict them, Narina was the closest thing
to an ally she had left. Tilla took a deep breath, kissed the top of
Mara's head, and said, "Let's go."

To her surprise there was no guard to argue with. Instead of
being confronted as they would have been when visiting any official building in Britannia, they walked unhindered past the gates
and followed the sound of hammering through a short passage into
a courtyard.

A couple of men were working on some sort of wheeled
pumping contraption with polished brass and leather that was
parked next to a stone tank. One of them was lying underneath
and trying to bang something into place. As she watched, the
other crouched beside him and poked at the underneath of the
vehicle with a stick. There was a clang as something metal landed
on the cobbles and the one underneath swore. Tilla drew Narina
back into the shadow of the walkway: This was most definitely not
the time to approach.

She was about to retreat into the passageway and try one of the
doors—there must be an office or a clerk—when she heard the
clatter of feet on wooden steps and a breathless slave appeared to
ask how he could help.

"I have come to visit one of my husband's comrades," she told
him. "Doctor Simmias."

To her amazement, the slave bowed and said, "Follow me,
mistress." He led them along under the covered walkway past
stacks of ladders and coiled ropes hung on the walls, knocked on a
door, and said, "Doctor, there is a lady come to see you."

It was that easy.

Doctor Simmias seemed very different now to when Tilla had first
seen him at the slave market. There, he had seemed very full of

himself. Now his chins wobbled with fright at the sight of her, and the first thing he said was, "Oh, dear."

"I have not said anything yet."

He backed away into the room, bumping into a stool and knocking it over. "Oh, dear. I am so sorry, dear lady, but I really didn't have anything to do with what happened."

Tilla handed the baby to Narina and told her to wait outside the door. Her lone presence seemed to terrify the doctor even further. He took another step backward, fumbled with the door of a cabinet, and pulled out a bowl. "Would you like, ah—?" The trembling hand held the bowl out toward her.

"I have not come here to eat cakes," she told him. "I have come here to talk to you."

"Yes. Yes, of course." The cakes disappeared back into the cupboard. "I was rather afraid you had."

"About the men who have come to our house."

"Oh, dear. Yes. A terrible thing. I was so sorry to hear about that, dear lady. How is your slave?"

Tilla blinked. "The slave?"

"Your husband told me someone was attacked."

"Yes." He must think she had come to talk about Squeaky and his friends, not the men who came to value the furniture. Whatever had happened between her husband and this man over in the gardens of Livia, it had clearly given him a serious fright. Now he seemed to think he was about to be attacked by a barbarian.

"It really was nothing to do with me, you know. I can quite understand why your husband was angry, but I didn't—oh, dear. There was no need for you to visit, you know. I was going to bring it over myself when I had a moment."

For a moment she thought he was going to offer the cakes again, but this time he delved lower into the cupboard, grunting with the effort of bending down. Finally upright again, he thrust a leather purse toward her. "There's almost three hundred sesterces in there. I'm afraid it's all I can manage. I was saving it to move to a new apartment. The stairs— You wouldn't understand. The stairs are too much for a man of my age." He jerked the purse up and down as if to prove from the chinking within that there was money in it. "You must have it, of course. I see that."

Tilla took the purse and pulled the drawstring open. A pile of denarii slid into her palm like silver fish. Times four to make sesterces . . . the number seemed about right.

She tipped them back into the purse without comment. She had come here to look for the missing doctor, but she was not going to turn the money down. "Where is Kleitos?"

"I really don't know. Please. You have to believe me."

She took a step closer. "You sent men to our house to collect Kleitos's things and sell them. You must know where he is."

Any remaining color drained from Simmias's face. He groped behind him for a chair and collapsed down onto it. "Oh, dear. Oh—"

"Stop saying *oh, dear!*" Tilla snapped. The whiny act was very irritating when you were the one who had to put up with it. "If you are dealing with Kleitos's affairs, you must know where he is. If you do not tell me, I will send the undertakers 'round to visit you instead."

Simmias gulped. "I know. Your husband told me."

Tilla turned and reached for a stool to buy some time while she tried to fathom what he was talking about. It seemed her husband had already used the threat of Squeaky to demand money. Now Simmias thought she had come here to collect it.

When she turned back there were beads of sweat glistening on Simmias's forehead. She began to fear that he would faint before she could get any sense out of him. Seating herself at what he might think was a safe distance, she lowered her voice and repeated the one thing of which she could be certain. "Some men came this afternoon to value Kleitos's things. They told me you sent them."

"Yes. Yes."

"You did send them?"

The chins wobbled frantically as the head nodded. "It seemed such a harmless thing—just a few sticks of furniture and some supplies—he would never know, and you would bring your own things anyway, and I needed the money. For the new apartment. It's more expensive to live at street level, you know."

Tilla gripped the sides of the stool. "You were trying to sell your friend's things?"

Again the frantic nodding.

"Holy mothers!" She was on her feet now, towering over him, not remembering how she got there. "You were stealing from him?"

The "Yes" was very faint.

"What?"

"Yes. Yes, yes! I didn't mean any harm!"

"So where is he?"

The head shook from side to side. "I don't know! I don't know where he's gone! Please, please—don't send those men!"

Tilla let Narina carry Mara home. Neither of them spoke. With each step, the purse she had slung beneath her clothing banged against her ribs like an accusation. She had deprived a not very clever man of his savings, and the trail that she had hoped would lead to Kleitos, and to the rediscovery of her husband's pride, was a dead end. It had not been a good afternoon's work.

53

R USO COULD TELL from the tone of Tilla's "There is some good news" that there was other news as well, and that he was not going to like it.

"Tell me," he said, briefly diverting his attention to correct Mara's cry of "Ah!" to "Pa!" and scoop her up from the sheepskin. *"Papa,"* he told her. "Say *Papa.*"

The chuckle that accompanied a fresh "Ah!" was one of the better moments of the evening. That, and the fact that the door had been fixed while he was out, so he was spared another awkward conversation with the carpenter. Better still, Tilla had somehow managed to extract almost three hundred sesterces from Simmias.

But, like his brief moment of being marvelous with a dying patient, the joy didn't last. Neither of them had managed to track down Kleitos, and now it seemed their one hope of finding him had ended in failure. The auctioneers who wanted Kleitos's belongings had been sent by Simmias. In addition, Tilla wanted to know exactly what he had said to Simmias that had made the man part with his savings, and when he told her, she said, "He says he did not tell Squeaky those lies about you complaining to the authorities."

"He must have," he pointed out. "He's the only one who knew what was going on."

"Even so. He acts like a man who is telling the truth."

He cupped the purse of silver in one hand, feeling the weight.

She said, "He was saving up to move to an apartment with no stairs."

"He was in on this barrel business with Kleitos," he reminded her, wondering if there was any way he could have been wrong about Simmias's betrayal. "And he was trying to sell Kleitos's property. He's got off lightly. What's for supper?"

It seemed Tilla had managed to fill Narina's afternoon with auctioneers and deceitful doctors. "But there is good bread, and some of that cheese left, and we fetched sausages and pastries from Sabella's."

"Hm. Remind me again why we bought a slave who can cook."

"Sabella says her husband wants to talk to you."

"I know," he said, not in the mood to listen.

In the indifferent light of the bedroom, he pulled out the box and lifted the top of the padded tunic that was wrapped around what Tilla always called *your soldier things*. It smelled of another life: of old sweat and leather and wool and the olive oil he had used when he cleaned the kit back in Deva. He placed the helmet on the bedpost. The empty space where his face would have been watched him as he buckled the segments together and lifted them so they rose into the shape of a man's chest. He lowered the shoulders and the metal soldier sank back into itself on the bed. The stiffness of the leather and the rough feel of the surfaces told him the armor had suffered in the damp of the sea voyage. It needed a cleaning it wasn't going to get.

The sword slid out of the scabbard and back in with reassuring ease. He laid it on the side where his right hand would be, and the dagger on his left. The metal strap ends jingled as he uncoiled the belt. The shield had gone to a needy recruit back in Britannia, but he had kept the rest of the kit, because who knew? Some Legion—perhaps even the Twentieth—might be short of a medical officer again soon. Whatever the official rules were about recruitment, arrangements could be made for the right medic. There had been a time when he was that medic. Now he wasn't so sure. Especially since he had managed to annoy Accius, the only man in Rome who was likely to recommend him for a posting.

For a mad moment he considered whether a trained legionary with a freshly honed sword and a sharpened broomstick for a spear could hold the door, defend his family . . .

The moment passed. There were no scouts to warn him when Squeaky was approaching; no trained comrades on either side of him to lock their shields with his, even if he'd still had one. The only reinforcements standing behind him were a British youth with a bang on the head and two women armed only with their personal knives and anything they could grab from the kitchen. And then there was Mara.

Most of the kit went back in the box. Ruso unthreaded his civilian belt and tossed it on the bed. The thick leather tongue of the military belt snaked back into its well-worn position through the buckle, like a man slipping on his favorite pair of boots.

As he walked toward the door, Ruso heard the familiar clink of the strap ends and felt the weight of the dagger resting where it should be. For the first time in weeks, he stopped feeling like a man who was pretending to be somebody else.

As Narina laid out this evening's food on the table in front of him, he leaned back and shouted, "Esico?"

The slave, whose black eye was developing nicely, appeared in the doorway.

"I'm making a few changes around here," he announced in Latin. "From now on, I only want to see patients who are going to make the doctor feel better. I don't want any constant grumblers, any nonpayers, anybody who decides they know better than I do, or anybody who won't do exactly what they're told. I don't want to see anything long lasting and incurable, and I don't ever want to hear that the other doctor didn't do it like that. All I want is patients who are going to be very grateful for anything. Or better still, for nothing. Can you manage that?"

When the full message had been conveyed by Tilla, Esico looked stunned.

Tilla murmured, "He is joking."

"No, I'm not."

Esico looked from one to the other of them, and intoned gravely, "Yes, master."

"Excellent!" He turned to Tilla. "You see how easy it is once you have good staff?"

"You are out of your mind," she told him, but he could tell from the way she gave him an extra pastry without asking that she was glad of the pretense.

54

THE GOOD MOOD lasted until after the lamps were lit. It lasted while talk of nothing important flowered and faded, and the household was getting ready to go to bed. It lasted right up until the moment when some drunk started banging on the door and slurring, "Ish me, Ruso! Lemme in!"

Esico grabbed the broken broomstick. Narina crouched beside the sleeping Mara, ready to snatch her up and flee. Tilla gestured to them to stay back. This was not a man she counted as a friend, but neither was he a threat.

"Lemme in!" repeated the drunk. "I'm losing her, Ruso!"

"Just a moment, sir!" The door shuddered under more hammering as her husband fumbled with the rearranged lock. Something more for the neighbors to complain about.

"Lemme in! I'm losing her!" Accius stumbled into the surgery, collided with the workbench, and told it, "I'm losing her! You've got to help me!"

"The master's rather tired, Doctor," put in one of the slaves who had arrived with him. "We're taking him home." The slave's hair and the clasp of his cloak were awry. It seemed Accius did not want to go home.

"Tired, yes." Accius slumped downward. To Tilla's disappointment, his other slave dived across and shoved a stool into position underneath him, saving him from landing on the floor as he deserved. Not even noticing the near miss, he swayed toward her husband and grabbed a handful of tunic. "You've got to help me, Ruso. I'm losing her."

"We've just come from Horatius Balbus's house," the first slave explained. "Some of the guests went back to the house for refreshments after the funeral."

Accius was hanging on to her husband's arm for support and gazing around the surgery. "Where are we?"

"In my treatment room, sir."

"Think I'm a bit drunk," Accius confided. "Don't tell the men. Got to set an example."

"I won't tell them, sir." He moved Accius's grasp to the edge of the workbench. To the slave he murmured, "No chance of getting a chair to carry him home, I suppose?"

"Not at this time of night, sir."

"What happened?"

The man's attempt to explain was drowned out by, "I love her, Ruso! I love her, and she loves me. I'm going back to find her!"

Tilla would have slapped some sense into him, and felt unreasonably let down when her husband put a friendly hand on his shoulder. "She doesn't need to see you like this, sir."

Accius pondered this for a moment, and then agreed. "You've always been straight with me, Ruso. You and that whats-her-name . . . Blond . . . That one." He swiveled 'round and pointed at Tilla. "You don't care what anyone thinks, you just tell them . . ." He groped for a word, and missed. "You just tell them."

After that he seemed to fall into a daze, his head nodding gradually toward the floor.

She sent his junior slave to the kitchen for some water. When he was gone the other one said softly, "Apparently the master overheard the young lady's new guardian asking Curtius Cossus to help the family with their business affairs, sir."

"Did your master say anything?"

"I don't think so, sir, but I was out in the courtyard with the other staff. Balbus's staff noticed the master getting rather, ah—"

"Drunk."

"Yes, sir. They told the master there was a message for him at the door to get him to leave, and here we are."

The water arrived. Her husband seemed pleased with Accius's efforts to drink it. There was talk of making up a bed. She said, "He can go in here with Esico."

Narina brought the spare blankets from the chest. The slaves were sent home to reassure the household that the master was under the care of his doctor, and to arrange a chair to collect him in the morning. No sooner had they left than Accius declared her husband to be his best friend in the whole world and the only man he could trust, and then he vomited all over the floor. As the best friend said, it was a good thing he'd remembered to ask Timo for a fresh bag of sawdust.

Finally everyone was settled down for the night, with one lamp still burning in the surgery and the snoring Accius propped up on his side in case he should vomit again. The best friend looked surprised when Tilla offered to sit with Accius for a while, but agreed to go to bed and leave her there in her night things, wearing a pair of winter socks and wrapped in a blanket.

He returned a moment later carrying the cloak he had not worn since they were on board the ship, and tucked it around her shoulders. "I thought you might be cold."

Gazing down at their unexpected patient, she said, "Tell me something, husband. Why, if he likes her and she likes him, do they not just bed each other and be done with it? The other man will not want her then, because your men always like to be the first and only, and they can marry in peace."

He looked at her with one of those how-foreign-you-are expressions. Like when he had thought she was going to serve him a suppository mixture for lunch. "A normal girl can't just marry whoever she likes, Tilla. She'll have to have her guardian's permission."

"I am not a normal girl?"

"Not at all."

She had thought he would bid her good night then, but instead he seated himself on the table with his feet propped up on the workbench so as not to tread on Accius. On the other side of the room the straw rustled as Esico rolled over and mumbled in his sleep.

He said, "I'm beginning to wonder if I'm as bad as they are."

Not sure who *they* were, she reached up and put a hand over his. "Never."

"Whether I'm actually guilty isn't the point," he said. "It's the possibility. The fact of the carelessness."

He was still worrying about that medicine. She said, "You thought you were the only person in the world who never made a mistake, and now you have found out you are not."

"It's not funny, Tilla. I was in a rush and instead of making the patient wait, I gave him something I couldn't vouch for."

"Whatever you did, you did it to help."

"I did it to hang on to this practice."

"You did it for us," she told him, patting his hand. "I am proud of you. Now go and sleep."

She felt the cloak being rearranged around her shoulders, then he eased himself down from the table and stepped over Accius. "Don't wait up too long."

She waited until she was certain he had gone to bed. Then she crouched on the floor and shook the former tribune by the shoulder. When he started mumbling about parades and morning briefings she said in his ear, "You are not on parade now. You are a drunk who is lying on a floor feeling sorry for himself. Tomorrow I will try to find out if that girl is still silly enough to want to marry you, and if there is any hope of it. But listen to me when I tell you this: No good will come of working with Metellus, nor of using my husband to make an enemy of that Curtius Cossus. I will not let you draw my family into danger like that. We have enough troubles already. Do you understand?"

Of course he did not. Neither would Esico, even if he were awake, because she was speaking in Latin. But as she settled back in the chair and pulled the cloak around herself, she felt much better for saying it.

55

I T WAS UNLIKELY that Accius understood much of what was said to him the next morning about the violent men who were demanding money from Ruso's family, but Ruso did not care. The man was so hungover that he would have agreed to anything in order to be left in peace, which was exactly what Ruso wanted.

Unfortunately, Tilla was less obliging. She did not want to go to the safety of Accius's house. She had already suffered enough malicious nonsense from his housekeeper, whom she had taken to calling the Witch before the first week of the sea voyage was out.

Besides, as she pointed out over the morning porridge, if the undertakers were not due to return until tomorrow, there was no reason to leave now.

"Accius's house is a lot better than this," he reminded her. "No neighbors to worry about, plenty of food from the kitchen, Mara can splash in the fountain—"

"And the Witch will want Narina to scrub it clean. So she can stand there watching and making comments."

"You wanted me to talk to him," he said. "This is what he's offered."

She looked up from making a valley in her porridge with the

edge of the spoon. "Do you know how many places we have lived in, husband?"

Surprised by this sudden change of direction, he confessed that he did not.

"Very many," she told him, perhaps not certain herself.

The sound of someone knocking at the door raised a fresh groan from the floor of the surgery. To Ruso's disappointment it was not four strong men ready to bear Accius away in a covered chair, but members of the night watch wanting to know if Doctor Simmias was here. Apparently he had not turned up for last night's duty.

Back in the kitchen, Tilla was in the mood to make speeches. "A proper family sows seeds in the spring and harvests in the summer," she told him, "and in the autumn they bring in logs for the winter and then they kill the pig. But our family has no land to plant, and no trees, and no pig. Because every few weeks, you come home and say, 'Time to go, wife!' and we put all the things back into the bags and boxes and move on."

"You married a soldier," he reminded her. "That's what soldiers do."

"You are not a soldier now," she told him. "You promised that if Kleitos did not come back, this place with no cockroaches would be our home. Kleitos is not coming back, and I am not leaving here just because some man with a squeaky voice wants money."

"I know I said that," he admitted, wishing he hadn't. "But things have changed. Apart from Phyllis's husband telling her to stay away from you and Sabella's husband wanting to evict us, three big ugly men are coming here tomorrow to collect more money than we've got. We can't expect the Christos people to be around next time, we can't afford to hire guards, and we've been offered a safe place for Mara. We should take it."

When she did not reply he said, "If you don't want to go there, Narina can take her."

"But she is my baby!"

"Do you want her here, then?" he asked. "When those men come back?"

She flung the spoon down in the bowl. "It is not fair!"

"No," he agreed, wondering why she had imagined that it might be.

More than once, he had watched his wife lavishing the attention on Mara that she had at least occasionally lavished on him in the past, and wondered *Why did I agree to this?* But then when he looked down at Mara's wispy hair and vulnerable little face he realized that it didn't matter why he had agreed to parenthood: He was just going to have to keep on doing his best at it until he found a young man good enough to take over the job of protecting her in marriage. And the gods alone knew where one of those might be found. He said, "I'm not going to order you to go, Tilla. But I may order Narina to take Mara."

She bowed her head and pinched the bridge of her nose as if her head was aching. He supposed that back in Britannia, when women went out armed with spears and swords there was always some grandmother or aunt left behind to mind the little ones. Then he remembered a terrible account he had read somewhere of a battlefield where a hungry baby was found crying at its dead mother's breast, and wondered if he was wrong.

Outside in the street there was a burst of laughter that rapidly deteriorated into a cough. Ruso held his breath, waiting to see if the cougher would call in for some medicine. The noise faded into the distance. With every sniffle and limp that passed the door, he was becoming more convinced that patients were deliberately passing them by because of gossip about the goings-on here.

"At home," she said, "the children are often there when the soldiers come."

It was true. He had seen children caught up in raids on civilian property. Whatever the troops did, it was messy. If they showed mercy it could be exploited as weakness. If they didn't, the Britons had yet another cause for seething resentment.

"They have nowhere to hide," he said. "We have somewhere. And Squeaky and his men aren't soldiers with an officer to keep them in check."

"If we go there," she said, "Those men have won."

"I don't care! I'm not putting our child in danger just so we can keep living in this apartment."

She said, "My people are always asking themselves this question about their home. Do you not remember the song?"

"Remind me." The best part of most of Tilla's ancestor songs was when they ended: a moment that was usually far too long coming.

"Some of my people wanted to leave when they knew the Legions were coming. But the rest of the people said, 'No, we will stay here, because here is all we have. The soldiers will come. They will steal our crops and take many of our lives, but if we are patient, they will also go. The winter will pass into spring, and when the peace comes, there will be a home for our children and our children's children.'"

"Wife, your people are hundreds of miles away across the sea." *And*, he wanted to add, *you cannot base a rational decision on a song full of ridiculous bravado.* Especially one with a tune that reminds you of autumn nights with old friends, when you were warmed on the outside by the bonfire and on the inside by too much beer.

"We stand our ground," she declared.

"Kleitos knew more about what's going on here than we do, and he ran. Now it looks as though Simmias has run too."

"Kleitos was not Brigante."

"And this isn't Britannia," he reminded her, regretting his promise not to order her to go. He had hoped the concession would persuade her to see sense. "Besides," he added, "refusing to move hasn't always worked too well for your people."

"We stand our ground," she repeated.

"Whoever composed that song was just guessing at how the story will end. The soldiers haven't gone. They're still there."

She lifted her chin. "And so are my people."

He sighed. Since her brief flirtation with being a Roman wife, Tilla seemed to have become more stubbornly British than ever.

"This is our home," she told him. "Tonight Narina can take Mara across to Accius's house to be safe. But if anybody wants me out—the neighbors or Sabella's husband or Squeaky and his friends—they will have to carry me."

Rather than point out that Squeaky would have no difficulty in carrying her, he went to see if Accius wanted more water. When he returned to the kitchen Tilla was busy emptying the shelves of all their wedding-present crockery. She said, "Promise me you will never tell your family where this went. How much do you think we will get for it?"

Very little, he supposed, since she would have to sell it quickly. He did not say that. Neither did he voice his own suspicion that paying Squeaky and his cronies might encourage them to come back for more. At least she was not hatching some mad scheme to try to fight them off. He said, "I'm sorry things haven't turned out the way you'd hoped."

She paused, caressing the smooth rim of a cup with one finger. Then she put it back on the table with the others. "I have more than I ever hoped for," she told him. "I have a husband and a baby. These . . ." She indicated the crockery. "These are just things."

The hug took her by surprise.

"What is that for?"

"Oh . . . nothing." He stepped back, eyeing the skinny girl he had bought in a back street, who had turned into this proud and brave and beautiful and exasperating wife.

"Then don't interrupt. I want to get this sold, and then I am going to see that poor motherless girl who wants to marry Accius." She bent down and pulled a fistful of fresh straw out of the hole she had slit in one of the new mattresses, then dropped it onto the top bowl in the box before reaching up to add the next one to the stack.

Just as she finished packing, Accius's steward arrived with a hired chair. The bearers bundled him in, pulling the curtains shut on him so that nobody in the street would know who was in there groaning.

56

Ruso could have got a better price back in Britannia, but if he had had the sense to stay in Britannia, he wouldn't have been selling his kit anyway. He turned away as two smug-faced Praetorians carried the box away down the corridor. *These are just things.* In their place was a second fat purse of coins.

A braver man would have made more of a stand over being blackmailed. Since there wasn't a braver man available, he would add this to the money from Simmias and the money from the sale of the crockery, and they would have more than enough cash to pay off Squeaky.

Ruso strode away from the barracks and cut south through the gardens on the way to the headquarters of the undertakers.

"Doctor!" Lucius Virius floated into the room with what might be the nearest thing he could manage to a welcoming smile. "So soon." The smile faded. "Not bad news, I hope?"

"Not for your staff," Ruso told him. "I'm about to give them quite a lot of money."

The eyebrows drifted upward. "Really?"

"To be honest," Ruso confessed, his hopes rising, "I'm not sure what the lad's name is. Big frame, small voice. He and a couple of friends came to visit the other day. After I'd been to see you."

Lucius Virius's face twitched, as if it was waiting to be told what expression to adopt.

"He seemed to think I'd been making things difficult for you," Ruso continued. "But I want you to know that I haven't. So I've come to reassure you personally, and to pay the compensation he requested."

Lucius Virius's head drifted down into a nod of acknowledgment, but his continuing silence suggested he still didn't know what Ruso was talking about.

"I was wondering," Ruso continued, sending up a silent prayer that the man wouldn't just take the money and have him chased off the premises, "if we could agree a discount for early payment." He slapped a heavy pouch of coin onto the table. "Since I've saved him the trouble of coming to collect it tomorrow."

The head bobbed up and down with more enthusiasm at the sight of the money. Lucius Virius was certain something could be arranged. How much, exactly, would the doctor consider a fair amount?

Ruso scratched one ear with his forefinger. This was going rather better than he had expected. Whatever Lucius Virius knew about the illegal supply of bodies for dissection, it was clear he didn't know anything about Squeaky's attempts at extortion.

The thing was, Ruso explained, his wife and several of the neighbors had been rather alarmed by the first visit and had begged him to make sure there wouldn't be another. "Your man and his friends are very large and very loud," he pointed out. "I'm sure they don't mean to be, but there it is. So I'd be grateful for his and your personal assurance that whatever we agree today is the end of it. Then I'll be able to promise everyone that they won't be back."

There was a pause while Lucius Virius might have been weighing up the damage that Squeaky's behavior could cause to the reputation of his business. Or he might have been wondering what sort of price Ruso might fetch if he were nailed up inside a barrel. Finally he said, "Excuse me one moment, Doctor," and flowed out of the room as if propelled by a strong current.

Ruso was left alone with a large sum of money and a display of dried flowers. He tried to concentrate on what he should say next, but was unable to push away thoughts of the conversation Lucius Virius might be having at this moment, and what Squeaky's response might be, and what sort of instruments might be stored here for the entirely legal disciplining of slaves.

There were footsteps crunching toward him across the yard. The door opened and the room shrank as Lucius Virius was followed in by Squeaky.

"Doctor," Lucius Virius began with uncharacteristic vigor, "let me say how grateful we are to you for coming here to reassure us in person."

Squeaky was looking from one to the other of them.

"My employee and I have discussed your kind offer," Lucius Virius told him, "And I must apologize for the misunderstanding. It seems someone had been wrongly informed that a payment was owing."

Ruso swallowed. They were going to cancel it? Just like that, after one meeting? After all the trouble he and Tilla had gone to?

"However . . ."

No, they weren't.

". . . my employee was given some very worrying information about a slander that, if it were allowed to pass unchecked, might affect our reputation and the renewal of our contract with the city authorities."

"It didn't come from me," Ruso told him.

"Yes, it bloody did!" put in Squeaky.

Lucius Virius put a hand on his arm. "My young friend is very keen to defend the reputation of the business. I'm afraid he's been a little overenthusiastic. But you see, we can't have slander circulating unchecked. And our source was very reliable."

"Simmias made it up to get you off his back," Ruso told Squeaky. "He doesn't want a home visit from you any more than Kleitos did."

Lucius Virius glanced at Squeaky. "Someone visited Doctor Kleitos?"

"That was Birna," put in Squeaky, "but Kleitos had gone."

Ruso added, "Simmias tried to deflect everything onto me."

"Doctor Simmias?" Lucius Virius sounded as though he could not believe it. "I must have a word with him when I see him."

Squeaky shuffled uncomfortably. "It wasn't him who told me this one was trouble."

Lucius Virius got there first with "Then who was it?"

Squeaky scratched his head and looked embarrassed. "I'll tell you later, boss."

Ruso said, "I think I have a right to know who's been spreading lies about me."

Lucius Virius held a hand out between them. "Doctor, I'm sorry you have been inconvenienced. Whoever it is, I will see they are spoken to. Now, please allow me . . ." He held out his other hand, which contained a fat purse not unlike the one Ruso had been about to hand over. "Perhaps you would allow me to make a small gesture on behalf of the business, with my apologies to your wife and neighbors. Can I hope the matter will now be forgotten?"

Ruso took a step back. "I don't want your money," he said, not sure what was being bought. "I want you to promise me that from now on this man and his friends will stay away from my family." Then as an afterthought, he added, "And from Simmias."

Lucius Virius inclined his head. "I think we can promise that, can we not?"

Squeaky said, "We were defending the business, boss."

"But, as I'm sure you're delighted to find," Lucius Virius told him, "the doctor is not an enemy."

"I'm very delighted, boss."

Ruso said, "Simmias didn't turn up for work last night. Do you know where he is?"

Lucius Virius raised his eyebrows toward his chastened employee. "Do we know where he is?"

But Squeaky did not. Or so he said.

57

HORATIA STILL LOOKED pale, but her hair had been combed and her dark mourning clothes were neatly arranged. She said she was pleased to have a visitor. "Yesterday it was everybody, now it's nobody," she confided. Tilla noticed the jet bracelet hanging from the girl's thin wrist as she pointed to the seat beside her. As Tilla joined her under the bower, Horatia declared she was chilly and sent the round-faced slave girl to fetch her stole. As soon as the girl was gone she whispered, "Quick, tell me! Is he all right?"

"Accius?"

"They told me he was ill. I've been so worried! All this talk of poisons! I should have told him to be careful."

"He wasn't ill," said Tilla. "He was drunk. He seemed all right this morning."

"You've seen him? What did he say?"

"He is never going to drink wine again."

"Anything about me?"

But before Tilla could reply, the servant was back to wrap the stole around her mistress's shoulders.

"Do stop sniffling, Gellia!" Horatia snapped. "It is not your father who has died! If I want miserable-looking people around the house I will send for the mourners!"

The girl apologized, but the sniffling carried on. Horatia sent her to stand farther away. "Another week of nothing but glum faces to put up with before the funeral feast," she said. "And then a whole twelve months dressed like this. I feel like a Vestal Virgin that's been buried alive."

Tilla asked if there were anything she could do to help, but Horatia's only suggestion—that she should send the new guardian back home—was impossible. "It's not as if he's ever shown any interest until now. He hardly recognized me, even though we're cousins. He thought I was still about ten. And now he's in the study with Creepy Cossus, going through all the records of the business, and Firmicus is walking around like a thundercloud because he always takes charge when Pa's away—I mean when he was . . . Oh, dear." She twisted the bracelet around her wrist. "Sorry. And the bodyguard's run away. Not that it matters. Pa doesn't need him now, does he?"

Across the courtyard, the round-faced girl was still standing to attention. The tears were trickling down her cheeks and dripping from her chin. There were dark wet blobs on her gray mourning tunic, under which the thickening of her pregnancy was beginning to be visible.

"I won't marry him, you know," Horatia said suddenly. "I'll kill myself first."

"Have you said this to your cousin?"

"He says I'll get used to it. I can stave them all off until the mourning period is over but by then Creepy Cossus will have his fingers so deep into the business that there'll be no way to prize them out."

Tilla said, "I am so sorry."

"Everyone is sorry!" Horatia cried. "Why don't they just do the one thing that would cheer me up, and let me marry Accius?"

Tilla said, "I don't know. Things are not done this way where I come from."

"I tried your husband's lettuce," Horatia's voice was calmer now. "I don't think it did any good, but I washed it down with a lot of wine, so who knows?"

"You look stronger today than you did in the funeral procession," Tilla told her, "but your slave girl is still very upset. Would you like me to talk to her?"

"Give her some lettuce," Horatia suggested.

Tilla was getting to her feet when she heard Horatia say, "Is it true there are medicines that are also poisons if you use too much of them?"

"There are," Tilla agreed. "But if you ask me about them, I will have to tell your cousin. And Accius."

"I thought you were on my side!"

"I am."

"You don't understand. I can't marry that man. If they try to make me—"

"I understand this," Tilla interrupted, "but no man is worth dying for. And there are far worse things than being married to a man you do not love."

"How would you know? You don't do things this way where you come from."

So then Tilla sat down again and spoke softly, and as busy slaves flitted in and out of the garden around them she told of the raid on the family farm, and how the leader of the men who had killed her family took her as a slave and used her for his pleasure. "All this is past and gone," she said. "I do not speak of it often. There are more and more days when I do not think of it at all. But when I was there, I saw no end to it. I wanted to die and join my own people in the next world. And then I thought, if I die, this man has won. So I waited. And then one day the gods smiled on me again and I escaped. So, no, I do not know how things are done here. But do not tell me that I do not understand."

Horatia gulped.

Wondering if she had said too much, Tilla added, "I cannot tell you what to do. Your guardian thinks he can, and there are a lot of powerful people here who will agree with him. If they try to force you to do something you don't want to do, you will have to choose how to answer them. But none of it is worth dying for. Now before I go and talk to your slave, if I see Accius, is there a message?"

Horatia sniffed. "Tell him . . ." She looked up. "They can't make me stay at home, can they? I'm not a prisoner. Will you make certain you see him?" When Tilla promised to visit him she said, "Tell him I shall have finished my book at the eighth hour today."

"I will."

"And tell him . . . Tell him I will be all right."

58

THE GIRL CALLED Gellia had stopped crying now and was sniffing and wiping her nose on the back of her hand. On hearing that the mistress had sent Tilla to talk to her, she looked very alarmed. Tilla steered her to the side of the fountain as the only safe place to talk in a house that was crawling with servants, and handed her a cloth. When the girl had finished wiping her nose Tilla said, "Is it your master's child?"

Gellia looked as if she had just been hit with a plank. "What?"

"You are making a good job of hiding it, but they will find out before long."

This brought on a fresh flood of tears, and, "Don't tell them. Please don't tell them. The housekeeper will tell Firmicus, and he'll have me whipped."

"I am not going to tell them." Holy mothers, another spare baby. There was something very unjust about the way the gods sent new lives into the world.

"It wasn't supposed to . . . to happen like this."

Tilla delved into her bag for a dry cloth, handed it to Gellia, and waited, watching the fish dart and glide in the basin of the fountain.

"He saw it in a dream. He said he would marry me."

"Men say these things." But not all women were stupid enough to believe them. Slaves were not allowed to marry. Surely Gellia knew that?

"No, he really did have a dream. He told me about it ages ago. He dreamed he was walking in a sunny meadow and he saw a mare giving birth to a foal. And he went to an interpreter who said he would be free when his son was born. Only it made no sense because he had no hope of a son. But then later on when I told him I was with child he said it was all coming true. He said he would be free soon and then he would buy me from the master and marry me. He said our son would be born a citizen."

"Because of the dream?" said Tilla, still trying to work out who *he* was.

"And it has come true, hasn't it? He's free all right. But he can't buy me now, can he?" She paused to blow her nose and wipe it with the cloth. "Firmicus says Latro ran away out of shame because he didn't save the master but I don't believe it. Anyway, the master didn't deserve saving. Balbus promised him his freedom in his will and then it turned out to be a lie." She screwed up the cloth and tucked it away in the folds of her tunic. "So, I've got to look after myself now." She indicated Tilla's healer bag. "You know about these things," she said. "You can help me get rid of it. Then they won't find out."

Tilla took a deep breath. There had been a time when she would have helped. She had once been given the same help herself. How could she deny it to others? But now that she had Mara . . .

"It is very late for that. It will be dangerous for you."

"I don't care."

"There are people who will help you, but I have not been here long enough to know them." It was cowardly, and she knew it. "I am sure someone in the household will know."

"But then I'd have to tell them!" The girl covered her face with her hands. "I don't know what to do!"

"Try to stop crying," Tilla told her. "Otherwise you will be in trouble sooner than you have to be. Make yourself useful to the family and maybe they will keep you."

"I could say someone took me by force and I was too frightened to speak of it."

"You could," Tilla agreed. "But it will have to be someone who is not here to be punished for it."

Gellia's voice hardened. "I know just the man. Lying bastard."

59

O N H I S R E T U R N to the surgery Ruso was delighted to find
a youth who had got into a street fight when somebody
insulted his girlfriend, and who had a bent nose and a cut over one
eye that needed a couple of stitches. For a few moments that were
doubtless more pleasant for him than for his patient—or for Esico,
who turned green at the sight of the needle—he was faced with a
simple and useful job that he felt competent to perform.

The patient paid without a quibble. Ruso watched him swagger
off down the street on the arm of the proud girlfriend. He washed
his hands before sharing with Esico—the only member of the
household at home—the good news that Squeaky and his friends
weren't coming tomorrow after all.

Esico's joy was restrained: Evidently he was not convinced that
his master knew what he was talking about. Ruso hoped Tilla
would be more appreciative. The sale of the crockery and his kit
and the unexpected reprieve from Squeaky meant that instead of
being bankrupt, they had more ready cash than they had seen
for a very long time. He fought down a pang of regret about the
kit, reminding himself that it had been sacrificed to save his
family. Squeaky had been dealt with. For a few brief moments

Ruso could be the youth with the swagger, and Tilla could be the girl on his arm.

That was the good news. Less pleasant was the fact that he couldn't find Simmias, either to apologize to him or to repay his savings. The stranger working in the treatment room at the night watch could tell him only that nobody had seen Simmias since yesterday morning when two women and a baby had come to visit, and that the absence was completely out of character. Some of the watch, fearing the worst, had gone up to the top of the stairs and taken an axe to the door of his apartment, but had found it empty.

As to who had told Squeaky that Ruso was threatening to report the trade in bodies to the authorities—Ruso had given that a great deal of thought on the walk back, and he was beginning to fear that Squeaky might have made the whole thing up in order to extort some cash. Which made his own attack on Simmias—and the threat to send Squeaky 'round to visit him—all the more embarrassing. Despite Tilla's reassurances, he really was beginning to wonder if he was just as bad as all the liars, cheats, and bullies around him.

Then there was the wretched business of the medicine. He had pushed the costly bottle of theriac Xanthe had sold him to the back of the shelf, but he could no longer push its history to the back of his mind. The best he could hope for was that Tilla would have got some sense out of Horatia, and that Accius might by now have seen reason and told Metellus to abandon his investigations.

He reached for the note Esico had just remembered to hand him, allowing himself to hope that it might be from Accius, apologizing for all the bother he had caused and confirming that he had given up his unwise plan to threaten his rival with a murder charge.

It wasn't.

Metellus Paullus to Ruso.
I have something of interest to tell you. Meet me at the Greek library in the Forum of the Divine Trajan this afternoon at the eighth hour. That is the Forum library, not the baths.

Telling himself Metellus could never resist the chance to look mysterious, Ruso snapped the message into small pieces and dropped it into the embers of the kitchen fire where he had disposed of yesterday's GO HOME.

Whatever Metellus had to say had better be very interesting indeed. The library was in one of the most distant Forums the man could have chosen. No doubt if Ruso tried hard enough, he could watch an anatomy demonstration on the way or a medical miracle or a public debate between rival doctors who were united only in their ignorance. But he wasn't going to try very hard. Somehow—since the body and the awful business with the medicine—the idea of critiquing the professional performance of his colleagues had lost its appeal.

Meanwhile, Ruso inspected the kitchen to see if there might yet be any evidence for Narina's claim that she could cook.

60

RUSO'S BRIEF MEETING with the Emperor Trajan had involved an earthquake, a collapsing wall, and a great deal of panic and confusion. It was hard to imagine the dust-covered figure of his memory being responsible for this gracious hall. The high walls echoed to the murmurs of hushed voices as the library slaves padded back and forth in the dusty shafts of sunlight from the high windows, taking requests and searching out scrolls. A sudden screech made him jump, but it was only a stool scraping across a marble floor. Ruso ran his eye down the rows of readers hunched over the long desks, but Metellus was not among them. He decided to climb the stairs to the balcony.

The twin library opposite—the one with its inscription over the door in Greek—had a matching balcony, positioned to give a similarly fine view of the column that rose between them. Ruso leaned over to see the base, where Trajan was buried, then craned upward to take in the grand bronze of the man himself. The tales of his exploits in Dacia filled the column in between: carved squads of handsome disciplined troops unrolling around it like a giant scroll. They said the architect had ordered a whole hillside cut away in order to build here, then had this column put back to show the height of what had been moved. It was an odd, perhaps defiant resting place for a man who had survived that catastrophic shift of the earth beneath Antioch. Tilla would have said that it was pointless showing off.

"Impressive, isn't it?" enquired a voice at his elbow. Metellus leaned out and surveyed the balcony opposite. "Not there yet. Good. It's best you know before they turn up."

Ruso said, "Who?" but naturally Metellus was not going to answer a straight question.

Moving away from a couple of youths who were leaning out over the balcony to comment on the girls passing beneath, he said, "You need to tell your man why he'll be giving up any claim to Horatia."

Ruso frowned. "The last time I looked, he was your man too."

"Sadly, after consideration of the facts, I've come to realize I made the wrong choice. Curtius Cossus is in the right."

So much for the loyalty of old comrades.

"Beneath that naïve exterior, Ruso, you're very good. You nearly had me fooled."

"Did I?"

Metellus glanced across at the balcony opposite. "Oh look. There he is. He's not looking well, is he? Now here comes Horatia."

The mourning clothes were unmistakable. Ruso guessed her chaperone had been told to wait downstairs. As he and Metellus watched, she ran up to Accius and flung her arms around him.

"She's undeterred, then," said Metellus. "That's interesting." When the lovers moved to stand side by side, gazing down over the balcony, he said, "She'll be breaking the news to him now."

"What news?"

"That she can't marry him. It's for his own safety— Yes, see? He's looking shocked and asking what she means. Tragically, if she loves him, she has to give him up."

"What?"

"I suppose once you—I'm guessing it was you, not Accius—found out what Kleitos was up to with the dissection, it was easy enough to blackmail him to leave so you could take his place. That was the secret opportunity you told me about, no?

It might look rather odd, an established man offering his job to a virtual stranger, but your reputation is good, so who could argue?"

"You think I got rid of Kleitos to take his job?"

But Metellus was raising questions, not answering them. "Everyone knew Balbus was afraid of being murdered. Dosing himself with theriac. You must have been dancing with joy when Balbus put on that show of handing over medicine in front of Cossus."

"I haven't the faintest idea what you're talking about."

"I don't remember you having much need for poisons and antidotes with the Legion, but suddenly here you are prescribing them. And making visits to a notorious poisoner."

"I wasn't prescribing them! I went to Xanthe afterward for advice!" Before he had finished the second sentence he was already regretting it, but Metellus was busy watching the lovers.

"What do you think? I'd say it's not going well. She'll have bruises if he hangs on to her arm like that."

"Are you saying—"

"Gently, Doctor." Metellus drew him farther away from the youths. "We don't want this all over the city."

Ruso lowered his voice. "Are you saying Accius and I murdered Horatius Balbus?"

"No. I'm saying you did. At his instigation."

"You're out of your mind."

"Please don't descend to insults."

"But why would he ask you to investigate if he—if we—were guilty?"

Metellus nodded. "I had to ask myself the same thing. Perhaps he assumed that even if I worked out that you'd done it, I wouldn't notice that he was behind it. He's a young man with a good background and fine education, but . . . I reached the conclusion in the end that he simply isn't very bright."

"This is ridiculous. I—" He stopped. Over on the far balcony, Horatia had escaped her lover's clutches and was running for the door that led to the stairs. Accius sprinted after her, but found his way barred by a couple of burly slaves.

"They'll have been told he was bothering her," Metellus observed as Accius and the slaves wrestled in the doorway.

"By whom? You?"

"Don't worry. Her own people will meet her downstairs and take her home."

"This is crazy," Ruso said, turning toward the stairs himself. "I'm going to talk to Accius. None of it makes sense. Why would he do something like that?"

"Because the father was standing in the way of his marriage plans. I think it could be made to sound very convincing in the hands of a good lawyer, don't you?"

Ruso spun 'round. For one terrible moment he saw himself lifting Metellus off his feet and pitching him over the balcony to crash on the paving below. Then he saw the youths sauntering toward him, grinning at some shared joke, oblivious to the drama all around them, and the vision faded.

"Cossus is unlikely to take this further," Metellus told him. "All he wants is the wife who was promised to him. And as long as nobody tells Horatia's cousin any of this, you're probably safe from prosecution too."

"You promised Accius—"

"A mistake. I should have known better than to be swayed by old loyalties. Especially after I warned you about him myself. The only way to get on in Rome is to back the winning horse."

"Or to switch horses in midrace."

"Besides," Metellus continued, ignoring him, "you and I were being asked to find evidence against an innocent man. We both know Cossus never had the slightest intention of murdering anyone. Horatia was only one opportunity among many."

"That's all he thought of her?"

"Don't be silly, Ruso. Daughters of rich families are part of the business. They're born knowing that. It's their duty to contribute, and since they can't do much else, the least they can do is provide helpful alliances and grandchildren. Not everyone can marry for love and live on beans like you do."

Ruso glanced across at the other balcony. Both Accius and Horatia had disappeared now. "I'm going to find Accius."

"Good idea," Metellus agreed, pushing the door open and standing back to let him pass. "She may not have remembered all the details she was meant to tell him. You'll be able to explain why he needs to keep all of this quiet. Horatia seems to believe he's innocent, but nobody else will."

"This is blackmail."

"Which is exactly what Accius intended to do to Cossus with our help," Metellus pointed out. "So unless you want to be brought down with him, you'll persuade him to live with it."

61

A LESSER MAN MIGHT have been literally thrown out of the
library doors for pestering a young lady and fighting with the
staff. The former tribune and his two bemused slaves were politely,
but firmly, escorted from the building and advised to read elsewhere in the future.

Seeing the white of Accius's face and the pink of his eyes, Ruso
withheld the suggestion of repairing to the bar around the corner.
Instead he attempted to guide him toward the nearest fountain
where he might dip his head into the water tank. But Accius was
in no mood to cool down. The conversation was conducted at a
smart military pace along the middle of the street, with awkward
and irritable pauses when the slaves scuttling along in front failed
to clear pedestrians and livestock out of the way.

"Why didn't you tell me you'd given him your own antidote
mixture when I asked you to investigate Cossus?"

Ruso's explanation that it hadn't seemed relevant was not well
received. *Because you only wanted to hear things that would support your
case* would have fared even worse.

Recriminations about the past were interspersed with glum
speculation about the future. "She says she'll try to stave him off

by claiming her full year of mourning, but after that—ugh! He'll be even older by then! It makes me shudder to think of him having her in his bed."

Don't think of it, then. "A lot can happen in a year, sir."

"Well, he might die, obviously, but what if he doesn't?"

"That's probably not the best thing to be discussing in the street in the circumstances, sir."

"I should have known Metellus couldn't be trusted."

Yes, you should. Because I told you.

"But he was the governor's security officer."

Precisely.

"Well? Say something, man!"

"I'm very sorry, sir."

"Sorry? That's hardly going to help, is it? I could be banished, and you could be—well, I expect they'll just cut your head off, and she'll be left alone with—What have we stopped for now?"

The slave stood out of reach while he explained that this was the place of sir's afternoon meeting.

"What meeting?"

"To discuss the appeal against the levying of fines on the fishmonger by the Theatre of Marcellus, sir. Because of the regular dumping of fish guts in the street."

"Fish guts?" Accius ran one hand through his hair. "Let him off. I don't care. I've got more important things to worry about."

The slave was immobile, his face carefully blank.

Ruso said as gently as he could, "You do need to carry on as normal, sir."

Accius glared at him for a moment, then muttered, "Fish guts. Gods above!" and executed a perfect parade-ground turn to face the direction his staff were indicating. As Ruso walked away he heard a voice floating down the street after him, "And don't even think about trying any of that boiled lettuce nonsense with me!"

62

S HE ASKED HIM to repeat the word, not daring to believe it
the first time.

"Home," he said again, scanning her face as if he were keen to
see how she liked this surprise gift. She threw the laundry she was
folding down on the bed, gathered him into her arms, rubbed her
cheek against his scratchy one and kissed him. "Home," she whispered, breathing in the scent of him. "Thank the gods!" Then,
drawing back, "Can I tell the others?"

But she could not—not yet—because there was much he
needed to say to her. About the visit to Squeaky's boss that had
unexpectedly left them with the spare cash for the journey. About
the shipping agent and catching a barge to Portus. About the
Notus, a ship due to sail from Portus to Massalia the day after
tomorrow. About the relative safety of traveling up through Gaul
by river. All details she knew she should take in, but she was
longing for them to be over so she could fling open the kitchen
door and announce, "There is good news!" and wait until she
had the slaves' full attention before declaring, "We are all going
home!"

He was talking about visiting his family. "I don't suppose you'll want to go there, but I'm sure Cass would be delighted to see you. And the nieces and nephews will all love Mara."

It was like a cold hand around her throat. "Me? What about you?"

"You'll have both the staff with you."

"Me?"

"I'll join you as soon as I can," he promised.

"Just . . ." She forced the words out. ". . . me?"

"And Mara." He cleared his throat. "I need to stay, Tilla. I can't leave Accius in this state."

And then she was pounding him with her fists, crying, "You promised, you promised!" And he was trying to fend her off and begging her to listen, but that was the last thing she was going to do.

"We stand our ground, together! This is our home! We sold all those precious things to save it!"

And now they were both shouting, and things were said that should not have been said, and then they were both shamed into silence by the sound of Mara crying.

So when Sabella's husband appeared a little later to say he wanted them out by the Ides, neither of them had anything to say. He repeated himself, perhaps thinking they had not understood, and Tilla said, "We are thinking about it."

"It's not a request," he told her. "We've had complaints. It'll be fifty for the rent plus damages. I'll inspect before you go."

He looked around at the four adults in the kitchen and at Mara in Tilla's arms, still red in the face from crying. Nobody answered him, so he turned and left the way he had come in, muttering something about bloody provincials.

63

THEY WERE BOTH awake before dawn. All the things that could have been said had been said last night, most of them several times, and the lovemaking that followed had been desperate and sweet and sad. Now all that was left was the making of arrangements and the passing on of information, and each of them was treating the other as if they were fragile.

"Accius will go and formally withdraw his offer for Horatia this morning," he said, sitting on the side of the bed and leaning down to grope in the space underneath for his shoes.

She said, "What will you do if what you say does not help him?"

He heard the swish of her pulling off her night dress. "Then perhaps I'll bring him to Britannia and we'll see if your relatives can find him a job." Except that if he failed altogether, there would be no chance of leaving Rome. Accius had not been joking when he'd said, *I expect they'll just cut your head off.*

"Promise me you will be careful."

"I'm always careful." Almost always. Rather than linger on that one moment of exceptional stupidity, he said, "The agent said you'll need to be down at the wharf outside the Porticus Aemilia by the ninth hour at the latest. He says there'll be plenty of barges to get you down to Portus, so ask two or three to get a decent price."

"I will."

He had never before noticed that you could hear someone combing their hair. He said, "Don't be afraid to stay at the farm as long as you want. Cass and my brother will make you welcome."

"It was a good letter."

She must have been awake during the night. Knowing she would read it—although not so soon—he had spent some time considering the phrasing, and ended up with

Gaius to his dearest mother, stepfather, brother, all three of my sisters, my brother by marriage, my nieces and nephews, fondest greetings.

That just about covered everyone. His stepmother would be pleased to be called *mother*, the idiot she had married was unlikely to care what he was called, and his sister-in-law Cass would be glad to be ranked with his two half-sisters. Families were a complicated business, especially when it was important to please them.

Unfortunately our stay in Rome has had to be cut short and we are returning to Britannia

(That would disappoint his eldest sister, who had been expecting him to find her husband a job here.)

but I am detained by some business. I am very much looking forward to seeing you, but in the meantime I am sending you this news via my most precious wife and daughter and our two slaves, who are looking after them.

Holy gods, he hoped he was right to trust her to the slaves. He had known them only four days. If things went badly for him here, they would be her only protection on the journey.

I know you will look after my household well until I am able to join you, and that if Tilla decides to travel on to join her people before then, you will give her every assistance.

Then all the usual waffle about everybody's health.

There were other letters that he had not told her about: the just-in-case ones he would leave with Accius to be sent via the Legion in Britannia: one to Valens and one to Albanus, entrusting his wife and family to their care.

They ate the morning's porridge from the pan. As Tilla pointed out, the sale of the crockery meant there would be one less box to carry. Then when Esico was out fetching water and Narina was changing Mara's smelly cloths in the surgery, she made one last attempt.

"I am not arguing," she whispered, "but I still think you have no reason to stay behind. It is not your fault you gave medicine when you were asked."

"There's a chance I'll learn something new from Balbus's body-guard," he told her, choosing to offer a hope so faint he had forgotten it himself rather than return to the old battleground. "I haven't spoken properly with Latro yet. He was there: He might have spotted something no one else saw."

She shook her head. "It is too late to talk to Latro. He ran away."

"Really?" With everything else going on, he had not even noticed. "There's a lot of it about."

"What?"

"Running away."

"He is a coward. He is the reason that slave girl is pregnant. His master promised he would be freed in the will, and he was not, and he cannot face the trouble he is in."

He upended the pan to scrape out the last of the porridge and tried not to envy the audacity of a man who ran away from his mistakes. "You won't forget to ask about Simmias?"

"I will go to the night watch," she promised. Simmias's flight was something they both felt guilty about. "He must have a family or something." But they both knew that if he had vanished as completely as Kleitos, the savings they needed to give back to him would never get there.

He could hear Narina talking to Mara in that singsong voice that women used to reassure children that whatever-it-was was almost done.

"Promise me you'll keep all of the business about Balbus's

death quiet," he said. "Wherever you are, whoever you're with. If the accusation gets out, Accius is ruined whether or not there's a court case."

Tilla took the pan from his hands and placed it on the table. "You have all those magistrates for making laws," she said. "Great bronze plaques with letters stamped into them as if they speak the truth and nothing can be changed. But this place is just like anywhere else. Everything depends on rumors and lies."

"I'm not even supposed to have told you."

"I shall keep it secret," she promised as Narina entered with a better-smelling baby. "I shall only tell one person, as you have. How about Sister Dorcas?"

His attempt at a smile felt exhausting. "I should never have brought you here."

"I could have said no," she told him. "I wanted to see what Rome was like."

He said, "I do love you, you know," as if there might have been some doubt about it, and then thought how strange it was that he could not remember ever telling her that before.

64

COSSUS WAS NOT there, of course. According to Horatia, who looked pale and exhausted, he had dropped by earlier to remind the cousin how happy he would be to help deal with any business that might arise during the period of mourning. "As if we didn't know that."

Accius was not there, either. Having visited the cousin first thing this morning and regretfully withdrawn his offer to marry Horatia, he was banned from the house both for upsetting her and for interrupting the privacy of the family's grief. On the way out he had seized Ruso in a clumsy embrace and promised to hurry across to the Palatine Hill and make an offering at the temple of Apollo to pray for his success: a promise which left Ruso even more nervous than before.

Guessing that the battle over Horatia would take place without either of the contenders present, Ruso had already sent a message to Metellus, who hurried into the inner courtyard not long after Accius had left.

"So you really can be contacted via the urban prefect's office," Ruso observed, to which Metellus replied that he had never spoken anything but the truth.

Ruso was sure that must be a lie in itself, but could not be bothered to work out why.

"I hope this is something important? I'm having a busy morning."

"I need a witness for Cossus," Ruso told him. "You'll have to do."

At Ruso's request the five of them gathered in Balbus's old study: Horatia, the cadaverous cousin—clearly annoyed at this latest disrespectful intrusion—and Firmicus, still loyally performing his role as Balbus's right-hand man despite his freedom. For once Metellus did not blend in: The plain tunic marked him as an outsider against the uniform black of the household's mourning.

The cousin said, "Well?"

Ruso took a deep breath. "I'm sorry to trouble you all with this," he began, ignoring the sudden thought that he might be the one who was sorry before long, "but I'm aware that the sad loss of the master of this house has been made even more difficult for everyone by the uncertainty over how he died."

He had their attention. Now for the difficult part.

"There's something I need to tell you," he said.

"Then get on with it," put in the cousin.

So he did.

When he got to the end he looked 'round at their faces. Metellus betrayed nothing as usual, although surely even he must have been surprised to hear Ruso confess his uncertainty about the medicine. The cousin was looking even more furious and bewildered. Firmicus looked stunned. Horatia, clutching the bracelet around her wrist, said, "It was you? All along, you knew it was you?"

"No, and I still don't know," Ruso repeated. "But I can't be sure what was in that jar labeled *poppy*, and I can't trace the man who put it there. And I can't go on listening to the sort of damaging accusations that are being spread around."

"Well that's not much help, is it?" demanded the cousin. "You don't know."

"I've come to ask your permission to find out. We need to take the medicine to an expert and have them check it. I think it's still—"

"It's in the master's study," put in Firmicus. "I'll fetch it."

Horatia said, "I'll go with you."

The bottle was still almost full. Cold now, of course, and the solids had settled into a dark sludge that undulated with the motion of the murky liquid above. It had not been one of his better efforts. Looking at this, Xanthe would probably classify him among those who knew nothing at all.

"There's an expert over at Trajan's baths." He had thought this part through, realizing they would believe nothing he said now. "But if you'd rather appoint your own . . ."

The cousin said, "That won't be necessary."

It was a small encouragement. Ruso turned toward the door. "She should be there now," he said. "She's called—"

"How much did you tell him to take?"

Ruso pointed to the label. "One small spoonful every evening."

"Then you can take four," the cousin told him.

Ruso froze. "But—"

"Four."

Only now did he realize he should have insisted on having another medic present. Not that he knew anyone who would have obliged. Both the doctors who had offered him friendship had fled. "It really does have poppy tears in it," he explained. "Four spoonsful could be a dangerously high dose."

"Cousin!" Horatia urged. "Cousin, if the doctor is telling the truth—"

"He should have told the truth a long time ago," Firmicus said before the cousin could answer. "My master might still be alive."

She said, "Perhaps an animal could be given it, or—"

"Four," repeated the cousin. "A dog proves nothing. And I'm not wasting a slave."

When he had drunk it they put him on an old couch in a bare little room off the garden courtyard. Stretching out, he wondered what Tilla was doing now, and if they were singing British songs in the kitchen. He was glad he had bought her those slaves. Even the one that had run away. It was not much to ask to please a wife whom you'd wrenched away from her own people. From everything she had grown up with or grown to love. A wife whom you had dragged around from one set of rented rooms to the next, eating food from cheap bars and living out of bags and boxes.

At least I mended her arm, he thought. And I gave her Mara. After a fashion. I did something good.

If he died tonight—which he might, even if it really had been just poppy all along, because he was drowsy already—it would all be fine. That was the thing with poppy. Everything was fine as your breathing slowed to a halt and you drifted away. Everything was fine. The trip to Rome had not worked out the way he expected, but Tilla and Mara would be safe. She was taking Mara home to family and friends. Sailing across the wine-dark sea.

His throat was dry. He could do with a drink, but that would pass.

There were faces above him, and they were looking much too worried. It was a shame for them. He tried to tell them he needed to sleep now, but they didn't seem to understand. A girl's voice said, "He's going!" and she sounded upset.

So he smiled and whispered, "No, fine. Really." He knew at last that the gods did indeed bring truth in dreams. He could see now how Horatius Balbus must have died, and if he hadn't been feeling so sleepy he would have done something about it.

65

TILLA DRAGGED AN empty wooden box out from under the bed and carried it into the surgery. Everything would be all right. Her husband would tell the truth about the medicine and people would understand. Even if it had been a mistake, it was an honest one, and who could condemn him for that? A healer who had tried to do good should surely not be treated like a criminal. Then, once they knew the whole story the family would have to agree that none of what had happened was Accius's fault. That would mean her husband had more than fulfilled his duty and could leave. Accius would renew his offer of marriage and things would follow whatever course the gods might choose.

There was a heavy price to pay, though. People would not trust her husband to treat them anymore. Not here. Perhaps not anywhere, if the story spread, and she had no doubt that Metellus would help it on its way. But that was a problem for the days ahead. With luck the business about the medicine would all be settled by tonight. Horatius Balbus's family would see that neither her husband nor Accius had tried to murder him. After that surely Accius could sort out his own problems? Tomorrow her whole household might go together down to the river and load their belongings onto a barge to travel down to Portus. The *Notus* would take them from Portus to Massalia, and from there it could not be more than two or three days to his family's farm. The nieces and nephews would play with Mara, and the sisters and the stepmother would make catty remarks, but the sister-in-law was a friend. The two brothers would greet each other with warm embraces and within the day they would be arguing again. That was what families were like, and suddenly she was desperate to be among them.

She was packing linen dressings around the weighing scales to protect them when the girl with the baby wandered in and sat on the stool to feed him and complain about the meanness of her mother. The baby, Tilla noticed, was called *he* now. It was progress.

The girl was too busy with her own troubles to notice that Tilla was preparing to leave, but Phyllis already knew.

"Timo has gone out," she explained as she sidled into the surgery and placed herself in the corner where he could not see her if he came back. "I had to come and talk to you. I am so sorry you are going."

"You're going?" demanded the girl, looking 'round her as if for the first time. "Where are you going?"

"Home," Tilla told her.

"What for? Don't you like us?"

"I like you very well," Tilla replied. "But—"

"Sabella's husband told them to go," Phyllis put in, moving to get a better view of the baby's dark head. "All because other people made trouble, and it wasn't even their fault. And Timo mended the door so it's not as if there's any damage to repair."

"It's that cow Sabella," said the girl. "Her stupid husband does whatever she tells him. My ma says somebody ought to slap her."

"There are many reasons why we are going," Tilla told her. "Not just Sabella." Sabella certainly had not helped, though. She said to Phyllis, "Your friends will need to take their furniture back by first thing tomorrow morning."

Phyllis said, "There must be rooms you can move to nearby. I'll ask around. Somebody will know a good place."

Avoiding the question, Tilla pointed upward. "How are things?"

Phyllis smiled. "Better than before. Thank you."

The girl said, "You ought to do what Ma did when Sabella tried to get us out. Ma said she would tell Horatius Balbus how her husband was cheating him on the rent. That shut her up all right. And Pa told the husband he would tell Sabella about him and the girl who delivers the laundry."

"Yes," agreed Phyllis, to Tilla's surprise. "You should try that. And— Oh!"

She ducked back into the corner as a shadow fell across the doorway, but instead of her husband it was a frightened young woman Tilla had never seen before. Her husband was on the way, bringing their son. He was three years old and he had climbed up onto the windowsill and fallen out.

The boy shrieked in pain as the father laid him on the operating table. His left foot was twisted at an impossible angle. The mother was sobbing, demanding that Tilla do something and wanting to know where the doctor was, while her husband was telling her this was what happened if you didn't watch them properly, and Tilla was silently cursing Publius Accius and his selfish problems, because this child really needed her husband's help, and her husband wasn't here. Worse, she had no idea when he would be back.

"If you couldn't help him, why didn't you say so?" demanded the father. "Now we've got to carry him somewhere else."

It was useless to explain that she had been hoping it was a sprain, that only when she'd seen the full extent of the injury could she see that there were delicate bones to be set, and that if she set them wrong, he would limp for life. Or worse. She was about to say, "You can leave him here: I will fetch someone"—Who? Phyllis might know—when a voice from the street said, "Am I interrupting, dear lady? I've come to look for Doctor Ruso."

"We were here first!" snapped the mother.

It was the last person Tilla had been expecting, but it was the first person she would have chosen. "Doctor Simmias! Please! We need help!"

To his credit, Simmias did not complain about how tired he was. Not until after the boy had been carried out with his straightened leg dressed with the linen she had removed from the weighing

scales and had soaked with wine and oil, and the last layer of
bandage had been coated with cerate. Then Tilla heard all about it:
how lucky Simmias had been to find some lads from the night
watch who were traveling down to the barracks at Ostia and who
could take him with them. How he had been unable to find a lift
back so he'd had to use some of the money for a carriage to get
here quickly, and how he had been traveling most of the night, and
it really was very tiring being bumped around for hours in the
dark when you weren't as young as you used to be. But anyway, he
was delighted to be back now.

Was she supposed to know why he had rushed to Ostia? She
could not remember. "You could not have come at a better time,"
she told him, handing him the drink and the cake Narina had
fetched from the bar.

"Glad to help." Simmias took a mouthful of cake before shifting
awkwardly on the stool to look around him at the confusion of the
half-packed surgery. "Oh, dear. I'm so sorry. I was hoping to get
here before they came."

For a moment she looked at him blankly. Then she guessed
what he was thinking. "This is our own mess," she explained.
"That man with the squeaky voice is not coming. My husband
went to see his boss and it is all settled and there is nothing to pay
because the boss told him to behave himself."

Simmias looked shocked. "Nothing to pay?"

"Yes, and I have to give you your savings back." She climbed
on a stool and groped for the bag of coins that was out of
sight, propped on two nails in the back of the rafter nearest
the wall.

"Nothing?"

"No. Really. It was very kind of you to help, but you can have
this back now."

He let out a long sigh and slumped his head into his hands.

"Are you all right?"

"Quite—yes, quite—oh, dear."

"You wanted to pay them?"

"No!" The head jerked up. "Certainly not, no. But I have been
all that way to fetch—ah well, never mind." He snatched another
mouthful of cake and washed it down with the wine.

"What have you been to Ostia to fetch?"

"I thought it was only fair to you and your husband," he said. "I went to fetch the rest of the money. From Kleitos."

She stared at him. "You have seen Doctor Kleitos?"

Simmias's jowls wobbled as he swallowed. "Yes. I explained what was happening here and he told me something I really do need to pass on urgently to your husband."

66

SIMMIAS WAS IN no condition to rush across to Balbus's house. Leaving him to mind the surgery and Narina to mind Mara, Tilla ran down the arcade and along past the shops and the council buildings and the lodging houses of the Vicus Sabuci. Beside her, Esico looked even more alarming than before with the bandage off and the stitched wound exposed above his red-and-purple eye.

"Left!" she called as they reached the shrine on the corner, and they both halted, breathless, at the door with the cypress bough over it.

She tried to knock in a way that was urgent but not disrespectful. "Look to one side so they can't see the state of you," she warned him. The last thing she wanted was to be refused entry. Her husband was in danger.

She could still barely believe what she had to tell him: that Simmias had known where Kleitos was all along, but had sworn not to tell anyone. That he really had been trying to sell his furniture for him. That he had only confessed this now because of what Kleitos had told him yesterday before boarding a ship bound for Alexandria. That Simmias had no idea what had been in the poppy jar, and that Kleitos really had gone now, so it was too late to ask. But it was not too late for the other thing. At least, she hoped not.

"Answer the door!" she muttered, knocking again. "Blessed Christos, make them answer the door!"

Finally there were footsteps, and the rattling of iron and the squeak of hinges, and the door scraped back a couple of inches to reveal the man who had let her in yesterday.

"The family are not at home to callers."

"I am sorry for the loss of your master," Tilla told him, "But I need to get a message to my husband, the doctor. There is a patient at home who needs him quickly."

"Wait there."

The door clamped shut in her face.

Clutching the little carved horse tightly, Tilla was muttering prayers to all the gods she could think of. Esico stood back, obediently facing away down the street. He had no idea what was going on, which, she thought, made him very lucky. "Holy mothers, bring him out safe."

Footsteps approached the door. She straightened. Any moment now—

Firmicus said, "He's not here. He might have gone to Publius Accius's house."

"Are you quite sure?"

He looked at her oddly.

"I mean—are you sure it was Accius's? Did he mention going anywhere else?"

"No," said Firmicus. "And no."

"He's needed urgently back at home. A patient is dangerously ill. If you see him, please tell him his wife said to hurry."

He said he would. Then he shut the door. She stared at its iron studs for a moment, trying to decide what to do. Then she turned to Esico. "We are going to another house," she told him. "And if you have any breath while we are running, pray for your master."

67

I T WAS NOT difficult to get into Publius Accius's house, where
she knew most of the staff, but it was useless. Her husband was
not there.

"I'd say, miss," said the witch housekeeper, addressing Tilla but
keeping her attention on the gangling Briton with the black eye in
case he ran wild around the entrance hall, "that if your husband
didn't leave word of where he was going, then he didn't want to be
found."

"Never mind what you would say." Tilla was in no mood to be
polite. "I need to know where he is."

The witch sniffed. "I'll see if someone can recommend another
doctor."

"I don't need another doctor. I need to speak to my husband."

"What about your urgent patient?"

"There is no patient!" Suddenly she was shrieking, and she
could not stop herself. "I made the patient up! Tell me where my
husband is, right now, or I will set my man on you!"

Esico was backing away in alarm, but the witch was so frightened of him that she squealed and ran anyway, knocking over a
palm tree in a pot and almost tripping into the pool.

Left alone with her slave, Tilla let out a wail of frustration and anguish that the gods must surely have heard, but they did not answer.

After a moment Esico said, "What do we do now, mistress?"

Tilla did not know. She could try asking some of the other staff, but it was unlikely that the housekeeper had lied. Her husband was not here. She was very much afraid that Firmicus was the one who was lying.

They were almost back in the street by the time Accius caught up with them, looking much better than he had last time she saw him. "I thought it sounded like you," he said. "Nobody told me you were here. What's happening? Where's Ruso? How did it go with Horatia's family?"

"He has not come home," Tilla told him. "And I need to tell him something. Now."

Accius ran one hand through his hair. "I left him over at Balbus's," he said. "He was going to talk to them." He leaned 'round to look at the angle of the sun slanting into the open roof of the entrance hall. "He can't still be there at this hour. He must have gone somewhere else."

"Would he not come to tell you what had happened at Balbus's house first?"

Both hands went through the hair this time. "Yes."

"I think he is still there," Tilla told him. "And I think Firmicus is lying. I do not know what is happening, but I do not think it is good."

68

Tilla had never realized until now how like a fortress a rich man's house could be. The door was solid oak, the fastenings were of iron, and nobody was answering her knock. When she called out that it was an urgent message for the doctor, a voice shouted back that he was not there. When she asked to speak to mistress Horatia or Gellia the slave girl, there was no reply.

Accius warned her it was useless for him to try because he was banned, but he tried anyway, and it was. He kept saying there must be someone with the authority to demand they open up, but when she wanted to know who, and how fast that person could be fetched, he fell silent.

The front wall opened out into shops on either side of them, but the scribe and the basket seller were telling the truth: Neither room had access to the inside of the house. She knew, because Accius sent his man in to check on both sides.

One side of the house was joined onto another two-story building. The alley that ran down the other side stank of piss and rotting vegetables, and from it the four of them gazed up at a painted wall that was completely blank all the way to the roof. She remembered how it was inside now: all those rooms opening onto the courtyards for light. No need for windows onto the street to let in noise or burglars or spies. Or wives who were afraid for their husbands.

"Did you not have some secret way in to visit Horatia?"

Accius looked shocked. "Horatia is a respectable girl!"

"Pity." Farther along, Tilla paused and put her finger to her lips. "Sh!"

All four of them stopped. After a moment Accius said, "What?"

She shook her head. "Only the fountain. Is there a garden door?"

It was amazing how blind the wealthy could be to what servants did and how they did it. Accius had no idea where the service entrance might be. When they found it, it was another heavy studded door that did not move when they tried to barge it open. It was set in another blank wall with weeds growing out of the bottom and tiles overhanging the top. Horatius Balbus had certainly not wanted unexpected visitors. The wall was so high that even if Esico stood on Accius's shoulders, he would not get over it. If he had, there would be a long drop on the other side. She said, "You are the soldier. How would you take this place?"

Accius said, "I'd put a spy in to open the gates." Seeing the look on her face, he added, "Create a diversion at the front and send men with ladders up over the walls."

The diversion would be easy enough. For a moment she wondered if Accius could persuade the night watch to lend them a tall ladder, but then she supposed they would send men with it, and the watch were surely not allowed to break into a house unless . . . "We could set fire to something," she said. That was how the soldiers forced people out of their houses at home.

When Accius said straightaway, "There's no thatch," she knew he must have been thinking the same thing. "Besides, they've got water. They'll put it out."

He strode back down the alley to the point where she had heard the fountain. "Doctor!"

The yell was so loud it made her jump.

"Ruso, this is Accius. Are you in there? Ruso? I need to talk to you!"

"We have come for the doctor!" Tilla shouted, her own voice weak by comparison. There were other, more useful things she could have shouted, but only if she could be certain who was listening. Otherwise she could make things very much worse. "The doctor is needed at home! There is a patient!"

A couple of pigeons fluttered up over the walls and flew away, but if any humans heard, none of them responded.

"This is hopeless," said Accius.

Esico said something she did not catch. She asked him to repeat it.

"We do not need to burn the house, mistress," he said. "Only the door."

"There are too many people about," she explained. "And that door will take hours to burn."

"But the smoke and the smell go through the cracks," he said in a way that told her he had seen it done. "And then what will the man inside do?"

69

Elysium. Paradise. Heaven. This was what all those inadequate words were trying to describe. He was a part of it at last. The joyful serenity that he had never understood, but secretly longed to share.

How he pitied the poor unbeliever that he had once been. How he pitied all the others, with their wizened brains and their tricky questions. If only they could see all the troubles of the anxious world in their proper place, as he did now.

An urgent thought came to him. He must share this. He must write it down. Others must know. Tilla. And the little wriggly one, whatever her name was.

But the voices were getting louder, starting to distract him with idle chatter. Something seized his shoulder and shook it. He tried to tell them to stop, but his throat was dry and nothing came out.

"He's waking up! Run and fetch my cousin."

He tried to say *No, I was awake then, but you are dragging me back into this body.*

Footsteps. A door banged. A voice said, "Water."

Blessed coolness was splattering across his parched lips but he pressed them shut. He must not be distracted. He must write it all down before—

"Take some water, Doctor," a voice urged him. "It will do you good."

A blurry face leaning over him, dark eyebrows and a faint gritty cascade of—was that ash falling on his skin? Then the water again.

He managed to raise a hand but he was not strong enough to push the cup away. A soft voice said, "He doesn't want it."

"It'll do him good," said the first voice. "Not that he deserves it."

A hand took hold of his. The soft voice said, "Welcome back, Doctor. We were afraid we'd lost you."

And then he was struggling to the surface, knowing something but not knowing why he knew it. He squinted upward. Faces. One, two, three faces. The one with the eyebrows. He was holding the water. The dark-haired girl with black around her wrist. And Metellus. Always Metellus, watching from the shadows.

Ruso said, "The water—"

"Here," The man was holding out the cup again.

More faces appeared: a skeleton still in his skin and a girl whose face held all the flesh that her companion lacked. The skeleton wanted to know what was happening.

Good question.

He had only to open his lips and liquid would soothe his rasping tongue and cool his throat. The man tipped it toward him. He turned his head away. "The water," he said, feeling it trickle over his jaw and down behind one ear. "Where from?"

"Firmicus brought it for you from the fountain," the soft voice said. "He thought you would be thirsty when you woke up."

"Don't want it. Don't drink it."

The man with the water said, "He's still groggy. He'll be all right in a moment."

And then, with a huge effort, Ruso managed to pull himself up onto one elbow and say, "Nobody drink the water. You, um—"

"Horatia," she prompted.

"You get some fresh. New cup."

"The mistress does not fetch water!" said the man.

"Fresh from the spout," he said, collapsing back onto whatever was underneath him and trying to remember how he knew that the man with the drink was dangerous.

70

ANYONE WHO GLANCED down the alleyway beside Balbus's house would know those people were up to no good: two slaves, a smart young man, and a blond woman all huddled around something on the ground, whispering. But unlike a real fortress, Balbus's house had no guards on patrol, and anyone who saw anything suspicious had more sense than to interfere.

Accius's man bought the oil from a supplier farther along the street and the basket from the shop next door, where he also managed to beg for dry offcuts of willow and reed to fill it. Tilla tore a linen cloth into strips and then pulled out her knife and cut the strips into small pieces. Accius struck the spark from the steel in his purse, remarking that if there was one thing soldiering had taught him, it was never to be without fire.

Nobody seemed to notice the clean flame in the sunlight. The slave carried the basket around the corner and knelt to place it in front of the door before standing casually in front of it, chatting to his master and a gangly youth with a black eye. Then Tilla dropped on the handful of weeds that Esico had fetched, and joined the others just as thick stinking smoke began to rise, along with shouts of alarm from the shops and people in the street.

The broom and the flapping cloths were easy enough to beat aside in the confusion, the owners of stamping feet not hard to knock off balance while more people were piling in to help and everyone was shouting at everyone else to be careful and get out of the way. Somewhere in the house, a bell was clanging. And then she heard Accius shout, "Now!" and through the smoke she saw the door open and Accius lunge forward just as the torrent of water came out and hit him. She screamed, "No!" and tried to claw her way forward but someone knocked her aside and the door was closing again and Accius was still on this side of it and she could not get there in time and—

And a big figure was shouldering his way in, his high-pitched voice sounding above the uproar, "Undertaker to see the steward!"

They slipped in unhindered in the wake of Squeaky, who reached up and stilled the bell. "Undertaker to see the steward," he repeated, and the doorman, stumbling backward away from him, said, "Just wait there, sir," but nobody did.

Several household slaves were running toward them, with Firmicus striding along behind.

Squeaky said, "I need a word with you."

Firmicus looked at him for a moment, then ordered everyone else back to work. Meanwhile Horatia came running across the entrance hall and flung herself into Accius's wet arms. "I knew you would come! I knew it!" The little woman who cried, "Mistress Horatia!" in shocked tones might as well not have bothered.

Tilla said, "Where is my husband?" but nobody answered. So she ran past Accius and the others, calling for him in the entrance hall, and past all the statues and out into the second courtyard, and there he was, being dragged toward the fountain by Metellus.

"Leave him alone!"

His clothes were creased, his hair was sticking up, and he was grinning at her as if he were a small boy. She held him tight and he started to giggle.

Metellus said, "It's the medicine. He says it'll wear off."

"It's all right," her husband assured her, reaching out to cup one hand under a stream of the fountain and slurping the water before wiping his wet palm over his face. "It's all right. It was just ordinary poppy all along." He glanced around before leaning closer to whisper, "Got to watch out for the steward."

"I know," she told him. "That's what Kleitos said to Simmias. I came to tell you."

He blinked. "Say that that again," he said. "Slowly."

71

IT DID NOT take Accius long to decide that since he was an aristocrat and a former military tribune and a man, he must be in charge. He unwound himself from Horatia, who was now very damp, gave his doctor a friendly slap on the shoulder that nearly knocked him over, and announced that he needed a word with the skull-faced cousin. The cousin muttered something about him being banned and about needing another bodyguard—and where was that steward when he was wanted?—but nobody seemed to take any notice. All the staff had either vanished or were scuttling about, making themselves look busy. When Horatia followed them into her father's old study to hear the word Accius was about to have, her cousin did not even try to send her away.

Tilla stood close to her husband as he scooped more water from the fountain spout. Gellia, very pale, was leaning over the opposite side and gazing at the fish as if she had nothing better to do. Esico was standing awkwardly by a pillar, trying to hide his black eye while he waited to be given orders. Metellus had disappeared, but he was like a pet snake: If you knew he was out of his cage somewhere you could never rest easy.

There was a cup abandoned on the marble seat. Tilla stepped

across to collect it and Gellia suddenly seemed to wake up. "Not that one, miss." The girl hurried across and snatched it from her. "I'll get you a clean one."

Tilla supposed that was the way they did things in a house with too many servants. People did not even know how to rinse a cup for themselves. She took her husband by the arm. "This is the last time you take your own medicine."

"It was only a very low dose of poppy."

"It could have killed you! Look at you! You are not even used to taking it like that man would have been."

"Only poppy," he repeated, grinning at her. "Four times the minimum dose, but only . . ."

"That was what I told you all along," she said, not entirely certain that she had. "Now, talk to me about that steward."

"Kleitos said not to trust him."

"I just told you that! What else do you know?"

So then he explained, with pauses to collect his thoughts that made her want to poke him to hurry him up.

When Gellia returned with the cup Tilla passed it to her husband and told her to stay.

"I need to talk to you about Latro."

Gellia raised her chin. "I am not talking about him."

"Yes, you are. This is important." Tilla was ashamed not to have seen the lie for herself yesterday. Nor even when she had repeated the story to her husband over breakfast. "Who told Latro that he would be freed in the master's will?"

Gellia frowned. "The master, I suppose."

"Think very hard about this, Gellia. Do you think it is likely that a master who depends on someone to help him stay alive would tell that someone that he will benefit from the master's death?"

Gellia did indeed look as though she was thinking very hard about it, possibly because she did not understand the question.

"Gellia, if I am your master and you are my bodyguard, will I tell you that things will go well for you if I die?"

"Oh, I see!"

"Are you quite sure it was the master?"

She was not. She had just supposed it must be.

"And if it was not the master, who was it?"

She said in a very small voice, "The only one who would know what was in the will was Firmicus."

The empty cup clapped down onto the side of the fountain. "That's what I thought as well," Ruso said. "The two men guarding Balbus when he died."

"Husband, not now!"

He said it anyway. "The steward who knew he would benefit from the death, and the bodyguard who . . ." He paused, scratched his head, and said, "The bodyguard who thought he would be freed too."

Gellia said, "Latro always looked after the master, he wouldn't . . ."

Tilla said, "My husband is just guessing."

But all the remaining color had drained from Gellia's face. Tilla reached out to take her arm but she spun away out of reach, racing across the courtyard and thundering up a wooden staircase. Tilla followed. By the time they reached the room beyond the courtyard balcony she was already shouting, "You! It was you! You made him do it!"

Tilla caught a glimpse of Firmicus and Squeaky staring at Gellia from either side of a pile of denarii before the slave girl stepped forward, and the desk rose up and silver coins were glinting in the air all around them and pattering over the floor like hail.

Gellia would have done better to press home the attack. Instead she faltered, hands covering her mouth, staring at what she had done.

Firmicus stood without speaking, and righted the fallen table. His eyes were cold. Gellia took a step backward.

"Get back to work," he told her, adding in a voice that Tilla could barely hear, "I'll have you brought to me later."

72

ACCIUS STRODE INTO the steward's office looking even more annoyed than usual. Meanwhile Horatia and her cousin had followed him up the steps. By the time Firmicus finished counting out the money he had rescued from the floor, the little room was crammed with people, and Ruso, who had got there before them, had to shift farther along to let them in.

Despite being only two paces away, Squeaky seemed not to have recognized either him or Tilla. Perhaps the big man was hoping they might mistake him for somebody else. When Firmicus handed him the newly filled purse he twisted the drawstring around his wrist, cupped the weight in his palm, and blundered toward the door.

To Ruso's surprise Tilla stepped into Squeaky's path. "What is that money for?"

Firmicus said, "Payment for the master's funeral."

She had picked the wrong fight. Even Squeaky could not be a money-grabbing bully all of the time. Now the big man was grinning down at her, and she was clearly wrong-footed. He knew he should say something, but *Be nice to my wife* didn't sound quite right.

Fortunately Accius took charge. "Nobody's to leave until we've cleared up what happened to Horatius Balbus."

Horatia looked up at him adoringly. Squeaky glanced 'round to see if anyone was going to tell Tilla to get out of the way, then backed into a corner. Ruso leaned against a cupboard and stifled a yawn. He was feeling faintly queasy, but he must stay alert. This was important.

Accius turned to address the cousin, who was looking more weary than impressed. Ruso guessed he would rather be back in his butcher's shop, hacking up carcasses.

"Sir," Accius began, "perhaps you'd allow me to inform our friends here of your kind acknowledgment that I had absolutely nothing to do with the sad death of the man I had hoped to call father-in-law and neither did my man Ruso."

This is what we need at a time like this, Ruso wanted to say. *A man who can make speeches.* For a moment he wondered if he had actually said it. But Accius was still talking, so probably not.

Then Firmicus said, "The tribune is innocent, sir, but the doctor isn't. My master collapsed and suffered a fatal injury after taking that man's fake medicine."

The cousin turned to Ruso and raised one eyebrow.

"The only potentially dangerous ingredient was poppy, sir," Ruso told him, stifling an urge to agree that making medicine with a dubious ingredient was a very stupid thing to do, and trying to remember where he had intended to go with this statement. Fortunately Tilla guessed.

"Horatius Balbus had been taking small amounts of poppy daily," she said. "Anyone who knows about poppy will tell you that if you take it every day, it is bad to stop, but if you take it that way it has a weaker effect. My husband does not take it often, and you made him swallow many times as much as his patient, and look! He is still here."

In body, at least. He was not sure where his mind was. "In any case, sir," he began, then paused. It was very distracting to be stared at by everyone like that. Ah, yes. "In any case, we've only got the steward's word for it that his master collapsed."

"Not true!" snapped Firmicus, not bothering to address the cousin. "Latro was there. He saw it too."

"But he's not here now," Ruso pointed out.

Tilla said, "You both thought you would be freed if Balbus died."

"The street was full of people!"

"You know, it's very odd," Ruso said, genuinely puzzled. "I couldn't find a single person who saw him before he fell. I spent a long time looking."

That sent Firmicus into a long speech about his lifetime of service here and how Ruso had blown in from the provinces only yesterday. Ruso could not understand why anyone was bothering to listen to this bluster, but he suspected he was still slightly adrift on the receding tide of the poppy. There was something else he needed to say, and it was important, and in a minute he would remember what it was.

"You waited till you were in the dark with nobody looking," Tilla interrupted, "And—"

"Sir!" Firmicus demanded. "Why are we listening to this—this woman?"

The cousin said, "Let her speak," but Tilla was already talking.

"In the dark," she insisted, "with nobody looking, you and Latro knocked your master down and killed him!"

What a woman he had married! She really was marvelous. This was like watching a boxing match.

Firmicus, on the other hand, thought she was talking nonsense and said so.

"You lied to Latro," Tilla went on. "You told him he would be freed when the master died, and he saw his chance to buy Gellia and marry her. He wouldn't have helped you otherwise."

Surely Firmicus would be floored by that? But no. When the cousin said, "Well?" he rallied. He had, he agreed, not been telling the whole truth. The fault did not lie entirely with the incompetent doctor, although he deserved to be punished for carelessness anyway.

Absolutely right, Ruso thought, then realized when everyone turned to look at him that he had spoken aloud.

Firmicus had not wanted to say this in front of the family, but that woman—why did people insist on calling Tilla *that woman?*—had forced him into it.

The whole thing, it seemed, had been planned by Latro. Firmicus himself had suspected nothing until they were passing the shoemaker's door and Latro suddenly stepped back and cracked his master on the side of the head with his club. Asked why, Latro said Balbus had refused to grant him his freedom, and if Firmicus didn't shut up and play along, he would get the same. To Firmicus's great shame, he had been too shocked and afraid to speak up at the time. Then later he had taken the difficult decision not to say anything out of loyalty to the family.

"Loyalty?" put in Horatia, incredulous.

"You need me, mistress." He looked around the room. "You all need me. Nobody else knows how the business works."

"What did Pa ever do to hurt you?"

"Nothing," Firmicus told her. "He was going to free me next year. The loss of me as well as him would have destroyed everything he built up for you to inherit."

A silence fell over the little room and this time it seemed even Tilla had nothing to say. It was too late now for *Doctor Kleitos said you weren't to be trusted.*

Finally the cousin turned to Horatia. "Is that three or four versions we have now of how your father died?"

Accius put his hand on her arm. "Let me deal with this. Sir, this is distressing for the young lady and we don't need all these other people here, either. I suggest you and I remain here with the steward and we'll get to the truth."

Or at least, thought Ruso as the rest of them trooped out onto the sunlit balcony, a version of the truth that would suit Publius Accius. Which was probably no bad thing.

73

GELLIA HAD NOT gone back to work. She was leaning over the side of the fountain again, staring at a dozen silver bodies floating and bobbing in the water.

"The fish!" cried Horatia, running down the steps. "All the fish are dead! We are cursed! First Pa, then Latro, now this!"

This seemed the wrong way around to Ruso: Surely the gods would start with the fish and work their way up?

Gellia stepped away from the fountain. This was a very different Gellia from the nervous creature he had first met, or the screaming fury who had thrown over the table, or the cowed servant expecting punishment. This was a young woman who clasped her hands over her pregnant belly and, with a clear voice, asked permission to speak.

Horatia said, "Of course."

"Firmicus did it, mistress."

Horatia frowned. "Firmicus struck the fish dead?"

"The water that he brought for the doctor," the girl said, pointing at the fish. "The water the doctor wouldn't drink. They said to take it away, so I tipped it in the fountain."

The queasiness returned as Ruso realized how close he had been to never waking up again.

"But why?" Horatia demanded of no one in particular. "Why did he do all these terrible things? Pa was going to free him next year anyway!"

Gellia said, "Your pa said that every year, miss."

Horatia was still staring at the fish. "We would have thought it was the medicine," she said, following the same train of thought as Ruso. "The doctor would have been blamed for everything, and poor Accius, and—"

At that moment they heard Accius yell, "Stop him!" but Firmicus leapt over the side of the steps and was past them and ducking in behind a trellis at the far end of the garden.

As they ran Tilla cried, "The door!"

But instead of the rattle of a lock there was a howl of pain, and a violent rustling of leaves as something hit the trellis, and a high-pitched voice shouted, "No you don't, pal!"

The surprise was not so much that Firmicus had escaped from Accius and the cousin—who probably hadn't thought to guard him—but that Squeaky, suddenly helpful, had known where the garden door was. It was where the undertakers had collected the other body. "The one he's just paid me for."

Ruso said, "What other body?"

Looking 'round at the baffled faces, Squeaky said, "Big muscular lad." He shook the immobilized Firmicus. "Matey here said he done himself out of shame 'cause he couldn't protect his master."

Firmicus said, "Latro was full of remorse. He took poison. I found the body." He looked 'round as if trying to find a sympathetic listener. "I was trying to protect the family from more tragedy."

In the silence that followed, Gellia stepped up to him and spat in his face. She watched the saliva trickle down the side of his nose for a moment. Then she walked away.

"I should've known he was lying," said Squeaky, who seemed to be enjoying his newfound celebrity. "He lied about you and all, Doctor. You never did say any of them things about us, did you?"

"I told you I hadn't," said Ruso, hoping Squeaky wasn't about to go into detail about the sale of bodies in front of the household.

Squeaky gave Firmicus another shake. "What did you do that for, then? Didn't you like him?"

It seemed Firmicus had run out of excuses.

"He didn't like me asking questions about his master's death," Ruso said. "He was hoping you'd provide a distraction." The poppy must be wearing off. Now that he thought about it, he had never liked Firmicus much, either.

"It's my belief," Accius told Ruso as they strolled back toward the inner courtyard, "that Firmicus had been jealous of Balbus for years. Horatia's cousin says they started out as equals, you know. Then Balbus is freed and ends up owning the whole place, including Firmicus himself. Apparently Balbus made him several false promises of freedom, and Firmicus must have finally had enough. Just think, Ruso—if I hadn't demanded an investigation, none of this would have come to—ah."

Ruso caught sight of a figure slinking down past the statues toward the entrance hall.

"There you are, Metellus!"

The figure paused, turned, and bowed as it approached. "Sir. Congratulations. I hear the young lady's guardian has promised to look with favor on your renewed proposal."

"No thanks to you. I'm deeply disappointed, Metellus."

Metellus's apology sounded genuine. Nobody, it seemed, could be happier than he was to be proved wrong. "I'm afraid the steward had me completely fooled, sir. And I felt compelled to protect the young lady—"

"You weren't supposed to listen to the steward," said Horatia, who had appeared from somewhere inside the house.

"I'll protect the young lady myself, thank you," put in Accius.

Horatia said, "You were supposed to be working for Publius Accius."

Metellus said again that he was sorry. "But the evidence did seem to be pointing in a very worrying direction, sir."

Accius linked arms with Horatia. "I've come to the conclusion," he said, "that evidence is a very slippery substance." Then he turned and escorted her away into the house.

Tilla was somewhere indoors tending to Gellia, who had collapsed into fresh weeping at the news about Latro. Ruso was surprised to be beckoned into the middle of the courtyard by Metellus.

Wondering if he was actually about to receive an apology, Ruso complied.

What he heard was, "Do you still want me to look for this Kleitos chap?"

"No."

"Good," said Metellus. "I would have done it before, but I've been rather busy."

Ruso said, "Lots of prayer meetings to attend?"

Metellus smiled. "Interesting people, the followers of Christos. When they're not squabbling, the best of them go to surprising lengths to support one another. I can see the attraction for freed slaves, people with no families, that sort of thing."

Ruso wondered if Metellus had a family anywhere. It seemed unlikely.

"Unfortunately there's also a core of fools who are stubborn to the point of self-destruction. Refusing to sacrifice to the emperor does nobody any good."

"So that's your real job? Infiltrating the followers of Christos?"

"My duty—the duty of any citizen—is to support the city prefect in keeping the peace on behalf of the emperor. For example, I took your recommendation about that charlatan causing trouble outside the amphitheater."

"You were the one who got rid of him?"

"Not me personally. A report was submitted. Decisions are taken much higher up."

"And who decided that you should undermine Accius?"

Metellus sighed. "Really, Ruso. You don't expect me to answer that, do you?"

"No," Ruso told him. "Not now that the poppy's worn off."

74

"CAN YOU SEE them, Doctor?" enquired the patient as Ruso conducted a silent and fruitless search for head lice.

Ruso ordered Esico to bring a comb, and the patient asked to have the door shut.

"I'm not going to be able to see nits in the dark, Quintus."

The patient shifted unexpectedly, leaning his head of graying curls closer. Ruso recoiled—head lice were notoriously agile—but Quintus turned his face toward Ruso's left ear and whispered, "It's all right, Doctor. There aren't any."

Realizing he would get no sense until they were alone, Ruso sent Esico to wait outside. "So," he said, turning back to peer at his patient in the poor light cast by the small windows above the doorway, "How else can I help?"

The man was still whispering. "If anyone asks, swear you will tell them I came because of the nits."

"I wouldn't tell them anything," he said.

"Swear!"

"You came because of the nits," he said. "Did I find any?"

"Would I have to pay extra for medicine?"

"You'd have to go shopping for radish oil or alum. I haven't got any in stock."

"Then you told me it was just dandruff," said the man.

"It *is* just dandruff," Ruso pointed out, baffled.

"Good."

Whatever this was, Ruso hoped it was not going to take long. Out in the kitchen, he heard the crash of cutlery being dropped into a box and the scrape and thump of luggage being moved about. They needed to be on a barge heading down the Tiber by the ninth hour. "So what can I do for you, Quintus?"

The man took a deep breath, but no words came.

Ruso said, "Do you normally see the other doctor?"

"No."

"I'll fetch a lamp," he suggested, "and then you can show me what the problem is." But before he could get to his feet, the man said, "It's not about me."

"Ah!" said Ruso. "Is it about a friend?"

"How did you know?"

"Tell me about him," he prompted, wondering which of the usual selection of embarrassing ailments he was about to be offered. "I'll see what I can do to help."

The man straightened. "You can't help," he said, his tone suddenly serious. "I just want to know if it was him. And I want to know where he is now and if he ever got a decent burial, because there's nobody else in this miserable city likely to care."

Ruso sat back.

"They said you found him here. They said he had blond hair."

"Shorter than yours," Ruso told him.

"A scar over his left eye," said Quintus.

Ruso nodded. "I'm sorry. We'd have notified someone, but none of us knew who he was." And clearly Lucius Virius had been lying through his teeth when he claimed that a family had identified and claimed the body. "The undertakers could tell you where his ashes are."

The head jerked up. "And have them tell my master I was asking?"

Ruso said, "Who was he, Quintus?"

The man gave a bitter laugh. "He was nobody," he said. "He was just a laborer. Overworked and underfed, like the rest of us. Last week he had a cough. This week it was worse. Then one morning he didn't wake up. We got sent off to work. When we came back he'd gone. The foreman told us he'd been cremated." The man was jiggling one knee up and down, unable to sit still. "Twenty-seven. That's all he was." He looked up. "He was a mate. Why would somebody do that to him? What sort of sick joke was that?"

Ruso said, "I don't know," because there was nothing else he could say. He supposed the master and the foreman had abandoned the body and sent no one to attend the rites.

"Bastards. I hope they rot."

"Who's your master, Quintus?"

The stool scraped against the floor as the man got to his feet. "You don't need to know," he said, moving toward the door.

"Is your name really Quintus?"

"Of course not," said the slave, snapping the latch up and dodging out past a surprised Esico.

Ruso stood beside his doorkeeper, gazing after the man who was not Quintus as he sprinted away and was lost among the pedestrians of the Vicus Sabuci.

Lucius Virius had lied in order to keep Ruso from asking more questions. The dead slave in the barrel had been buried with no name. He was, as his friend had said, nobody.

"Have you got a moment, Doctor?"

It seemed everyone wanted the doctor now they knew he was leaving, but there was something he needed to say to Timo anyway. "Of course. We appreciate the help you've given us. We went a long time with no children of our own, so I want to do the best for the one we chose."

It sounded clumsy and contrived even to him. The carpenter placed his bag down beside the pillar of the arcade and straightened up before asking, "Has my wife been talking to you?"

"No," Ruso said, truthfully. "How can I help?"

"There's this skinny kid up on the fifth floor with a baby. I was going to ask you what you think."

"You'd have to ask Tilla about babies."

"About adopting. The wife said you'd know."

Ruso thought for a moment. He had assured Metellus that parenting was marvelous, but somehow that did not seem the right thing to say. "It's like any other sort of parenting, I suppose. Although not having tried the other sort, I don't really know. Sometimes, it's exhausting. Most of the time, it's—well, I can't imagine being without her now." He suspected there was a silly grin on his face as he added, "She had another tooth come through this morning. And I'm almost sure she said *Pa*." Seeing the expression on Timo's face he added, "Sorry. That's not really what you were asking, is it?"

Timo nodded. "That'll do." He bent to pick up the bag.

Ruso was glad Tilla hadn't been listening. He said, "Be careful with Brother Metellus. I've known him a lot longer than you have. He's not everything he seems."

Timo heaved the bag up onto one shoulder. "We're all sinners, Doctor," he said, turning and making his way along under the arcade to the stairs.

No sooner had he gone than a breathless figure turned up at the head of a string of porters carrying boxes and furniture. He flung his arms around Ruso. "Dear boy! This is so good of you! No stairs, not a single step! But are you sure you won't stay?"

"The wife's never going to be happy here," Ruso told him.

"Ah, yes!" Simmias followed him into the surgery and made sure Tilla was not in it before adding, "Magnificent lady. Truly magnificent."

"I like to think so." Ruso went to the door and asked the porters to wait a moment. They lowered their burdens to the pavement, looking resigned. Another set of clients who hadn't finished clearing out by the time they were supposed to.

Safe in the privacy of the surgery, he said, "Tell me, did Kleitos ever say exactly why he left?"

"Not exactly," Simmias admitted. "He just said he had no choice. And then he told me to tell you to be careful of that steward. He glanced around him. Is there something I should know about this practice?"

"Nothing you don't know already," Ruso assured him. "But I don't think your secret was as safe as you thought. I think Firmicus knew what was going on here. I think he was trying to blackmail Kleitos into poisoning Balbus for him."

"Oh, dear." Simmias blinked, perhaps for the first time seeing the wider implications of what he had been involved in.

"Kleitos had a choice all right. He could stay here and murder somebody, or stay here and be disgraced. Firmicus didn't expect him to run."

"But why didn't he tell me? I'm his friend!"

Ruso shrugged. "Perhaps he didn't want to drag you into it. There are several things I wish he'd told me about too."

Simmias said, "Oh, dear!" and sat down on a stool.

Ruso put a hand on his shoulder. "It's all right," he assured him. "It's over."

He left Simmias supervising the distribution of his belongings and went to tell the magnificent lady it was time to leave. He found only Narina with the luggage outside the back door, pulling the twine taut around a box. He crouched down and put a finger on the knot. "We'll be leaving in a moment," he told her. "Are you looking forward to seeing Britannia again?"

It was impossible to tell from the tone of her "Yes, master" whether she really was or whether she was saying it out of duty.

The magnificent lady was bearing down upon them, carrying the three-toothed daughter who might or might not have called him Pa this morning. "I have said good-bye to Phyllis," she said, "and I have told Sabella what she can do with her threats."

"Just as well we're leaving, then," he said, noticing Phyllis and Timo strolling across the courtyard behind her. They paused to clasp hands before entering the darkness of the stairs that led to the apartment of the girl with the baby. A woman was watching them from the water fountain, and above the sour expression he recognized the frizzy hair of Sister Dorcas.

"You are not listening."

"No," he agreed.

"Sabella guessed what Kleitos was doing."

Now he was paying attention. Sabella was not above spreading vicious rumors that could taint any doctor using the premises. If someone like Sister Dorcas got hold of it . . .

"It is all right," Tilla assured him. "I told her we know her husband cheats on the rent collection for the landlord and we know it was her own idea to leave that body in another street and not the slaves', because she told me that's what we should do, and I said we are going to tell Simmias all about it. And anyway, next time she has to take one of her children to a doctor she might be very glad of him knowing where everything inside is supposed to go."

"Well done."

"So I think she will be nicer to Doctor Simmias than she was to us. And if her husband makes trouble, Simmias is to ask him whether Sabella knows what he gets up to with the girl who delivers the laundry. Also, I have told Simmias that if a skinny slave from the Brigantes ever turns up and says he is sorry he ran away, tell him we are not sorry at all, and he has missed his chance to go home."

He touched the end of Mara's nose with his forefinger. "Your mother," he told her, "is a magnificent lady. Everyone says so."

Mara rewarded him with a flash of the new tooth. Top right.

As the four adults and a couple of hired men lumbered out of the courtyard with the luggage that had been brought in less than a week ago, he caught sight of the women who had come to the door to complain. He gave them a warm smile. "We're leaving!" he called.

They scowled and turned away. There really was no pleasing some people.

75

A CCIUS WAS WAITING below the vast vaulted warehouses of the Porticus Aemilia as promised. Horatia sent her apologies: It was not appropriate for a family in mourning to be chasing about all over the city. "You don't have to go, you know," Accius urged, surveying the luggage being loaded onto the barge by a couple of men and a skinny boy. "I'll need all the good men I can find when I run an election campaign. I'm sure I can find you something else in the meantime. I'll need a personal physician, for a start, and there's Horatia's household . . ."

"You're never ill, sir. And if you are, Simmias knows what he's doing."

"I hope you're not going back to that ghastly island because of your wife. Who's in charge here, man?"

Ruso changed the subject. "You're standing for election?" he asked.

"Not yet, obviously. But sooner or later. It's expected."

It might be expected, but it was also horrendously expensive, and given Accius's dubious standing with the emperor's friends it might well be doomed to failure.

"You could always do something else, sir." He was tempted to add, something useful, but he did not have time for a debate on the usefulness of magistrates and politicians. "Who's going to look after Horatia's properties without her father or Firmicus?"

Accius looked as though Ruso had just slapped him across the face. "I hope you're not suggesting—"

"Yes." He would have liked to be more subtle, but already the boatman's hand was steadying Tilla and Mara across the gap between wharf and tethered barge.

"There are—she will hire—there are people to do that sort of thing."

"Yes, sir. And I've seen how they do it."

"You're offering to stay and run the rental properties?"

"I'm asking you to take an interest in how Horatia's money is made. You're a decent man, sir. If you saw some of the conditions people in those apartments are living in—"

"It's their choice, Ruso. They pay very low rents, you know. And lots of them cram in far more friends and relations than they're supposed to."

"It was Balbus's choice to let his caretakers exploit them, sir. It was Balbus's choice not to keep up with repairs. It was Balbus's choice that led to my wife and daughter sleeping in a room crawling with cockroaches." Ruso stopped, aware that he was getting louder. "Sir."

Accius took a long breath in through his nose. "You never told me that."

Tilla and Narina were both on board now, unrolling a mattress along the top of a stack of red bricks. "I didn't like to seem ungrateful, sir."

"He said the tenants complain whatever you do."

"Not all of them." The boatman was shouting at Esico to get a move on—was he coming or not?

Accius said, "A man in your position can't possibly understand what a step down that would be."

"Probably not, sir." Esico was standing at his elbow, and he could hear Tilla calling him from the boat. "Sir, I have to—"

"My father would have been appalled."

He sent Esico toward the waiting boatman. "You were a good officer, sir. You've got a sharp clerk, and you can hire the help you need. And I'm sure if you threaten him with Squeaky, Firmicus will be happy to brief you on how things are done while he's awaiting trial."

"Hm."

"Your young lady is very well educated. I'm sure she could help."

"Oh, no. Oh, no. We don't all live like Britons, Ruso."

"No, sir." He paused with one foot on the solid wharf and the other shifting with the water.

The boatman called, "In or out, sir?"

"I can just imagine what Horatia would say."

"Yes, sir." Already the gap between him and his patron was widening. He made the step before it was too late, feeling himself taken up by the motion of the barge. He said, "Who's in charge here, sir?"

Accius reached out, but the grasp was brief. "Bugger off, Ruso. And may your gods bugger off with you."

Ruso raised a hand in salute. "It's been an honor, sir." Because in a strange way, it had.

76

WORKING ON THE barges was much better than working
for Uncle Birna. For the first couple of days the boy had
hung around the wharves, making himself useful. Tying a tarpaulin
over bales of wool when it looked like rain. Holding a restless mule
while its load was repacked. Helping to sweep up the broken bits
of used amphorae and lugging them up to the top of the dump that
was turning into a mountain. One night the reward for snatching
up a toddler before it fell in the water had paid for his and Ma's
dinner and raisin cakes afterward.

Then someone had sent him upriver with a message to deliver
to the brickworks, and on the way back he had squeezed into a gap
in the cargo to rescue a lost gold coin, and the man who lost it had
given him bread and bacon, and after that he just stayed on board
and nobody seemed to mind as long as he did what he was told.
The sight of a barrel still made him shiver, but he told himself it
was only oysters in there, or maybe foreign wine, and he sent Ma
a message with a smaller boy to say he had found honest work.

Already he was starting to get the hang of it: the long pull
upriver to collect the bricks, then back into the stink of the city to
load passengers and boxes and crates, then down the river and into

the canal to Ostia or Portus, where there were huge ships that went out all over the world. After a long time away—they went right out of sight: The sea was bigger than anyone could imagine— they would be guided back by the lighthouse, bringing amazing things. Wild animals in cages. Silks and furs and marble. Merchants with jewels on their fingers. Sandalwood and soldiers and slaves who prattled in tongues nobody could understand. Pink stacks of amphorae to be loaded up and rowed back to the city. People said, "Sometimes they bring in elephants." People said, "Wait till the grain ships arrive from Africa. Then you'll see a sight."

The passengers were settling down for the long evening now, surrounding themselves with their bags, trying to make them- selves comfortable. He would wait until they had had nothing to look at but flat water and reeds for a long time and then try them with the honey cakes and the watered wine, and perhaps they would even buy the baby one of the little dolls someone had shown him how to make from plaiting the reeds. Bored people with money would buy anything.

It wasn't time yet. They were still talking. The man—the older one, not the gangly one with the black eye—was lying back on one of the mattresses watching the sky go past. He said, "They thought I was asleep, but I wasn't. I was thinking." He tried to sit up without moving the baby dozing in the crook of his arm. "And then it happened," he said. "The whole world came clear and sharp and there were colors I'd never noticed before—I mean, I had, but they were themselves, only more so. And that's when I realized the gods had given me the answer to everything."

The blond woman looked up from the fleece she was spinning and said, "Your own medicine was the answer to everything?" as if she didn't believe him.

"Probably the poppy. I wanted to rush out and tell you."

"Tell me now."

The boy carried on with his plaiting, not daring to breathe. Hoping they would not notice him. If he was sent away now, he would never know the answer to everything.

"Well?" said the woman.

"I can remember knowing it," the man said. He reached up to scratch one ear with his forefinger. "I just can't remember what it is."

AUTHOR'S NOTE

Writing about Roman Britain usually involves a great deal of guesswork and invention to fill in the gaps. Writing about Rome presents the opposite problem: too much information and a terrifying number of ways to get things wrong. But as with every novel, there came a time when the research had to stop and the story had to be written. Here are a few of the points where the two joined together. Or didn't.

Some of the locations in the story were inspired by fragments of the Forma Urbis, Rome's ancient and fascinating street map, which is currently online at http://formaurbis.stanford.edu/.

Other locations are still visible on the ground. The building site where Ruso first sees Curtius Cossus supervising the crane team became Hadrian's Temple of Venus and Roma, and its remains are a fine sight from the Colosseum. A short walk uphill from the Colosseum leads to a park where sections of the walls around Trajan's vast bathing complex still stand. Farther west, Trajan's column is a splendid memorial to him, although the grand libraries and their balconies on either side of it are long gone.

Sadly the Pantheon was built too late to fit into the story, and while Trajan's shopping center and market halls are a delight for the modern visitor, I failed to find a reasonable excuse to send any of the characters there on a spending spree.

Roman-style apartment blocks can best be seen in the port city of Ostia Antica, as can street bars and the local headquarters of the Vigiles—Rome's night watch/fire brigade—which regularly sent its men downriver to serve there.

Lured by shopping opportunities, bars, and sunny courtyards with fountains playing in them, it is sometimes tempting to imagine that we might feel at home in the Roman empire—at least in those parts well away from the horrors of the amphitheater. Yet the reliance of the whole edifice on slave labor is a sharp reminder of how alien some of the ancient world's thinking was to our own. Although numerous attempts were made to refine the law, often for the slaves' benefit, abolishing slavery itself seems to have been unimaginable.

The lot of a Roman slave was not always as dreadful as we might imagine, nor as predictable. Slavery was not connected to race, and neither was it always a life sentence: Many of the leading citizens of Pompeii were freedmen and freedwomen, who presumably saw no irony in owning slaves themselves. For some, though, the situation could be exceedingly grim. An inscription from Puteoli sets out the duties of the local undertaker, a contractor who was expected not only to conduct funerals, but also to carry out punishments on behalf of the magistrates, or indeed of anyone who wished to have a slave punished privately. The list of equipment the contractor might deem necessary makes for gruesome reading.

There is no shortage of good books on Rome. Here are some of them:

The Roman Household: A Sourcebook by Jane F. Gardner and Thomas Wiedemann

The Roman Guide to Slave Management (also published as *How to Manage Your Slaves*) by Marcus Sidonius Falx with the modern assistance of Jerry Toner

The Colosseum by Keith Hopkins and Mary Beard

Roman Architecture: A Visual Guide by Diana E. E. Kleiner

Ancient Rome: City Planning and Administration by O. F. Robinson

ACKNOWLEDGMENTS

For guidance, encouragement, admin, editing, and lunch (not in that order) I'm grateful to the professionals: George Lucas at Inkwell; Araminta Whitley, Peta Nightingale, and Jennifer Hunt at Lucas Alexander Whitley; Lea Beresford, Glcni Bartels, and the folks at Bloomsbury who do the jobs authors rely upon but can rarely name; Ashley Polikoff for copyediting; and Susie Pitzen for proofreading.

Many thanks to the kind people who answered my requests for bizarre information—including Mike Bishop, Drs. Vicki and Mike Finnegan, Annelise Freisenbruch, Dr. Martin Mather, and members of the Roman Army Talk Facebook group.

Andy Downie's patience has been nothing short of miraculous. At least he had a trip to Italy this time, instead of having to tramp up and down wet hillsides in England.

Finally—there are always mistakes, and they are always mine. So, to the person I'm sure I've accidentally left out, apologies.

A Note on the Author

Ruth Downie is the author of the *New York Times* bestselling *Medicus*, as well as *Terra Incognita*, *Persona Non Grata*, *Caveat Emptor*, *Semper Fidelis*, and *Tabula Rasa*. She is married with two sons and lives in Devon, England.